Myrtle G.
D0427269

The Hearth and Eagle

by

ANYA SETON

1 9  4 8

HOUGHTON MIFFLIN COMPANY BOSTON

PRINTED IN THE U.S.A.

The HEARTH and EAGLE

AUTHOR'S NOTE

MARBLEHEAD, Massachusetts, the background to this story, is typical of many of our New England seacoast towns in the development and decline of two out of three of the industries which have supported it through the years, and at first I had no intention of naming it specifically. But as I began research over two years ago, I soon discovered that Marblehead is far too vivid and fiercely individualistic to be flattened into a type. As I returned there again and again, and studied the material more deeply, the town itself produced the story of Hesper and her family and the old Inn. I have tried to be accurate in presenting every event which affected actual town history. There is a wealth of fine material, and I am extremely grateful to all the Marbleheaders, old-timers and (comparative) newcomers, who have generously given me of their help and interest. I also want to thank the staff members at the Essex Institute in Salem, the Abbot Hall Library, and the Historical Society in Marblehead, for their co-operation.

There are many published works treating of the town, but for the period I was trying to cover, the most valuable were Samuel Roads, Jr.'s *History and Traditions of Marblehead* and Joseph S. Robinson's *The Story of Marblehead,* and, of course the files of the *Marblehead Messenger* and other contemporary newspapers.

For the early part of the story I studied many fascinating source books, but I am particularly indebted to Sidney Perley's and James Duncan Phillips' histories of Salem, and above all to Governor Winthrop's own careful, detailed journal in which I was able to follow the day-by-day incidents of that historic voyage.

The Honeywood family and all the main characters are fictitious though I have made use of some of Marblehead's typical names.

A. S.

CHAPTER 1

ON THE NIGHT of the great storm, the taproom at the Hearth and Eagle was deserted. Earlier that evening men had wandered in for beers or rum flip—shore men all of them now, too old to go out with the fishing fleet. They had drunk uneasily, the pewter mugs shaking in their vein-corded hands, while they listened to the rising wind. Ever more boisterous gusts puffed down the big chimney scattering fine ash over the scrubbed boards. In the Great Harbor two hundred yards away, the mounting breakers roared up the shingle, muffling the clink of mugs on the table and the men's sparse comments.

Hesper, crouching on her stool in the kitchen hearth, could see into the taproom through the half-open door. She watched her mother's face. Ma stood stiffly behind the counter at the far end of the taproom, and she was listening to the storm too. Even while she made change for the beer drinkers or turned the spigot over a mug, her eyes would slide away to the windows, and her big freckled face grow glum and watchful.

This seemed queer to Hesper, because she herself loved the storm. She luxuriated in the delicious feeling it gave her because it was safe and warm in here. The kitchen, and the whole house, closed around and held her safe the way Gran did sometimes when she was feeling good. Outside, the storm was roaring and stamping like Reed's bull roared and stamped in the pasture over on the Neck, but the bull couldn't get at you, nor could the storm. The house was stronger.

Hesper pulled her stool outside of the fireplace and leaned her head against the paneled oak cupboard where Ma kept the spare pots and skillets.

The kitchen smells lulled her. The molasses-and-pork smell from the beanpots in the brick oven, the halibut stew bubbling softly on the trivet near the blazing pine logs, the smell of beeswax that had been rubbed into the long oak table, and the benches and hard pine settle that was dreadful old-fashioned, Ma said. The settle had been right there by the fireplace near two hundred years, an eyesore Ma said, all scarred like that from jackknives and pitted with spark burns. But Pa wouldn't get rid of it. He liked the old things that had always been here.

Another crash hurled itself on the house, and a new sound mixed in it. A slapping wetness. The window panes ran with water.

"Rain's come," said old Simon Grubb, wiping his mouth on the back of his hand. "Dor-r-ty weather makin'. Don't like 'em from the sou'west. Means they start in the Carib. This is goin' to be worser'n regular September line star-rm." He heaved himself up from the table, slid three pennies on the counter by Ma's arm. She picked them up and dropped them in the tin cashbox.

"Think it'll travel up to the Banks?" she said. Her voice was just the way it always was, quick and rough, but a quiver ran through Hesper. The fear in her mother slid across the taproom, through the door into the bright kitchen. Now Hesper saw fear in all of them, in the three silent old men who did not answer her mother's question but filed out the door, their steps slow and careful, feeling the floor as if they were pacing a heaving, slippery deck. While the door was open to let the shoremen out the storm blew into the house with the boom of the waves just across Front Street.

"Ma—" whispered Hesper, "I'm scared—" She ran to her mother, burying her face in the brown calico skirts. "Maybe the sea'll get in—don't let it get at us."

Susan Honeywood shoved the heavy iron bolt across the door. "It might," she said indifferently. "But the house'll stand." She gave the child a brisk shove. "Get the mop. Floor's all wet. Nothing'll happen to *us.*"

"But you was scared, Ma—" persisted the child, though already her panic had passed, the house closed around again, comforting and protecting.

Susan wiped the beer rings from the table in the taproom, shut that door, too, and stirred the halibut stew in the iron pot before speaking. Her words when they came seemed to spring from an angry compulsion. "Have you so soon forgot Tom and Will?" she snapped over her shoulder to the puzzled child.

Hesper stared up at her mother's closed face, hurt by the sudden hostility, and yet she had always known Ma loved the boys better.

"But they're away off on the Banks with the fleet—" she whispered.

Susan slapped the pewter plates onto the table. "And so will this storm be—tomorrow or next. It's like the one in '20, afore I met your Pa—" Her full lips folded themselves into a pale line. She untied the apron from around her stout waist. "Call your Pa—supper's on. I'll go in and see of your Gran's got enough wit for eating tonight."

Hesper swallowed, listening to her mother's heavy tread entering the kitchen bedroom. Ma didn't like Pa's old granny but she didn't usually sound so angry when she spoke of her—most times when Gran acted queer, Ma'd be kind enough, feeding her from the silver porringer with the special silver spoon Gran always used, even rocking her in the long cradle when Gran got one of those fits when she'd cry and cry and think she was a baby again. Hesper loved Gran, loved her stories and her warm comforting arms on the good days, and accepted the bad days without wonder.

Hesper walked across the kitchen and knocked on her father's door. He spent the greater part of his life in that little lean-to room that had been built for a loom room years before even Gran had come to the house. Only now it was just called "Pa's room." It had a desk and a Franklin stove, and so many books piled on the floor and up the walls that there was hardly place to stand.

Roger Honeywood opened the door at once—sometimes he didn't—and smiled down at the child. His near-sighted eyes puckered around the corners, and his stooping shoulders seemed too frail to hold up the long thin body.

"It's a wild night, Hesper." He spoke dreamily, lingering over her name. From the moment of her birth in an April twilight he had loved this child as he loved no one else, and he had overridden his wife's impatient objections, to name the baby Hesper, after the western star.

He touched the child's red curls with his bony ink-stained fingers, and shambling after her into the kitchen, sat down at the table.

Hesper filled his plate with the steaming fish stew, which he pushed away absently, still held in the dreams that brightened his solitary hours.

Rough wind that moanest loud
Grief too sad for song;
Wild wind, when sullen cloud
Knells all the night long. . . .

he repeated slowly.

Hesper was used to his quotations, and usually she liked the sound of them and the vague enchanted pictures they made in her mind, but to-night she felt sympathy with her mother, who entered the kitchen to hear the last lines.

"God-blost it, Roger!" she cried, "I'll not stand for that quiddling poetizing tonight. What do you know of grief, or knells, or aught else, forever shut up in your room with them books!" She shoved his plate back in front of him, and banged the coffeepot down on the table.

Roger lifted his head and looked at her. "I merely thought, Susan, that Shelley had rather well expressed the mood of the night." His tone strove to be sarcastic, and to show a gentlemanly reproof, though his hands trembled and he looked toward the child for the eager response she usually gave him. But Hesper was staring at her mother, who made a strange rough sound in her throat. "To hell I pitch your Shelley, whoever the bostard may be. D'you hear that storm out yonder? D'you have wit enough to know what it may mean, you buffleheaded loon?"

Her eyes were blazing, her heavy freckled face suffused with dull red.

Hesper saw her father retreat, seeming to shrivel into himself, but he said, "Spoken like a true Marblehead fishwife—"

Again Susan made the sound in her throat—" 'Tis what I am. I come from fisher folk and so do you for all you never set foot in a dory these thirty year—for you weren't no good as a fisherman—nor no good at being a tavern keeper, neither—nor at being a fine gentleman at the college—"

Hesper saw the color leave her father's face, and she hoped for anger to replace it—anger to match her mother's. Why couldn't he shout too—hit out, even strike at that flushed, furious face across the table.

But there was silence in the kitchen except for the woman's heavy breathing. Then outside, another gust threw itself against the house and a branch crashed off the big chestnut tree.

Susan's hands unclenched, she lowered her head. "Don't mind me, Roger," she said. "Eat your supper. I'm grouty tonight with the storm." She walked to the fire, and poked the smoldering logs. "But they be your sons too," she added very low.

It seemed that Roger had not heard. He sat staring at his plate, his thin hand turning and twisting the tin fork. Around and past the child there flowed an emotion which she dimly felt. There had been anger as there often was, and now it was gone, replaced in her mother by an unexpected appeal—that carried with it no hope of an answer.

But Roger did answer after a minute. "I see no cause for worry about the boys. The fleet's weathered many a storm, if this should reach to the Grand Banks, which I doubt."

Susan carried her plate and Hesper's to the wooden sink across the room. "I saw Old Dimond on the Burying Hill last night," she said.

"He was waving his arms and beating about the gravestones, pointing towards the Banks."

Hesper felt a thrill of awe. All the children knew about Old Dimond, the wizard, and his queer daughter, Moll Pitcher, who lived long ago.

"Nonsense," said Roger standing up. "There aren't any ghosts. It's not like you to be fanciful, Susan."

His wife pumped water into the sink and the pewter plates rattled against the spout. "He came to warn when our men're in danger, same as he always did. You know naught about it. You're a landsman."

"I'm a Marbleheader the same as you. Eight generations of Honeywoods have lived in this house. Don't forget that, Susan."

The woman's massive shoulders twitched. "I'm not like to—with you dinging at it day in, day out."

The child stared anxiously from one to the other. Now Ma was getting angry again. Not on account of the Honeywoods exactly—Ma was a Dolliber and her family had been here as long as any—but it was because Pa—

Hesper went to her mother and tugged at her skirt. "I wish the boys *was* here at home, Ma—" she said, trying to fill the need and forestall the renewed attack.

Susan frowned. "Well, it wouldn't be fitting if they was. Men must go far to work and fight—and the women must bear it. *Most* men," she added looking at Roger.

The child's hand dropped. Her impulse had done no good. Pa's face had its cold, shut look. He walked back to his room, and the books and the pages and pages of writing that he never talked to people about. They heard the bolt slide in the door.

Susan trod around the kitchen, placing the pewter dishes behind their racks in the old built-in dresser, adding water to the beanpot in the brick oven, scattering the embers in the great fireplace.

"Go to bed," she said to Hesper, who had long been expecting this command, and could measure by its tardiness the extent of her mother's preoccupation. She obediently picked up the candle her mother had lighted. It flickered wildly in the drafts that blew down the chimney and from under the door.

"Here, give it me. You'll burn the house down." The big middle-aged woman and the small red-haired girl mounted the stairs. Susan waited until the child stood in her long cotton nightgown.

"Say your prayers."

The child knelt by her cot. "Now I lay me down to sleep—" and at the end she added timidly, "Please dear God, keep Tom and Willy safe." And looked up to her mother for approval.

By the guttering light she saw the grim face above her soften. "Amen," said the woman, and Hesper crept into bed comforted. Her mother bent over with a rare caress, and as she did so they heard a muffled thud below, and the house trembled a little.

"What is it—Ma!" cried the child struggling up again. Susan went to the window and pressed her face against the small panes.

"It's the sea," she said. "The water's over the Front." Hesper crowded to the window beside her mother; together they watched the heaving blackness outside. There was no lane, nor yard; the thin film of shiny blackness lapped up to the great chestnut tree before the house, showing here and there the jagged points of rocks pushed up from the Cove. "Ma, what'll it do—" whispered Hesper. The woman lifted the child and put her into bed.

"The house'll stand," she said. "Go to sleep." And Hesper knew instant security. Ma was always right. Ma was strong. Strong as the house that had been here so long. Gran was strong too—even when she cried and wanted to be rocked, you felt it wasn't really her, it was as if she was making believe. And Pa—he wasn't strong, but he had Ma and Gran and the house—and me too, she thought.

All night the storm blew, and sometimes waves swirled around the rock foundation of the house and poured into the cellar, but Hesper slept.

It was three weeks before they got the news and for Hesper the night of the storm was only a shadowy memory. Driftwood had been gathered, rocks rolled off the road, and seaweed thrown back to sea. The small craft which had been blown high on shore and on the causeway to the neck had been salvaged. At the Honeywood home no sign of the storm remained, except the scar on the big chestnut tree where the limb blew off.

The news came to the Honeywoods first. A boy flew into the taproom crying that a schooner had been sighted off Halfway Rock. Zeke Darling, the lighthouse keeper, had sent word it looked like John Chadwick's *Hero*.

Susan shut the taproom, threw a shawl over her shoulders and ran to the nearest high ground, on the ramparts of ruined Fort Sewall. She paid no attention to Hesper, who trotted after her, much interested. All over town people were hurrying to vantage points, up to the lookout on the Burial Hill, and crowding up the steeple on the Old North. Silently the women and children watched the schooner round the Point of the

Neck and glide into the Great Harbor. Some of the children started to cheer, greeting this vanguard of the overdue fleet in the traditional manner. But there was no answering cheer from the men on board. The tiny figures on the deck seemed to move about in a listless and mechanical way.

Susan made a sound under her breath and began to walk down the path. Hesper looked up at her curiously but did not dare speak. They threaded their way around the fish flakes at Fort Beach, and up Front Street past home, and then Lovis Cove and Goodwin's Head, and at each step others joined them, silent shawled women like Susan, excited children held in check by the tension of their elders. They reached Appleton's wharf as the *Hero* made fast. No one spoke as Captain Chadwick walked solemnly down the plank, the plod of his heavy sea boots thumping like hammer strokes in the stillness.

"It's bad," he said, shaking his head and not looking at anyone. "Tor-rible bad." Above his beard his face was gray-white as a cod's belly.

The crowd stayed silent another minute, then Susan pressed forward into the empty space near the Captain.

"How many're lost?" she asked quietly, as she had been quiet since the night of the storm.

The skipper pulled off his sou'wester. "Eleven vessels I know of, ma'am. All hands."

"The *Liberty?*"

He bowed his head. "I saw her go down not half a mile away. We could do nothing. Our own mains'l went like a tar-rn pocket han'kerchief."

Susan stepped back, and others filled her place. The air grew harsh with despairing questions. The *Sabine,* the *Pacific,* the *Trio,* the *Warrior* —the agonizing list grew. Sixty-five men and boys had been lost. Scarce a home in Marblehead that had no kin amongst the drowned, and from the crowd behind, a woman's voice raised in a long moaning wail.

Susan turned and pushed her way back through the people. Hesper followed close. She was awed and excited. Ma had been right. The great storm had got the fishing fleet, and Tom and Willy. She felt no special sorrow. Her brothers had been big men of sixteen and eighteen, away fishing half the year, and with no time for her when they were home. Cousin Tom Dolliber had been on the *Liberty* too. So he was gone with the others.

Hesper followed along behind her mother filled with a sense of importance and drama. By Lovis Cove they met her father hurrying towards them, his thin face anxious, his vague eyes peering into their faces.

"What is it, Susan? Why didn't you tell me there was news?"

The child watched them nervously expecting her mother's ready anger, because Pa had somehow failed again. But Susan was even quieter than she had been on the wharf. She laid her hand on her husband's arm. "Come back home, dear."

He gave her a startled, uncertain look, as surprised by this gentleness as Hesper was. They moved away from the child, and though Susan's hand still rested on her husband's arm it was as though he leaned on her, his long body drooping over the broad figure beside him.

Hesper trailed after them. She paused at Fort Beach a moment to watch a sea gull catch a fish, and felt a rough hand on her hair, and a painful tug.

"Don't—" she cried, whirling around, tears smarting her eyes. Two boys had crept up behind her, Johnnie Peach and Nathan Cubby. It was the latter who had pulled her hair, and he now began to caper around her jeering—"Gnaw your bacon, gnaw your bacon—little Fire-top's head is achin'."

Nat was a skinny boy of eleven with watery yellow eyes and a sharp nose. Already Hesper was used to being teased about her flaming red hair, but she had not yet learned any defense. She shrank into herself and tried to keep the tears from rolling out of her eyes.

"Oh, let her be," said Johnnie, carelessly. "She's just a little kid."

He was a year younger than Nat, a handsome boy with curly dark hair. He shied a stone at the water and watched it skip.

"What for you're blubberin'—Fire-top?" taunted Nat coming closer. "Blubberin' cause your head's on fire?" He made another grab at her hair.

Hesper ducked. "I'm crying 'cause Tom and Willy's gone down with the fleet—" she wailed.

Johnnie turned. He raised his arm and struck down Nat's outstretched hand. "That's so—" he said. "They was on the *Liberty*. My uncle's lost too, on the *Clinton*. Reason enough to cry without you roilin' her."

"Oh, whip!" said Nat contemptuously, using an obscene Marblehead expletive. "I betcha my Pa's lost too. Leastways he hasn't come in from the spring fare yet. Ma, I think she's give him up."

Young as Hesper was, she was conscious of an obliquity in Nat, and that his speech about his father sprang from something stranger than bravado or the callousness of childhood. Though he was of normal height for his age he had a hunched and wizened look, and malicious brooding eyes. He reminded her of a picture of an evil dwarf in the Grimm's *Fairy Tales* her father had given her.

"You shouldn't talk like that—" said Johnnie severely, "and you shouldn't say 'whip' front of a little lass. Run along home, Fire-top."

Hesper caught her underlip with her teeth, though she didn't mind the hated nickname from Johnnie. She looked at him adoringly, but the two boys had lost interest in her. They had sighted Peter Union's dory pulling around the rocks to his landing, and they clambered down to the beach to see what luck the fisherman had had.

Hesper wiped her face on a corner of her white muslin pinafore, threw the trailing ends of her shawl over her shoulders in a gesture duplicating her mother's, and continued homeward. The old house awaited her, and she thought as she often had when approaching it from the water side that it looked like a great friendly mama cat. It's unpainted clapboards had weathered through two centuries to a tawny silver, and the huge chimneys, one on the old wing, one on the new, stuck up like ears. And the inn sign above the taproom door swung back and forth like the cat's tongue. There had once been painted emblems on the sign, a pair of andirons and a flying bird above the letters "The Hearth and Eagle," but they had all faded into a rusty red blur.

Hesper, moved by a feeling of special solemnity, went through the east door under the sign instead of around to the kitchen entrance as usual. The taproom door was closed, but she could hear her mother's voice, slow and thick with long pauses. So Ma and Pa were shut in there. Hesper wandered into the kitchen. It was still warm with the sunlight from the windows over the sink, but there were clouds building, and the wind rising on the harbor.

Beside a small bright fire in the great hearth, Gran sat huddled in her Boston rocking chair. She was wrapped in fleecy gray shawls and she looked like a tiny old seagull. Her sharp black eyes were sea-gull eyes too. "What's Roger doin' in the taproom with Susan?" she asked querulously when she saw Hesper. "And why'd he run out before?" Her voice was high and thin, but on a good day like this it had a snap to it.

"There's been a tor-rible thing happen to the fleet," said Hesper importantly, imitating Cap'n Chadwick. "Tom and Willy aren't never coming back. Ma's telling Pa."

The old woman's wrinkled eyelids hooded her eyes. She stopped rocking. "They ain't never comin' back?" she repeated, seeming to consider. Her eyes opened and stared unseeing at the child. Her mouth drew itself into a pucker. "No more did Richard. He didn't come back." She shook her head. Her gaze slipped around the bright kitchen to rest on the hooked rug by the entry. "Right there I stood when I last saw Richard. I hooked that rug myself. 'Ship and sunset' we called it."

Hesper stared at the rug on which she had walked a thousand times. "It's real pretty," she said, then drew in her breath. There was a queer noise from the taproom. A broken cluttered sound as if someone was crying, and mixed with it Ma's voice, firm and comforting. Pa was crying? thought the child in amazement, when he hadn't seemed worried at all about Tom and Willy before. The sounds frightened her, and she puzzled over them until she found the answer. It wasn't that Pa didn't feel, it was that he lived so far away he didn't believe in real things, and when they happened he didn't know what to do, except turn to Ma, and let her comfort him.

Old Sarah Honeywood did not hear the sounds from the taproom. She kept on staring at the rug, and the misty present dissolved into the vivid emotion of seventy years ago, emotion she had thought long outrun, and yet it was still strong enough to rush forward again and overpower the changed body and the dim mind.

She saw Richard as he had stood that July day, boyish and handsome in his regimentals. The "handsomest man in Essex County," she had said that herself—that long-forgotten Sally Hathaway when Richard first came a-wooing to her father's house in Cunny Lane. She had said it again on the rug, her arms around his neck, the tears running down her face on to her red linsey-woolsey. With the memory of the red linsey-woolsey the scene grew sharper and brighter. From outside she heard the shouts of the other men in Glover's regiment. Orders had just come from General Washington, saying the Marbleheaders must proceed to New York. Already half of them had sailed over to Beverley. Richard must hurry, yet she clung to him begging and sobbing. He hadn't wanted to leave her, an eight-months bride, and carrying his child. Yet he had been in high spirits.

"Us Marbleheaders'll show the stinking redcoats how to fight, show the rest of them quiddling farmers too from back country. And so be it they've water down around New York, we'll show 'em what a boat's for too." He had said that even while he kissed her again, and pulled her clinging hands down from his neck.

"Fare ye well, Sally lass—I'll be back by snowfall."

But he hadn't come back. He had helped row the retreat from Brooklyn to New York after the dreadful battle of Long Island, and he had written her a letter, cocky as ever—"We saved the army, us Marbleheaders, we muffled the ors and rowed the poor lubbers acrost that little millpond they got down here-along. Don't fret, sweetheart, it'll be over with soon."

How long had she kept that letter sewn into her bodice? Years it must have been, because she had nursed little Tom for two years, and long after that the letter was still in her bodice. It was the only letter she had ever got from Richard.

The Marbleheaders had rowed again on the night of December twenty-fifth. The old woman, caught by a single-minded urgency, got out of the rocker and walked gropingly toward her own room, the warm kitchen bedroom near the great chimney. In the bottom drawer of the pine chest, she unearthed beneath piles of flannel nightcaps an ancient tea box, its purple roses and green daisies still glowing on the lid after seventy years. Richard's letter was inside, tied up with black ribbon and rosemary, but it was not that she wanted. She shuffled through other keepsakes until she found a yellowed newspaper clipping. It was headed "Speech by General Knox," and she held it at arm's length, squinting her eyes.

"I wish the members of this body knew the people of Marblehead as well as I do. I could wish that they had stood on the Banks of the Delaware River in 1776 in that bitter night when the Commander in Chief had drawn up his little army to cross it, and had seen the powerful current bearing onward the floating masses of ice which threatened destruction to whosoever should venture—"

The remembered anguish of a few minutes ago gave place to the old thrill of pride. Sorrow was a solitary business, but pride must be shared. She put the clipping on her knee, and called the child.

"Hessie—I want you should come here."

Hesper obeyed slowly, a little rebellious. The strange noise in the taproom had stopped, and she had been amusing herself seeing pictures in the fire, the red leaping castles peopled by tiny golden fairies.

"I want you should listen to this. Set down, child."

The high quavering voice read the first paragraph out loud, and went on from Knox's speech. "'I wish that when this occurrence threatened to defeat the enterprise, they could have heard that distinguished warrior demand "Who will lead us on?"' That was General Washington speakin', Hessie."

Hesper's attention came back with a jerk. She nodded politely. The clipping trembled in Gran's hand, "And you listen what Knox says next. 'It was the men of Marblehead, and Marblehead alone, who stood forward to lead the army along the perilous paths to unfading glories and honors in the achievements of Trenton. There went the fishermen of Marblehead, alike at home on land or water, alike ardent, patriotic and unflinching, whenever they unfurled the flag of the country.' "

The long words meant nothing to the child, but she was impressed by the way Gran looked, shining as if somebody had lighted a candle behind her face.

"Richard was the first port oarsman right back of Washington, Bill Blackler commanded the boat. Josh Orne told me all about it months later. He said there was Richard, the sweat freezin' on his face, and cussin' something dreadful, but tryin' to swallow his oaths on account of General Washington there."

The old woman gave a sudden cackle of laughter. "Richard was a terrible one for bad language. Anything he didn't like, he'd yell, 'To hell I pitch it and let the devil fry it on his rump!' I used to beg him to talk gentle, but pretty soon I give up," she sighed. "But he was a good boy."

Hesper frowned, struggling with a new impression. Gran often told stories, often changed like this, going from sad to glad so they didn't make much sense. Half the time she didn't listen. But something in the way Gran had said, "He was a good boy . . ." made it real.

The child put her hand on the bony gray knee. "Who was Richard, Gran?"

The old woman twisted her head. An immense futility engulfed her. Explanations—why didn't people know without being told, why didn't anyone remember. . . .

"He was your—no he was your *great*- grandsir, I guess—" she said dully. "And he was killed at the Battle of Trenton."

Killed, thought Hesper. A queer word. A quick rippling word. It didn't sound very scary. Not like drownded. That was heavy and black.

Sarah had been wandering back again, not to clear-cut scenes, but to a long confusion of strivings. The striving to give birth here in this room—give birth to Tom. And forty years later his own hopeless striving for life, there on this very bed. Then the striving to make a living, running the tavern alone, until Tom grew up enough to help before he went off fishing with the bankers as a cut-tail. And another striving to give life, in this old Birth and Death room, the night Roger was born, and the niminy-piminy daughter-in-law, Mary Ellis, whimpering she couldn't get through it. Nor did she. Death again. Opening and shutting, opening and shutting the door of this room. I wish it'd open for me, Sarah thought, I'm getting mighty weary. And she looked at the long cradle which stood in the corner of the room. Built two hundred years ago for Mark, the first Honeywood, who had something wrong with his spine. Rocking would soothe him, 'n' it soothes me too. In the cradle you could let go all this memory of striving, the beautiful gray peace folded over you, you floated back and forth, back and forth in the gray peace, and sometimes the rocking brought your mother's voice humming a soft little spinning song—and sometimes it brought Richard's voice singing above the lap of waves against a boat in the harbor.

"He sang real nice—" she said out loud, and she began to quaver—

> A pretty fair maid, all in a garden,
> A sailor boy came passing by.
> He stepped aside and thus addressed her,
> Saying "Pretty fair maid, won't you be my bride?"

"Gran!" cried Hesper, tugging at the old woman's arm, for Gran had got up still singing and was going toward the long cradle. Her eyes had sunk back in her head and there was a silly little smile on her face. She was sliding into one of the bad times, when she wasn't Gran at all, just a helpless old baby wanting to be rocked.

"Gran"—the child repeated urgently—"don't get in the cradle—Tom and Willy are drownded."

The old woman paused, the appeal in the child's voice reached her. Tom and Willy are drownded. Tom and Willy? She groped through the clinging gray peace, and shook her head half in annoyance that the child's voice was detaining her, half in sympathy. "Well don't take on, dearie. There's a many drownded here, and off the Banks too. Hark! I can hear the keel gratin' on the sand, that's what folks used to say, when Death's comin' for them."

Death—the soft grayness floating down through peaceful waters that rocked you back and forth.

Hesper saw that the answering look had gone from Gran's face. Shaking off the child's hand she climbed into the long high cradle. She settled down with a sigh like a swish of wind through leaves.

"Rock Sally—" she whispered plaintively. "Sally wants to be rocked."

Hesper looked down at the small face on the pillow beneath the sheltering oak hood. The wrinkles were smoothed away, the lips smiling in anticipation.

The child put her foot on the rocker and gave it one sharp push, but misery welled up from her tight chest. She jerked away from the cradle, and stumbled into the kitchen.

Gran had gone back to her secret world. Ma and Pa were together behind a closed door. They were talking about Tom and Willy. It was an awful bad thing had happened. But *I'm* here, she thought, don't they care that I'm here—

She crept to her special stool on the hearth inside the fireplace and leaned her head against the bricks, sobbing quietly.

The small flames kept shimmering and dissolving between the huge andirons, the black balls that topped the andirons stood quiet above the noisy little fire like two proud, strong people. She watched the andirons and her sobs lessened as she began to think about them. Pa and Gran used to talk of them sometimes, though Ma thought they were dreadful ugly and liked the brass ones in the parlor lots better. Pa called these tall black andirons Phebe's fire-dogs. Phebe'd brought them on a ship across the sea, so long ago that there wasn't any Marblehead here at all. Phebe was Mark Honeywood's wife. The first *American* Honeywood, Pa always said, though nobody ever would listen except Hesper. Most everyone in Marblehead had families that went way back too.

But Pa thought there was something very special about Phebe, because of a letter. Pa said a great lady had written it, and it was something to be very proud of. He kept it wrapped in a yellow Chinese silk square in a carved wooden box in the secret drawer of his desk. He'd read it to Hesper on her last birthday, but she hadn't understood it very well, even though he made her repeat some of the phrases about being brave: "She hath a most sturdy courage," and "it is such as she who will endure in my stead."

Hesper had been much more interested in the embroidered yellow silk and the black box carved with the faces of slant-eyed men. These had belonged to Moses Honeywood, Pa's great great grandsir who had owned three schooners in the China trade, and made a lot of money. The only Honeywood who had.

But Pa wouldn't let her play with the box, and he kept on talking about Phebe and Mark. He spoke of them as heroes and gods, comparing Mark to Odysseus and Phebe to a radiant all-conquering Hera. Sometimes he was bad as Gran, making her listen to old stories when she wanted to be playing hide and seek between the fish houses with Charry Trevercombe.

Hesper watched the andirons, and the small leaping tongues of fire between them, when suddenly a thought struck her with the thrill of revelation. It was over two hundred years since Phebe'd brought those andirons here, but she must have sat just like this sometimes and watched them too. Phebe was dead—all those others after her—Isaac and Moses and Zilpah and Richard, and now Tom and Willy too. They were all dead. But the andirons were still just the same. They're letting *me* watch them now, she thought, with awe.

Then there were some things like the fire-dogs, the letter, the house itself that went on and on even if people did die. Things that didn't draw away from you and leave you alone the way people did. Things that didn't change from day to day. Miss Ellison at Sabbath school said God didn't either. But you couldn't touch and see God.

She frowned, struggling with a further concept. For had not Phebe and Mark, being dead, become as enduring as the andirons? Neither could they change now, and yet it was because of what they had been that Hesper, sitting by the hearth in the old house, was as she was.

Pa had said something like this when he read her the letter, but she had not understood. Now a great yearning came to her.

What were they like, Phebe and Mark? Why did they come here? What made the great lady write the letter?

She rested her head against the brick facing, and her eyelids drooped. But it seemed to her that on the flagstone hearth she saw the image of a ship, the size of the schooners in the harbor but of a strange and quaint rig, and it seemed to the child that on the deck of this ship she saw the figure of a girl in blue. She could not really see the girl's face, and yet Hesper knew that there were tears on it. Frightened, anguished tears, and this seemed strange to her too for she knew the girl was Phebe, and did such brave people cry or shrink like that?

Hesper sighed, and the image on the hearthstone blurred and faded. Her head fell forward on her chest, and she slept. Outside, the nor'easter with its whistling blasts ripped up the harbor, piling the leaden waves against the wharves and causeway, but the house gathered around to protect the dreams of still another Honeywood.

CHAPTER 2

The rising wind brought restlessness and a sense of danger. Already Phebe Honeywood had learned that. It brought the crudest physical misery as well. Phebe raised her swimming head above the wooden rim of their bunk and groped again for the tin basin.

The *Jewell* rolled and lurched and rolled once more, and Phebe, still retching, fell back on the straw pallet. Mark had risen long ago and gone off to the fo'c'sle with the crew. These shipboard days he was always eager and interested as she had never yet seen him in their six months of marriage, nor was he seasick.

From the bunk above Phebe, Mistress Brent gave a long groan, followed by a grunt from her husband and little Rob's wail. There were three of them up there, wedged into a bunk like their own which, as Mark said cheerfully, was "sized exactly to a coffin." But they had all been fortunate to get space in the only small cabin. The other fifty passengers slept as best they could on layers of rickety shelves in the Great Cabin, or in hammocks between decks.

This was Friday, the ninth of April, 1630. They had been twelve days at sea and not yet quitted England, still near the Isle of Wight. Dead calms and adverse winds had prevented. Twelve days of cold and bad food and seasickness, and the journey not begun. It seemed to Phebe that already twelve weeks had passed since she kissed her father farewell and boarded the *Jewell* at Southampton, where the vessel lay in the channel with the other three ships in this vanguard of Governor Winthrop's fleet—the *Talbot,* the *Ambrose,* and their beautiful flagship, the *Arbella.*

Phebe raised her head again, then inched gingerly to a crouching position. The dark cabin swirled around her, and she leaned her head against the rough planking. She heard Mark's laugh from the deck outside and he burst into the cabin.

"What, Phebe—" he cried between laughter and reproach, peering into their dark bunk, "not puking again!"

Over feeble protests from the sufferers in the top berth he flung open the wooden shutter of the deck window, to let wind and gray light rush through the noisesome cabin.

"Aye, you do look green, poor lass," he said, examining his wife, "but you should cheer now. We've a fair wind at last. Come dress yourself—we'll soon be passing Portland Bill."

She tried to smile up at him, this great, swaggering handsome youth in his red leather doublet, so tall that he must keep his dark curly head bent low to stand in the cabin. She loved him dearly, but his words brought her lacerating pain which he would never understand. Portland Bill was but a few miles from Dorchester—from home.

If they must leave England, she thought, turning her face from him, why could it not be clean and sharp as they had thought in Southampton—instead of this long-drawn, ever-renewed parting.

Mark, seeing her hesitant and thinking it the seasickness, scooped her from the bunk, stood her on the planks in her night shift, and held up his scarlet cloak to screen her from the inert Brents above.

Phebe clenched her teeth and hurried through her dressing. Mark teased her for her modesty, but she suffered deeply at the public nature of all private acts on board the ship. She put on her everyday gown of French serge, blue as the cornflowers in the meadow at home, and her white lawn falling collar, its points embellished with rows of tucks, in elaboration exactly suitable to a prosperous yoeman's daughter. The collar was limp from the sea air and hung badly. Phebe sighed, thinking of the care her mother had lavished on fine linen for the journey. Mark impatiently wrapped her in her blue hooded cloak and hurried her out on deck.

The Easterly wind had not brought rain, nor was it cold this April day, as the little *Jewell* bounded across the waves, seeming as eager as Mark was to hurtle herself toward the Western sea and be quit of Old England forever.

There was scarce room to move on deck, since all the passengers who were well enough had come out to wedge themselves amongst the water barrels, the chicken coops, and the long boat, and they were heartily cursed by the harassed sailors. But there was no other place to take the air. Only Mark by dint of his exuberant interest and treats of strong water to the crew was allowed on the fore deck, and Captain Hurlston permitted no one but his officers on the poop.

Phebe leaned against the starboard rail, her eyes on the shadowy coastline. She was always quiet, even in their moments of passionate love, but Mark's jubilance was checked by the expression of her face as they neared the headlands of Dorsetshire.

He put his arm around her. "Take heart—" he whispered, bending down, for she was small and her smooth brown head barely reached to his shoulder. "It's a great venture, Phebe."

Her indrawn breath dilated her nostrils. Her fingers twisted in the folds of her cloak. "I know."

How well she knew, for him, the restlessness, the discontent at home, and the zest for the untried which had all compelled him to this venture. His nature was made for struggle. It had been so with their marriage. She had not loved as soon as he did, but her indifference had excited him as much as her father's opposition had angered him.

Mark's father was but a small Dorchester clothier, never prosperous, and of late oppressed by the new taxes, harried by imposts and restrictions to the verge of bankruptcy, while Phebe Edmunds was the child of a wealthy yoeman farmer, who was distantly connected with gentry and freeholder of the same Dorsetshire acres which had been granted to his ancestors after the Conquest.

But when Phebe's love had at last grown strong as Mark's, her indulgent father's opposition wore itself out. Six months ago on her eighteenth birthday they had married and found great joy in each other. Yet she had known Mark still unsatisfied.

He detested Dorchester, and the clothier's trade to which he had never given but grudging attention anyway, preferring always the wharves and sea eight miles away at Weymouth. That she understood, but she long fought against another realization. Her own beloved home, the great sprawling half-timbered house set in gentle meadows and warm with the affection of a close-knit family—this he detested even worse.

"Yet what *is* it you want so much?" she had cried, as she began to see the extent of his unrest. "What can New England give us better than we have here? It's not as though we were Separatists."

Mark's underlip had jutted out in the stubborn way she had come to dread. "No need to be Puritan to build new and free in a new land." He had thrown a resentful glance around the Edmunds' great Hall where they were sitting, at the sparkling casement windows newly curtained in a delicate rose sarcenet, at the carved oaken chairs, the gilded court cupboard, the polished floor cloth painted like a chequerboard and warmed by a Turkey rug.

"Soon, perhaps," she suggested timidly, "we can build for ourselves."

His face had blackened and he flung his head up like a spurred stallion. "Aye, on your father's land! Where he'll o'ersee all I do." He jumped to his feet and began to pace the Turkey rug. "Look, Phebe. I mean to be my own master. Nor account for what I do to King or Bishop or Commissioner or father—yours or mine. I'll never make a clothier nor—" he glanced contemptuously toward the window—"nor sheep farmer."

Phebe's family, after the first dismay, had accepted Mark's plan. For was there not fear and insecurity everywhere, now that the King had rid himself of parliament and given ear to his Papist Queen who might yet force back the terrible days of Bloody Mary?

"Aye, times are mortal bad," Phebe's father agreed, wagging his grizzled head. "Were I younger, Phebe sweeting, I mought come with 'ee." Yet even as he spoke he cast a complacent look about his comfortable house and through the window to the rolling downs dotted with his sheep. And she knew that come what might her parents would never leave home. They would bend a little here and there under necessity, and conform to any order, secure in the hundreds of years which had rooted them to these acres and this life.

And I too, she thought, as she had thought many times during the weeks of preparation, though once the decision had been taken she had never troubled Mark with her doubts. Her love for him deepened as they became isolated together by their shared enterprise. She listened anxiously while he spelled out the Planter's list of requisites suggested by the Massachusetts Bay Company; bellows, scoop, pail, shovels, spades, axes, nails, fish hooks, and lines. All these were Mark's concern; for their purchase, and the passage money of six pounds each, and the freightage costs, he used most of the hundred pounds left him by his mother. To buy the remaining requisites, warm clothes, household gear, and provisions, Phebe used her dowry, since Mark stubbornly refused any help proffered by his father-in-law.

In only one thing had she combated her husband's will. She had insisted upon bringing her wedding andirons. They had been made for her by a master blacksmith of more than local fame. They were tall and sturdy, fit to hold the greatest logs, yet graceful too in the deceptively slender shafts and the crowning black balls.

Fire-dogs were not on the Planter's list.

"But I want them, Mark," she insisted, near tears. "I want them in our first hearth wherever it may be."

He had given in at last, though he had not understood. Only her mother had understood, that the andirons ordered in love for her by her parents to grace a new hearth would always be a link with home, the twin guardians of the precious flame; like man and wife, English-born, transplanted and yet enduring with steady purpose. But indeed those were womanish thoughts, unfitting to a man, and standing now on the *Jewell* deck beside Mark, she shifted her weight and pressed against him, glorying in his strength and bigness, waiting for the quick response of his arm to the pressure of her body.

But Mark was not thinking of love. He made a sharp movement, swinging on his heel, and stretching his hand above his head. "God blast, the bloody wind is slacking off again!"

She followed his scowling gaze up to the sails that now were flapping fitfully, where they had been taut-bellied before. She turned and looked again toward the land and saw, jagged and sharp against the sky, the crenelations of Portland Castle where she and her sisters had so often played, gathering moss roses around the ruined walls, then galloping over the strip of shingle on their little moor ponies. Behind the castle and over that rounded ridge of hills—lay home. Mother would be in the stillroom at this hour, sugaring the new cowslips for her famous wine, or maybe helping the dairy maids skim the cream. And painted clear against the sky, Phebe saw the sweet comely face, rosy as an apple beneath the graying hair, heard the loving admonishments and the ready laughter. She'd had a bad cough when they left home a fortnight back, what if it had worsened and gone down into the lungs, what if . . .

Phebe clutched at the wooden rail, and shut her eyes.

"Satan himself must be in it—" said Mark morosely, staring across the league of water to the North. "Back where we started. One might lower the long boat, row ashore and be at your father's in a couple of hours."

"Oh, don't!" cried Phebe, so loud and sharp that Mark started and gaped at her. She held her head rigidly turned from him, her small brown hands clenched on the rail, but beneath her cloak he saw her shoulders shaking.

He leaned over her with clumsy and puzzled tenderness. "Phebe—what ails you, sweetheart?"

She gathered herself tighter and whispered through her teeth. "Let me be. Let me be awhile."

He patted her shoulder, and left her, heading forward to the fo'c'sle.

After a few minutes the capricious wind returned, the sails filled and the *Jewell* gained headway. Phebe moved her body, so that she might no longer see the diminishing shore, and stared ahead doggedly towards the other three ships of their company, all drifting still becalmed almost within hailing distance. She had no interest in the *Ambrose* and the *Talbot,* her brooding gaze rested on their flagship the *Arbella,* and gradually as she fixed her thoughts on it she felt solace.

The *Arbella* was by far the largest ship of them all, near four hundred tons burden; she had been newly painted for the voyage in gay reds and whites and shining black, and her figurehead, the flying gilded eagle on her prow, glinted proudly in the uncertain sunlight. There were great folk aboard; Governor John Winthrop who was to head their colony, Sir Richard Saltonstall and his children. These were gentry indeed, but she knew little of them except a glimpse in the distance when they embarked at Southampton. In the most noble passenger of all, however, Phebe felt vivid interest, because she had talked with her.

Three days ago while they still awaited favorable winds off the Isle of Wight, many from all four ships had put ashore at Yarmouth, that they might walk about and refresh themselves. Mark had been away at once, eager to explore the little town, but Phebe found no such energy. She was content to walk along the beach, relieved by the feeling of earth beneath her feet. She had wandered a short distance around the bend and up the mouth of the Yar when she came upon a low bank covered with beach grass and shaded by the ruin of an ancient lookout. She prepared to sit down on a block of fallen masonry, when she saw a young woman standing near by. The woman was richly dressed in garnet-colored paragon, somewhat stained with sea water, and beneath the fur-lined walking hood, her shadowed blue eyes gazed out to sea with an expression of both yearning and resolution which touched immediate understanding in Phebe. She was too shy to accost a lady, obviously high-born and still further protected by intense preoccupation with her own thoughts. But the lady heard, and giving a slight start, turned. Seeing a girl some years younger than herself, staring with admiration, she smiled, and made a gentle gesture of welcome. "You are on one of the ships, mistress?"

Phebe smiled too, and curtsied. "Yes, your ladyship. From the *Jewell.*"

"You know who I am?" asked the lady in some surprise.

"I guessed," said Phebe gently. "For I've heard that the Lady Arbella is tall, has golden hair, and is fair as the mayflower."

Arbella withdrew a little. The words touched a memory of many venal flatteries. But she examined the quiet young face upturned to hers, saw that the brown eyes were honest and clear as brook water, and she smiled again.

"Sit down, mistress, and tell me of yourself, since we are fellow travelers."

Phebe hesitated. "I intrude, I fear. A moment alone is so precious now. Already I've learned that."

Arbella nodded and sighed, but checked herself. "Our gracious Lord has harder lessons than that in store for us, but with His Mercy we'll conquer."

Why, she is homesick as I am, thought Phebe with sharp sympathy. "It means much to us all to have you venture with us, your ladyship," said Phebe earnestly. "It gives us courage."

"Ah, child—only God can give you that." But Phebe saw that her words had pleased. Arbella took the girl's hand and drew her down on the stone beside her. "Are you with your husband, mistress? You're not truly of our Puritan congregation since you wear a wedding ring."

"No," said Phebe glancing at the gold band on her finger then at the lady's ringless hands. "Forgive me, but I can't think it wrong."

"Nor I," said Arbella faintly, "but it's a Papist symbol for all that and we must purify our church. My beloved husband thinks it very wrong," she added, half to herself, thinking of Isaac and his burning zeal to cleanse their form of worship from corruption. He had denied himself even this hour's respite from the ship, and was now as usual closeted with Governor Winthrop planning and praying for the success of their colony in the New World.

She turned to Phebe. "But tell me of yourself, mistress." She was much interested in this girl who obviously came from a class she hardly knew. Neither gentry nor of the lower orders.

Phebe, always self-possessed, willingly answered Arbella's questions, and when she spoke of Mark, Arbella smiled, accurately building an image of a handsome impetuous youth, eager for adventure, but well knowing how to hold a woman's love.

"But if it's not for conscience' sake he emigrates, what is it he hopes to find in the New England?" she asked at last, and Phebe, who had herself often been troubled by this question, found the answer promptly.

"Freedom, milady—and—" her lips parted in her rare smile, "and—I believe—fish."

"Fish! Is he then a fisherman by trade?"

"No, milady, a clothier, but he hates it. He has been much influenced by the clergyman, Master White, at Dorchester, who believes that in fishing New England will find great fortune. Mark is drawn to the sea, he ever loved the docks and boats at Weymouth."

"But you—mistress—" said Arbella frowning. "You're bred to gentler ways, I cannot see you as a fishwife."

Phebe hesitated, fearing to seem forward. "I think, milady, there will be no gentle ways for anyone out there in the wilderness, no matter what we be."

A darkness deepened the lady's blue eyes. She rose from the stone. Phebe saw that the long pale hand which drew together her fur cloak wavered, but her answer was firm. "You're right. I pray that I may have the strength."

As they stood there, they heard the far-off boom of a cannon.

"The signal—" said Arbella, turning toward the water. "We must get back to the ships. With God's mercy we shall meet again at Naumkeag. God keep you, mistress."

"And you, milady—" said Phebe softly. She watched the tall figure walk down the beach, and she felt again the glow of pride she had tried to voice earlier. The Lady Arbella Johnson was the daughter and sister of an earl, the most noble Earls of Lincoln. What if many of the malcontents did now sneer at title, what if the new dissenting creeds averred that all are equal in the sight of God, was there not special courage required of such a one as the Lady Arbella, sheltered, delicate, and accustomed to delicacy. The first noblewoman to venture toward the New England. For conscience' sake, thought Phebe, docilely echoing the Puritan lady's own words. But from deep within her a surer voice spoke. Not only for conscience' sake, she goes for love of her husband—even as I.

As if in answer she saw Mark racing down the beach towards her, waving his Monmouth cap, his curly dark hair disordered, his eyes alight. "Phebe—Phebe—make haste—the shallop's leaving. I couldn't find you."

Warmth and gladness at the sight of him rushed through her body; she held out her arms and he caught her hard against him, kissing her on the mouth. "A fair welcome, sweetheart. But hurry." She ran with him down the beach, his arm around her waist. Those already waiting in the shallop eyed them sourly as they arrived laughing, their cheeks flushed, and about them the glow of warm love.

Mistress Bagby, the midwife from London, made grudging room for Phebe on the after seat. "You pleasured yourself in Yarmouth?" she sniffed. "At a pothouse maybe?"

Phebe shrugged, indifferent in this moment of new courage to the spiteful fat face beside her. "Nay, mistress. I only walked up the Yar a way, and there I met the Lady Arbella."

Mrs. Bagby stared, then masked her envy with another sniff. "And being noticed by quality has gone to your head, I see. I've heard she's but a meaching, mincing thing."

"She is very fair, and winsome and brave," said Phebe, and turning her back looked over the other heads to the bow where Mark pulled on a larboard oar. He caught her eye and they smiled at each other.

This sureness and warmth between them sustained her that night through their first quarrel. As they lay cramped together in their bunk, she tried to tell of her meeting with the Lady Arbella, and he would not listen, speaking to her roughly and telling her that she was fool indeed to think that the daughter of an earl had shown true good will. It was then that she remembered that he had cause to hate the lady's class. Once as a boy of eight he had snared a rabbit on lands belonging to the Earl of Dorset. He had been caught and punished by the Earl's order, cruelly beaten, and his left ear cropped. Of this he had never spoken but once. His abundant hair hid the jagged wedge space cut from his ear, and she had forgotten.

She soothed him with soft murmurs and the tenderness of her body, but their disagreement was not yet ended. Mark too had something to tell of their stay in Yarmouth, and she felt sharp dismay when she found that he had spent some of their small horde of silver for a strange purchase.

He pulled his prize from under the straw at their feet and made her feel sundry bumpy objects in the darkness.

"What are they?" she whispered, though the snoring of their cabin mates, the creaking of the ship, and the rush of water made secrecy needless.

"Lemons," he answered triumphantly, stuffing them back beneath the straw.

"Whatever for?" she cried. She had hoped at least for sugar plums to vary the dreadful sameness of their food.

"I met an old sailor in Yarmouth, he's been fifty years at sea, to Cathay and back. He says if we suck one every day we'll not get ship fever. He sold them to me for eleven shillings."

"Oh Mark—and you believed him! He was but diddling you to get the profit."

He drew his arm from under her. "They've come from Spain," he said with anger. "Lemons are always dear. You must not question my judgment, Phebe."

"No, Mark, I won't—" she said after a minute, hurt that he had turned from her again. "Forgive me."

And she hid her worry. For it seemed to her ordered mind that his buying of the lemons touched things in him that her love would rather forget, a recklessness and improvidence.

But after they had at last bade final farewell to England, and the journey became a plodding, ever recurrent nightmare of storm and sickness, it did seem that she and Mark were stronger than many of the others.

All over the ship the passengers complained of sharp pains in their bones, of swollen mouths and tongues, and teeth so weak they could not chew upon the hard salt meat the cabin boy flung into the wooden trenchers. She and Mark had none of this, and now that her young body had become accustomed to the pitching and tossing of the ship, even seasickness no longer bothered her.

On May Day, during a great storm and cold, Phebe helped a frantic mother tend her sick child in the great cabin, and while she wiped the little girl's swollen blue lips, she mentioned hesitantly the lemons. "I don't know if they do good, but Mark thinks so and we *have* kept well."

Mrs. Bagby had also been tending the child, and now she hooked her fat arm around the upright of a bunk to keep her feet on the lurching floor, and said scornfully, "Lemons, forsooth! You think the child doesn't suffer enough already, Mistress Honeywood, that you must parch her poor mouth. Give her beer, Goody Carson, beer and wormwood. That'll help her."

And Goody Carson listened to the midwife who was a determined woman of reputed skill, for Goody Carson was big with child, and near to term, and she feared that she would need Mrs. Bagby's good will before the journey was over.

Phebe said nothing more. She was unsure herself if those shriveling little fruits were contributing to their health, but each morning before they pulled themselves out of the damp, moldering bunk straw, Mark split two lemons with his hunting knife, and they sucked and swallowed the bitter pulp.

The journey went on, and the weeks went by. Long since, the memory of home had faded to a haze as unreal as the impossible visioning of the future scene. Nobody thought of either. The ship life alone was true, and its incidents the only interest. Bad food, increasingly scanty, bad weather, bad smells, bad air and bitter cold. These made the dun thread on which the days slid by, but now and then it seemed to knot itself and pause for a more vivid pattern. There was the Sabbath service, held on deck if the weather permitted or, as it usually did not, in the great cabin, smoky from the cook fire and stinking from some fifty unwashed bodies. On the *Jewell* there was no ordained minister, but a godly little clerk, Master Wenn, from Norwich, made shift to read the Bible, lead the prayers, and even preach. Mark always escaped the services, being welcomed by the sailors where he listened to sea lore instead. But Phebe perforce listened with the other passengers, and was much irritated by the canting nasal voice. She missed the candles and the rituals and prayers to which she was accustomed, and found Master Wenn's bald manner of exhorting God shocking in its crudeness. But this and many other matters she kept to herself.

In mid-Atlantic a sailor died, one who had been incessantly drunk and blasphemous, and many thought it a judgment on him and were pleased.

It was a matter of comfort, too, that usually they were in sight of the other ships, the *Arbella* and the *Ambrose,* though the *Talbot* had disappeared after they left the Scillys. Phebe would sometimes push her way to one of the square portholes in the great cabin, and gaze across the heaving gray waters to the *Arbella,* thinking of the beautiful lady for whom the ship was named and wondering how she endured the hardships. It seemed that the ships made no progress, gales and storms followed each other; the passengers, forbidden the deck for fear of the pounding waves, became some quarrelsome, some apathetic.

On Thursday the twenty-seventh of May came a day of special trial. They had been seven weeks in the open sea; all night a stiff gale had harried them. The little *Jewell* climbed the mountainous waves, shivering as if in fear at the summit, then pitching down to drive her prow a fathom through green water. All night Phebe had clung to Mark, while his long legs braced against the sides of their bunk, and at dawn they dragged themselves to the great cabin for food, both bruised and dizzy. The glum faces of the few passengers who were on their feet announced a new disaster. The beer had given out. Nothing to drink but the slimy, fetid water which all knew was unwholesome. "We must ask Captain Hurlston to broach us a cask of spirits," said Mark. "That alone can make the water safe."

The others nodded and murmured. The sailors had beer, but their supplies too were running low, and to stint them had caused mutiny at sea before this.

The gale had continued and now the rain sliced like silver knives at the rigging. By noon the cold in the cabin was bitter as winter. Teeth chattered and faces turned blue and pinched. Many coughed from the smoke of the cook fire which could not escape through the closed portholes.

For dinner there was the watery pease porridge in which floated chunks of salt beef. Most had no appetite, and Phebe gave her portion to one of the young boys.

In midafternoon Mark came in with news. Since the sailor's death he and another passenger had been pressed into filling some seaman duties. The *Arbella* had managed to send over a skiff to borrow a hogshead of meal, and in return had sent back brandy. There was a feeble cheer, and anxious faces lightened a little.

By dusk all had forgotten themselves in pity and a new fear. Goodwife Carson suddenly started into active labor. Mrs. Bagby kept her head and habit of firm command, but even the children knew that matters were not going right. The laboring woman's shrieks tore through the main cabin, until Phebe, horrified by the public exposure of the poor woman's ordeal, had helped to carry her to the Honeywood bunk in the small cabin. Two of the older women followed, crowding close in the cold, airless space, trying to help the midwife. Anguish and death crowded with them. Helpless, they watched the agonized body wracked not only by labor pains, but by the violent wracking of the ship too. Between pains the woman lifted her head, the hair matted and wet, the eyes like an animal's. "Can ye not make it still an instant?" she wailed. "An it were quiet an instant, I might—" But a wave so big hit the ship that her body was flung against the bulkhead, and again that thin animal scream splintered the air.

Phebe, repulsed by the midwife, stumbled into the great cabin and going to the latrine bucket vomited a little. I must get out, she thought. I must. And running to the ladder, she climbed it and pushed with all her strength against the hatch above. She pounded on it frantically. It would not move. She crouched on the upper step, clinging to the rail. The dreadful screams were growing weaker.

"She can't endure," thought Phebe. In the great cabin a steady murmuring had begun. She lifted her head and listened. Master Wenn was reading from the Bible.

Above the hissing of the waves, the creaking of the joists, and the groans from the cabin, she heard the dry nasal voice intoning—

"Unto the woman he said, I will greatly multiply thy sorrow and thy conception; in sorrow thou shalt bring forth children; and thy desire shall be to thy husband—"

THAT will not help her, thought Phebe, with a sudden hot anger. She ran down the ladder, and burst in on them, the little group of women and children and a few shamefaced men who listened.

"Can you do nothing for her besides *pray!*" she cried.

They stared at her. Mistress Honeywood had seemed always so composed and aloof.

Mr. Wenn rested the ponderous Bible on his lap, his tight little face with its peaked gray beard seemed to consider her. His eyes were unexpectedly kindly. He did not rebuke her for interrupting the word of God, even though he disapproved of the Honeywoods as irreligious, careless conformists.

"And what can we do for her but pray, mistress?" he asked quietly.

The anger left Phebe and she bowed her head.

"I don't know," she whispered. "Forgive me." She shivered and drawing her cloak tight around her sank on the edge of a bench.

Master Wenn bent his head again to the Bible, screwing up his eyes to see the text by the flickering light of the iron lanthorn. Phebe tried to fix her mind on the droning voice, but she could not. From the small cabin now, there came at times a long choking moan. Phebe's hands gripped each other and she floundered through the black wash of fear. Fear for Goody Carson, that stupid but well-tempered woman reduced now to a thing less than human—and that other fear which she had not dared face. I too, next February maybe—like that creature in there—no!—it is but the hardships have delayed me. I cannot have conceived in that bunk where she lies now, conceived in the moldy straw—the lice—the ignoble stealthiness, watchful even in the unguarded ecstasy because the Brents might hear.

The ship lurched onward through the falling night, though the howling of the wind had abated, and the motion. On the deck above her head heavy footsteps passed. She heard the muffled shout of orders.

Around Master Wenn a group still listened, their heads bowed. Phebe looked down at her wedding ring, and into the confusion of fear there came the thought of the Lady Arbella. *She* would not give way like this, possessed of inner panic, resentful that her husband did not somehow divine a need and fly from man's work to comfort her. The Lady Arbella was strong and invincible.

Phebe moistened her dry lips, got off the bench, and went to the fire. No one had thought to replenish it, and the logs had fallen apart to smoldering ash. Yet food must be cooked for the children.

Her head throbbed as she bent over, but she shoveled the ashes into a heap, careful not to disturb the thick coating of dirt and brick dust which protected the wooden planking under the fire. She studied to lay each stick of pitchy kindling fair and square. As she finished and the flames aided by wind from the bellows crackled upward to the oak logs, a new sound came from the small cabin which had long been quiet. The acrid cry of the new-born.

Master Wenn closed his Bible. They all pressed through the door. Mrs. Bagby met them triumphantly. Her falling band was stained with blood, her fat face haggard, her hair in wisps. She held a swaddled bundle. "A girl. Never have I so needed my skill."

"But the mother—" cried Phebe, staring at the still mound.

"She'll do." Mrs. Bagby shrugged, put the baby at the foot of the bunk. "Fair lot o' trouble she gave me. Has the strongwater been broached?"

A sigh ran over them all. The moment of unity passed; they fell apart into their separate groups. Master Wenn and the two old men went to find the brandy. The children fell to quarreling beneath the ladder.

Most of the women gathered around, asking the midwife eager questions, while she cleansed herself a little in a cask of sea water.

Phebe had no taste for spirits, but when the brandy came she helped the others to mix it with the river water they had taken on at Yarmouth, and like them drank thirstily from the dipper.

Later when Mark appeared at last, bringing with him the freshness of damp sea air, she had hidden all trace of her fears.

Mark was in high spirits and full of the day's happenings on deck. The skiff from the *Arbella* had nearly foundered on her perilous trips between the two ships, but the wind had turned in the nick of time. They kept fairly well on board there, though many were dying on the *Ambrose*.

"And the Lady Arbella herself?" asked Phebe, braving Mark's displeasure. But he was in an indulgent mood. "I daresay she bears up like the rest—" he said carelessly. "I heard nothing contrary. Is that woman and her brat to have our bunk?" he looked toward their cabin.

Phebe nodded. "We can't turn them out tonight."

"Well. Then I must have me another noggin, and you too; 'twill soften our couch."

Phebe was grateful for the brandy haze as they lay down on the planking wedged into a space between a hogshead of dried pease and the forward bulkhead. The stink of the bilges was stronger here, and a rat scuttled about their feet. Mark put his arm close around her, and she lay with her head on his shoulder, trying to doze. But she could not.

The brandy and the stench brought back the seasickness she had thought conquered.

"Why must the ship forever roll so—" she whispered plaintively, trying to control her twitching stomach, and thinking Mark asleep.

"Why, it's your thrice damned fire-dogs, poppet—" he answered, chuckling. "No doubt they overbalance the ship; didn't you know that?"

She forgot her stomach, happy that he should tease her, glad that she had forborne to trouble him with the panic and forebodings she had suffered.

Ah we will endure, she thought, and all be well. It can't be for much longer. And she closed her eyes.

But the journey went on. Another week of cold and sudden gales and calms passed by. There was more sickness; not only the frequent purging and gripes in the belly from which all suffered at times, but an epidemic of feverish colds that left its victims with a strangling cough and a purulent discharge from the nose. The daily food rations shrank, but few cared, for the pork had spoiled, the stringy hunks of beef induced a thirst which there was no beer to quench, and the hard biscuits were coated with blue mold. They lived on pease porridge and water gruel.

Goody Carson, the new mother, was up from childbed but her wits seemed befuddled; she neither spoke nor smiled, and she had scanty milk for her nurseling whose wails were incessant. The baby had been named "Travail," and as the passengers' tempers grew ever shorter there was many an acid jest as to the appropriateness of its naming.

Everywhere on the ship small feuds had risen. Master Wenn led a clique of Separatists who joined in disapproval of those whose reasons for emigrating were not primarily religious.

Mrs. Bagby, from malice and boredom, headed another faction held together by resentment towards Phebe, because she kept herself apart, because she was young and more gently bred than they, because she wore a small lace ruff around her neck on Sundays, because she and her wild young gawk of a husband—naught but a tradesman either—seemed set far from the rest by a wanton show of passion for each other.

Phebe heard the whispers and knew herself shunned, but she was too weary and indifferent to care. She silently took her turn at the communal duties, the cooking of whatever food the cabin boy flung in the trenchers, the emptying of chamber pots and slop pails, the care of the sick, and otherwise lived for the moments of dubious privacy in the bunk with Mark. She had not told him of her fear, shamed that she should think it a fear. Besides, as long as it remained unvoiced it remained unreal. And there might yet be a mistake. Time enough to face it when they reached land. *If* they reached land. That was the thought in all their hearts. Day after day the soundings touched no bottom. Day after day the endless ocean stretched on ahead. And then one day they could no longer see the water, for an icy gray fog, colder and thicker than any they had met before, swathed the *Jewell* in a sinister quiet. The incessant blare of the horn sounded muffled and impotent, and no sound came back except the purling of sea at the barely moving bow.

The passengers, at first relieved to find steady decks beneath their feet, soon caught the contagion of renewed and sharper anxiety. The sailors had turned surly and would not speak. Captain Hurlston, briefly glimpsed on the poop deck, kept thereafter to his quarters in the roundhouse, and returned no answer to anxious messages.

Even Mark lost his optimism, and from his few glum words Phebe learned their peril. They must be near the Grand Banks; there were dangerous shoals to the south. They had lost the other boats four days ago, and in the fog the Captain was unsure of his bearings.

No, Mark answered impatiently, to her frightened question, of course there was nothing further to be done, except wait—"And I dare say you women and Master Wenn might pray on't." He escaped soon to the fo'c'sle, where at least there were no foolish questions, and where he had become proficient at knots and splices and learned the knack of the marlin spike.

The fog continued that night and on into the next day which was the sixth of June, and colder than any January day in Dorset. After a basin of porridge Phebe lay down in her bunk, shivering. The matted straw pallet beneath her was damp as a dishcloth and seemed to have vanquished even the lice which were less troublesome. She lay wrapped in her cloak and with their two bed rugs piled on top. She shut her eyes tight, trying to escape for a while into sleep, when she heard the thumps of running feet on the deck and men's voices raised in a resounding cheer. "Land Ho! Huzzah! Huzzah!"

She jumped from the berth and went out on deck.

The fog had suddenly lifted beneath a pale watery sun, and far off to the north rose a black line of cliff. Her heart swelled with wild relief. "Oh, thank God it's Naumkeag!" she cried crowding with the other excited passengers to the starboard rail.

"No, sweetheart"—she turned to see Mark laughing at her—"you push us too fast. It's Cape Sable, and many days yet ahead of us. But it is the New World at last!" He bent down and kissed her exuberantly, unnoticed for once by Mrs. Bagby and Master Wenn, who were united in the general elation.

They were indeed off the Grand Banks, the famous fishing banks to which European boats had been sailing for centuries. And the sea being most providentially quiet, they lay to while the sailors and most of the male passengers commenced to fish. They were abundantly rewarded; in less than two hours they had taken near fifty giant codfish. The women retreated to the poop deck, as the main deck became a mass of silvery flopping bodies. Phebe watched Mark, and ignorant as she was of the art, saw that he seemed more apt than the other landsmen. His movements in casting out the hand-line were quicker, he seemed to know by instinct the instant for the sharp jerk, he caught more fish than they did, and he caught the biggest of all—a yard long and near to that around the middle.

She thought of the Lady Arbella's remark, "I cannot see you as a fishwife," and smiled. Far across the water to the southwest the *Arbella* lay ahead of them, also hove-to, and doubtless also fishing. Later when they had glutted themselves with the sweet fresh fish, so delicious a change in their fare, she thought of Arbella again, and said to her—"You do not despise the occupation so now, do you, milady?"

The fish were good omen, not only for the bodies which they strengthened, but for the voyage. The winds at last grew fair and the weather warm. Off to starboard high land and mountains streamed by. All might spend the day on deck in the sunshine, and pleasant sweet air drifted to them from the land like the smell of a garden.

The strain relaxed from Mr. Hurlston, the ship's master, and he, who had been grimly aloof during those endless weeks at sea, grew affable and pointed out to them the landmarks they passed. Mount Desert, Agamenticus, The Isle of Shoals. Off Cape Ann a stiff southwest gale delayed them but now, so near to land and having weathered so many worse gales, the passengers scarcely minded.

On June 13, the Lord's Day, the *Jewell* slid gingerly through the passage between Baker's Isle and Little Isle, and at two o'clock the whole ship's company again let forth a mighty cheer, for there to the north of them rocking at anchor rested the *Arbella,* seeming as placid and at home as she had seemed so many weeks ago in Southampton Harbor.

"And THAT *is* Naumkeag—" cried Phebe staring with all her eyes at the wooded shore behind the *Arbella*.

"Nay, Phebe," said Mark laughing as he had laughed a week earlier when she miscalled Cape Sable. He took her by the shoulders and swung her around toward the southwest. "Down there is Naumkeag. Here is Cape Ann shore, we are still a league away. You must have patience."

"I can't wait to land," she said, smiling that their characters should be thus reversed, she chafing at delay and he counseling patience.

"See—" he said, pointing to the *Arbella,* "they're manning their skiff. They mean to waft us in, though being so much larger they must wait themselves for high water and a fair wind."

At five o'clock of the soft June afternoon the *Jewell* reached Naumkeag at last, and dropped anchor in the South Harbor. The low wooded shore was dotted with people waving, and the Huzzahs came now from their throats, not from those on the ship. These pressed together silently gazing at journey's end. Master Wenn raised his voice in a prayer of Thanksgiving, and Phebe, caught like the rest of them by the solemnity of the moment, bowed her head while the tears started to her eyes.

Mark was busy helping to lower the long boat, and she was in the first load to leave the *Jewell.* As he lifted her down from the ladder, she was astonished to feel a sharp nostalgia. The battered little ship which she had so much detested was now friend and home. She looked back at it with misted eyes, and the faces of those still on board, even that of Mrs. Bagby, seemed transfigured and lovable.

But it was good to set foot on the land though it seemed to sway and heave beneath her like the ship's deck. Delicious to refresh the eyes with the brown of earth and the brilliant green of the trees, loftier than any at home.

A score of men and three or four women had gathered at the landing place to greet them, but they held back in respect for the two ministers. Mr. Higginson and Mr. Skelton, tall and solemn in their flowing black prunella robes, bowed to each arrival saying "Welcome to Salem." It seemed that the Indian name "Naumkeag" had been replaced by the Hebrew word for "Peace."

Phebe held back a little, shy of these strange faces and waiting for Mark to discover what was expected of them, and as she watched, her joyous excitement dwindled. They looked haggard and ill, these people who had already been settled for a year in the land of promise. Mr. Higginson, though only forty-six, seemed like an old man. She noted the trembling of his hands, the eyes sunk back into the sockets, the unwholesome red on his cheekbones. Nor did his fellow minister, Mr. Skelton, look much stronger. They were all thin, ill-clothed, and hollow-eyed, these men and women of Salem, and after the first cheer they fell silent, drawing together on the bank and watching with somber looks while boatloads of passengers disembarked from the *Jewell.*

"Come—" said Mark, returning to Phebe. "We go to Governor Endicott's." They and the others moved along behind the ministers up a trampled path.

Phebe stared around her curiously, noting some rough earth dugouts roofed with bark, and tiny log huts beneath the trees, and thought with a thrill that these must be Indian dwellings. "I wonder how far it is to town?" she said to Mark. But Mr. Higginson overheard her, and to her mortification stopped and turned looking down at her. *"This* is the town, mistress—" he said; his burning eyes showed reproof and a faint amusement. "This the highway—" He pointed down the path, "and these our houses—" His long thin hand pointed to the bark dugouts.

"Oh to be sure, sir—" she stammered, turning scarlet. The minister nodded and continued to walk. Phebe followed silently, striving against dismay. On her father's land these dwellings would not have been thought fit to house the swine.

They came to a clearing of uneven grassy ground and near this clearing there were three wooden houses. The largest was two stories high and fairly built with windows and gables, almost like those at home. It was the Governor's house.

John Endicott met them on his stone doorstep and spoke a few gruff words of welcome, but he seemed out of temper, a sharp frown between his bushy brows, his pointed beard waggled irritably. For he was Governor no longer, as he had yesterday discovered upon the arrival of the *Arbella* with the royal charter, and his successor, John Winthrop.

"You'd best return to your ship," he said, "till your new Governor lands and can regulate your proceedings. We've little food or shelter for you now and there is much sickness."

Even Mark's enthusiasm was quenched by this, and after further consultation between Endicott, the ministers and the *Jewell's* master, the new arrivals trailed disconsolately back to the ship. So Phebe and Mark slept again in the cramped cabin they had foolishly thought to have seen for the last time.

The first day on shore was filled with a feverish activity. When the *Arbella* had been warped up to the town dock near the *Jewell,* the great folk on board, the new Governor, the Saltonstalls, the Phillips, all moved majestically down the gangplank ahead of its lesser passengers. Phebe watched eagerly for the Lady Arbella, until she landed last of all, walking slowly, her tall figure swathed in the fur-lined cloak, though the day was warm. She was leaning on the arm of a tall, fair young man who was her husband, Mr. Isaac Johnson.

Phebe drew back shyly as the lady passed, but Arbella noticed her, and smiled with great sweetness. "Why, it's Mistress Honeywood, Isaac, I told you of her." She held out her hand. "How was the journey, my dear?"

Phebe took the thin white hand and curtsied. "I thought it would never end, milady, but now I scarce remember it, there's so much to do here."

Arbella nodded. Her blue eyes wandered past Phebe to the dusty lane which disappeared amongst the trees by the first earthen dugout. " 'Tis good to be on land," she said vaguely. "I'll soon gain strength again." This was to her husband, and Phebe saw the quick anxiety in his eyes.

"To be sure you will." He clasped the hand which rested on his arm. "Do you know where we're to go?" he asked of Phebe. "Governor Winthrop was to return for us, but he must have been detained."

"Oh yes, sir, they've prepared a fair wood house for you, down by the green, 'twas built last year by some gentleman of Mr. Higginson's party—at least," she added, her lips indenting with a rueful humor, "it's a fair enough house for Salem."

Isaac nodded, and she thought how much alike those two were, both tall and fine-drawn, both informed with an idealistic courage.

"We don't look for a castle in the wilderness," he said. "Will you guide us, mistress?"

Phebe gladly complied, but as she trudged up the path ahead of them her heart was troubled. They did not expect a castle, but did they expect the hardships and the actual hunger which already Phebe had discovered in Salem. This morning when filling a pot with water for the cleansing of their garments, she had talked with a gaunt middle-aged woman near the spring. Goodwife Allan acted half-crazed as she told of the previous winter; the wolves, the savages, the bitter bitter cold, the hunger and the sickness and fear. Her high thin voice whined through her drawn lips as though against its will. She had no pity, nor desire to frighten, either. It seemed she could not stop from touching again and again like a festering tooth the horror of her memories. And Phebe could not get away, for the woman followed her about until another woman came and spoke sharply.

"Hold your tongue, Goody. 'Tis cruel to so frighten the young mistress here," and turning to Phebe she spoke lower. "Her two babes died this winter. She returns to England when the fleet goes—and so do I."

Home to England—! Phebe had clamped her mind down hard against the great leap of longing and envy she had felt, and hope too. Surely Mark would soon see how different all was from his expectation.

Yet now, watching the Lady Arbella and her husband, she felt some shame for her own faint heart. *They* would never falter, thought Phebe proudly, nor turn back home in fear and failure.

Governor Winthrop came hurrying across the green to meet them, and Phebe curtsying and drawing aside noted the Lady's gracious words, how she praised the beauty of the countryside, and even praised the compactness of the rough-planked two-room house which had been prepared for her.

The Governor and Mr. Johnson plunged at once into frowning consultation, and Phebe, warm from Arbella's smile of thanks, slipped away, back down the lane to the South River. A hundred yards up the slope from the Landing Place, near to the Burial Point—Mark had found them a shelter. He had bought it for a barrel of meal from one of the men who wished to leave Salem. It was twelve feet long and eight wide, made from a sapling frame; the walls and roof were of woven rushes and pine bark. Its floor was the ground, its door a single batten of hewn oak planks, and its end fireplace of piled field stones cemented with fish-shell lime provided the only daylight through its wide square chimney.

It had been copied like its fellows from an Indian wigwam. It was dark and damp and smoky, but it was shelter.

Aye—but how will it be alone here—she thought, entering the wigwam to start their supper preparations, and the new trouble which the sight of Arbella had momentarily banished came back to plague her. For Mark was leaving her to sail southward with Governor Winthrop and most of the company and search for better lands.

At no time had Winthrop considered permanent settlement of his company in Salem, but he had found physical conditions far worse than he expected, nor were spiritual matters to his liking. The ministers Higginson and Skelton had unaccountably changed during their year here. They had come over as Puritans, averring their loyalty to the Mother Church and interested only in freeing her from certain forms of Papist corruption.

Had not Mr. Higginson upon taking the last sight of England a year ago cried, "Farewell the Church of God in England, and all the Christian friends there. We do not go to New England as Separatists from the Church of England—but we go to practise the positive part of Church reformation, and propagate the gospel in America."

And yet upon his arrival in Salem, Winthrop found that these same ministers had adopted the congregational polity and affiliated themselves with the Separatist Church at Plymouth. And so strict in conscience had they become that Winthrop's company, being no members of the Salem Church, were not even invited to worship with them on the Lord's Day.

There were besides many jealousies; the earlier settlers under Endicott and the ministers felt themselves dispossessed by new authority, just as Roger Conant and his settlers had been literally dispossessed, in 1628, by the arrival of Endicott.

So Winthrop would sail again tomorrow on the *Arbella* to explore Massachusetts Bay and decide on a more welcoming site for the new settlement. Most of the male passengers would accompany him, and Mark too of course, already impatient with Salem, but ever hopeful and eager for more adventuring.

I must be reasonable, thought Phebe, sighing, I can manage alone for a time. She moved around the wigwam trying to make it more homelike. Though all the *Jewell's* freight had not yet been unloaded, the Honeywoods had found some of their household gear, and together carried it to the wigwam. There were blankets to sleep on, the two chests of clothing, a skillet and spoon, and an iron pot which Phebe, feeling very housewifely, hung from the green lugpole left by the earlier tenant. And there were the andirons. They gave an incongruous and elegant air to the rough Indian fireplace, and Mark had been impatient with her insistence that they must be used. But when their first fire blazed and they sat down on the blankets to eat, he admitted that they were sturdy, well-made dogs and did better than the stones the other new settlers were using.

They supped that night on pease porridge and a large catfish which Mark had caught in the river. And they had beer, bought with one of the precious shillings, from a sailor on the *Arbella*. But the shillings were not so precious here, Phebe had soon realized—only to those who were returning to England. Here nothing mattered but food.

It had not occurred to Mark that she might be short of food during his absence, since they had brought barrels of pickled meat, flour, and pease, but already Phebe had seen enough of the conditions to realize the vital importance of conserving supplies as long as possible—in case they stayed long. Always that reservation whispered in her heart.

But there were wild strawberries in the woods, and mussels and clams at low tide for the picking.

"You'll not be frightened to be alone, Phebe?" said Mark suddenly, seeing her pensive. "I'll be back soon. You know how little I wish to leave you—but I must."

"I know dear—" she said gently, for she saw that he was shaken from the bustle of novelty and action which had made him thoughtless, and that there was anxious awareness of her in his eyes. "No, I won't be frightened. Why, I can see the ships from our doorway, and then there are all the other folk—so near."

"The Lady Arbella—" he said with a curt laugh. "I vow you dote upon her noble ladyship. I never thought to find you so fawning—God's blood, Phebe—it's to be rid of such as her, I quitted England!"

She had been sitting beside him in the bed-roll, and now she rose and walked away from him to the doorway. "It has nothing to do with her rank, Mark." She spoke with coldness and dignity.

"What is it then?" he asked in a quieter tone, standing up beside her.

She could not answer. Never had she found it easy to speak of the secret things in her mind. The Lady Arbella was like a shining silken banner for the humble heart to follow. She was beauty, she was courage, and she was England here on this alien and unfriendly soil. Mark would never understand that, nor need to. He needed no symbol to strengthen him.

She shook her head. "I cannot say."

But Mark was no longer attending; he had forgotten his question in watching the curve of her rosy cheek, and the roundness of her neck and bosom. He picked her up and sat down with her on his knee, where he held her fast, pulled off her cap and tossed it in the corner, rumpled and loosened her smooth brown hair.

"Not so solemn, sweetheart—" he whispered. "We must be merry in our fine new home."

She resisted at first, being still grieved by their difference. But he began to caress her playfully, teasing her with mock anger, kissing away her protests until at last he had her laughing too and as eagerly amorous as he.

The *Arbella* and Governor Winthrop came back in a few days, he having decided to gather up his company and establish a temporary settlement at Charlestown. It was not an ideal site since the peninsula was small and the water supply very scanty, but it would serve as a base for further exploration.

Phebe had been bitterly disappointed that Mark had not also returned to Salem. He had however sent her a letter which was delivered to her wigwam by a friendly sailor.

She carried the letter inside her dwelling and stared at it with a mixture of apprehension, embarrassment, and pride. Mark knew—or had he forgotten—that she could not read—that was an accomplishment deemed useless to a yeoman's daughter. She turned the half-sheet of folded paper, admiring the red seal stamped with a small signet, and guessed that he, never backward in fulfilling his impulses, had borrowed all from one of the great folk on board.

At last she broke the seal and stared at the lines of cramped and blotted writing:

> "Swete wife be not vext I linger too finde us setlment. Ther is muche to see but the peple are not so as we ded expect. Ther is good stor of feishe but harde to come bye and not enuf provisseyenes.
>
> Bee stout harted.
>
> Thy lovinge husband
>
> M. Hunywood."

She followed each word with her finger, her brows drawn together. Almost she got the sense of it, but she was not sure. A certainty born of love told her that here was no particular bad news, and that he had written the letter so that she might have an immediate token of him, and for this she bent her head and kissed the paper. But it was exasperating not to know precisely the meaning.

She considered a while, then nodded her head with decision. There was but one person in Salem who could read the letter, yet who would not smile at it or Phebe's ignorance, one person to whose delicacy of understanding one would not shrink from exposing intimacy.

Phebe took the hearth shovel, dug into the earth in the corner of the wigwam, and pulled from its hiding place the key of her bride chest. This and Mark's oaken chest stood in the wigwam with the precious provisions.

She drew out her best dress, a soft crimson gown with slashed sleeves, made of a silk-and-wool fabric newly fashionable in England, called farandine. She put on her wedding ruff and cuffs made of cobweb lawn trimmed with Mechlin lace, and she rejoiced that the day being so mild, she might dispense with the heavy hooded serge cloak which had done hard duty on the ship and was her only outer garment. Before donning her best lace-trimmed cap, she pulled her hair forward into loose ringlets about her ears and examined the effect in a small steel looking glass.

Then she set forth up the road toward the common, happy in the feminine consciousness of being suitably dressed for her visit. Not so elegant as to affront the gentry, nor in coarse sad-colored clothes like the goodwives and maid servants.

The weather was very hot, warmer than it ever was in England, and the lane was dusty. Soon she came to the village "green," no green now but a square of trodden earth and brownish stubble. Some women clustered as usual around the well, gossiping while they drew water for their households. At the other end near the stocks—unoccupied today—three young men played at stool ball, ceasing frequently for thirst-quenching at the Ordinary near by. Idleness like this was naturally frowned upon by the magistrates, but the return of the *Arbella* and Governor Winthrop's intent to remove all his settlers had relaxed supervision.

Phebe continued past the two-room houses belonging to Mr. Higginson and Mr. Skelton, past the Governor's larger frame house, where there was much bustle of coming and going, for Winthrop was inside and holding conference, and on a little way up the lane to the next house which was that of the Lady Arbella.

She knocked timidly and waited. There was a scuffle within and suppressed giggles. At last the door was opened by a frowsy maid, her cap awry, her holland apron stained with the claret she had evidently been sampling. She stared sullenly at Phebe, impudence just held in check by Phebe's clothing and dignity.

"Might I have a word with the Lady Arbella, if it's convenient?" said Phebe.

" 'er Ladyship's resting," answered the girl in her flat Lincolnshire twang. "She wants no company," and she made to shut the door, staying her hand at the sound of a clear firm voice calling, "Who's at the door, Molly?"

"Mistress Honeywood," supplied Phebe. The maid shrugged, and walking two steps to the shut door on the right, imparted this information.

"Let her enter," called Arbella. Molly stood aside long enough for Phebe to pass, then darted back to the house's other room, the hall or kitchen where she rejoined her two companions by the wine cask.

Phebe entered the other room which was also the bed-chamber. The servants slept above the kitchen in the unfinished loft.

Arbella lay on a feather bed raised a foot from the planks by a rough pine frame. She wore only a bedrobe of transparent blue tiffany, but her pale face was bedewed. Her golden hair as it branched from her forehead was dark with sweat, and there were bistre shadows beneath the large blue eyes. But her smile as she greeted Phebe had its usual gallant sweetness.

"Welcome, mistress, it's kind that you come to visit me. How comely you look."

"To do you honor, my lady—" said Phebe, accepting the ladderback chair indicated by Arbella. " 'Tis most good of you to receive me."

Arbella shook her head. "Nay, I'm much alone. My husband still at Charlestown, and my friends who returned, the Governor and Sir Richard, so much occupied. And my servants—" She shook her head again. "But you saw Molly, how she was. And the others worse. It's hard to believe a new country or a sea voyage could so change them. And I've not—not yet—the strength to rule them properly. I must save my strength."

As she said this a light came into her eyes, and her lips lifted in a joyous and secret smile. She looked at Phebe and saw in the younger woman's face the eager admiration which had been there from their first meeting in Yarmouth, and the need to speak overcame Arbella's reticence.

"I'm with child—" she said very low. "At last. Wed seven years and I had lost all hope. Our dear Lord has rewarded me for braving the new land."

Phebe swallowed. For an instant she could not properly answer the lady's confidence. It pierced through the foolish barrier Phebe had built against her own realization. And through the rent, like the mounting sound of tempest waves, she heard the rushing of fear.

And again Arbella had shamed her, by the radiance in her thin face, and thrill in the low voice.

"I'm happy for you, milady," Phebe said gently. She hesitated. "I think I too am with child."

Arbella gave a little cry and stretched out her hand until Phebe came to the bedside and took it in hers. "We have then that great bond between us—" said Arbella. Her pale cheeks flushed, and she sat up, her long braids of wheat-colored hair falling back across her thin shoulders. "Tell me—" and she asked eager questions, and as they talked together, she seemed the younger of the two women.

Both babies would be born in the winter they decided, Arbella's the earlier, in January, for she had reason to guess it had been conceived in England before the sailing. "And you will stay near me, Phebe—

won't you," Arbella said—"that our babies may know each other and grow together in the new land?"

"Indeed I hope so, milady." Now Phebe's eyes too were shining, Arbella's courage and Arbella's pride had become hers too. "But I don't know where Mark will decide our settlement. He—he wrote me a letter, I brought it—" Phebe stopped and blushed. "I hoped—" She stared down at the letter in her hand.

Arbella was briefly puzzled. She had been talking to this girl as she would have talked to her own sister, Lady Susan, and had forgotten that there was difference between them. Nor did the rigid class distinction seem to matter much in the wilderness. She covered Phebe's embarrassment at once by taking the letter and calmly reading it aloud.

" 'Tis evident he takes thought of you and loves you," she commented smiling.

Phebe smiled back, unable to suppress the leap of hope again. If Mark continued to be disappointed in conditions as he found them—perhaps after a few months of roving and striving . . .

"I too had a letter this morning from my husband—" said Arbella. "He favors a place called Shawmut—it's across a river from Charlestown—and is starting to prepare for me. You must bear on your Mark to settle there too."

Phebe was silent for a moment, glad that the lady did not guess her unbecoming hope, and considering this new idea.

"Why, is there fish at this Shawmut, your ladyship?" she asked with her sudden quiet twinkle.

Arbella laughed. "There must be. Is he still set on fishing?"

"More than ever. He is most apt." But he might fish from Weymouth at home, she thought, it was scarcely farther to the great fishing banks from there than it was from any part of this unwelcoming wilderness.

"I shall speak to Mr. Johnson," said Arbella with decision. She said nothing more but she was thinking. She would use her influence to settle the Honeywoods in Shawmut, or Boston as Isaac proposed to call it from their own shire town.

"When the Governor leaves again," she said, "he'll bear a letter to my husband. I shall request that he find your Mark and take interest in him."

Phebe gratefully acquiesced, nor voiced her doubts of Mark's reception of this affectionate and natural patronage.

That was the first of many visits. As the days passed and the heat wave lessened, Arbella grew stronger, and together Phebe and she stood on the bank by the landing place and watched the ship *Arbella* sail down the river, bound southward to the new plantations with two hundred aboard her.

Except for the few like Phebe and Arbella who remained to wait for their men to fetch them, and the very few who desired to settle there, Salem reverted to its earlier population. In the North Village there lived a handful of the first planters who had not followed Roger Conant across the river to Beverley; and in the south or main village, lived those who still survived from the companies which had come with Endicott or the two ministers. True, throughout June and July many ships touched at Salem, as the rest of Winthrop's fleet straggled into port. But the passengers were not disembarked. All sailed again at once for Charlestown to join the others.

On July 3, Phebe, asleep in her wigwam, was wakened by the now familiar shouts and creakings and bustle which meant the arrival of another ship. She dressed hastily and opening her door was delighted to see that it was the *Hopewell* which had in England been destined for freight. Mooings and cracklings and bleatings echoed in the early morning air, and the inhabitants of Salem crowding down to the dock let out a cheer. Most of them were disappointed. The livestock must go on to Charlestown, where already there was famine. But Phebe, finding courage to board and seek out the master herself, discovered that her milch-cow had survived the trip, and demanded that it be landed.

In this she would not have succeeded, between the Captain's haste to be on to Charlestown and finish this tedious trip, and her lack of the necessary papers, had not Arbella, hastily summoned by Phebe, come down to the boat and straightened the matter.

Phebe coaxed and tugged the terrified cow down the gangplank; and when her prize was safely on shore could not resist kissing the soft fawn-colored muzzle. Betsey was living link with home. Phebe had last seen her standing in the Edmunds' barn, her new calf beside her and placidly munching while the younger children decorated her with a wreath of early primroses, "because Betsey was a cow princess and going to America with sister Phebe."

Phebe soothed the cow with soft whispers—"So-o-o-o, Betsey—Hush, Betsey, it's on land again you are. Ah poor beast, you're nearly dry. Didn't they milk you right or was it the seasickness?"

The cow looked at her mournfully, and Phebe threw her arm around the warm furry neck.

The Lady Arbella had been watching with some amusement. "Aren't you afraid of its horns?" she asked. "I've never seen a cow so close before."

Phebe looked from the cow to her friend. Friend, yes, the only one in Salem, and they seemed to share much together. But in truth they did not. The lady's fine white hands had never labored with anything rougher than the embroidery needle. A spasm of homesickness overpowered Phebe. For her father's hearty laugh and broad speech, for her mother's kindly bustle. "Phebe, child, do you finish the milking, the dairy maids are at the churns." For the fresh voices of the younger children singing "Oh Lavendar's green, dilly, dilly—" and tumbling about the grassy courtyard, while the doves cooed accompaniment from their cote.

"I've milked Betsey many times, milady," she said very low, and pulling on the halter, she began to lead the cow up the path from the dock to her wigwam.

Arbella followed. "Will the animal not be a great care?" she asked gently. "And how will you feed it?"

Phebe considered. "I'll arrange with little Benjy, the herd, to take her each day to the common to graze with the other stock. At night I can tether her by my door. 'Twill be well worth it, if I can coax her milk back."

"For butter?"

Phebe nodded, "If I can borrow a churn, but mostly for milk. That will do us good. You too, my lady."

Arbella looked so astounded that Phebe smiled. She knew that except on farms neither milk nor plain water were considered wholesome. Arbella like all the gentry drank wines, often diluted. The lower classes drank strong liquor, beer or cider or mead. But milk was considered valuable only for its ability to produce cheese and butter.

Nor did she ever persuade Arbella to try it. By the time the cow had adjusted herself to her new home and the coarse pasture land on the common so that Phebe's persuasive handling would fill a night and morning pail, Arbella was confined to her bed again with a mysterious illness. And the *Arbella's* physician Mr. Gager was in attendance.

Those were grim days that set in after the middle of July. Many were sick besides the Lady Arbella, some with the ship fever which swelled mouths, loosened teeth, and sent cruel pains through the body. Others like the Lady herself were afflicted by excessive languor, headache and colic, and these though often able to get about seemed to grow burning hot towards evening, and day by day to lose strength. The weather too ceased to be pleasant. There was much heavy rain. The lanes turned to quagmires. The reed thatching on Phebe's wigwam leaked in a dozen places, and when there was no rain, the mosquitoes swarmed through the new-made crannies and attacked voraciously. Phebe set her teeth and settled to day by day endurance as she had on the boat. The friendly Naumkeag Indians came and went in town. She had quickly become accustomed to their nakedness and dark painted faces, and she learned to barter with them as did the others. A little of her meal she had exchanged for corn and pompions, the great golden fruit which might be baked or stewed into good food.

Sometimes she dug clams or made a hasty pudding from the corn, but mostly she lived on corn cakes baked on a shovel over the flames—and Betsey's milk. She grew very thin, and sometimes felt light-headed, and that the wigwam and the rain and the mosquitoes, the heavy-eyed people in the village, the close pressing forest—and even Arbella lying white and silent in her house, were all painted on smoke. Shifting figures without reality that a strong breath might blow away. Still Phebe had few pains. She even found a way of lessening the surface discomfort from the mosquitoes. On the lane to the common she had spied a small herb, pennyroyal, much like that which grew at home. Well instructed by her mother in the making of simples, she had gathered a horde of it, and distilled it over boiling water. The pungent mint odor, when rubbed on the skin, repelled fleas at home, and did discourage the mosquitoes here.

She carried some of it to Lady Arbella on one of her daily visits. There was now no need to knock. Molly, the impudent maid servant, was herself ill and lay groaning in the loft. The manservant and the other maid gave only grudging and frightened service, held from actual escape by the knowledge that there was no safe place to go.

Phebe's daily arrival was heartily welcomed for she did much of the nursing.

Today Mr. Gager, the physician, was there, bleeding Arbella. He acknowledged Phebe's quiet entrance by a curt nod, and went on with his task. Phebe took off her muddy shoes and placing them in a corner of the room, came to the foot of the bed. Arbella started to smile a greeting as she always did, but at once her gaze slid past Phebe, and into the staring blue eyes came a distant intent look. "Think you, madam, 'twill be a fine day for the chase?" she said. "I hear the huntsmen winding their horns. Will Charles ride the gray stallion?"

Phebe's breath caught, and her eyes met the physician's. His mouth set, and he nodded his gray head. "She wanders." He sighed heavily. "It's enteric, I believe. There are the rose spots." He drew the coverlet down a little. The delicate white skin of the swelling abdomen and slender waist was sprinkled with pinkish dots.

"I must find someone to help you and the servants," he said, rising, "but so many are sick. Each day a new case. Would that her husband were back—" he added half to himself.

"I'll not leave her," said Phebe.

William Gager picked up his leech bag and threw in the lancet. "You're a good girl, mistress. I'll come back later—I—I must rest. Give her nothing but wine and this oil of fennel." He indicated a flask on the rough stool by the bedside. He put his hand to his head, and swayed a little as he stood up. Phebe saw his lips twitch, and fear pull at his face. "This thrice cursed country," he said under his breath, and went out.

Phebe went to the kitchen for a pewter basin. The little maid sat on a stool, listlessly turning two spitted rabbits above the flames. The man-servant had gone to the forest for firewood. Above in the loft the sick maid, Molly, whimpered incessantly. Phebe climbed the ladder, and did what she could to bring comfort, changing the fouled linen, holding the mug of claret while the girl drank. Then she hurried back to the other patient with a basin of rain water, washed Arbella's thin fair body, then rubbed it with the pennyroyal. Despite the tight-shut windows mosquitoes whined in the dark little room, and the rain beat without ceasing on the roof.

Arbella was still wandering. Sometimes she thought herself a child in Tattershall Castle, or riding through Sherwood Forest. Sometimes she relived her bridal day and spoke to Isaac, her husband, with such poignancy and passion that Phebe flushed and murmured, "Oh, hush my dear lady. Hush!"

Worst of all as the long gray day wore on, Arbella began to talk of her child, thinking that it had been born, and demanding of Phebe that she bring it in to her. "I wish my son," she said imperiously. "All in this new land rejoice that he is born. Why don't you rejoice? How dare you look so sad, wench! Bring me my son."

Phebe soothed her, replacing the cool cloths on the burning forehead, stroking the restless hands that plucked at the coverlet.

At dusk Arbella became quieter; it seemed the fever eased. She lay still a long time, her eyes closed, her hand clinging to Phebe's. Then the blue eyes opened and gazed at the girl with full recognition. "You must rest, dear," she whispered. "You do too much for me. You must think of your babe."

Phebe shook her head, smiling. "No, I'm strong. Nursing is nothing for me. I've done it often at home."

Her last unconsidered word seemed to crash through the room, like the first toll of a passing bell. A spasm twisted Arbella's face, while the word went echoing and swelling around them.

Blundering fool, cried Phebe to herself, and she spoke again with cheerful resolution. "Here now is home, my lady, and soon 'twill feel so." She rose to smooth the bedding.

Arbella stopped her. "Do you remember, Phebe, Mr. Higginson's sermon on the Sabbath? 'What went ye out into the wilderness to see? A reed shaken with the wind?' We must not hark back. Promise me, Phebe—" she rose painfully on her elbow, her eyes beseeching. "Promise me, you'll not give up—no matter what may happen."

Phebe tried to speak, to give easy assurance, but she could not. Mr. Higginson had died the day before. Arbella did not know that. There was death in every dwelling—and hunger and despair. When Mark came, tired perhaps of the new adventure, restless again, and wishing to go home,—home—home—home—The forbidden, the exquisite music.

Arbella sank onto the pillow, the light faded from her eyes. "I had no right to ask you that, child. Your future is in God's hands—as is mine." She drew a shaking sigh, that ended in a sudden cry of pain. The brief interval of peace was ended. The pain and noises in her head returned, and the cruel gripings in her distended belly. Phebe almost welcomed the mounting fever, for it gave surcease from the pain as Arbella's mind escaped again, back—now always back, into the tranquil, the sheltered days of her childhood.

All the interminable night, Phebe watched beside Arbella, refusing the little maid's reluctant offer of help. "You look after Molly," she told the girl, "and keep the fire up for hot water. I'll look to her ladyship."

Once in the evening, a neighbor, Mistress Horne, hurried in, saying that Mr. Gager the physician had told her how very ill the Lady Arbella was. Mr. Gager himself was suffering with headache and vomiting so that he could not rise from bed.

Phebe thanked her but said that she could manage alone. Mistress Horne's kind, worried face showed relief. "I'm glad to hear it, my dear, for I've heavy duties at home, my little girl puking blood, and my youngest most feverish. You've none but yourself to consider, have you, mistress?"

Phebe shook her head. The two women stood by Arbella's bedside together. Mrs. Horne made a sound in her throat, and whispered—"Dear—she do look bad. Such a sweet woman. I was watching from my window the day she landed and come walking down the street with her fine young husband. She looked so kindly and so fair. But I feared then 'twould take rougher clay than she is to stand the roughness here—"

"She'll get well," said Phebe sharply. "Many do have the burning fever and get well."

Mrs. Horne sighed and turned from the bed. "We can hope so. But many do not." She walked to the wall and peered into Arbella's looking glass. "What a frump I've grown," she said pushing distractedly at the lank hair around her perspiring face, then seeing Phebe's expression, she said, "I'm not unfeeling, my dear, but one gets used to death here. Needs must or go mad." She straightened her linen cap, gave a tug to her collar. "They say there's a ship sighted way off down the bay. If it's another from England, I hope they bring us provisions as well as more mouths to eat 'em."

"But maybe—" cried Phebe, "it's from Charlestown—from the Governor—maybe it's her husband at last—" she looked toward the bed, "and mine," she added very low.

"Mayhap it is," said the woman kindly, and without the slightest conviction. "Pray on't," she advised, opening the door. "Miracles are wrought by prayer."

Through the night Phebe thought of this. They did live by prayer, here, and they did seem to have special understanding and closeness to God. At home God stayed in church. He lived in the candles and the incense and the golden cross, in the voices of the choir boys, in the slow solemn movements of the lace-frocked priest. But she had never thought to find Him elsewhere.

She tried to pray, but no words came, nor could she remember the words of the prayer book. Neither could she believe that any prayer might change the identity of that ship in the bay. The prayer, therefore, which came to her heart but could find no utterance was for Lady Arbella. And she made a foolish covenant. If the lady recovered it would be easy to join in her Church, for had they not in a dozen conversations agreed to stay near each other, and Phebe to follow her in all things.

In the first rose light of the new summer day, she heard the sound of running feet on the road outside. She darted to the door and flung it open. She saw five men crowding upon the threshold, and gave a cry to the man in front. "Oh, Mr. Johnson, thank God." The blond young man gave her a frightened look and pushed past her as she clung to the door frame. She saw a curly head behind and higher than the others, she tried to speak again, but a rocking giddiness swept through her head. The sunlit road billowed and darkened. She felt strong arms seize her, as she slipped down to the ground.

She opened her eyes to the familiar ragged thatching of the wigwam. Her bemused gaze wandered from a chink between the reeds and the slit of blue sky it revealed, to Mark's frightened face bending close to her own. He knelt beside her on their mattress and his arms still supported her. She gave a little sigh of content, and turning her head, nuzzled for her accustomed place on his shoulder.

"Sweetheart!" he cried sharply, feeling her body relax against him, and seeing her lids droop. "Don't swoon again. Phebe, are you ill?"

He almost shook her in his anxiety. She raised her head and kissed him on the mouth. "Not ill," she said drowsily. "Hungry, and so glad you're safe back."

His frown cleared. Always and so easily she could reassure him. He smiled and kissed her, hard and long. She submitted, willing enough to drift with him to that moment which ensured forgetfulness of all else.

But Mark had been alarmed when she slid off Lady Arbella's stone step into his arms, and he saw now how pale and thin she was. He shook his head and put her from him. "Food first, poppet," he said standing up. "I've no wish to bed a wraith. You lie there, I'll do all."

He had brought a venison steak, gift as he explained of a Mr. Isaac Allerton of whom he had seen much, and in whom he had great interest. She watched him with some surprise, as he hacked off slices with his hunting knife and broiled them over the fire. He had learned much, apparently, in those weeks he had been away. Never before had he had anything to do with cookery.

He fed her the rich gamy meat, and brought her mugs of beer until she could hold no more, and she sighed deeply and loosened her belt to enjoy the delicious fullness.

Mark chuckled, glad to see the color come back to her cheeks, and amused that she who was always so fastidious should loosen her clothing. But as he gazed at her a new look crossed his face.

"Phebe—" he said half teasing, half startled, "did the venison fill you so much, or can it be—aren't you more full-bellied?"

Phebe looked down at her gown. "You have sharp eyes, love," she said quietly. "I had not thought to show yet." She spoke so quietly because, still, the old fear leaped at her, and now the new fear too, the fear for Arbella which her exhaustion had put aside for this past hour.

Mark, puzzled by her voice, and uncertain as all young husbands, persisted, "You mean I've got you with child—?"

At this, despite her fears, she could not help laughing. "Oh, Mark, you great goose. Who else? Nor should it surprise you, you're lusty enough, the Lord knows."

She saw him adjusting himself to this new idea. He bent and kissed her cheek, carefully, as though she were of a sudden turned to crystal. Then his natural exuberance returned and he gave a great roar of mirth. "You had better not let any of those mewling Separatists hear you call on the Lord to witness lustiness! They'd sew a letter "L" to your bodice for lewd, and very like add a "B" for blasphemy—Pah—" he cried scowling, "they're a narrow canting lot. I've no stomach for all this Godly talk and conscience-searching. Nor was it what we were led to expect when we came. Why else did Master White get 'em to sign 'The Humble Request' on the *Arbella* back at Yarmouth except to show we would not separate. Promised we were we'd be let alone in our own beliefs. Now Winthrop's getting sour as the rest of them."

"They're not all so bad, Mark," Phebe said softly, but he scowled even harder, staring at the earthen floor.

"You've no say in running a town unless you're a freeman, you can't be a freeman unless you join the Church, you can't join the Church without the minister permits. I'll never make Churchman, and I've seen no minister I like here yet. 'Tis cramping in its own way as the Old Country."

Phebe drew in her breath. "Then what will you do, Mark," she asked, watching him very close, "if you've found no place to your liking for our settlement?"

He raised his head and looked at her. "Aye, but I think I have."

Her heart slowed, and her mouth grew dry. "Tell me then—no tell me first about your journey, from the beginning."

For she dreaded to hear of any decision, and well knew how much harder it would be to change his mind after he had voiced one.

He nodded, for he was himself unsure as yet, and glad to clear his mind by talking. "Well, as you know, we set off from here with fair winds—"

He described the two-day voyage in somewhat more nautical detail than she could understand. They had passed a place called Nahant, threaded their way amongst a great many little islands, entered the mouth of the Charles, and landed passengers at the ramshackle collection of tents and wigwams called Charlestown. The place appealed to nobody; it was cramped and barren but it was necessary to stop somewhere while the leaders searched further.

The minister, Mr. Phillips, set off to explore with Saltonstall up the Charles in search of a new site, the Governor went up the Mystic for the same purpose. Mark, however, had no intention of settling inland, and crossing the Charles by canoe, he had been amongst the first to explore the peninsula known as Shawmut with its three rounded hills. They found a settler there, a taciturn well-lettered man called Blackstone. He had lived there quite alone five years, and made himself snug in a two-room cabin filled with books and surrounded by a small garden and three apple trees.

He was a man, said Mark, who liked solitude, and had been watching the activities across the river with considerable dismay. But he was also a gentleman, and his greeting was not uncordial.

The Lady Arbella's husband, Isaac Johnson, was much taken with the site, and when Governor Winthrop returned from the Mystic River, both men held long conferences with Mr. Blackstone, who unselfishly agreed that they might settle at Shawmut if they wished. He would stay a while and help them, since he knew the secrets of the country, the best springs, the most fertile soil, and was also well-liked by the Indians. "But," said he gravely—all his speech was slow and grave, but in this instance his eyes twinkled a bit—"I'll soon be off to the wilderness, for I doubt not I'll grow as weary of the 'lord brethren' here as I did of the 'lord bishops' in the old England."

Mark had heard this speech and applauded it.

The town planning began at once, Shawmut was rechristened Boston, land was allotted, Master John Wilson was appointed minister, settlers poured in as the ships from England docked almost daily, and Mark found it not at all to his liking.

It was then that he met Isaac Allerton. There was a makeshift ordinary in a hut on the beach at Charlestown, and Mark had gone in one evening for a tankard of metheglin from a cask just arrived by the *Success*.

He had been tired and discouraged, but the strong fermented honey liquor put new life in him. Perhaps it also had something to do with his immediate interest in a man who entered the smoky little room, and also called for drink.

He was a man in his middle forties, rather short, and comfortably plump. His round face was clean-shaven, his full cheeks a healthy red, doubtless from the seafaring life, but Mark found it pleasant to see again a man who appeared well fed and sanguine, the type of beef-eating country squire who seemed seldom to emigrate. He had grown so accustomed to the half-starved gauntness of his fellows, that the newcomer's appearance and smile was an agreeable shock. Then he was well-dressed too in a slashed doublet of green serge lined with leather, glossy calamanco breeches, and a silver filigree buckle on his beaver hat.

They fell into conversation, and Mark was astonished to find that this Mr. Isaac Allerton was a Separatist from Plymouth, of importance to that colony, having been Assistant Governor for many years, negotiator of Colony business in London, and having recently taken as a second wife Fear Brewster, daughter of the Elder.

Mr. Allerton had been trading in Maine in his ship the *White Angel*. He had been twice to England in her, he had just stopped at Salem, but was returning to Plymouth with a cargo of stockings, tape, pins, and rugs, on which, though he did not say so, he expected to make handsome profit. Nor did he say that he was becoming extremely unpopular at Plymouth, where a growing disquiet at the sharp increase in the colony's floating debt began to focus attention on the vague activities of their agent, Mr. Allerton. True, he always had satisfactory explanations, and there was about him an ingenuousness that disarmed criticism, but even his father-in-law, Elder Brewster, was becoming aware that Isaac's successful trading expeditions always seemed to impoverish the colony.

Mark did, however, gather that Mr. Allerton, being somewhat wearied of life in Plymouth, intended to settle elsewhere. And that having investigated many lines of commerce, he had decided on a new one which would certainly make his fortune. Fishing.

"Here—" said Mark, smiling at Phebe, "you may be sure I pricked my ears, and questioned him narrowly." He paused, and she knew that now would come something of importance, by the off-hand tone in his voice. "You know the point of land across the little harbor here?"

"You mean that they call Derby Head?"

Often she had stood on the Salem wharf and gazed at the low headland across the water. For her as for the earlier Dorset people it aroused a poignant memory, being by some trick of nature shaped exactly like the headland at the mouth of the River Wey.

She brought her thoughts back for Mark had gone on. "He told me he had land and a fishing stage at the other side of Darby Fort. He calls the place Marblehead, and says it is the best harbor for fishing on the coast. He will remove there himself soon, and he says I may share in the venture with him."

"Is it there you mean to settle, then?" asked Phebe slowly. "But are there others there, Mark?"

"Oh, a fisherman or two, I believe— They do say a Guernsey wight named Dolliber wintered there last year in a hogshead." He chuckled as he saw her expression. "But when Mr. Allerton comes it'll make all the difference. I go there with him tomorrow to look at the place."

"Is it far from here—?" she asked presently, because Mark seemed waiting for her to speak.

"Not by water, an hour's sail with a fair breeze. Come, poppet—don't look so dismal. I vow it'll be the very place for us. I'll decide when I've seen it."

He got up, stretching his long legs and yawning. His black curls grazed the thatching, and under the worn red leather doublet she saw the strength of his shoulders, the bulge of his arms. Yes, he was a proper man, and it was right that he should rule. But there was another love for which she felt allegiance, small indeed, beside her love for Mark, but still an insistent claim, and she would have no peace until she spoke of it.

She watched him shamble about the wigwam, then pick up his fowling piece. He settled on the stool, scooped up a handful of tinder, and whistling through his teeth fell to cleaning his gun.

Her heart beat fast as she rinsed the pewter beer mugs in a cask of rain water outside the wigwam, burnished them to silver with a fair linen cloth as her mother had taught her, and placed them on top of her bride chest. She tended the fire and the hearth, sweeping the ashes neatly behind the great andirons with a twig besom she had made.

"Mark—"

He nodded, intent on the hammer of his fowling piece.

"While you were gone, I've come close to the Lady Arbella. . . ."

He clicked the hammer again, and his lips tightened. "So I suppose since you swooned on her doorstep; it angers me to see you headstrong. You knew my wishes."

Phebe sighed and attacked obliquely. "But didn't you like Mr. Johnson? You saw much of him at the Bay."

Mark shrugged. "He's well enough for one of the canting East County folk. He talks overmuch about the state of Grace."

"If we should settle in Boston near them, I'm sure he'd find you preferment, you might be freeman at once—nay wait, dear—" for he had shaken off her hand and his lower lip jutted out, "I ask only that you open your mind to the thought. True, they can help us advance but you can also help them, they've need of a great strong man like you in the new plantation."

He made a derisive sound, "What cozzening is this, Phebe! You think I don't smell some womanish plot. You and your meddlesome peeress!"

Anger struck through her, and she took a step back. But she looked at his stubborn side-turned face, at the fall of his hair which covered the sickening mutilation of his ear, and her anger died.

She came close again and spoke very soft. "Our babes will be born near the same time, Mark. Their interest would mean much. It's not us I think of, but of our child."

His hand fell from the fowling piece, and he turned his head. "God blast it. I'd forgot the child." He reached out and pinched her cheek in unwilling contrition. "Poor lass—small wonder you seem so dithering."

He rose and walked to the doorway of the wigwam. The coming of a child was a problem he had not anticipated in his enthusiasm for Allerton's proposal. Nor had he till now thought of the danger for Phebe. It crossed his mind that he should have left her home. Safe she would have been, comfortable—and no encumbrance, until he had made permanent settlement. But he thought too of her softness and warmth. The full, curving mouth that always spoke gently, and yet parted in sharp desire to his kiss.

"It may be the Marble Harbor'll not suit me at all," he said. "Let's forget the matter for now."

He set sail with Isaac Allerton the next morning in the *White Angel* for Marblehead, and while he was gone one problem was settled.

For the Lady Arbella died that evening in her husband's arms. There were many crowded into the small room, and Phebe huddled into the far corner by the door. Mr. Johnson himself had sent for her earlier, saying that the Lady called for her. Arbella had had one excruciating sharp pain, and then all pain had stopped. The fever red had left her thin cheeks, and they became yellow-white as the sheet on which she lay. Master Gager, the physician, himself very ill, had been carried to her bedside and carried away again. He had recognized the symptom which he hourly expected in himself. The intestine had been perforated and there was no hope.

Almost at once the delirium left Arbella, and she knew what was going to happen. Before she sank into a stupor she greeted Phebe with the old sweet smile. "So we cannot plan for our babes together since God has other plans for me and mine. Nay, don't weep, Phebe, I am content to obey His will, there is no other happiness, child."

This, Phebe filled with grief and rebellion could not believe. She tried to pray when the others did. Isaac Johnson, though himself distracted with sorrow, could pray, and Master Skelton the minister and Master Endicott, and the hushed neighbors who stood by the entry and on the steps. But Phebe could not. She envied them their certainty of being able to pierce the iron wall of death, but Phebe helping to shroud the body of her dearly loved friend could find no comfort.

The Lady Arbella was laid near Master Higginson on the burying point that jutted close to the South River. And atop the grave they placed a heavy flat field stone—for fear of wolves. Phebe standing apart from the others, watched the hasty ceremony with a misery so bitter that it was near to disgust. Everywhere on the point there were new mounds; even now before the final words had sealed the lady's last rest, two servants waited with shovels for the digging of another grave. Doctor Gager had died, and Mrs. Phillips. Arbella's maid, Molly, had outlived her mistress but an hour. Goodman Bennett, Goodwives James and Turner, and Mr. Shepley, and some indentured servants, all had died this week.

And to what purpose—thought Phebe. What had they accomplished here? Where were Arbella's beauty and courage now, and where her babe that might have been born to gentleness and happy childhood in the castle of its ancestors? Buried in the wilderness beneath a stone for fear of wolves.

She turned and started up the path across the fields. I'm going home, she thought. I'll make Mark see reason, and if he won't—I'll go alone, until he's ready to come back to me. Nothing can make me bring forth my poor child in this enemy land. She stopped and leaned against a tree, seeing against the coarse dry stubble at her feet a shimmering vision. She saw her mother and father holding out their arms to her from the doorway, and smiling welcome. She saw the great hall behind them garlanded with roses and ivy as it had been last Saint John's Day, and heard the blithe singing of her sisters at their spinning.

She felt the smoothness of the lavender-scented sheets on her own carved oaken bed, and she saw herself and the babe lying there together, safe and tended by her mother's knowing hands, while the mellow sunshine—not fierce and scorching like here, flickered through the mulberry leaves and the diamond-paned windows. She had not cried before, but now a sob burst through her throat, and she stumbled blindly on the path, until a hand touched her shoulder.

She raised her bowed head to see Mr. Johnson beside her. His cheeks, no longer pink, had fallen into sharp grooves. His thin blond hair was uncombed, and from his black habit he had cut away every button and shred of lace.

"Mistress Honeywood—" he said, speaking through stiff lips—"will you come back with me, I've something to give you."

She nodded a little, and they walked silently together along the

Highway past the green to Arbella's house. Phebe cast one look at the plank bedstead on which the Lady had died, and turned away, standing by the door.

Isaac Johnson opened a drawer of the little oak table. "She loved you much," he said, his voice so hoarse that Phebe had to lean forward to hear.

"And I her, sir—"

He fumbled among several letters which he brought from the drawer. "I go straight back to Boston. There's so much to do—I doubt that I've much time before I join her. The sickness gripes at my bowels. It is the Lord's will. Here are letters she left—one that treats of you. You shall have it."

He held out to her a folded sheet of paper. Phebe took it, and opened it, stared at the lines of clear, delicate writing.

"I cannot read it—sir," she said, very low.

"Aye—to be sure." He snatched it back from her, and she saw that he was impatient to be alone with his sorrow.

" 'Twas meant for her sister, Lady Susan Humphrey, but never finished." He steadied his voice and began to read.

" 'No word yet from home, so I write thee again, dear sister, perchance to send this by the Master of the *Lion*. I try to keep my thoughts from harking back, but ofttimes I cannot, this to my shame for there be many here who are braver.

" 'There is great sickness, and I do pray for the babe I carry. I am much alone and endeavor to strengthen my spirit in the Lord God who led us here. He gives me solace, and in especial hath vouchsafed to me a friend. This, one Phebe Honeywood, wedded to one of the adventurers, and naught but a simple yeoman's daughter, but a most brave and gentle lass. She is not as illumined by Grace as I could wish. . . .' "

Isaac paused, started to say something, but sighed instead, and went on. " 'Yet she is of fine and delicate spirit, and God is closer to her than she knows. She hath, I confess, been inspiration to me—having a most sturdy courage to surmount any disaster and follow her man anywhere, and found a lasting home.

" 'O, my dear sister, it is such as she who will endure in my stead, to fulfill our dream of the new free land, such as she whose babes will be brought forth here to found a new nation—while I . . . too feeble and faint-hearted. . . .' "

Isaac's voice cracked. "That's all." He held the letter out again. "Keep it in remembrance of her."

Phebe could not raise her eyes, red had flooded up her cheeks beneath the slow tears, "Our dear lady misjudged me—" she whispered. "I have no courage—indeed she did not know—"

Isaac was stirred from his own grief by her face. "God will strengthen you, mistress," he said. "Trust in Him."

He rose, putting out his hand. She took it and curtsying, turned and left him alone. She went back to the wigwam, and throwing herself down on the pallet lay staring up at the ragged rush thatching.

Arbella's letter rested beneath her bodice on her heart, and seemed to whisper its words. "It is such as she who will endure—to fulfill our dream. . . ."

She thought of the promise Arbella had asked of her in the first days of her sickness. "Promise me you'll not give up, no matter what may happen." She had not promised.

It's not fair—cried Phebe to the gentle yearning voice, and lying there alone on the pallet, she vanquished the voice with a dozen hot refutations. This founding a new land, this search for a purer religion, was not *her* dream. To her, God had made no special revelation. And as for Mark—would it not be wiser to free him for a while from her hampering presence—hers and the babe's, until he either tired of the venture or had made a really suitable place for them. It was no disgrace to go home, every home-bound ship was crammed with those who had seen the pointless folly of the venture. The Lady Arbella, herself too weak for survival, had no right to appoint Phebe her surrogate.

The August afternoon flattened under a blistering sun. Beneath the wigwam's thatching the heat gathered stifling, and fetid with the smell of the swamps. Once, slow footsteps plodded down the path outside toward the Burial Point. Phebe heard the sound of sobbing and one low cry of anguish that faded into nothing. Then again there was no sound but the rasp of locusts, and the rustle of the close-pressing forest.

I shall find the Master of the *Lion*—she thought, starting up at last. The *Lion* would sail as soon as there were fair winds.

Phebe washed her face and hands and smoothed her hair. She took the letter from her bodice and flung it in her bride chest, slamming the lid. She threw open the batten door, and on the earthen threshold stopped dead.

"Oh dear God—" she whispered. "I cannot," and she sank to her knees between the oak door frames. She kneeled there, facing the eastern horizon, while behind Salem the sun sank slowly into the untracked forests of the New World.

God did not seem to speak to her. She felt no exaltation or comfort. But there was certainty.

When Mark returned from his expedition to Marblehead he found Phebe changed, very silent and with a grim set to her mouth. She listened acquiescently but without comments to his enthusiasm for his new plan, and his satisfaction that through Mr. Allerton's influence he had obtained a grant of five acres in Marblehead from the Salem authorities, who had little interest in that remote section of their plantation.

She remarked only that it did seem wise to move from Salem Town, and the sooner they could move the better, but otherwise she submitted to the remaining weeks in Salem and to Mark's frequent preparatory absences in Marblehead with an unquestioning fortitude. Since the day when she had received Arbella's letter, and finally put all thoughts of going home behind her, she had passed beyond personal fear. Yet the stench of fear hung over the whole colony. Daily disasters battered all the settlements, and no day passed without a death.

In Charlestown it was no better. Governor Winthrop sent word that they were starving, rotted with disease and lacking medicine. He proclaimed a Fast Day throughout the colony with a view to softening the Divine Chastisement. But Providence still scourged them.

Four weeks after Arbella's death a home-bound ship touched at Salem and brought news from Boston, that Isaac Johnson too had died and had been buried in the lot by his unfinished house.

When Phebe heard this news she went to her bride's chest, and drawing out Arbella's letter gazed at it long and earnestly. What else besides this piece of paper was there left now of the Lady Arbella? Phebe raised the letter to her cheek, then wrapped it in her wedding handkerchief and put it back at the bottom of the bride chest. Nor did she ever mention the letter to Mark.

The Honeywoods were fortunate in escaping illness, but as September went by, they did not also escape malice and envy from their fellow townsmen. Their last days in Salem there were murmurs against them and slanting dark looks. They had not tried to join the congregation, they were virtually, by their own admission, no better than Papists. And why, in this case, should the Lord allow them immunity from the general sickness? Unless indeed it was not the Lord, but some Satanic power in league with them.

Phebe, openly goaded one day at the town spring, by an old crone called Goody Ellis, answered that perhaps the milk from her cow and the abundance of fish caught by Mark filled their bellies and made them better able to withstand sickness. Goody Ellis brushed this aside as nonsense, and made vicious allusions to witchcraft. Phebe was glad enough to be leaving.

There were no women at Marblehead yet, Mark told her, except the squaws in the Indian Village over Derby Fort side. And he worried about this for the time when her pains should come upon her. "But I'll get you a midwife from Salem, if I must give her all my silver," he promised and she agreed indifferently.

On the eighth of October the Honeywoods left the wigwam and descending the path to the landing place, set out at last for their new home.

Mark had hired a shallop and boatman from the fishing settlement on Salem Neck, and this also conveyed all their goods, except Betsey. The cow must wait in Salem until Mark could lead her around by land. Six miles of rough Indian trail through the forests.

It was a fair sparkling day of a kind new to them, for autumn in England held no such vibrance. There was freshness of blue and gold on the water, freshness of red and gold on the trees. This buoyancy in the air seemed to bathe one in a tingling expectation, it smelled of salt and sunshine and hope, and Phebe knew a faint return of youthful zest for the first time since Arbella had died.

Scudding before the wind they swished by Derby Fort Point, and Phebe was pleased to see that from this offshore angle it no longer resembled the headland at home. At Marblehead all would be new, and there would be no memories.

They rounded another heavily wooded point where Mark said there lived a fisherman called John Peach. They veered southwest between two small islands and lost the wind. The boatman and Mark took to their oars, and presently, the tide being high, their prow grated far up on the shingle of a little harbor.

Phebe jumped out, careless that she wet her feet or the hem of her blue serge skirt. While the men unloaded the boat she stood on the beach, staring. The sunlight fell warm on her back, matching a warmth in her heart. For in that first moment she felt a liking for the place. It was snug here in this little harbor with its two guardian points and tiny sheltering islands, and just beyond them there was grandeur; the whole blue sweep of the Atlantic stretching to the white horizon. Her senses seemed sharpened to a new delight. The sucking of the wavelets on the shingle, the water-borne cry of a seagull gave her pleasure, and in her nostrils there was the smell of pine trees and salt, mingled with faint pungency of drying fish. She looked for its source and saw on the northern curve of the little cove two spindly wooden frames, and a shabby hulking figure crouching over them.

"The fish flakes," said Mark, seeing her puzzled gaze. He laughed. "That'll be Thomas Gray turning the splits. He's a bit of a knave and generally in liquor, but I've cause to be grateful to him."

Phebe nodded. Mark had told her of the help given by Thomas Gray and John Peach in the building of a shelter. Phebe had resigned herself to making do with another wigwam, but seeing Mark's air of mystery and excitement now her hopes rose.

He led her a hundred yards back from the beach through a tangle of ruby sumach and wild asters to a modest clearing. Then he paused and waited, and Phebe did not fail him.

"Why Mark—it's a real mansion you've builded!" she cried, clapping her hands together. Indeed it was hardly that. A two-room cabin, topped with thatching, but the walls were solid, framed in sturdy New England pine, faced by pine weather-boarding, and all hewn by Thomas Gray who had knowledge of carpentry.

Together the three men had built the central chimney of the field stone so abundant here, and cemented the chinks with clay. The six small windows were still unfinished, the thatching of rushes pulled from a near-by pond was ragged and thin, but the thatch poles were of good barked hickory, and the rafters all ready for a permanent roofing later. Inside, Phebe was delighted to find a real floor of wide pine planking, and the walls snugly sheathed with soft pine boards.

"It's marvelous!" she cried, running between the two rooms. "I never thought to find you so skilled," and she kissed Mark, indifferent to the grinning boatman who was busy hauling their goods from the shallop.

Mark accepted her delight, and gloried in it. He well knew that her family had thought him feckless, and unlikely to provide good care for their daughter. The quick building of this solid house was something of a triumph. To be sure he had had help; from Allerton's men on the *White Angel,* and then from the two fishermen here.

Exultantly he showed her around their kingdom. Their land adjoined that of Allerton's where he proposed soon to establish his fishing stage, and also that of the Bay Company's English Governor, Mathew Craddock, who had never left or proposed to leave the Old Country but bought many likely parcels of land in the new.

Mark pointed out to her their well, so convenient to the house door. How fortunate they had been to find sweet water so soon, and so near the salt. Here at a distance would be the privy—here the shed for

Betsey. See how many trees they had, three great chestnuts, four elms, and a pine, rare luck for this rocky promontory.

Here behind the house on the slope to the Little Harbor was rich soil for a vegetable plot. And to the south a stone's throw from the house was the sea again, the restless deep waters of the Great Harbor. Phebe longed to return to the house and start the placing of their furniture, but Mark held her beside him on the rock-strewn beach.

"This harbor is big enough for a fleet, and deep too. Better than six fathom at ebb tide—and mind you—look how sheltered it is! See the spit of land across?" She nodded obediently. " 'Tis a great neck with pasture and marble cliffs on t'other side to quell the sea—and down there to the south, a most fair haven, and Master Allerton says the day'll not linger when we see it teem with shipping."

"For sure it will," said Phebe, and tried to speak with interest. While they stood there the sun had set behind them, and the air grown chill. The harbor filled with shadows, and the ceaseless muted sighing of the waves seemed to increase the solitude. Mark, deep in musing, did not move. Then from the far-off forest side toward Salem she heard the long-drawn howl of a wolf. She shivered and put her hand on Mark's arm. "We have much to do inside."

He turned and helped her up the little bank. She was growing somewhat clumsy and uncertain in her steps.

That winter was one of plodding hardships and now and again a sharp peak of danger. But Phebe found comfort in her home. She kept her two rooms swept and garnished with housewifely pride. When all their goods were at last unpacked, and supplemented by Mark's carpentry of plank table, bedstead, and stools, it was not ill-furnished. She had a shelf for her shining pewter, the mugs, platter, and salt cellar. The wooden trenchers were ranged beneath with her pewter spoons and candlesticks. To be sure, she had no candles as yet, nor means of making them. The fire gave light enough, or in emergencies pine-knot flares as the Indians used them.

Her kitchen hearth was her special pride, wide and deep enough to have roasted an ox, furnished with the much-traveled andirons, and a stout green lug pole from which hung her two iron pots. There was color too in this common room from the ears of red and orange Indian corn hung up to dry, and a sparkle of cleanliness from the white beach sand on the floor.

The other room held, besides the bed, chests and provisions until a lean-to could be built for the latter, but it too had its cheerful fire, and plenty of iridescent flamed driftwood to burn in it.

The two fishermen, Thomas Gray and John Peach, found cheer in the Honeywood home and were grateful for such hospitality as Phebe could provide. They were unlike each other in every way, and before the visit of Isaac Allerton with his great plans, and the subsequent arrival of the Honeywoods, had had little to do with each other. Each had built himself a cabin on the shore a half a mile from the other, each had in England learned something of rude carpentry and fishing. There was no other resemblance. John Peach was a meager wisp of a young man from the West Counties, who spoke rarely and wore a look of settled melancholy. Some early tragedy had soured him and made him emigrate. He never spoke of the past, and the Honeywoods learned nothing of his early life.

Thomas Gray was as garrulous and rowdy as his fellow settler was restrained. No inner love of solitude had driven him to this secluded point, but the intense disapproval of the Salemites, who wanted none of him. He had come over with Roger Conant in 1623, and sober or half drunk he was an excellent fisherman. Wholly drunk, he embodied all the failings most abhorred by the ministers.

He brawled, he wenched, he blasphemed, he was given to fits of lewd and unseemly mirth directed at godly members of the congregation.

During the seven years since his landing he had roistered his way through most of the new settlements, from Cape Ann to Beverly to Nantasket and Salem. In none had he found welcome. Marblehead had been the answer. Though under Salem jurisdiction, the authorities were, so far, too busy with their home problems to concern themselves with the outlying districts. Gray found good fishing, and convenience to Salem where he might sell or barter his fish, and obtain enough supplies of "strong water" to make his solitary nights more cheerful.

He was a large shambling man and except when liquor released a violent temper, a good-natured one. Phebe deplored his coarse speech and coarser jests, but both she and Mark liked him.

The Honeywoods kept Christmas Day, a celebration which would have outraged the rest of the colony, had anyone known it.

On the twentieth of December, Mark had most providentially shot a wild turkey which had wandered down to the shore in search of shrimps. Phebe invited the two fishermen to dine and plunged into preparations.

At first the contrast between these preparations and those last year had saddened her so that she almost lost heart and she weakened into thoughts of home for the first time since August. Christmas had always meant weeks of excited anticipation, in the kitchen—where she and her mother supervised the making of the mincemeat, the cakes, and pastries, the boar's head, the snap dragons, and the wassail bowl, and outside—the ceremony of cutting the Yule log, the gathering of holly and mistletoe, the midnight procession to the sweet-smelling candlelit church, the visits of the mummers in ludicrous costumes, the waits gathered outside the windows and singing the old carols, while inside and out there were dances and kisses and laughter.

Here, a two-room cabin in the wilderness, and no sound but the waves and a bitter winter wind.

"It's folly to try—" she said to herself while she stood in the raw cold and pulled pine boughs from one of their trees. Tears sprang to her eyes and chilled on her cheeks. She wrapped her cloak tight around her swollen figure and walked back to the house. It was Mark who cheered her. Seeing her despondency he made her sit and drink a cup of sack. He applauded the pine branches, and stuck them on the pegs that held his musket, telling her they were as pretty as holly.

He seemed always lighthearted these days, and was full of plans. With Tom Gray's sporadic help he was building himself a rude shallop; it should be finished by spring, if the winter were not too severe. He looked forward to Allerton's coming. He had been fortunate in finding food. Oysters now, and he pointed to a piggin full of gnarled bluish shells. He had found a bed, which was exposed at ebb tide. "They'll do well to stuff the turkey with, sweetheart," he said, and she smiled again, heartened by his eagerness.

So she stuffed the turkey with oysters and corn meal, and roasted it on a green sapling spit hung on the andiron hooks. The boiled pudding was also of corn meal, sweetened with all her remaining store of currants and enriched by Betsey's milk. And in one of her iron pots they concocted a makeshift wassail bowl of beer and brandy and a pinch of her jealously guarded spices.

The guests arrived at noon. Thomas Gray already something unsteady on his feet, lurched over the rocks through a fine sprinkling of snow and singing at the top of his voice. "Here we come a wassailing, among the leaves so green!" He had stuck a gull feather in his monmouth cap, tied a bunch of cedar to his filthy leather doublet, and he held in his hand a fishing pole from which dangled a huge slab of dried cod.

"Merry Christmas to 'ee—mistress," he roared at Phebe. "I've brought un a gooding, my best dun-fish. 'Twill be fine for thy belly and what's within it."

Phebe colored and thanked him. John Peach came in quietly, but even his melancholy eyes lightened at the sight and smell of the great turkey, golden brown on the spit.

"We maun sing—sing—sing," shouted Thomas, helping himself from the wassail bowl and banging his mug on the table. "Raise thy voices, split uns' gullets 'till they hear us in Salem. The sniveling pewking whoresons."

Mark laughed and, clinking his mug against Gray's, complied in his melodious baritone.

Wassail, wassail all over the town,
Our bread it is white and our ale it is brown—

Phebe joined in, and even Peach after a while in a whispering monotone. They sang all the verses in the old, old way, lifting their mugs and bowing to each object mentioned. For "A good crop of corn" they bowed to the drying ears by the hearth. "Here's health to the ox," and they bowed toward the shed where Betsey munched her Christmas ration of salt hay.

For "Here's to the maid in lily-white smock," they gave Phebe courtly bows. "In truth—" shouted Thomas slapping his thigh, "she's no maid by the look of her, but we'll greet 'ee nonetheless."

They ate and they drank and they sang. The snow stopped and the wind roared louder. It blew from the northeast and piled the mounting breakers into the Great Harbor. The men grew still a moment, all listening. "Are the boats pulled up high enough, d'you think?" asked Mark uneasily.

"For sure they be—" answered Thomas. "This'll be no storm. Coom sing again—we havena had 'The Bellman,' nor the 'Boar's Head,' yet."

But the other two men looked at each other and stood up. Peach nodded and buttoned his doublet. Mark, full of wassail and none too steady, followed the fisherman out into the cold dusk to see to the boats.

Thomas Gray promptly fell off his stool and lay on the floor snoring. Phebe began to straighten up the room.

The feast had gone well. For an hour or so they had almost captured the richness and gaiety of a real Christmas. She had thought of them at home almost in triumph, saying to them, "See, we are not so barbarous here, nor to be pitied."

But now she saw how flimsy a shell had held their gaiety. The wind rose, and the shell was shattered. At home the rising wind meant another log on the fire, another round of punch and a heightening of snug comfort.

Here it meant danger. She pulled her cloak around her and went out into the raw bitter cold to the shed to milk Betsey. She leaned her forehead against the warm flank while her aching fingers fumbled on the teats. Thank God, the cow had proved sturdy. She did well enough on the salt hay and bran they had brought from Salem.

Above the hissing of the milk into the wooden bucket, and the increasing pound of the waves, both woman and cow heard another sound. Betsey shivered and tossed her head.

"Hush—" whispered Phebe, though the flesh on her spine crept as it always did. "The wolves can't get at you here."

The shed was strong, and the wolves had never yet come down on the Point; they remained near Forest River.

To soothe Betsey she began to sing the old children's carol of "The Friendly Beasts." Often she had heard her mother sing it to the baby.

And next Christmas, thought Phebe, will I be singing it to mine? But the baby did not seem real.

"Aye, dear God, I wish it was over," she whispered. Her hands fell from the udder. She picked up the heavy bucket, and staggered with it back to the house. She must leave for Salem soon, if the baby were to be born there.

But on each succeeding day the journey was impossible. It could only be made by boat. Thomas Gray's shallop had been battered, though fortunately not lost in the Christmas storm. John Peach had only a skiff too small to fight the winter gales which blew steadily through January.

On the first day of February the wind dropped at last and a glittering sunshine dazzled on the snow patches. The waters of the two harbors calmed to glancing ripples filmed along the shore by brittle ice, and Phebe knew that they might set forth for Salem.

She knew also that it was too late. An agonizing backache had awakened her at dawn. By noon she was in full labor. Mark, helpless and frightened, paced back and forth, from the bed where he clumsily smoothed her forehead and murmured endearments which she did not hear, to the kitchen where he tended a roaring fire and kept a pot of water boiling.

Boiling water he had heard was needed in childbed, but he did not know why and he knew nothing else of the procedure. He dared not leave Phebe to summon the other men, but John Peach presently came of himself to tell them he had the skiff ready.

"No good now—" Mark groaned. "Her pains are already monstrous hard. I don't know what to do."

A smothered cry came to them from the bedroom, and the sweat sprang out on his forehead. He ran to Phebe. She was panting, her eyes stared without recognizing him, the pupils dilated to black holes.

An hour went by and he knelt beside the bed. Sometimes she seized his hand as though it were a block of wood without life, and clutched at it so violently that his great bones cracked.

Sometimes she tore at the stout coverlet and her nails ripped gashes in the material.

At five the pains seemed to lessen a little and Phebe drowsed. There was a knock on the door. Mark opened it to see Thomas Gray and an Indian squaw.

Gray, sober for once, stepped forward. "Look 'ee, Honeywood, John Peach come to me cot saying thy good wife's pains're on her, and 'ee fair distraught. This squaw's got brat of 'er own, and must know summat of birthing. So I brung 'er."

Mark's intense relief at the sight of a woman, any woman, was nearly eclipsed by astonishment. Only a few Marblehead Indians had remained to brave the winter, and they kept severely to themselves over by Tagmutton Cove. Nor did they allow their women to roam. This young squaw in her doeskin dress, with a mantle of beaver fur on her shoulders, was not uncomely, though her bronze skin was faintly pitted by the smallpox. She gave Mark a deprecatory smile, which showed even white teeth.

"Name's Winny-push-me, or summat like that," said Thomas. "I call her Winny." As Mark still looked astonished, he added, "She's my doxy." He gave the squaw a pinch on her backside and she giggled.

"But Tom—it's rash!" Mark cried. "We darn't offend the Indians, we're so few here—"

Thomas went to the fire and rubbed his hands. "Ah, ye needna fret. She's widder woman, they care naught wot she do. I've bedded with her off and on, for better'n a year."

A moan from Phebe recalled Mark. He took the squaw by the arm. "Go see what you can do." The woman understood his gestures, and Mark followed her to the bed.

Phebe cried out and shrank as she saw the dark face and felt the alien hands on her, but through the red surges of renewed pain she heard Mark's voice. "She'll help you, sweetheart. Let her do what she will."

Winnepashemic was a skilled midwife, a rôle which often fell to the tribe's widows. She watched Phebe's pains carefully, nodded, and produced from her bosom a leather pouch. From it she drew a sharp bone knife and a small leather thong. These she laid on the floor to be used later. She got hot water from the kitchen pot and mingled with it a powdered herb which she forced Phebe to drink. In a few minutes Phebe's pains increased in violence and frequency. Winnepashemic nodded again, satisfied, and pulled down the blankets.

Half an hour later the baby was born. The squaw cut the cord with her bone knife and bound the stump with the thong; then she wrapped the baby in her own beaver mantle and carried it to the kitchen.

She thrust the bundle toward Mark. "Man," she said, beaming. Mark, whose body dripped with sweat and whose hands shook, stared at her blankly, but Thomas jumped up and pulled apart the beaver wrapping.

"So it be!" he shouted. "A fine boy, red as a strawberry an' plump as an oyster." He clapped Mark on the shoulders. "Ye can smile now, m' hearty young stud."

Mark looked at the baby, at the smiling faces of the fisherman and the squaw. He mopped his forehead with the back of his sleeve and went in to Phebe, walking on tiptoe. In his great chest was a hard fear. The sound of her screams was still in his ears.

She lay so quiet and flat on the bed that his mouth went dry and he could not speak. Then he saw her drowsy lids lift, and she too smiled at him.

"No need to fear, Mark—" she said dreamily. Her smile seemed to come from secret distance. But she saw his need and made greater effort. "It's all over. Aren't you content we've a fine boy?"

"But Phebe—it w-was fearful. I thought—thought—"

He fumbled for her hand, clumsy in his pity, and amazed that she could smile that little secret smile.

"Aye—" she squeezed his hand, quieting his restless fingers, "it was bad, bad as I always feared. But I got through it—and the babe. We're strong."

He was humbled by the triumphant pride in her last words. He saw her exalted, and far from him. Nor did he know that above the natural triumph of accomplished childbirth, she had private cause to exult. Though her next words might have given him clue.

"You won't mind, Mark, if we name him Isaac?"

"Isaac?" he repeated. He had thought, in the few times he thought of it at all, that the baby if a boy would be Mark again, or perhaps for her father—Joseph. Isaac? Isaac Allerton. His frown cleared. It would be fine compliment to the man who had settled them here, it would increase his interest in them when he finally arrived himself.

"For Master Johnson," she said softly. "Please." During the hours past, the pain had wiped out all thought of anything but itself. She had not thought of her mother, she had not thought of God. She had been as beastlike as Goody Carson on the ship. But now she knew that did not matter. And since it had finished she had felt the Lady Arbella near her, smiling a happy smile.

Mark was not pleased, but he could deny her nothing now. And later, if he cautioned her to silence, Mr. Allerton would believe the boy named for him. Mark bent over and kissed Phebe on the mouth.

In the September of 1636, Phebe, dressed in her crimson farrandine and bridal cap and neckwear of the Mechlin lace, hurried along the Harbor Lane to Redstone Cove, as eager as little Isaac for the day's festivity. The child danced with excitement and she held him tightly by the hand or he would have darted on ahead and maybe soiled the new suit she had made him from her blue serge gown. Yet, were it not for the cooing baby she carried on her left arm Phebe felt she might have run and danced like Isaac.

The sun warm and golden as brandy poured down from an azure sky, but it was not too hot. A small crisp breeze blew down the harbor, and the Neck had moved so near in the September air, it seemed a reaching hand might touch the massed green trees across the water.

"There she be—there's the ship!" shouted the child. Phebe nodded and smiled, and paused to look a moment before scrambling down among the rocks to find a sitting place for the launching.

There she was, finished at last, the pride of all Marblehead. A great fair ship, one hundred and twenty tons burden, the largest yet built in the colony as Mark so often boasted. Fully rigged, she poised lightly on the ways like a black swan, and across her stern ran her name in glowing red letters, *Desire*. Ah yes—well named, thought Phebe, settling herself on a rock and spreading her crimson skirts. For more than a year the village had centered its hopes and dreams upon this ship. And Mark more than any of the others.

She saw him now leaning against the taffrail on the high poop deck, talking to Jemmie White and John Bennet, and they all held mugs in their hands. He waved to her and shouted—"Hulloa—Phebe, I'll be right down to you. Does the boy know his part?"

She waved back, and made little Isaac wave. As the first child born in Marblehead, he had been appointed to christen the vessel. As the son of a man of consequence too, thought Phebe proudly. Mark had thrown himself heart and soul into this venture, and contributed every penny he had and labor too, working day after day with the other men on the sturdy oak hull. He dreamed of his share of the profits from her cargoes, and he announced that he had found his real profession at last. He would be shipwright and owner.

He had, during these six years of their settlement here, done fairly well at the fishing; he had his own shallop and his own fish flakes at the foot of his land on Little Harbor, but Isaac Allerton's larger projects had never been realized. True, Allerton came to Marblehead and established his fishing stage, but soon the remote little settlement bored him, there was small scope for his ambitions, and then misfortunes beset him, his house burned down, and the *White Angel* was lost with all her cargo. He became morose and restless, and in 1635, having deeded all his Marblehead property to his son-in-law, Moses Maverick, Master Allerton disappeared in the direction of the New Haven Colony, and Massachusetts knew him no more. Then Mark had said "Good riddance," feeling that he had misjudged Allerton's worth, and having in any case small interest in working for someone else.

How many changes here, in how short a time, thought Phebe. Eleven women now in Marblehead besides herself, and twenty-eight men, and the children. She looked down at the sleeping baby on her lap, small Mark. His birthing had been aided by Dorcas Peach, a jolly stout widow from Saugus, suddenly and surprisingly married by the melancholy young fisherman, John Peach. And the birthing had been easy, very different from that of Isaac.

And there were other houses now in Marblehead, huts and cabins strung along the waterfront all the way from John Peach's Point to Bartol's Head, but no house except Mr. Maverick's so fine as the Honeywoods'.

Aye, I'm content, thought Phebe, watching Mark clamber down the ladder from the ship and come toward her. How handsome he looked as he swaggered along the shingle, taller and stronger than all the other men, and how boyish still for all his thirty years. He had a streak of pitch across his cheek, and some of the points on his doublet hung loose.

"You're heedless as the boy is—" she scolded fondly, wiping at his cheek. "Nay—don't tumble him about." For Mark had seized his elder son and thrown him high in the air. "You'd not have him queasy for the launching."

"God blast it—No!" cried Mark with a boisterous laugh. "But he's no get of mine, trollop, if he hasn't a strong stomach." He lowered the delighted child in a great swoop, then stumbled and caught himself.

"Oh Mark—" cried Phebe between reproach and amusement—"not

tipsy so soon! Had you nothing better to do up there on the ship than guzzle."

"No. All's ready and waiting for high water, and I'll drink as I please. Come, Phebe, no long face. This is the day to rejoice. I'm happy as I never thought to be." He put his arm around her waist and squeezed it hard. "All goes well for us, at last."

"Aye, for sure it does—" she said, smiling back at him. For whence but from womanish cowardice had come that little moment of foreboding? A chill that crept along her spine and vanished in the brightness around her. Mark patted his wife's shoulder, poked a finger at the baby, then drawn as by a lodestone, walked back to the ship and climbed aboard.

The cove was filling now, in the village all work had ceased, and they came over the cliff and down the rocky path, each dressed in best attire, the Marblehead women and the children and the few men who were not about the ship. Some were shouting, some singing, and all elated by the completion of their community project.

Young Remember Maverick, Moses' bride, radiant in her green paragon ran toward Phebe, crying, "What here already, Phebe?—Look d'you see up there upon the ledge? I vow those are Salem men."

Phebe followed the girl's gaze to see two peering figures in sad-colored clothes. They were approaching the cove tentatively.

"They've sailed over to view the launching, no doubt—" said Phebe, laughing. "Just so they keep their distance. They'll get short shrift if Mark sees them."

"Or any of our men—ah, I thought so." For Tom Gray reeled down the path, and stopped short at the sight of the strangers.

"We want no foreigners here—" he shouted. "Sniveling whoreson spies. Get ye back to your psalm-whining and your magistrating. Ye couldna build a ship like thisun, if ye strained till your arses burst."

And he picked up a large stone. The Salemites retreated hastily behind a tree. "Oh hush, Tom—" whispered Phebe, not for disapproval of his sentiments, but because he would certainly be hauled up before the Salem Court again. Salem considered this rocky outpost of its own tight community to be a godless and intractable stepchild, and concerned itself with the renegade only for purposes of discipline. There was as yet no meeting house in Marblehead, nor preacher, and few who felt the need of either.

Tom let fly the rock, which bounced off the tree, and would have thrown another, but Mr. Maverick appeared, and taking in the situation shrugged his shoulders, saying, "Let them be, Tom, we've better matters to be about."

The tide was nearly high. There were shouts from the men on the ship, and the half-dozen who remained on shore swarmed over the ways and began to knock at the retaining planks. The women clustered together staring at the ship, their hearts beating with pride and expectancy.

They stared at the oak hull made from their own trees, at the two towering masts cut from the finest stand of spruce in Essex County, the quarter-mile of rope in the rigging, all imported from Bristol, the shining paint on her hull, tediously mined from the Indian paint mine back of Beverley, and the furled sails—their cloth had come from England too, and for its purchase there had been many a sacrifice made.

How many feet of cloth, thought Phebe, were represented by the sale of poor Betsey's only calf? But every Marbleheader there had had part in the building of the *Desire;* poor as they were—and even the Mavericks were poor by Salem or Boston standards—they had willingly pooled their hard-won shillings.

They had done it all by themselves with the fierce independence which had drawn them here, men and women from Cornwall and the other West Counties, and from the Channel Islands—disparate beings, some as rough and uncouth as the savages, some of tenderer stamp, but held together by a dual bond, the love of freedom and the sea.

The harbor water lapped up to the pitch mark they had made upon a rock. The hammering increased in volume. Little Isaac tugged at his mother's skirt. "See Dada—" he cried shrilly, pointing his plump finger and hopping up and down. Phebe tilted her head high to see Mark, foremost of three young men who were swarming up the rigging on the mainmast. Phebe caught her breath but smiled. How like Mark! He would never submit to standing tamely on the deck while the beloved ship was launched. But the others stopped at the crows-nest, while Mark went on, until he perched astride the yard of the top-gallants'l, and waved his cap in exultant gesture. Again a chill touched her. Why must he always be reckless, in everything excessive, and trying to best the others? Why could he not . . .

"Well, Mistress Honeywood, is the boy ready?" Moses Maverick stood before her, holding out the uncorked flask of wine.

"Oh yes," she said quickly. "Go with him, dear."

Isaac's chubby fist closed on the bottle's neck, and while Maverick held him up on the platform he obediently lisped—"I christen thee *Desire,*" and sprinkled wine on the great wooden wall of the stern.

The ship started, she slid gently down the greased ways, and the tide leapt up to meet her, but as she settled into the blue harbor waters she gave one sideways lurch, and from the watching crowd there came a hissing gasp of horror. The ship righted herself at once, but Mark who had leaned far out to see his son perform the triumphant ceremony, lost his balance on the yard and came hurtling down to the deck below.

Mark was unconscious for many days and after he came to himself his mind was clouded, and he could move neither of his legs. Moses Maverick sent a shallop to Salem and brought back a physician, but that worthy gentleman, after examining Mark, shook his head, said he believed the backbone was crushed. He could do nothing.

Phebe received this verdict in silence. Her brown eyes took on a chill and stony look; she neither prayed nor lamented, and the physician thought her unfeeling. So did others who, stopping at the door to give sympathy and food, were received with tight-lipped thanks.

Dorcas Peach, who helped her with the nursing, and Tom Gray, who neglected his own livelihood to save Phebe from the rougher tasks—these knew better.

They saw the unfailing tenderness which she showed to Mark, who was often fretful and sometimes swept by violent rages in which he cursed Phebe or little Isaac, making of them objects to be battered for his helpless rage at fate. While his mind was clouded from the fearful pain he babbled incessantly about the ship, thinking himself on board, and it was Phebe, who—indifferent to the ridicule of some of the townspeople—asked Tom to fashion a giant-sized cradle. And after he had done so and they had lifted Mark's shrunken body into it, Phebe rocked it very slowly, and the gentle motion mingling in his thoughts with the motion of a ship, did bring him relief from the pain.

After a while as he grew stronger the pain receded, and he no longer needed the cradle: then he would lie propped up in bed silent for a day at a time, and once when Phebe came to feed him the evening meal his brilliant hazel eyes sought hers with a violent determination. And he commanded her to bring him his gun. "Bring it to me, Phebe! I can't live like this—" and he struck down at his wizening nerveless legs. "Half a man. No man." His face contorted and he clutched at her arm. "Phebe, bring me the gun, and when you're widowed there'll be plenty of men to take you and the children. . . ."

Then she slipped her arms around his neck, and held his heavy head against her breast, whispering to him as she did to the little ones, soothing him with a hundred gentle words. "Nay, darling, hush. We'll manage, I know we will. You'll get better. Why, I warrant by spring you'll be back in your shallop fishing the Bay."

But she knew he would not. Nor for some months, while they lived off the neighbors' offerings, did she know how the black future was to be endured.

The *Desire's* first voyage had been successful. Spain and Portugal welcomed the cargo of salt fish, cured by the New England sun, and tastier than the native bacalao. The *Desire* returned with oil, wine, and salt—and a moderate profit. Mark's share was small, and in it he had now no interest. Phebe dared not mention the ship, for all reminders of his accident provoked attacks of pain and violence far worse than the dull apathy into which he had gradually lapsed.

Phebe spent many days in hesitation and nervous anxiety, all the more acute since she must hide it from Mark, and many nights—she slept now in the loft with the children—she lay till dawn staring up at the black outlines of the rafters. Then she awoke one bleak February morning with her decision made.

She hurried through her tasks fearful of losing that moment of certainty. She nursed the baby and bundled him in his cradle, she replenished the kitchen fire, and heated the porridge for their breakfast, she tended Mark who lay heavy as a log of yew. He would neither open his eyes nor speak, but he ate a little when she coaxed him, and when she said she must go out for a while, he seized her hand and held it tight—as though in fear to have her leave him.

When Dorcas Peach came over to help, as she did each day, being warmhearted and having no children of her own as yet, Phebe was waiting already cloaked. She left her household in Dorcas' care and set out northward along the icy rutted lane until she came to Moses Maverick's.

Mr. Maverick was at home, sitting at a writing table near to the kitchen fire, for the day was bitter cold. He received Phebe kindly, but she saw the corners of his mouth sink in, and in his eyes a wariness. This did not surprise her. She well knew that her problem was a burdensome one to the settlement.

"And how is your good man today, Mistress Honeywood?" he asked, pulling up a chair for her and seating himself again at the table which was covered with sheets of foolscap.

Phebe's hand twisted itself into a fold of her homespun skirt, but she spoke quietly, seeming to consider the matter. "Why, he's neither better nor worse. His mind is no longer much clouded, but he cannot move his legs. Nor do I think he ever will."

Maverick shook his head. "That's bad. Bad— And he so tall and strong he used to do the work of two. Had he only not been so rash . . ."

He had spoken his thought without regard to the listener, for he was one of those to whom Phebe's composure had always seemed unwomanly. He was therefore shocked to see a spasm cross her face, as a stone convulses the still waters of a pool, and in that instant grief looked nakedly from her brown eyes.

"Pardon, mistress!" he cried. "I didn't mean to cause you pain. It does no good to think of the past."

"No," she said, controlled again. "It's because of the future that I came to you."

He drew back into his chair. The wariness returned to his gaze, and he sighed. His young wife, Remember, was fond of Mistress Honeywood, and had much troubled him with questions and speculations as to what would become of the stricken family. Food was not so plentiful that anyone should be asked to provide for four extra mouths. Mark Honeywood's affliction was indeed a cruel drag on the struggling little settlement which could ill afford to have one of its strongest assets reverse the ledger and become a debit. Far better had he died, thought Maverick; women were scarce and she might then find a man to take her, for all she was so small and thin and reserved in her ways.

"I think there is but one solution, mistress." He spoke with exasperation and decision. "Return to England! You have people there to care for you?"

Phebe lowered her head and stared at the fire. She was silent so long that he began to feel discomfited. Then she spoke very low, so that he leaned forward to catch the words.

"I've thought of it many times. Many times—" she repeated slowly.

Then she raised her head and looked at him. "But I cannot go back— Nay—" she added with a faint smile, seeing that he thought there was some discreditable reason, "my family would welcome us. They'd care for Mark, and provide for me and the children."

"Then why—" he began, frowning. "You've no puritan scruples."

She shook her head. "But I can't go. Two things prevent." He waited, still frowning, and tapping on the table. After a moment she went on with difficulty, loath to bare her heart.

"I can't go because Mark, the real Mark, wouldn't wish it. He's lost courage now, but I can't take advantage of his weakness. This place was his choice. Our children were born here. We've endured much—and Marblehead has become—home." She paused a moment, then went on swiftly. "The other reason is a promise."

A promise I never made, she thought, seeing the dark stuffy little room in Salem and on the bed the dying lady. And she thought of the letter that lay wrapped in the lawn handkerchief at the bottom of her bride chest.

Maverick crossed his legs and cleared his throat, seeing that she had finished speaking. "Admirable reasons, no doubt, and do you honor—but Mistress Phebe—"

She nodded and cut in. "I know. I've a plan. I want you to apply to the Salem Court for me, for license to run an ordinary."

"An ordinary?" he repeated slowly, relieved by something practical at last. "You mean to run one in your house? But have you room? Could you do it alone? There are many considerations. Our plantation is yet small to support one."

"I think not." Phebe smiled. "The fishermen and the sailors will certainly welcome one. Tom Gray'll help me. We can build a room for Mark off the kitchen, our other room to be the taproom. Mark will, some day, take an interest, I hope. He can keep the books, and there'll be people around to divert him."

"And how will you buy your stock?"

"From Mark's share in the *Desire*."

Moses stared at her. He had misjudged her. She was neither deficient in feeling or character, and the color had come into her thin cheeks as she talked, and he saw that she was not deficient in comeliness either.

"You have courage, my dear," he said.

Phebe looked puzzled. "But indeed I haven't—" she said earnestly. "Not in myself."

Maverick smiled, understanding why his wife was so fond of her. "Perhaps we never know ourselves, our virtues or our faults—" He uncrossed his legs and stood up. "I believe that you'll somehow manage to keep your home together here, and your plan is good. I'll give you what help I can."

That May of 1637, Phebe opened her ordinary. Mark had been carried to a chair beside the beer keg in the taproom, and though his face had fallen into deep grooves and bitterness pulled his mouth, he managed to speak to the first customers, Moses Maverick and John Peach. Phebe in white apron and cap stood behind the counter, near to Mark, where sometimes, when the strain was too much for him, she touched his shoulder and whispered encouragement.

The taproom, with its rush-strewn floor, its shelves of wooden mugs, its casks of brandy and sack, its table and benches, showed little resemblance to the bedroom where the Honeywoods had spent their first years. Their bedroom now, duly built by Thomas Gray, lay off the northern side of the kitchen, and its window gave onto the Little Harbor. From it Mark could look across Phebe's garden and watch the landings of slippery cargo at the fishing stage. He could also watch his elder son who escaped whenever possible from the chores set him by Phebe to splash in and out of the shallops.

Above the front door of the house Thomas Gray had nailed a small dried hazel bush, as was required by the law to show a licensed ordinary. But Phebe had wished a sign as well, and though her advisers had thought it an extravagance had commissioned a roving painter. The figures beneath the straggling letters were inconclusive, two rigid objects topped by spheres and between them a bird. The legend was clarifying. It said "The Hearth and Eagle," and though the Marbleheaders ignored the sign and referred to the tavern as "Honeywoods'" it gave Phebe a secret content. Even though she must now receive strangers into her home, yet the andirons were still guardians in the kitchen and on the sign. As for the eagle—that was from the gilt figurehead on the ship *Arbella*.

CHAPTER 3

A DESCENDANT of the first Hearth and Eagle sign creaked and rattled on its iron bracket outside Hesper's window, awakening her at sunrise on the morning of April 23, in 1858.

"Drat that sign!" she said out loud, and muffled her ears with her pillow to shut out the piercing squeal-bang, squeal-bang. Needed oiling again, or better yet take the stupid thing down, as Ma kept saying. Inns didn't have signs like that nowadays, and Johnnie Peach had once made fun of the blurred drawings on it, called it a spitted chicken.

Only Pa wouldn't take it down. He would never change anything. Hesper yawned and gave up trying to sleep. Ma'd be hollering for her to get up pretty soon anyway. Awful lot of chores to be done before school. The Inn was crammed full, and there'd be big doings tonight what with most of the ships crews sailing for the spring fare to the Banks tomorrow. If this fair wind held. The sign banging away like that meant a good stiff offshore breeze.

Johnnie'd be tickled pink, couldn't wait to sail again now he'd be full sharesman on the *Diana.*

Hesper sighed. Silly to think about Johnnie when he didn't pay her any mind now she was a great girl of sixteen, nor for a long time before that either. Not since she'd gone to dame school and he'd given up schooling and sailed off on his first fare to the Grand Banks as a "cut-tail." That was five years ago when he was fourteen, and he'd suddenly gotten ashamed of playing with a girl, even when the rest of the boys in the Barnegat gang didn't know about it.

I wish I was a boy, thought Hesper passionately. Johnnie'd taught her to sail, and she could handle a dory almost as well as any boy, and once when she was ten, Johnnie'd lent her some of his clothes and smuggled her on the *Balance* when the ship went down to Boston for the salt. They'd been gone two days, and there was a terrible hullabaloo when they got back. Ma'd tanned her backside so she couldn't sit for a week, but it was worth it.

She heard her mother's heavy tread on the old boards outside in the hall, and there was a sharp rap. "Hurry up, Hes. It's gone six."

Hesper said, "Yes, Ma—" and reluctantly slid out of bed onto the braided rag rug. It had been made by poor old Gran just before she died, out of scraps of sprigged calico and homespun and torn stockings Gran had hoarded like a magpie. It kept the floor's chill off the feet and it was pretty enough and spotless clean because Ma made her wash it once a month, but Hesper despised it. Charity Trevercombe had a red turkey rug so thick you could sink your fingers in it at *her* bedside. But then the Trevercombes were still rich. They'd made a fortune in the China trade and kept some of it too, which was more than the Honeywoods had done. The Honeywoods had only been rich for a while in the middle of the last century, when Moses Honeywood, the shipowner, had built the great new wing to the house, and married off his daughters into some of the foremost families: the Hoopers and the Ornes and the Gerrys. Then the Revolution came and he lost every penny. Charity was pretty too, the prettiest girl in Marblehead.

Hesper slipped off her long flannel nightgown and shivered. She poured water from a dented pewter pitcher into a chinaware basin, moistened her arms and face and neck, deciding with relief that there wasn't time to wash all over. I wish I wasn't so big, she thought, her discontent growing. She had only recently become conscious of her body, and the consciousness brought nothing but disappointment. She was taller than any other girl at the Academy, five and a half feet—near as tall as Johnnie. And suddenly in the last year, a lot of—well, bosom. She dried herself and flung on her underclothes. She brushed her hair with violence. Red. Brick-carrot-red, curly and springy as wood shavings, and so much of it, below the waist and thick enough when braided to make a hawser, and she had been teased about it since she was a baby. She skinned it all back from her face and slicked the wiry little tendrils down with water, and she stared into the small mirror, exasperated by a new reminder. It was bad enough to have the Lord afflict her with tallness and that hair, and a squarish face with high cheekbones, and a wide mouth, and light hazel eyes that looked almost green in some lights, but why must He refine still further upon an effect already so far removed from prettiness, by endowing her with thick dark eyebrows? She flung the brush and comb onto her bureau, buttoned herself into her brown serge school dress. Well, anyway, the Lord spared me freckles, she thought forlornly. Ma and some of the Dollibers who had sandy hair had the freckles too. Hesper's skin was a thick, dense cream, like, as a schoolmate had once remarked, "the insides of a clam shell." Hesper had tried to believe it a compliment.

She threw her bed together, not bothering to untuck the sheets and hoping Ma would be too busy to look. She slapped on the counterpane and paused at the sound of hoofs and the rumble of heavy wheels outside. She peered through the tiny-paned window at the street and saw that it was the delivery dray from Medford. Two men were unloading casks of molasses and rum and carrying them into the taproom. Early, thought Hesper, surprised. They must have driven the team all night. And she hurried downstairs to the kitchen.

Susan called from the taproom where she was supervising the delivery of the casks, "Turn the sausages, start the fish cakes, and the milk's ready for skimming in the butt'ry, and hurry for once. The two drummers've to be off for Lynn."

Hesper nodded and flew to the little pot-bellied cookstove. The fire in the great fireplace would be lit later, but the brick oven was still warm from yesterday and contained pans of swollen bread dough, ready now for baking. She took them out, and put them on the table, stirred the grounds in the huge-spouted can of coffee, turned the sausages and fish cakes again, then ran into the taproom to set the table for the drummers' breakfast. And she was amazed to find her mother standing, stock-still in the center of the floor, staring at a piece of paper.

"What is it, Ma?" Hesper tried to crane over her mother's shoulder and saw what appeared to be a regular bill for the rum and molasses, with some lines of brownish writing across the very bottom of it.

"Mind your own business—" said Susan, folding up the paper, but she spoke with a hesitancy most unlike her. "You're too young . . ." She scowled at the paper. "Today of all days with the house full, and a crowd tonight . . . but it must be done . . . someway. . . ."

"*What* must, Ma?" cried Hesper.

Susan put the piece of paper in her apron pocket. "You'd be a blabber-mouth. . . ."

"No, no, Ma. . . ."

Susan shook her head, pursed her lips. "Get on with the chores, you'll be late to school." She walked from the taproom, through the kitchen to Roger's study door, and threw it open without knocking. Hesper, seething with curiosity and the resentment which her mother often aroused in her, followed close. The door to her father's study was ajar a crack; she put her ear as close as she dared and listened.

"—and it's the U.G.," said her mother's voice, finishing a sentence.

"Written in milk on the bill like the last time. I held it to the fire. There's two of 'em, I guess, and they're coming tonight."

"I'll have nothing to do with it!" cried her father's voice sharply. "I absolutely forbid it."

"Forbid—indeed!" the other voice harshened with anger. "You did it last time and you'll do it again."

"That was different, years ago, before they passed the act. I'll not break the law. I told them I wouldn't."

Hesper heard her mother's heavy hand strike the desk. "Blast and domnation! Since when do Marbleheaders cringe at a law if it's a bad one! They must be desperate or they wouldn't be trying *us*. It maddens me to have you turn niminy-piminy, chicken-hearted. . . ."

"That's enough, Susan. I disliked the last episode and after all my own ancestors were slaveowners—Moses Honeywood owned several blacks," said Roger in his nervous, irritable voice. "I'll not have my house used as a station again."

Hesper gasped, pressing closer to the door. So that was it! The U.G. was the underground railroad.

"You hold with slavery, then?" shouted her mother.

"Why no, but I doubt abolitionism's the answer, let the South take care of its problems, and remember too there are many Southern sympathizers here in Marblehead."

"Bah! Some of the shoemen, and maybe the Cubbys, because poor Leah has no mind of her own since her man was drownded, and Nat, that young whelp of hers'd swarm to any view that'd roil decent folks."

"There's no use arguing, I've no more to say."

Hesper heard the familiar sound of a pen scratching on paper, and drew back from the door, but not fast enough. Susan burst through, her cheeks red, and her little eyes snapping. She stared at her daughter's guilty face, and banged the door behind her. "So you've been eavesdropping, miss! You heard it all?"

Hesper opened her mouth and shut it again, but oddly enough Ma wasn't mad. She sank down in the old Windsor chair, and said very low—"Well, Hes. We'll have to do it alone. The poor things'll be coming, and we can't send 'em back, despite your pa."

Hesper instantly stifled a pang of loyalty. For surely Pa was wrong in this. It was because he wouldn't read *Uncle Tom's Cabin* though nearly everyone else in Marblehead had, he wouldn't even read any of Mr. Longfellow's stirring poems like "The Slave in the Dismal Swamp." He only read books by dead people who had lived across the ocean long ago. So he didn't know how terribly the poor slaves suffered, and anyway this was so exciting.

"How can we do it, Ma—" she whispered eagerly. "The house'll be full all evening with the 'Bankers' who sail tomorrow . . ."

"Hush—" said Susan, glancing at the banjo clock. "There's those drummers a coming downstairs. Feed 'em their vittles, and then I'll tell you what to do. You can skip school today."

Hesper waited on the two men, banging plates and spilling coffee in her haste, and for once unrebuked by her mother, who moved automatically through her kitchen work, her sandy brows pulled together in a scowl of concentration.

Her decision once taken, Susan had not the slightest scruple in deceiving Roger. She had many times before this had to take command, ignoring his uncertainties and evasions, allowing, though with scant tolerance for his increasing retreat from life. For fifteen years he had been engaged on a rhymed metrical account of the town titled "Marblehead Memorabilia," but as his treatment of the work entailed so many classical allusions and consequent detours into reference books and source material, he had progressed no further than the French and Indian Wars.

That this poem was to be apology and justification for a life of outward failure, both his wife and child dimly understood, but to Susan the fecklessness of the project was added exasperation. All his life it had been the same story. As a matter of course, he had been sent to sea on a banker as cook, when he was twelve. During the whole of that six weeks' fare he had lain in his bunk in the fo'c'sle seasick and entirely useless.

"I doubt he'll ever make a seaman—" the skipper had said contemptuously on returning him to his father. Nor did he. He was a clumsy unwilling fisherman, he had no knack for boats.

Thomas Honeywood, his father, finally accepted these strange shortcomings, though there had never been a Honeywood since the days of Mark and Phebe who had not spent a great part of his life at sea. Thomas decided on a new course. The boy was brilliant at the Academy and was forever piddling about with ink and quill, when he was not hidden in the attic with a book. Let him be a scholar then. No matter the money, young Roger should go to Harvard. But nothing came of that either. At Cambridge he made no friends. The other students thought him a queer fish and mimicked his Marblehead dialect, which in fact he hadn't known he had. He responded with anger, and secretly practiced many hours to rid himself of it. He studied little, cut many classes, spent all the time he dared in the Library, and then he fell ill; he had dull headaches and sudden spasms of unexplained terror in which he sweated and vomited. At the end of his fourth term he failed all his examinations.

Home he came to Marblehead, and the illness ceased. His father, though bitterly disappointed, said little but tried to make him useful in the business end of innkeeping. Here, too, Roger was vague and inattentive, having no interest in figures. Then when he was twenty, attracted both of them by the law of opposites, he married Susan Dolliber, and all Marblehead agreed that it was the only piece of gumption he ever showed.

"Ma—they've gone . . ." whispered Hesper coming into the kitchen with a tray piled high with dirty dishes. "Have you planned?"

Susan cast a sharp look over the tray, picked up the two quarters which were payment for the breakfasts, and put them in a hinged lacquer box which she kept in a drawer of the old dresser.

"Come in here—" she said very low. She pulled her daughter to the left of the great fireplace and through the door of the "Borning Room" —the kitchen bedroom, unused since Gran died, because it was sacred to birth and death and grave illness. She shut the wide-planked oak door. "You'd best read the message—" she said, taking the Medford bill from her pocket, " 'fore I burn it."

Hesper peered eagerly at the faint brown letters at the extreme bottom of the page. They said—"2 packages tonight by nine P.X. Brig off Cat. Cat."

"What's it mean, Ma?"

Susan took the paper back. "It means—" she said dryly, "two runaway slaves'll be dumped here tonight by some means, that the pursuit is hot behind 'em, that we're to keep 'em until we can get 'em aboard a brig that'll be waiting off Cat Island to run 'em to Canada, and the password is 'Cat.' " She took a small pair of scissors from her pocket, cut off the bottom of the bill, lit a match, and burned the sliver of paper.

"But where could we hide them—" asked Hesper, suddenly a little frightened.

Susan shrugged. "Same place as we did before. No, you didn't know about it. I doubt you've sense enough now to be mixed up in a thing like this, but I've got to risk it."

"Oh Ma—I *have* sense—I'll not breathe a word. . . ."

Her mother snorted. "You'd better not. You don't want us jailed, do you? You don't want the dom copperheads setting fire to the house?"

Hesper's jaw dropped.

Susan snorted again, but now there was a twinkle in her eye. "You look as scairt as though you'd heard the Screechin' Woman. All you need is a bit of spunk, and you've got that, I should hope.

"Now listen—you know the long cupboard next the brick oven in the kitchen?"

"You mean where we keep the brooms and the old guns?"

Susan nodded impatiently. "Come, I'll show you. I reckon you've got to be told."

Hesper followed her mother back into the kitchen. It was quiet and empty as they had left it, the banjo clock ticking, the cookstove giving off a subdued crackling, Roger's door closed.

On the walls either side of the fireplace the wide pine sheathing was darkened and glossy from the smoke of countless hearth fires, but otherwise exactly as it had been placed by Mark Honeywood, except that a shallow cupboard had been cut through two of the planks. Susan touched the latch and the door moved silently open on its wrought-iron snake hinges. Hesper watched dumbfounded while her mother pushed the brooms and the old muskets to one side and wedging herself into the narrow space, reached high over her head groping for the head of a tiny iron pin which was hidden at the top and back of the closet. She pulled the pin up, releasing the two-foot-wide plank which she slid sideways to disclose a narrow opening, and some wooden steps.

"Go on up—" she said to Hesper, "I'll keep watch down here. Wait, take the dust rag with you, here—and a can of water, and some of this." She dumped gingerbread, and the remains of the sausages and fishcakes into a wooden trencher. "We mayn't have as good a chance again to provision."

"But Ma—" whispered Hesper, "where's it go to? And what is it? I never knew—"

Susan twitched impatiently, then relented. "It's a pirates' hidey-hole. 'Twas built about 1700 by Lot Honeywood, he'd a sister married Davy Quelch. This Davy and his brother John pirated 'gainst the Portygees, or some such. They'd hide the loot up there. Honeywoods wasn't so domned law-abiding in *those* days—" she added with a glance towards Roger's door. "Now, hurry, child."

She draped Hesper's arm with the dust rag, added the water, trencher, and a lighted candle. The girl walked nervously into the closet while Susan shut the door behind her. The flickering light showed narrow wooden steps thick with gray dust. The steps circled to the back of the central chimney and mounted steep as a ladder to a cubicle about six feet square. It had been built from space cunningly filched from the attic and from her parent's bedroom which had once been the loft of the original house, and in a structure so full of irregularities and additions, its existence had never been suspected after Moses Honeywood had added the large gambrel-roofed wing to the house in 1750. Moses had left a notation about the pirate's hidey-hole amongst his private papers, but no Honeywood until Roger had bothered to look through these.

The candle trembled in Hesper's hand; she saw a lumpy shape on the floor and gave a stifled cry, but it was only a straw pallet. What if there was a ghost? Ma believed in ghosts—Old Dimond—the phantom ship—the screechin' woman who'd been *murdered* by pirates. So did lots of other people. Her heart thumped on her ribs, and she put the candlestick on the floor. It burned calmly. An inch-wide crack, running along the ceiling, took in air from the attic. Hesper dabbed at a few cobwebs, put the food and water on the pallet, picked up the candle and retreated.

In the bright sunny kitchen, Susan was mixing cornmeal for johnny-cake, as though nothing out of the way were happening at all. She showed Hesper how to slide the false panel, and drop the iron pin that held it rigid. "Your Pa's gone out—" she said in an acid tone, "to the depot. Seems he's expecting a package of his everlasting books from Boston. Pity *our* packages can't be handled so easy. I've been thinking, Hes, and I've made the plans. First I want you should find Johnnie."

"Johnnie Peach!" cried Hesper, her eyes shining.

"Aye, I thought you'd not object. His family's abolitionist, and he's just the boy to help with this business. We'll need a good seaman, and a lad with spunk. You *can* tell *him,* but no one else—mind!"

"No, Ma," she breathed. Find Johnnie, share a great secret with him. He'd have to notice her then. She gave an irrepressible skip, starting toward the entry where her cloak hung.

"Stop, bufflehead! That's not all. We'll need more than Johnnie. Go to Peg-Leg and ask him to come here, but don't say why. I'll tell him myself."

Hesper nodded, slightly dampened. Peg-Leg was Susan's brother Noah Dolliber, and a stop at his house meant boring delay, for his wife was an interminable talker.

"Don't let your Aunt Mattie catch wind o' anything"—she waited while Hesper nodded again—"then go on up Gingerbread Hill, try at Ma'am Sociable's and Aunty 'Crese's if they know a fiddler I can get for tonight."

"Fiddler!" cried Hesper—"Oh Ma—you'd never mean we're going

to have dancing here!" She stared at her mother with incredulous joy. Susan, a staunch church member, did not hold with frivolity of any kind. She ran the Inn with stern decorum, always limiting drinks when she saw fit. And there had been no party at the Hearth and Eagle since the Fourth of July celebration two years ago.

"Stop teetering around like a chicken with the pip," Susan snapped, ladling the corn batter. "You needn't think I'm going to hold a regular tidderi-i, but since the crews'll be here, and I daren't stop them coming, for they'd think it strange, there'd better be as much rumpus as possible to cover the arrival of them two packages."

"Oh Ma—what a grand lark!" Hesper clapped her hands, intoxicated with this succession of excitements. The secret room—find Johnnie—a fiddler and dancing.

Susan turned her bulky body and confronted her daughter squarely. "It's not a grand lark, Hesper. There be two human lives at stake. And there's danger. For them, and maybe for us too."

The girl flushed. She'd never heard Ma use that solemn churchy voice before except once. That was the way Ma spoke so long ago at the wharf, the day they got the news that Tom and Willy were drowned.

Hesper got her cloak silently and went out the kitchen door to find Johnnie. She stood a moment in the yard, considering. It was past eight o'clock, so he'd likely be down at Appleton's Wharf by now or on the *Diana* making ready to be off tomorrow. She walked under the chestnut tree, new-leafed in tender green, and on Franklin Place turned left to the Great Harbor. The land breeze had slackened and the tide was out so the water lay in quiet seaweed-fringed pools amongst the bare rocks on Fort Beach. There was an April softness in the salt air that smelled of drying fish from the flakes and of oakum and tar from the wharves. There were other smells, too, less pervasive than the key odor, whiffs from privies and pigsties back of huddled houses, and a pleasanter scent of cordovan leather from the cordwainers' shops. Along Front Street the unpainted houses, weathered long ago to silver—some clinging catty-corner to rock ledges, some squared with the street—presented a melody of angles and gables and gambrels, each man having built as he pleased and as he could find tenure in the scanty soil.

On the waterside, past the blacksmith's, where Mr. Murchison hammered on a small anchor, and the grovers and ships' chandlers, three schooners and a square-rigger from Portsmouth rode quietly at anchor in the harbor, the gaudy colored stripes on their hulls gleaming in the sunshine. And behind them again, hugging close to the Neck, a huge Nova Scotian coaler edged up towards the coal wharves past Bartol's Head.

As Hesper neared Appleton's Wharf at the foot of State Street, Swasey the fishmonger began to blow "Poko White," the Marblehead "Bankers" call, on his fish horn, thus announcing his wares, and a dozen mewing cats precipitated themselves from adjacent doorways.

Hesper picked her way briskly around the cats. The accustomed smells and sights and sounds of Marblehead made no impression on her. She was looking for Johnnie.

The wharf was teeming with busy seamen in red flannel shirts and knitted Guernsey frocks, and they all wore clumsy leather fishing boots made by Mr. Bessom in his wharf shop. Hesper threaded her way among kegs and coiled rope, passing two other schooners, tied up along the wharf, the *Ceres* and the *Blue Wave,* before reaching the *Diana.*

The *Diana* was an old ship of seventy tons burden, a "pinkie" with high-peaked stern, high sides, and a saucy uptilted bowsprit. She was sluggish as an old turtle and even her newly tarred rigging and fresh-painted blue hull and gold stripe could not disguise her air of obsolescence, but she had weathered the Great Gale of '46 and many another too, and her Master and crew were fond of her.

Two of the crew were toiling up the gangplank carrying a cask of water. Hesper knew them by sight, but a sudden shyness prevented her calling to them, nor did she dare go on board without invitation. Bred as she was to the waterfront, she saw that they were stowing in the hold the last of the Great General, which consisted of the salt, the water, the fuel, and tackle. The Small General, which consisted of provisions, would be already on board.

She walked to the end of the dock trying to peer into the *Diana's* square dark portholes, when she heard an unwelcome drawl behind her. "Well, now if it isn't Fire-top! Have you come to ship with us, my lass?"

Hesper frowned and turned around. It was Nat Cubby staring at her morosely, one foot resting on a stanchion, and his jaws champing a plug of tobacco. He was twenty now and still an undersized and scrawny youth, but there was a quality in Nat which canceled all impression of youth or smallness. He had wiry strength, the stubble of beard on his narrow jaws was heavy as a full grown man's, and his yellowish eyes were wary and unyielding as those of an old lynx. As hc contemplated Hesper his mouth set in its perpetual slight sneer. It was a thin red scar that drew up the right half of his upper lip, but it was hard to allow for that, because the resultant snarl was so in keeping with his usual manner. Nobody knew for sure how his lip had been split open, it might have been some boyish accident, but many thought it had been done by Leah, his mother, in a fit of the madness with which she had been afflicted after her husband was lost at sea. Yet Nat adored his mother, never leaving her alone when he was ashore, and she was the only person to whom he did not show a brooding malevolence.

Leah was but sixteen years older than her son, her curly hair was a glossy black, her mouth full and red as a girl's, and her magnificent dark eyes were luminous and unstained by the agonizing tears they must have shed. Strangers seeing her beside Nat might have taken them for almost the same age.

"Well, what d'you want?" repeated Nat to Hesper, spitting into the water. "*We* want no women cluttering about the wharf at loading time."

"I came to find Johnnie Peach—" said Hesper with spirit. "I've a message for him."

"You won't find him here. Likely he's gone home. I gave him leave."

"*You* gave him leave . . ."

The small eyes, cold as yellow glass, surveyed her without interest. "I'm mate on this ship now." He hunched a shoulder towards the *Diana*.

"Then for sure Johnnie'll be a mate soon too—" she cried hotly. Or skipper over you, she added to herself.

Nat shrugged and shifted his tobacco to the other cheek. "Very likely he will. He's an apt seaman." You couldn't tell whether he was mocking or not, but Hesper was silenced. There'd always been a queer sort of companionship between Johnnie and Nat. Queer because as boys they'd belonged to different gangs, Johnnie a "Barnegatter," Nat a "wharf rat," and they'd fought each other many a time, and while everyone liked Johnnie, nobody else had a good word for Nat. Still, you couldn't tell what Nat was really like. He seemed indifferent now, remote—but you always had the feeling there was a lot going on in his head. And he was known for a troublemaker; known for a copperhead too, she thought with sudden disquiet, remembering an argument in the taproom when Nat had sneered at all the abolitionists gathered there, and obviously from no motive but malice and the desire to annoy.

"You coming to the Inn, tonight?" she asked quickly. She felt herself flush and tried to look indifferent.

The yellow eyes shifted and rested on her. "I might." He took his boot off the stanchion, and walked up the gangplank onto the *Diana*.

Lord, thought Hesper, if he should get wind of anything he'd turn us in sure. For the reward, if not just for deviltry. But Johnnie'll know what to do.

She gathered her cloak around her and hurried down the wharf and along State Street. The Cubbys' house was in the middle of the block; she glanced at it and saw a slender black figure standing on the roof behind the railings. The white face was turned towards the sea, and even at that distance gave an impression of stillness and patient waiting. Hesper felt a thrill of horror. Had Leah taken to standing in the "scuttle" again, as she used to, day in, day out during her madness, watching for her drowned husband's ship? Hesper hurried faster, but the eerie fear subsided before common sense. Leah's madness was over long ago. Surely she had merely climbed to the scuttle to look for Nat on the wharf so that she might know when he started home.

Hesper turned down Washington Street and now her progress was impeded by traffic on the narrow sidewalk. Old seamen, past sailing, were wandering uptown to bask in the sun on the steps of the Town House, or on chairs outside the firehouses, and shawled women carrying wicker baskets were market bound to the shops around Mechanic Square. Two of these, Mrs. Cloutman and Mrs. Devereux, stopped Hesper to ask her if her ma was going to provide the cakes for the church supper at the Old North on Wednesday.

"I don't know, I guess so—" said Hesper distractedly. "I'll remind her." But the women didn't yet let her pass. "What you doin' out o' school, Hes?" said Mrs. Cloutman, eyeing the girl's flushed haste.

"Errands for Ma. Going to be terrible busy tonight."

"Humph," said Mrs. Cloutman, unsatisfied, but Hes Honeywood wasn't the kind to be up to mischief. Big homely girl, and a good student at the Academy she knew through her own daughter.

Hesper escaped, but only for a block when Cap'n Knight came bearing down on her. She bobbed her head and stood aside for him to pass, as all children must for a sea captain, but this skipper, whose ship was not sailing for the spring fare, was in no hurry.

"Mar-rnin', child—" he said. "Be'nt ye Hes Honeywood?" He rested on his briar-thorn stick, his fringe-bearded face turned towards her amiably.

"Yes, sir—" she tried to edge around him but he lifted his stick and held her back. "Gr-reat stroppin' gur-rl ye've gr-rown to. Oi moind when ye was no bigger'n a minnow tumblin' about the wharves. Ye favor the Dollibers, Oi see, wi' all thot carrot hair."

"Yes, sir—" repeated Hesper. "Please, I must be off—"

"Sweethort-rt waitin' fur ye?— Ye'd best drap hobnails in the tallow pot, n' see if he loves ye true, lass. Aye, well—shove off if ye must." The captain lowered his stick. " 'Tis a stavin' spring mar-rnin'. Oi can't blame ye."

Oh dear—thought Hesper, hurrying past the Old North and up the hill on Orne Street. It's getting so late—suppose Johnnie isn't home any more, suppose he's gone out in his dory.

The Peach house was set back from the street in the old section of the town called Barnegat, perched on the cliff that overlooked Little Harbor. It was a small house and quite new, being built only thirty years ago, but already its clapboards had weathered to a buff-toned silver like the older houses.

Johnnie's mother, Tamsen Peach, opened the door to Hesper. Mrs. Peach had a baby at her breast, a weanling tugging on her skirt, and the five-year-old twins scrambled on the rush-strewn kitchen floor behind her. Johnnie was the oldest of nine living children. Not a large family for Marblehead.

"Well, Hessie—" said Mrs. Peach, her kind rosy face breaking into a smile. " 'Tis donkey's years sense Oi've set eyes on ye. Come in an set. Oi'm bakin' the sable cake for Johnnie's sea chest."

"Where *is* Johnnie—" said Hesper so anxiously that his mother gave her a startled look. "I mean, Ma—" no that wasn't right, why would Ma summon Johnnie—"I wanted to say good-bye to him," she finished, lamely, since Johnnie had sailed for many a fare when she hadn't seen him at all.

A smile twitched at the mother's mouth. So many girls after Johnnie, and he'd scant use for them.

"Well, ye may, then," she said. "He's out back in the shoe shop."

Hesper thanked her and went outdoors. The Peaches' shoe shop stood in the back yard between the privy and the shed. It was a small wooden shack lighted by two windows and warmed by a pot-bellied stove, as were all the hundred other backyard shoe shops in Marblehead. Here the men worked during the winters and at other times when they might be in port, skiving and lasting and sewing and finishing shoes for delivery to the manufactories, the uppers having been earlier stitched and bound by the women in their kitchens during moments snatched from cookery and baby care.

Hesper heard the sound of tapping and men's voices inside, and she hesitated at the door. The shoe shops were male sanctums like ships, where women intruded only with haste and apology. Then she heard Johnnie's easy laugh, and she knocked.

"Come in, then—" called the gruff voice of Johnnie's father, Lem.

Hesper opened the door, and paused choked by the thick air. Smoke poured from the cracks of the pot-bellied stove where they were burning scraps of shoe leather, and it poured too from the four men's white clay pipes. The warming glue pot on the stove exhaled its own stench, and the visible air that swirled around the three cordwainers' heads was white with chalk dust.

"Why 'tis Hessie Honeywood—" said Johnnie, who had been lounging on a stool, smoking and reading the *Essex County Gazette* to the shoemakers.

Lem Peach looked up from his last. "Well—come in, gur-rl, an' shet the door, ye're makin' a domned draft." He coughed long and hard, ejecting the blood-specked spittle against the stove. His face was pinched and his thin shoulders were peaked in the shoemakers' stoop.

"Will ye set down?" said Johnnie, laughing a little, and pointing to the stool he had vacated. "It's rare we have a visit from a lady."

Hesper smiled timidly and shook her head, her heart beat fast as it always did at the sight of Johnnie—his close cropped dark hair, the thick muscles of his neck rising careless and easy from the open red flannel shirt, and his blunt white teeth grinning at her.

She glanced at Lem Peach, hunched on the cobbler's bench, and at the other two cordwainers, Barnegat men whom she did not know. "Might I speak with you a bit—" she said to Johnnie—"Are you busy?"

His father snorted. "He's not that! He's no hand for shoemakin', gr-reat clumsy loon. He's good for naught but the sea." Lem drew his sparse brows into a scowl, but a baby would have heard the pride in his voice. "Afor-re ye go out, Johnnie—hand me me long-stick and a cup o' grog. Can't stop work for a minute if we're to deliver all these pairs to Porterman's on time." He took a pull from the tin cup of grog and handed it to the man on the next bench. "I mislike that Porterman," he added gloomily—"hulkin' penny-pinchin' furriner from Danvers, nor do I like his foreman neither, ever a-huffin' and a-dingin' at us to horry up with the consignment. We be free men here in Marblehead, not nigger slaves."

"Right you are, Pa—" said Johnnie, puffing on his pipe. "Don't you let 'em boss you, cordwainers've always been their own masters, slow or fast as they willed, and where'd the manufacturers be without you —tell me that?"

The three men grunted, Lem coughed, polishing a gleaming chalk-white sole with his mahogany long-stick. "And the bostard talks of lower wages too. As it is, we barely keep body and soul together at three dollars the case." He picked up a pigskin bristle and waxed his thread.

"Johnnie—" whispered Hesper, fearing this talk of prices and Porterman, whoever he might be, might go on forever.

"Oh aye, aye, lass," said Johnnie kindly, putting his pipe in his pocket. "Mustn't keep a lady waitin'." He made a bow, and stood aside for her to precede him into the sunlight.

"Well, Hes—what's on your mind?" He glanced with amusement at her worried face and twitched the long auburn pigtail that swung down her back. "You been filchin' your ma's pasties again? Or come to think on it, why be'nt you in school? 'Tis very wrong to play hookey."

"Oh, Johnnie, I'm not. I'm not a child any more. It's a grave matter. We mustn't be overheard."

He chuckled. "You don't say. Well, come up Burial Hill then, the gravestones'll not listen."

He shambled along beside her but his rolling seaman's gait was fast, and long as her legs were she had to trot to keep up with him. Much courting took place at night on Burial Hill among the old graves, and more than courting too, but this April morning there was no one in sight.

They climbed the sharp hill to the highest spot by the Seaman's monument. It commemorated many a drowned seaman, and Johnnie's uncle and Hesper's two brothers among them, but neither of the young people glanced at it. Johnnie, squinting out to sea, immediately forgot Hesper. There was one of the new clipper ships beating to windward off Little Misery, Salem bound, she'd be. He shaded his eyes with his hand until he was sure of her. She was the *Flying Cloud,* for he saw the angel figurehead plain under the bowsprit. Then her master'd be Cap'n Josh Cressy of Marblehead. A pretty enough craft but over-flimsy and tender, a toy for feverish transporting of landlubbers. She'd never stand up in even a half-gale off the Banks, he thought, jealous for the old *Diana* whose masts he could see swaying gently above the shed on Appleton's Wharf in the harbor below.

"Johnnie—" cried Hesper tugging at his arm. *"Please* listen to me."

He lowered his head, and patted the hand on his arm. "Sorry, Hes. Out with it." He threw himself down on the bank, and pulling a grass blade began to chew.

"Johnnie, you *are* abolitionist, aren't you?" she cried, abandoning all subtle approaches.

He sat up straight, his indulgent gaze sharpened to surprise. "I am. You've not got me out here to start political argument?"

"No, but Ma wants your help, tonight. There's two—two packages being delivered at the Inn, and we've to hide them."

He stared at her and gave a long whistle. "The Underground?" She nodded and he drew his brows together. "Where are they to go, after?"

"Canada. There's to be a brig off Cat Island, waiting. Lucky it's the dark of the moon."

"To be sure. They're allowin' for that. They always plan well."

"Then you've done this before?"

He smiled and spat on the grass. "It's often best not to question if you don't want to hear lies. Now tell me all you know about this thing."

"I know *all* about it—" she said hotly. "Ma and I are doing it together. Pa wouldn't."

"So? Well, get on with it."

She had his full attention at last, and he listened gravely, nodding sometimes as she told all that had happened that morning, and her mother's plans. "But—" she added as she finished the account, "I'm afeared of Nat Cubby, he'll be at the Inn tonight."

"Oh, he's all right," Johnnie said. But he wasn't so sure. There wasn't the old free understanding between them. Nat was a bit like a cat, you never knew which way he'd jump, except it'd be to his own advantage. But Nat was smart at anything he'd turn his hand to. Johnnie didn't begrudge him the mate's berth, he'd worked hard for it, he'd be a good mate, maybe, if he didn't get one of his savage vindictive notions when no man could make him see reason. "All the same—" he said out loud, " 'twould be best he knew nothing of this matter tonight. Run along Hessie—get Peg-Leg like your ma said, and find a fiddler. I'll go ready my dory for her trip. Peg-Leg'll have to help me row. Tide'll be racin' in against us, and there's wind makin'." He squinted at the sky.

"Yes, Johnnie—" she said, turning slowly to go. Johnnie had taken over, masterful and sure, as she knew he would, but this hadn't brought him any closer to her. He hadn't looked at her once, to really see her. And why should he, she thought bitterly. I'm not so much to look at. Why didn't I take time to put on my good dress and pin my hair up?

An inkling of the girl's dejection reached Johnnie, and he thought she was frightened of the dangerous project tonight. "Hes—" he said, chuckling, "d'you mind the time we stowed away on the *Balance* to fetch the salt?"

"Oh, yes—" she breathed.

"You were a plucky one, got the makin' of a seaman too, shouldn't wonder." Her eyes shone, dazzled by this highest praise, and then Johnnie spoiled it. "It's mortal shame you're only a girl."

She put her lips tight together, and walked away. Johnnie, after a moment's surprise, forgot about her and started down the hill towards Little Harbor and his new dory.

Hesper continued in the other direction along Beacon Street to Dolliber's Cove, and Peg-Leg's neat cottage. She was startled to find her uncle wrapped in a red blanket and lying propped up on a bench in his yard. Peg-Leg for all the strapped-on wooden stump that served him for left leg and despite his increasing plumpness was nimble as a jack rabbit. He still went out dory fishing in the bay, and he was a great gardener. From May to September his little yard bloomed with daffodils, or cinnamon roses, moss pinks or asters.

"Why, Peg-Leg . . ." cried Hesper pushing open the gate, and hurrying up to the red cocoon on the bench—"Whatever's the matter?"

The round face above the fringe of sandy beard surveyed her sourly. "Where's yore manners, chit? Yore Grandsir Dolliber hear ye callin' me thot, he'd guv ye a stroppin', he would. Susan'd ought to raise ye better."

"I'm sorry, Uncle Noah," said Hesper, rightly deducing great stress from this unusual cantankerousness. Half the town had nicknames everybody used, and Peg-Leg never minded his. "Ma wanted to see you at the Inn, right away."

"Well—she won't then. Nor see me at all, lessen she comes here. Oi'm thot kinked up wi' t' rheumatiz, Oi wouldn't budge fur Old Nick hisself."

"I'm sorry—" said Hesper again. So Peg-Leg wouldn't be any use to Johnnie tonight; who then could he get to help him? Well, he'd make another plan, Johnnie was never at a loss, but—a blinding and thrilling idea struck her. She straightened her strong young shoulders. If only she could persuade him. . . .

Her uncle saw the sudden brightening of her face and was naturally annoyed.

"Me pains're far worser now than after the God-domned shark bit me leg off," he said peevishly, scowling at her.

"It's a mortal shame—Peg—Uncle Noah. Have you tried the goose grease?" She was in a fever to be off on the rest of her errand, and dismayed to see her aunt come bustling through the door into the yard.

"Who're ye a gabbin' with, Noah—Oh, I see, 'tis Hessie. How be ye child, an' how's your ma and pa? He's real grouty wi' t' rheumatics—" she jerked her double chins in the direction of her husband. "Oi'm cookin' him up a garney stew. Me father-r useter say there was naught like tongues and sounds and fins well seethed in a bit o' broth fur strengthenin' the belly. D'ye 'member me pa, Hessie? Master o' the *Rebecca* he was." The insistent babbling voice paused an instant—

"Oh, yes, Aunt Mattie I do—" cried Hesper with complete untruth. "I must be—"

"Nay, to be sure ye don't—" went on her aunt, whose pauses were always for breath and not for response. "Ye wasn't barn yet when he died, an' speakin' o' dyin'—does yore ma know Puff-Ball Thompson expoired yester e'en? Oi was there, an' 'twas the drink did her in, wi'out doubt, fur she stank loike a dram-shop, but maybe we've no cause to blame her fur drownin' her troubles, when ye think there's her brat Cassie, eight months gone by Rob Nichols and him China bound out o' Salem, an' not loike to wed her even—"

"Mattie!" Peg-Leg opened his eyes. "Ye forget yore hearer." His wife was no way discomfited. "Well, Oi should hope Hessie's old enough to take warnin' from the sins o' others, an' Cassie's not the only one either, Oi have grave doubts about—" The acrid odor of scorching fish swirled out the kitchen door. Mattie sniffed reluctantly and said "Crimmy—there's me garney a-cautchin' itself—wait, Hes—Oi'll be back directly," but Hesper did not wait.

As she climbed the narrow sharp lane up Gingerbread Hill she briefly considered Aunt Mattie's last remarks. What had Cassie and Rob Nichols done exactly, that Cassie should be "eight months gone?" That it was something shameful and to do with a baby, Hesper understood. But people had babies after they were married, not before. Sows and bitches could be "eight *weeks* gone," not months, there was perhaps some connection, but for Hesper not a convincing one. She couldn't ask Ma who'd slapped her once for mentioning the old sow's tits. The girls at school were always whispering and giggling in corners; they might know, but she had no intimate friend she cared to ask. Her interest lagged and reverted to Johnnie, and the adventure tonight.

She reached the top of the hill by Black Joe's Pond, and hesitated in the lane between the two rival taverns. The Widow Bowen, "Ma'am Sociable," lived in one, and "Aunt 'Crese" lived in the other. They both ran cent shops, and sold election cakes, gingerbread, and Gibraltars as well as grog. Both women were shrewd and easy-going, both held frolics and jigs and reels and penny-pitching contests, in an endeavor to lure customers away from each other's establishments. "Ma'am Sociable" was a spry little elf of a woman with faded flaxen hair. "Aunt 'Crese" was fat and dark as soot, the widow of "Black Joe" who had been a free Negro and fought in the Revolution. Marbleheaders in search of gaiety patronized them quite impartially.

At Hesper's approach the flock of white geese on the pond set up a raucous cackling and honking. The Widow Bowen fled out the door and down her stone steps. "Come in, come in, dearie. Your ma send ye fur my rosewater? I've got a bottle or so left—" over Hesper's auburn head she saw Aunt 'Crese waddle through her own doorway, and she raised her voice to a high wheedle, "I've got fresh gingerbread nuts, or some mighty pretty ribbons, you've pennies with you, haven't you?"

"Only two—" said Hesper fumbling in her pinafore pocket. Maybe a red ribbon tied into a bow at the neck of her best dress for tonight—

Aunt 'Crese reached the lane and her thick molasses voice flowed over them—"Mornin', young lady—ah got some tasty nice pep'mint drops today, some purty pitcher cyards too, they'se got li'l pink hearts on 'em an' li'l gol' doves. Sho' you want to see 'em." She ignored her rival and bestowed on the girl a dazzling smile.

Hesper, flanked by the small insistent white woman in a sunbonnet and the large determined black one in a yellow turban, suddenly giggled. "I didn't really come to buy. Ma wants to know, will you send her a fiddler for tonight?"

Both women stopped looking persuasive, and drew together in a momentary bond of caution against outside competition.

"What's Mrs. Honeywood want a fiddler for?" snapped Widow Bowen. "She never has jamborees at her Inn."

"Well, she's holding a farewell for the men on the *Diana* and the *Ceres;* thought they'd like maybe to dance a bit," said Hesper pacifically.

"I'm holdin' a frolic myself," snapped Widow Bowen, who had just thought of it, "I'll need Pipin' Willy here."

"Yo' kin have Ambrose—" said Aunt 'Crese, referring to one of her grandsons. "Ah expecs yo' ma'll pay well? Ev'body know Ambrose es the bes' fiddler in Essex County."

The Widow Bowen sniffed, shrugged her shoulders, and retreated. Those Honeywoods, uppity they were, hardly give you the time o' day —let 'em just try to liven up their stuffy old inn, that moony ink-stained Roger, and Susan Dolliber glum as a haddock—they'd not get far. She slammed her front door.

"Thanks, Aunt 'Crese," said Hesper. "Could Ambrose be there at seven?"

The old Negress nodded, her yellowed veiny eyeballs rolled and focused keenly on the girl's face. "Yo' got su'thin' on yo' min', chile. I can see it plain."

"Oh, no I haven't," said Hesper quickly, but the old woman put two fat black hands on her shoulders and held fast. "Wait, chile, I can read a powerful lot in yo' face. Yo're goin' to go through a heap o' livin'."

Hesper tried to back away; all morning people had been detaining her, and the old woman's breath was fetid.

Aunt 'Crese's gaze rolled inward—her purplish lips stuck out. "Le'me tell yo' fortune chile. Yo' got coppers, ain't yo'?" Hesper nodded, "But—"

One black hand slid down to her arm, and Aunt 'Crese pulled Hesper into her little tavern. It was dark inside; from the smoke-blackened rafters there dangled hams, bunches of dried herbs, and strings of corn ears. Next to the rum keg there was a glass case containing rusty pins, a spool of thread, faded picture cards, and a cracked dish of miscellaneous taffy balls, peppermint drops, and Gibraltars all filmed with dust. This was the cent shop. One of the grandsons, a lanky bullet-headed young Negro, sprawled on a pile of corn husks near the fire, snoring fitfully. His grandmother stepped over his legs and Hesper followed. Her unwillingness had given place to interest. She'd heard that Aunt 'Crese told fortunes when the fit struck her, but Charity Trevercombe and Nellie Higgins had sneaked out here once after dark, and Aunt 'Crese' hadn't told them any fortune at all, she'd made them spend all their coppers on moldy candy they didn't want.

"Set down," ordered Aunt 'Crese, pointing at a sticky bench spotted with candle grease. Hesper did so gingerly, and the old woman pulled a lean pack of dirty playing cards from a niche under the tavern trestle.

"Cut with yo' left hand." Hester imitated the other's gesture, staring at the cards and suffused by an agreeable feeling of excitement and guilt. She'd never seen playing cards before. Ma wouldn't allow the devil's playthings in the house.

"Make a wish—" Instantly, Hesper thought "Johnnie," and as instantly suppressed it; she ought to wish for something noble and unselfish—like the success of the venture tonight.

Aunt 'Crese shuffled and slapped the cards on the table. Outside on the pond the geese quacked incessantly. The young Negro snored by the hearth. These were comforting noises, nor was there anything eerie about the old Negress in her grimy yellow turban, even when she began to speak and her voice had gone high and thin, drifting through her pendulous lips and scarcely moving them. "Yo' goin' ter see a heap o' trouble, chile—Heartbreak. Heartbreak. Yo'll think it won't mend, but life's got a hull lot up her sleeve for you. It'll mend an' yo'll fin' out how many ways a woman's heart can break."

Hesper drew in her breath. "I don't want to hear things like that. I don't believe you anyway."

The thin singsong continued unheeding. "Yo'll know three kin's o' lovin'. They's three men here in yore life."

"Three?" cried Hesper, relaxing again. This was the sort of thing a fortune should tell. "Will I get—get married?"

But Aunt 'Crese stared at the cluttered cards and heeded nothing else. "There's fire aroun' yo', fire in yore hair, fire in yore heart, fire that makes a beautyness, an' real fire fearsome in the night. An' there's water too. The ocean salt's in yore blood. Yo' cain't live without it."

What rubbish, thought Hesper, and she looked around the tavern for a clock, but she could not see one.

The old woman stooped closer over the cards. "Ah see yo' scribblin' away, pen on paper, puttin' down words . . . puttin' down words."

Hesper brightened. That was her secret ambition, poetry like Pa. Like Mrs. Hemans or Mrs. Sigourney. She had a pansy album half filled with little verses.

"All them words won't do yo' no good—" said Aunt 'Crese with contempt. "No good at all. Yo' want things too hard. Always hankerin' an' a-ravenin' after su'thin'. Yo' can't holp it, Ah reckon, but yo' should listen to the house."

The girl sighed. "I can't listen to a house," she said crossly.

"It's yore home—an' it's powerful wise effen yo'll listen to it, yo' kin hear the Words o' God through it."

"I don't see how—" cried Hesper, shocked at this blasphemy. "Listen, I've got to go, Aunt 'Crese, and you haven't even told me about my wish."

The old woman waggled her head, she poked at a red spotted card. Her voice dropped from the high whine. "Yo'll get yore love-wish, chile, but someplace there's heartbreak. Heartbreak," she repeated with solemn unction. She spattered the cards into a circle, heaved herself to her feet staring at Hesper with a blend of malice and pity. "That's yo' fortune. Gi' me the coppers."

"But, you didn't tell me anything, really." Hesper's hot hand clutched the two coppers in her pocket. One was for the Sabbath collection, and the other was her weekly allowance. She felt cheated and disgruntled. Heartbreak. Fire and water. Listen to the house. Three men, when all she wanted was Johnnie. Get your wish—but—

"Ah tole yo' plenty," said Aunt 'Crese, "Ah tole yo' de truf." She drew herself up sharply until she towered over Hesper, and the shiny face went hard like black marble. "Yo' think Ah cain't see things others cain't? Yo' think Ah don't know what's hidden in the secret heart?" The fat good-natured Aunt 'Crese had become an outraged priestess—"Yo' think Ah don't know what yore up to tonight? Why yo' want Ambrose an' his fiddlin'?"

Hesper's mouth dropped open. What'll I say? Does she really know? Can she read my thoughts? Or is she part of the Underground too?

Aunt 'Crese watched her through slitted eyes and gave a throaty chuckle. She held out her pinkish palm, and Hesper slowly dropped the coppers into it. Aunt 'Crese tucked them in her turban where they jingled with other coins on the grizzled wool. "Run along, chile, Ah don't meddle with nobody, an' nobody meddles with me. Run along."

Hesper nodded uncertainly and obeyed. As she walked down Gingerbread Lane, she felt a little like crying. Her two coppers were gone, and there'd be a scene with Ma about the one for the collection. The fortune had been horrid, queer and vague, and Aunt 'Crese had been horrid, queer and vague, too. How did one learn to take people, not to feel lost and inadequate when they suddenly acted different from what one expected? Like Peg-Leg this morning, too. She'd never known he could be so cross. Hesper had always lived in a childish world of certainties, of black and white, and she felt rebellion and resultant helplessness at the first dim, adult perception that many things must be endured without certainty. Take Aunt 'Crese, was she good or bad, did she guess or know about the Underground, or were her words just a lucky hit? Serves me right for dawdling and listening to that silly fortune.

She ran down Orne Street, as distant church bells clanged twelve times. Lord, dinner'd be on, and Ma frantic to know the result of the errands. Hesper cut left between the houses and scrambled down to the Little Harbor Beach. Above highwater mark on the shingle and in the adjacent field, fishermen tended the semicircle of fish flakes, the slated wooden frames on which the cod splits, glittering with salt crystals, dried in the April sun. Hesper looked for Johnnie's green dory amongst the dozen boats drawn up on the beach but it was not there. She hurried off the beach, across a lane and into the Honeywood lot, in back of the Inn. Here there were four apple trees, remnant of Moses Honeywood's fine orchard. Here too were Susan's herb patch and vegetable garden where old "Looney" Hodge was hoeing, his vacant half-witted face drooping over the stony soil with mournful patience. Since Roger never lent a hand, Susan hired Looney to help with the rougher chores. He slept in the barn above the pigsty and the empty stable where the rare Inn guests who did not come on foot from the depot, or by water, might shelter a horse and buggy.

To Hesper's great relief she found her father alone in the kitchen. He sat at the scarred oak table, with his dinner of salt pork and pickled beets still untouched on the pewter plate before him, and a book propped up against the mug of coffee. He looked up smiling as the girl flew into the kitchen, throwing her cape on the entry hook, patting her ruffled hair and casting a quick glance around for her mother.

"Hail, radiant daughter of an April Morn—" Roger said with the affectionate playfulness he never showed to anyone else. "Sit down, my dear—I want to read you some magnificent lines." He indicated the book before him. "One of Horace's Odes—translated by Dryden. It well expresses what I—what I'm trying to instill into my own poem."

She heard the uncertainty and yet the pride in his voice, and she put her hand on his thin alpaca-covered shoulder. "Not now, Pa—" she said. "Where's Ma?"

"In the taproom or the parlor, I believe—making some sort of a to-do." He compressed his mouth, and frowned again through his spectacles.

"Descended from an ancient line . . ." Ah, Hesper was too young to know the subtle comfort of that, but she might have listened. He turned the page to the last stanza, reading to himself.

> For me secure from Fortune's blows,
> Secure of what I can not lose
> In my small pinnace I can sail
> Contemning all the blustering roar;
> And running with a merry gale
> With friendly stars my safety seek,
> Within some little winding creek
> And see the storm from shore.

That was the way to take life, in contemplation and serenity.

"Eat your dinner, Pa. Do—" said Hesper coaxingly seeing that she had hurt him. She nudged his full plate. "I'd love to hear the poem tomorrow."

Susan came bustling into the kitchen. "So you're back, miss—" she said scowling at Hesper in a preoccupied way, her broad freckled face was flushed from the exertion of cleaning the always immaculate parlor and moving furniture out of the way of tonight's celebration. "My God, Roger, you're that gormy at your vittles, I'm like to go mad. Have you not enough reading shut up in your room all day? Step to the buttery—" she added under her breath to Hesper.

She thrust a cheesecloth into the girl's hands and took one herself and they both wrung water from the waiting pats of butter, while Hesper gave a whispered account of her morning, deleting, of course the fortune-telling episode.

"So Peg-Leg's out, we must trust to Johnnie alone—" Susan said, shaking her head, "I daren't trust anyone else. The baker's boy told me there was a big nigger hunt in Lynn last night. The slave catcher might come here, next."

Hesper squeezed the butter until it jutted in ridges between her fingers. "Ma, I can row. I could help Johnnie."

"Rubbish. You'll do nothing of the sort. No, hold your tongue, I've got enough to fret me without your buffleheaded notions."

Hesper turned her back on her mother; hot mutinous tears flew to her eyes. No uncertainties about Ma, anyway. She always said No.

The knocker on the side door between the taproom and the kitchen resounded with two heavy raps. Susan's hand paused, she put the butter in its crock. "Who's that, I wonder?" she said slowly. "Not a regular customer, or he'd 've walked in." She wiped her hands on her apron. "Well, there's naught yet for anyone to find—" she gave her grim chuckle and pushed past her daughter. Hesper dabbed at her eyes with the buttery cheesecloth and followed.

She heard a deep voice say, "Mrs. Honeywood? May I speak with you a moment?" and knew from the enunciation it was no Marbleheader. Her mother answered, "In the kitchen then, sir. We're expecting some of the men off the ships tonight, and the parlor's at sixes and sevens."

A very tall and heavy-set man entered the room after Susan. He was dressed in frock coat and striped silk waistcoat; across it a massive gold link watch chain ran from pocket to pocket. He held a glossy beaver top hat in his hand, and there was a big dent in the top of the hat. His hair, clipped short and square above his ears, was of so light a flaxen color that it almost seemed white, and made him appear older than his twenty-six years.

Roger looked up in surprise, and rose from the table as the stranger entered saying, "Good day, sir. I'm sorry to disturb you. My name is Amos Porterman. I now own the old Allen shoe manufactory on School Street."

"Oh, do you indeed, sir?" answered Roger with vague hospitality, and not the slightest interest. "Will you sit down?" He glanced for help to his wife, a trifle surprised at her silence and a wariness in her bearing.

Hesper and Susan were both more enlightened than Roger by the stranger's identification of himself. Hesper thought, with immediate antagonism, Oh, it's that dreadful shoeman from Danvers, Johnnie's father was talking about. What nasty cold blue eyes he has, and what's he want butting in here? Surely Ma'd give him short shrift.

But Susan, though she sat down when Mr. Porterman did, said nothing. She sat waiting. This then was the foreigner who'd bought up the Allen factory last fall, when Mr. Allen and all the other shoemen in town, except Bassett, went bankrupt in the panic. This big young man looked honest and open enough, but you never knew. The shoe manufactories had a large trade with the South, and many of them were copperheads.

Amos Porterman was irritated but not surprised by his reception. He'd met nothing but varying shades of hostility all the months he'd been coming to Marblehead. "I came today, ma'am—" he turned back to Susan, "because I've been told you keep a very fine inn."

"Well—" said Susan. She continued to regard him steadily. He had very bushy blond eyebrows, and when he drew them together as he did now they gave to his blue eyes a quizzical expression, mitigating the frown. "Well, ma'am, now I've bought a factory here, I must spend some time in Marblehead to look out for it. I'm not comfortable at the Hotel, and I thought I'd take a room with you."

Hesper made an involuntary gesture and said "Oh, no," under her breath. Amos heard it and was annoyed. He gave her a quick glance. Unmannerly redheaded chit, gawky and untidy. Surely that was a dab of butter on her cheek? And what right had those greenish eyes to stare at him from under those peculiar dark eyebrows with such a frank dislike.

"I've no rooms just now, Mr. Porterman—" said Susan after a pause. "I seldom let 'em out, anyhow, except to drummers for a night. I've all I can do with the taproom."

"You mean—" snapped Amos, all at once losing his temper, "that you don't want me here! You confounded Marbleheaders . . . my factory's giving work to your folk who need it, I don't see why you . . ." He clenched his big hand, and shut his mouth with a snap, thinking of his walk here down Washington Street. A gang of small boys had thrown rocks at him from ambush behind the Town House, yelling "Rock him outa town! Squael the dor-rty furriner!"

To Hesper and Roger's amazement no less than Amos', Susan suddenly laughed. "Maybe we be a mite hard on furriners, and maybe some of us like the old ways best when we didn't have to depend on shoes for work, the sea did it all. But times change and I don't know as I blame you for being grouty."

Why, Ma likes him, thought Hesper dumbfounded. Ma always liked a bit of spunk and temper in a man, but a *shoeman*—from Danvers, bad as Salem and so big and sleek and fancy-clothed. Why he actually smelled of bay rum, she thought, sniffing, instead of fish and rum, as a man should.

"Well, ma'am, I'll be going," said Amos, only slightly mollified by Susan's speech. "Sorry to trouble you folks." He bent his big body in a stiff bow.

"You want a place to board—" said Susan, who had made up her mind that this man had come here with no sinister intent, "you might try Mrs. Leah Cubby, on State Street. She takes roomers."

"Oh, really." Amos turned from the door, grateful for any softening. The manufactory did well, but aside from his foreman he had no one to talk to in Marblehead. These people with their peculiar words, and rough burring dialect kept so tightly to themselves on their rocky promontory, you'd have thought them living in a fortress. Opposition always roused his dander, and he'd have moved here altogether, forced them to accept him, if it weren't for Lily Rose.

"Cubby's an odd name," he said at random, conversationally.

At this Mr. Honeywood raised his head from the book he was reading and spoke in the tone of a tolerant schoolmaster. "It's derived from Cubier, a Guernsey name. We have many such here, though not quite as old as the English stock, like mine." He bent his head again.

"Oh," said Amos. Queer Dick, this Honeywood, with his ink-stained fingers and long, thin, baldish head. Pride of family, evidently. Well you met that in Danvers too, and damn silly it was.

"You're married, a'nt you, Mr. Porterman?" said Susan glancing at his wide gold wedding band. She had been thinking that Leah was a mighty handsome woman.

"Yes, I am. But my wife is an invalid. She stays at our home in Danvers." Lily Rose, and her lacy pink negligees, and her medicine bottles and her strained, sweet smiles. Must remember to buy her a present before I go home.

"Well, will you try the Widow Cubby's?" asked Susan sharply, and Hesper was relieved to hear her mother's normal impatience returned. This stranger was interrupting everything, holding up the preparations for tonight, standing there like a hulk, not sense enough to go. Let him go to Leah's, or back to the Hotel, or sleep on the wharves, so long as he got out of here. A bore he was, and patronizing too. She hadn't missed the disdainful look he cast around the kitchen when he came in.

And in this she was quite right. After Amos had bowed himself out he walked along Front toward State Street to interview the Widow Cubby, and he thought with pity and contempt of the Honeywoods. Older than the Ark, that house, wouldn't you think they'd make shift somehow to get some new furniture, and at least cover the rough plank flooring with some decent oilcloth? Shiftless, run to seed, except perhaps the mother. She had a briskness and toughness about her that appealed to him. That Honeywood, no gumption, well educated obviously and done nothing about it. Amos thought of his own career. Father came to Danvers about 1818, from where? New York, New Jersey? Amos didn't remember, had never been interested. Married a Scotch hired girl, set up a tannery, did well. Died worth ten thousand. And I'm going to do a sight better than that. I know shoes from the hides up, and I know manufacturing. When I die I'll leave a hundred thousand—more. Leave it to whom? He sighed. If Lily Rose would only get stronger. Maybe the sea air would help if he could only persuade her to move here. Could a tart, sensible woman like Mrs. Honeywood make Lily Rose pull herself together? He thought again of the antiquated Inn, smelling of sea air and smoke, of the dominating rough-voiced wife, and the vague bookworm of a husband, wondering if all Marbleheaders were as strange. Of Hesper he did not think at all.

CHAPTER 4

BY SIX O'CLOCK, the guests, having finished their supper, began to arrive at the Hearth and Eagle for the evening's frolic. The fishermen off the *Ceres* and the *Diana* were spruced up in their best double-breasted red flannel shirts, knitted "Gansey" jackets, and flowing black silk ties, and their oiled rubber boots were discarded tonight for shiny black brogans made in their own little cordwainer shops. Those men who had wives brought them, of course, for this was a social gathering, and Susan had extended invitations through little Benjie, the grocer's boy.

Hesper, upstairs in her bedroom, heard the frequent tinkle of the bell that hung over the taproom door, and tried to hurry.

Her best dress was a dark blue poplin, made over from one of her mother's. It was trimmed, on the skirt and sleeves, with rows of Turkey-red rickrack, bought cheap by Susan from a peddler. Hesper, never much aware of clothes, had been satisfied with the dress. Now she wasn't so sure. It didn't seem to fit just right, tight across the bust and bunchy on one shoulder. She loathed sewing, always impatient to get outdoors or back to the book she was reading, but now she wished that she had paid more attention to the pattern her mother had cut for her. Charity Trevercombe was coming tonight, and she always wore lovely dresses.

Her last anxious look into the mirror ended in dissatisfaction as usual. She had tried her hair in three different ways, determined that no matter what Ma said, she would not wear it in a long pigtail like a little girl. The flamboyant masses of fiery tendrils refused to conform. They wouldn't sleek down over her ears from a center parting and they wouldn't make a neat knot on the nape of her neck. She finally coiled the heavy braid around her head, skewering it with slippery bone hairpins, and the result made her scalp ache. She put on her only jewel, a mourning brooch, onyx and silver, inherited from Gran, and went nervously downstairs.

Her father met her in the hall. Roger, too, had taken unusual pains with his appearance, and his antique and seedy frock coat was redeemed by a snowy stock, and old-fashioned gold-button waistcoat. Although in general he never mingled with the Inn's customers, this was different. This farewell to the crews was part of tradition. He had no intention of staying long amongst the company, nor much interest in any of them, but he wandered from group to group greeting them with misty benevolence, and pleased to see his house in gala mood. The oldest house in Marblehead, and certainly the finest, he thought complacently, now that it's erstwhile rivals, "King Hooper's" house and the Lee Mansion, had deteriorated from their last-century glories and been converted to commercial purposes, a drygoods store and a bank.

Susan had thrown open all of the "New" wing tonight, he was delighted to see. He wandered through the great hall with its fluted and white-painted paneling, illumined by candles in gilded sconces. He gazed with deep pleasure at the elaborate carved stairway, its newel post like a thick white icicle. It led up to the four large bedrooms that were never used except by the infrequent overnight guests.

Susan had even opened the small second parlor across the hall from the main entrance, though it was but inadequately furnished, and she kept it as a box room.

Roger returned from his prowl of inspection, and drifted up to the two sea captains, Caswell from the *Ceres* and Lane of the *Diana,* who stood chatting together near the punch bowl in the taproom.

"Good evening, sirs, good evening," Roger said heartily. "You're most welcome, and your men too. Have you sampled the punch? Susan took pains with it, I know." The refreshments were on the house tonight, so Susan had closed the bar and provided a five-gallon tub filled with rum punch.

The two Bank skippers, who had each been boasting of the merits of his own schooner, the smartness of his particular crew, and the unprecedented number of quintals of cod they were sure to catch, broke off and turned politely to their host.

"Why sure, Rahger-r—" said Cap'n Lane, who had sat on the same bench with him forty-five years ago in the little Orne Street schoolhouse, "punch is a stavin' foine dr-rink, war-rms a mon's belly, an' per-rks his sperrits."

"It is Lot Honeywood's recipe—Moses' father—" said Roger, gratified, never doubting that his listeners would know which ancestor he referred to, as indeed they did in a general way. Most of the old Marbleheaders knew the names of each other's grandsirs and great-grandsirs, and they shared many in common.

"Lot wrote the punch recipe down up there—" continued Roger, pointing to some lines of crooked letters which ran along the great "summer" beam athwart the taproom, and quite oblivious to his hearers' interest proceeded to recite—"Punch."

> The name consists of letters five
> By five ingredients 'tis kept alive
> To purest water, sugar must be joined
> With these the grateful lemon is combined
> When now these three are mixed with care
> Then added be of spirit a good share
> And that you may the drink quite perfect see
> Atop the musky nut must grated be.

And that's exactly how it's made here to this day a hundred and fifty years later—" he finished with pride.

Hesper heard this from her seat on a hassock in the big parlor near her mother, and was touched and amused. Poor Pa, he didn't know Ma didn't make the punch that way at all. She used tea instead of water and molasses instead of sugar and a whole bottle of port wine as well as the rum. But Pa didn't know lots of things, and he didn't see that he'd checked all the easy talk there'd been amongst the seamen. The two skippers and those of their men who had arrived stood now in a stiff row waiting for his precise voice to stop.

She sighed. He doesn't know how to get on with people, and I guess I don't either. But there wasn't anything for her to do right now, except wait. It wasn't seemly for her to go into the taproom where the men were until the dancing began, and anyway Johnnie hadn't come yet; she kept watching through the door. So she sat bleakly on her hassock and listened to her mother and Mrs. Cap'n Lane discuss the church supper and the Ladies' Fancy Work Sale.

Susan and Mrs. Lane sat upon the long horsehair sofa, their somber bombazine skirts arranged in decorous folds, their voices subdued as befitted the dignity of the seldom-opened parlor.

This large square parlor was Susan's great pride, and compensation for the rest of the house. The parlor was quite up to date and elegant. None of its furnishings were earlier than Moses Honeywood's time, and of those only the French wallpaper, with its hunting scenes in faded maroon, the spinet, and the biblical tiles around the fireplace. The what-not, loaded with shell work, scrimshaw, and china figures, had been acquired by Roger's father, as had the horsehair chairs and sofa, while the bright green and cabbage-rose carpeting, Susan had scrimped to buy herself. There was a center table with fringed yellow-plush throw, and on top of that the Bible, and the Family Album, flanking a large oil lamp with a white globe chimney frosted in ferns. There were candles too, in sconces along the wall, and in china candlesticks on the mantelpiece, though Susan always preferred lamps when possible. Candles dripped wax and made a mess.

At a quarter to seven Charity Trevercombe arrived with her mother. They entered by the formal front door on the harbor side of Moses' wing, and Hesper hurrying to greet them felt a new despondency. Charity wore a dress of ruffled cherry-colored taffeta, her chestnut hair fell over her shoulders in soft perfect ringlets, from her ears dangled little gold earrings shaped like butterflies, and she looked extraordinarily pretty.

Nor could Hesper help seeing the quiver of attention that ran through the men in the taproom, a sort of kindling; even old Cap'n Lane patted his tie and shifted position at the punch bowl so he could watch the little cherry-colored figure.

"Oh Hessie—isn't this a lark!" trilled Charity, flitting around the parlor and settling as near the men as she dared. "I do love dancing. What other girls are coming?"

"Why, I guess Nellie Higgins and Bessie Bowen, and I think Ma asked the Selmans and the Picketts—" She broke off, staring into the taproom.

"There's Johnnie Peach!" cried Charity. "My, he looks almost handsome. Haven't seen him in ages. Guess he'll ask me for the first reel."

She dimpled and fluttered her eyelashes as Johnnie walked into the parlor, but though he grinned at the girls and made them a mock salute he went past them to the horsehair sofa. "Evenin', ma'ams—" he said bowing to Susan, Mrs. Cap'n Lane, and Mrs. Trevercombe. "Fine night for a party. It's blowin' up a bit outside though. Wind's shifted."

Hesper watching and straining to hear, saw her mother's eyes meet Johnnie's for a thoughtful second. "I hope 'twon't blow hard enough to hold you in the harbor—tomorrow." The pause before the last word was obvious only to Hesper and Johnnie.

"Why no, ma'am, I don't doubt we'll get out."

Mrs. Lane bridled; after all her husband was master of the *Diana* and Johnnie only one of the crew. "That's for Cap'n Lane to say—John Peach. He'll do as he thinks best."

"Yes'um," said Johnnie submissively. Mrs. Trevercombe rearranged her bonnet strings and looked bored. Johnnie Peach was a nice enough boy for a fisherman, but she hadn't missed her daughter's flutters and dimplings as he came in. She doubted the wisdom of letting Charity come tonight; not likely to meet any of the few really eligible young men in Marblehead.

Now the two large rooms began to fill; Nellie Higgins and Bessie Bowen arrived together with their families, then the Selmans and the Picketts from up Franklin Street. The men, having fortified themselves, temporarily abandoned the punch bowl and mingled with the ladies. Ambrose, the fiddler, arrived promptly at seven and was stationed on a box in a corner of the taproom, where he set up a premonitory squeaking and scraping, upon which Roger, feeling that he need do no more in the interests of hospitality, vanished to his study.

The girls clustered together in the parlor by the spinet, trying to look unconscious as the young seamen began to edge towards them.

"Here he comes—" whispered Charity, referring to Johnnie, of course. But Johnnie looked right over her head to Hesper, who had drawn back to the wall, miserably conscious of her height and the inadequacies of her blue poplin.

"Come on, Hes—" said Johnnie, holding out his hand, "we'll start 'em off."

Charity said "Oh" under her breath, tossed her head, and accepted Willy Bowen, who was mate on the *Ceres*. Hesper found herself still clinging to Johnnie's square brown hand, and dropped it with a furious blush. "I don't know many steps—" she murmured, "I—"

"It doesn't matter, no more do I. But I wanted a word with you."

They took their positions at the head of the seat, and while the other couples formed beside them, Johnnie muttered out of the corner of his mouth—"Where's Peg-Leg?"

"Sick. Couldn't come," she whispered back.

Johnnie frowned, while he seized her hands and they galloped down the aisle of jigging, clapping young bodies, and said, "This job'll take a bit of doin'. Is your ma keepin' watch?"

She nodded, for Susan had seated herself in the parlor so that she might see through the west window which overlooked the street. " 'Tisn't time yet." And I wish it never would be, Hesper thought.

This business tonight now seemed to her an unwelcome and foolish interruption. She was happy with Johnnie, leading the set and dancing better than she had hoped to. The music was exciting, "Money Musk," "Sir Roger de Coverley"; Ambrose was a good fiddler, the round mellow notes winged from his fiddle and filled the old taproom with the essence of gaiety. The light from a dozen candles flickered on smiling faces, the oak planks, glistening with a fresh coat of beeswax, resounded under stamping exuberant feet. Later there'd be forfeits —maybe Johnnie'd still be her partner, and if the forfeit was a kiss—

She completed a left and right around the circle, stood again before him, panting a little—her eyes shining, but Johnnie didn't see her. He stared past her toward the entry, his lips tight. She followed his gaze and saw Nat Cubby with a strange man. Oh dear, she thought, for Johnnie muttered and dropped out of the dancing; she tagged along behind him as he sauntered up to the newcomers. "I was wonderin' if you was comin' tonight," he said to Nat, and raised his eyebrows toward the stranger.

This was a lanky man with a black mustache, a flowered waistcoat, gray pantaloons, and a broad silk belt from which protruded the handle of a revolver. "Good evening—" the stranger said easily—"Hope I'm not intruding. Happened to have a bit of business in Marblehead tonight. Ran into my young friend here on the pier, asked him where I could find a little drink, so he brought me along." The black mustache lifted in an ingratiating smile.

"Taproom's closed to the public," said a sharp voice. Susan had squeezed past the dancers, and she stood behind Hesper and Johnnie, arms folded across her black silk bosom.

"Why, I'm sorry for that, ma'am—" drawled the stranger bowing to her, "but you'd not turn away a weary traveler, would you? It's been a long journey, first and last—from Carolina I started, but there's been many a stop since." He smiled again. "At Swansea—" he added, "at Medford—and last night at Lynn. You see, ma'am, you might say I've been searching for something."

No muscle moved in Susan's broad freckled face, as she heard the insinuating drawl tick off the nearest stations on the "Underground." Hesper, for a moment not understanding, felt Johnnie beside her take a quick breath. Why, it's a slave-catcher, she thought suddenly enlightened. She stared at the revolver. The stranger gently buttoned up his coat. Nat leaned against the wall, watching all of them from his sardonic yellowish eyes, his mouth lifted in the lifeless smile.

The music stopped with a flourish of twirling dancers, and a burst of clapping.

"You're welcome to a mug o' punch," said Susan, "since you've come so far, and Nat brought you, but—"

"I'm glad of that, ma'am—" interrupted the stranger, "for I'm expecting my friend, your sheriff, to join me here. A convenient meeting place you might say."

"Aye—to be sure—" Susan said, with perfect calm. "Here's Jeff now." She walked forward to greet the weedy, apologetic little sheriff, who came sidling in, torn between the necessity of upholding the law and embarrassment at affronting the Honeywoods. "Nat—" Susan went on smoothly, "you 'n' Johnnie take care of the sheriff and Mr.—"

"Clarkson, Harry Clarkson—" supplied the stranger.

"and Mr. Clarkson, see they get acquainted 'n' have some punch. I'll fetch some more spices from the kitchen."

"Wouldn't dream of troubling you, ma'am—" said Mr. Clarkson, "unless I went with you and helped you. Down South we don't let our ladies lift a finger, 'deed we don't. Besides I don't like my punch too spicy." He stood squarely in front of Susan. The sheriff gave an embarrassed cough and moved away.

The situation was now quite clear. The slave-catcher had no intention of letting Susan out of his sight. During the course of his work he had become a shrewd judge of character, had often encountered her type during his raids on underground stations—forceful, steely-eyed women fanatical in their determination to meddle with other people's property. She'd be the ringleader, all right. But he had to go slow, no evidence that this was a station, nothing but a rumor that had reached him in Lynn after his disappointment last night. He'd been sure the nigger wench and her brat were heading to Lynn, but he hadn't been able to find them there. It had been good luck at last to meet up with this young Cubby on the wharves. He'd been quite friendly and helpful, though with that snarl on his face you couldn't tell what he was thinking; anyway he'd led the way here.

The slave-catcher's sharp suspicious eyes darted over the faces while he accepted a glass of punch. Lot of rough fishermen jabbering away in that crazy brogue most of 'em talked; some old women, and a handful of gawky country girls. It was then that he discovered Charity, who had withdrawn to the far corner of the taproom to giggle with Willy Bowen until the music started again, and she could make Johnnie dance with her.

Charity decided that Johnnie had lost interest in Hesper, since he was lounging glumly near the parlor door, and Hesper was standing in back of her ma near the interesting-looking stranger. As a matter of fact the stranger was staring in her direction, and Charity arched her neck and gave him a sidelong glance. The slave-catcher's eyes gleamed. He sauntered across the room, not neglecting to keep Mrs. Honeywood in sight with the corner of one eye. But this gave Susan a needed opportunity. "Hes—" she whispered under cover of stirring the punch, "he's not watching you. Go to the kitchen and wait for 'em. You know what to do. I'll keep him in here. Hurry, slip out while he's talking to Charity."

"Oh Ma—I can't." Leave the fun and dancing, leave Johnnie to Charity's wiles, just when things were going so well. And what for? Some old niggers who probably wouldn't come, and in whom she didn't actually believe. This wasn't an adventure at all, it was unpleasant and stupid, and she heartily agreed with her father. Except that the whole thing seemed unreal, everyone playing a part like Bible charades. The slave-catcher and his pistol didn't seem any more convincing than Old Pharaoh and his spear when Willy Bowen had played it. "You'll go *now*—" whispered Susan savagely. "I knew you wasn't fit to be trusted." If they'd been alone she would have slapped the girl, shilly-shallying like her father.

Just then Johnnie turned in the doorway where he had been watching both rooms, Nat in the parlor and the slave-catcher in the taproom. Johnnie saw Hesper's unhappy face beyond her mother's flushed and angry one, and he caught something of the situation. He smiled at Hesper, a smile of warm encouragement, and his lips formed the words "Good Luck!" Then he turned his back again.

So that was different. Johnnie expected her to go. Hesper backed quickly and noiselessly toward the wall behind her, where a door led to the buttery passage. Ambrose the fiddler had sat silent on his box since he had stopped playing, his fiddle resting on his knee, his dark face expressionless, staring up at the beams. Yet at the moment when Hesper opened the buttery door and slipped through he lifted his fiddle and brought the bow across it in a crescendo crash tearing into "Pop Goes the Weasel." So that nobody noticed Hesper's departure.

Hesper went along the passage into the kitchen. It was chilly in here, the little cookstove nearly out, and no fire in the great hearth. She lit a candle and put some more wood in the stove, and wished she might light the logs that "Looney" had piled in readiness on the big andirons. But Susan certainly would not hold with wasting fuel, when here it was almost May, and anyway if those niggers really showed up, and she had no idea how or when, it would be wise not to have too much light in here. She sat down in Gran's old Boston rocker and watched the shadows flicker over the bright pewter on the oak dresser. The sounds of music and dancing came to her faintly, muted by the thick doors and the huge mass of the central chimney. Clearer than the music she heard the intermittent rattle of the shutter from the borning room; that meant some wind from the northwest. The iron spigot dripped plink-plunk into the stone sink, and the banjo clock gave forth its unhurried tick. She turned her head and watched the brass pendulum as it swung behind its glass window. It was past nine. They're not coming, she thought, relieved. I won't have to stay much longer. She continued to stare at the clock, tracing in the gloom the familiar painted pictures, a white and gold barkentine sailing on a translucent green sea, and above on the lyre-shaped neck a panel of stars and roses. The clock had come into the family with Mary Ellis, Roger's mother, who had not survived his birth. I wonder what makes women die when babies are born, what happens exactly, thought Hesper trying to lighten the boredom of exile by forbidden speculation, and it was some seconds before her mind registered a new impression. There was a cat miaowing outside the back door.

Must be the Pickett's Tom, she thought, mildly curious, but he wouldn't be apt to come here if he was hungry. Susan discouraged cats. The miaowing continued faint and insistent, and suddenly she jumped from the rocker, listening. Cat! "Cat" was the password, but she had applied it only to Cat Island. Her heart beat against her ribs, she picked up the candle and opened the back door. There was nothing to be seen in the darkness but the barn wall and the shadow of the nearest apple tree. And there was silence. She strained her eyes but nothing moved. "Is someone there?" she whispered. No answer. Then she realized she should give the password, if indeed there was any truth in all this. "I thought I heard a cat," she quavered into the darkness, feeling both nervous and foolish.

At once two cloaked and hooded shapes glided round the corner of the house from behind the lilac bush. She held the door silently and they went past her into the kitchen.

The taller shape bent close to her, peering from under the concealing hood, and she saw that it was an old bearded man, a white man. "Is it safe?" he whispered. She shook her head. "Then hide 'em quick!"

Hesper turned to the other figure, and with that glimpse beneath the hood, her daze shattered. The haggard golden-brown face was upturned in terrified appeal, the black eyes held fear so naked and defiant that Hesper gasped. And against the colored girl's breast above the shrouding cloak lay a baby's head.

Lord, this *is* real—the thought flashed through her like a galvanic shock; she pushed the woman and the baby toward the broom closet. These were real people in terrible danger. Her trembling fingers released the pin, she slid the panel back and gave the girl a candle. "Up the steps—" she whispered, "there's food. Don't let the baby cry. The slave-catcher's here."

The colored girl gave a stifled moan, then noiseless as smoke she vanished up the narrow stairway. Hesper slid the panel, dropped the pin, and shoved the brooms and musket back in place.

The old man stood in the dark, silent until she lit another candle, then he stepped forward, and his steady wise eyes ran over her. "They safe?"

"I think so, nobody knows the hidey-hole, but—"

"You're not in this alone?" he interrupted anxiously. "The brig's waiting off the Island, the *Scotia* from Halifax, someone's got to get 'em out there."

"I know, we've arranged, Ma and a fisherman—"

He nodded quickly. "Then I'll be off, left the wagon outside of town in a covert. Should've got 'em off at Lynn, but the chase was too hot. So we had to use you people. Poor things—" he shook his head, looking toward the broom closet. "She's the most pitiful of all those I've helped —God'll help you to help them too. The cause is just."

He gave her a smile of great sweetness and dignity and wrapped his cloak around him. The door from the taproom was thrown open with a bang. Hesper jumped, and her mouth went dry. The slave-catcher walked in to the kitchen.

"Pardon me, Miss—" he said, not looking at Hesper, but at the old man who stood motionless by the settle. "All of a sudden I had a fancy for a drink of water."

I mustn't show anything, I mustn't—she clenched her hands on the folds of her skirt. "Well, take it then—" she said tartly, in her mother's voice. "There's the sink and a cup."

Clarkson did not move. "You've a caller, it seems—"

Before she need answer, the old man shuffled forward, and spoke in a feeble whine, "I seed t' young lass through t' winder, she's a pokin' up t' stove, so I knocks n' axes her fur a handout. No har-rm in that—mister. Me pore ol' belly's empty as a cask." He seemed to have shrunk to half his size, his shoulders hunched, and there was a vacant look on his wrinkled face.

Gratefully accepting her cue, Hesper hurried to the stove and felt of the coffeepot which always stood there in readiness.

Clarkson stood his ground staring at the old man. His sharp lower teeth gnawed on his mustache, his fingers through a gap in his buttoned coat twitched on the handle of his pistol. Suddenly he swung out a long arm and grabbed the old man's shoulder, yanking him into the full light of the candle. "God damn it, you old bastard, I'm sure I've seen you before. In Medford, that's where. You've got a farm with a mighty convenient haycock on it, keep it filled with blackbirds, don't you!"

Hesper's cold hands grew clammier. She clattered the poker against the stove lid.

"Lemme be, mister—" quavered the old voice. "I ain't done nothin' but ax for some vittles. I ain't got no farm no place. I ain't got nuthin'."

The fiddler in the taproom blared louder for a moment, and then the noise was shut off, as Susan came into the kitchen and closed the door.

She paused for a second taking in the scene. The slave-catcher bent menacingly over a trembling old tramp, and Hesper, white as the plaster wall, prying at the stovelid with the wrong end of the poker.

"What're you doin' in my kitchen!" She brought her fat freckled hand down sharply across Clarkson's arm, which dropped involuntarily from the old man's shoulder. "Quit bullying this pore old man."

"So you know who he is!" cried Clarkson turning on her.

"Never saw him afore in my life," answered Susan.

"I say you did! I say you knew he was coming, and you know what he's brought. I'm going to search this house." Clarkson jerked out his revolver, beside himself with fury. His arm tingled from the blow this woman had given it, her cool contempt enraged him.

"Sheriff!" he shouted at the top of his lungs. "Sheriff, come here!" But Ambrose was playing as hard as he could, and singing too, and many of the dancers sang with him—"As I was walking down the lane, down the lane, down the lane—"

"God damn that caterwauling nigger—" said Clarkson through his teeth, he looked at the three in the kitchen with him, and he dared not leave them. He cocked the pistol with his thumb, deliberated a moment, then shot through the west outside wall of the room. The old plaster starred and cracked a little around the black hole, the bullet buried itself in a stout oak upright beneath the clapboarding.

That brought them. The fiddle stopped. The sheriff ran in looking scared, and with him Johnnie, Nat Cubby, and as many of the guests as could squeeze through the entry. And it brought Roger too. He rushed out of his study to see his kitchen crowded with people, and a slimsy black-mustached fellow in the middle of them holding a smoking pistol.

"*What* is this rumpus?" shouted Roger. "What's the meaning of that shot?" His eyes were no longer vague, but bright with anger. He looked at the bullet hole, and his marred wall. "I'll have you arrested!"

"Who's this man?" Clarkson growled to the sheriff. The others crowded around open-mouthed.

"Why, that's Mr. Honeywood. Ye didn't oughta go shootin'," answered the sheriff unhappily.

"Oh you're *Mister* Honeywood, so I reckon you know all about it, but I'd be glad to clear your mind anyhow. I represent the law and I represent Mr. Delacort, owner of the Albemarle Plantation on the Santee River in South Carolina. One of his best nigger wenches lit out with her brat four weeks ago, and he's commissioned me to find her. She's a good breeder and smart too, worth two thousand dollars. I've reason to believe she's hidden in your house."

"Indeed she is not!" said Roger, quivering, but in a quieter tone. "You may take my word for it." He glanced at Susan's blank face. How glad she must be now that he had forbidden her to receive the fugitives.

Clarkson was a trifle nonplussed. This one spoke more like a gentleman than the rest of these oafs, and his voice had the ring of truth; still, the women might be trying something on their own.

"I'm going to search the house and grounds," he said doggedly. He turned his back on the Honeywood family and the old man to confront the silent group of fishermen. A dozen pairs of eyes stared back at him, unwinking. "Any of you men lend me a hand?" he asked, "Can't *all* be god-damn traitrous abolishers."

Cap'n Lane gave an angry grunt, and his fists clenched, otherwise nobody moved.

"You?" said Clarkson at random, pointing at Johnnie with his pistol.

"Why, no—" said Johnnie, "I'd rather not."

Clarkson scowled and pointed to Nat—"You then, you were eager enough to bring me here."

Hesper held her breath and it seemed to her that the others did too. Nat stood beside Johnnie, staring at the slave-catcher. He shifted his feet a trifle. His eyes were speculative. "What's there in it for me?" he asked.

"A hundred dollars if we find 'em—"

Johnnie swung around looking down at his friend. "Dirty money, Nat, I never thought it of you. I'm sure your ma'd not think it of you, either."

A strange expression flickered across the sardonic face. Nat twisted his head and met Johnnie's eyes, "You're a soft fool—" he said very low, but he turned on his heel, shoved his way amongst the watching men, and strode through the outside door, slamming it behind him. The little bell jangled and faded to stillness.

"All right, all right," said the slave-catcher, "I'll do it alone. Sheriff, you keep 'em in the taproom. You know your duty?"

The sheriff nodded and coughed, staring at the floor.

"Well, get moving! And there's any hanky-panky, I'll set the federals on you, after I've done with you myself."

The sheriff sullenly motioned with his hand, and the fishermen moved back into the taproom to be met by excited or frightened questions from those who hadn't been able to understand what was happening.

"This is an outrage!" cried Roger, while Clarkson himself saw to the bolting of the doors. "You've not the slightest shadow of excuse—I told you there's nobody hidden here."

The slave-catcher twisted his pistol and paid no attention. Susan sat down on her regular stool behind the counter. Her face was white as Hesper's and the freckles stood out between beads of sweat. The old man in the cloak huddled himself into a dark corner between the fireplace and a keg of beer. Ambrose still sat on his box, staring again at the beams, his fiddle quiet as Clarkson had ordered. Even Charity was subdued and had squeezed herself on a bench beside her mother.

"You—girl—" said Clarkson suddenly pointing at Hesper. "You're coming with me. You can hold the candle, and you know the house."

Hesper glanced at her mother, Susan gave a helpless shrug. Helpless, and she looked frightened. Ma! Ma couldn't do anything, and she didn't rightly know what had happened in the kitchen before she came in. Hesper felt an unexpected surge of pity, and then a headier intoxication. Her heart stopped pounding, warmth returned to her hands. She picked up a candlestick, and walked toward the slave-catcher.

"Come then—" she said, cool and easy. "And you might stop waving that pistol about. You're not like to use it."

Clarkson looked startled, and she heard Johnnie's laugh. "Good for you—Hessie!"

"We'll start with the outhouses—" commanded Clarkson, shoving Hesper ahead of him. She gave him a freezing look and he muttered something that might have been apologetic. He thrust the pistol back in his belt. They went through the kitchen door, having picked up a lantern from its shelf in the entry. Clarkson searched every inch of the barn and the hay loft, thrusting a pitchfork again and again through the scant heaps of straw, and disturbing only poor "Looney" who was asleep on a mat in a corner. He looked in the pigsty and even the privy, then returned to the house. He hadn't expected anything of the barn, anyway—much too obvious for experienced agents like that old graybeard, if he *was* the man from Medford. Not quite sure. Not sure of anything except that two thousand dollars worth of human merchandise was secreted somewhere along this infernal rocky coast.

He hustled Hesper back to the kitchen, where she stood in the middle of the floor holding the candle while he opened cupboard doors, peered into the Dutch oven and the bottom of the china closet. Once he tapped the plaster wall on the north side between the kitchen and the lean-to, but the sound was dense and flat.

Then he opened the broom closet, and motioned her nearer with the light. Hesper's courage ebbed, and her palms grew wet, but he scarcely glanced at the brooms and mop and musket in the shallow closet, and had he bothered to sound the false back, he would not have been enlightened. Lot Honeywood and his brother-in-law the pirate had built cannily. The oaken slab was nearly two inches thick and would give out no resonance.

Hesper went from room to room as he ordered her. They entered her father's little study; she saw that when he had been interrupted by the shot, he had been working on the "Memorabilia," and while she held the light for Clarkson, she read one line—

"In olden times in Marblehead, there was many a deed of valor—" The thought did not come clear to her, but as she led the slave-catcher from the buttery, through the larder and into the borning room, pausing in each for him to poke and pry and open cupboards, she was puzzled by a question. Why did the olden times seem so romantic—while the present never did? She had a vague realization that this night's work would also seem romantic someday, but it didn't now. That's because I don't know the ending—she thought. Things you hear of from the past, you know what's happened, you don't have to worry. Yet at the moment, she wasn't worried. She felt contempt, mastery, inner excitement, not worry, as she led the slave-catcher through the rambling house, even pointing out cupboards and crannies he might overlook. They descended to the cellars; the shallow, crude excavation under the old part, the capacious dry rooms under Moses' wing. Clarkson picked up a long stick that was used for stirring the brine in the salt-pork barrel and thrust it into the potato bin and the apple bin. He moved the spare casks of rum, and the kegs of beer. He kept a sharp eye for any suspicious marking in the masonry.

The cellars and attics of these old houses were prime choice for hiding places. He found nothing. He kept a sharp eye on Hesper too for any signs of tension, but he could see none. Queer sort of a girl with all that tumbling red hair, her squarish white face set in an expression of chill indifference. Younger than he'd first thought too, not more than sixteen, and innocent-looking for all her loftiness. His certainty that Delacort's fugitive nigger wench was hidden in the house began to weaken, but he pursued the search.

Hesper led him up the newer cellar stairs, to the parlor, still brilliantly lit. From the other side of the door they could hear the uneasy shufflings and murmurs of the company imprisoned in the taproom. They continued to the second floor up the beautiful mahogany front staircase. She waited for him to look under the canopied beds and into paneled cupboards in the four spacious bedrooms built by Moses. They descended two steps to the back passage and the old wing. Here there were three bedrooms, her own, her parents', and a spare room, all small and low-ceilinged, sparsely furnished with the rough pine bedsteads and rush-seated slat-back chairs they had always contained.

Clarkson shook his head and snapped, "Now the attic—if that's all down here. House's a regular rabbit warren—up and down, little rooms, big rooms, crazy way to build."

Hesper said nothing, but she saw that the slave-catcher was losing hope, and her spirits rose higher.

There was a bad moment in the attic. Clarkson stumbled around amongst the accumulated lumber of centuries, the spinning wheels and flax carders, the long cradle and the wooden chests and brass-studded cowhide trunks. Hesper held the candle for him as he demanded it, and he halfheartedly opened a few lids, shook those trunks and chests which were locked. He groped around the masses of the huge central chimneys, the old one of stone, the newer one of bricks. He took the candle himself to examine the roof and the rough-hewn rafters, and did not discover so much as a cobweb, so thorough was Susan's housekeeping. "I'll take oath there's nothing here—" he muttered when a strange little sound came to them, a small, choked wail.

"What's that?" cried Clarkson, his hand flew to his pistol, he swung the candle this way and that, peering. The sound had seemed to come from the floor near the old chimney.

It's the baby, thought Hesper petrified. Pray God it doesn't do it again.

"I didn't hear anything—" she said. "For the Land's sake aren't you through up here yet?"

"Shut up! *I* heard something. Keep quiet."

They stood in the old attic, listening. There was no further sound. Hesper saw plain what must be going on down there, the terrified mother crouching on the pallet in the little cubicle beneath the floor muffling the baby's mouth with her hand, or her breast.

"Very like you heard a rat, or the wind in the chimney—" said Hesper in just the right tone of boredom and impatience. Strange how easy it was to lie. Stranger yet that these lies were allowed. Ma herself, who was so strict, had been telling them all evening.

As though the slave-catcher had caught an inkling of her thought, he suddenly held the candle to her face. "Look, honey—" he said quite gently, "you people don't act like you realized I'm only doing my duty and my job, and the law's solid behind me, remember that. You seem like a smart nice girl. I'm going to put it to you fair and square." His mustache lifted in an ingratiating smile, the hand that held the candle touched and pressed against her shoulder. "Have you seen, or do you know of, any fugitive slave hidden anywhere on these premises?"

"No," said Hesper, moving her shoulder away. Clarkson made a disgusted sound through his nose. He turned and stamped down the attic stairs in glum silence. Maybe the wench was telling the truth, maybe the whole business was a mare's nest after all. Thing to do now, was let the old graybeard loose and follow him. See what he did, come back here later, when they were off guard, maybe find a clue then.

He unlocked the taproom door. "You can all go now—" he said sulkily, entering. He had put the pistol back in its holster, and he didn't look at anyone; not even Charity, who thought him most attractive, and had spent this imprisoned hour envying Hesper her opportunities, rambling alone all over a dark house with a handsome, sophisticated man like that. What if he was a slave-catcher! Who cared about the silly slaves anyway. Ma'd often said they were far better off on the plantations than they'd be anywhere else. Now that Mr. Clarkson had satisfied himself he wasn't going to find whatever he'd been looking for, maybe he'd relax and enjoy the party, come and sit by her again, repeat that she was the prettiest little piece he'd laid eyes on in many a long day.

Charity's hopes were dashed. Mr. Honeywood, who always seemed so meek and spineless, suddenly pulled himself up until his head grazed the beams, and stiff as a flagpole, pointed a long bony finger toward the door. "Your behavior has been outrageous, sir," he said in a high quivering voice. "Get out of my house."

And Mr. Clarkson picked up his wide-brimmed black hat and went without a word. The minute he left all the others started leaving too. Charity sighed. First to last the party'd been a failure. She'd only danced two dances, there hadn't been any forfeits, and Johnnie Peach hadn't been near her at all.

The sheriff left next, murmuring a sheepish apology. The others followed quickly. No one mentioned the evening's interruption.

"Oi misloike leavin', ma'am—" said Cap'n Lane, shaking first Susan's hand then Roger's—"but Oi needn't tell ye, a seaman keeps ear-rly hours. We've to be abar-rd by cock-crow. Thanks for the good cheer-r."

His wife, Cap'n Caswell, the other couples, the girls and the young fishermen all made similar farewells and filed out.

The Honeywood family was left with Johnnie Peach, and the old man who seemed to be asleep by the fire.

"Disgusting occurrence—" said Roger. "Put a hole right through the kitchen wall. Molesting innocent people. I'd like to have the law on him. That's what comes of ever having gotten mixed up with—" He checked himself, remembering that he was not alone with his wife. He scooped a mugful of punch from the depleted bowl, and swallowed it irritably. "What's to be done with that old tramp?" he said, pointing.

Susan had started piling the used mugs on a tray, and crumbing the table. There were mounds of gingerbread, brandy snaps, and saffron tarts still untouched.

"Never mind him, Roger," she answered quietly. "I'll care for him. You go to bed. Hes and Johnnie'll help me clear up."

Roger grunted. "Well, good night, all. If that bostard comes back, don't let him in." And his use of the universal Marblehead epithet marked the extent of his perturbation. He stalked out.

Susan put down the tray of mugs; she and Johnnie both looked at Hesper. "What happened, Hes? Tell us quick, from the beginning."

Hesper complied, speaking in short, nervous whispers, while Johnnie and her mother listened anxiously.

"Now what's to be done—" said Susan shaking her head. "How'll we get 'em out o' here?"

The old man raised his head, pushing off his hood. "Where's the fiddler?" he said.

Susan jumped. "I'd clean forgot you, sir. The fiddler bolted the minute Clarkson opened the door, he looked pretty skeered."

The old man nodded. "Too bad. He knew something of what was up. But he'll be no use now. You got your boat ready?" he asked Johnnie.

"Aye. She's pulled behind a rock, windward side o' Gerry's Island, nobody'd see her there tonight. I calc'lated we could sneak 'em down through the Honeywood lot, and across Little Harbor to the island near dry-shod before the water rises much. Row 'em over to Cat from there."

"Good. But can you manage alone?"

" 'Twill be hard. Tide and wind's both against."

"I'd help you—though I've a feeble back and no knowledge of the water—except that I'm worse needed for decoy." His bearded lips lifted. "I know our friend the slave-catcher's mind better than he knows it himself. Having drawn a blank here, he's lurking outside to follow me. I'll lead him a good chase, make it interesting enough to keep him with me, it'll give you time." He stood up and went to the table, crammed a tart into his mouth, and a handful of gingerbread into his pocket. "By your leave, ma'am."

"O' course—take all—you've got spunk, sir. I hope we've as much. We'll do our best. But after this the U.G. mustn't use us. Roger's dead agin it. I had to diddle him tonight."

"Yes, I saw." He smiled his singularly sweet and warming smile. "Anyway we're building up the overland line, westward to the border. I must hurry, but who's to help you row, young man?" he added frowning.

"I am," said Hesper firmly. "I'd thought of it earlier."

Johnnie's worried face cleared. "Gorm—I guess you could at that, Hes. You used to be right handy for a girl."

Susan opened her mouth and shut it again. It was the only solution now, but her heart misgave her. There was always danger on the sea—who to know better than she who had lost sons, and her father too? If anything should happen to Hes, and Roger not knowing either. Still, what was right was right and risks must be taken.

"You sure o' the brig, sir?" she said rolling up the brandy snaps in a napkin and handing them to the old man.

He nodded. "Cap'n Nelson never fails. He's heart and soul for the cause and well paid too. Good luck. God'll rejoice in you for this night's work. I daren't shake hands, for I believe our bloodhound's lurking by that window. Give us twenty minutes, then move fast." He wrapped himself in his cloak and shuffled across the floor and out the taproom door.

"Hes," said Susan briskly, handing Hesper a diluted mug of punch. "Drink this."

Hesper obeyed, startled. Ma'd never let her touch anything stronger than dandelion wine. It tasted awful, for a second she thought she must retch, then a pleasing tingle of warmth glowed in her stomach.

"Change your clothes—I'll give you Willy's oilskins. Johnnie, keep watch outside, be sure he's gone." Susan bustled her daughter upstairs. As soon as Hesper had taken off the blue poplin, her mother reappeared with a flannel shirt and complete set of oilskins. She kept her drowned sons' clothes in a locked sea chest in her bedroom though the fact was never mentioned.

"Good thing you're tall—" she said grimly. She pulled down the braid of red hair and tucked it inside the stiff yellow jacket, jammed on the stiffer back-brimmed sou'wester and fastened it under Hesper's chin. "Anybody at ten paces 'd take you for a fisher boy—" and suddenly she leaned near and kissed Hesper on the cheek, an occurrence so unprecedented that they were both flooded with embarrassment.

"Well, are your feet glued to the floor—" snapped Susan. "Get moving—hurry."

They found Johnnie pacing up and down the kitchen, also attired in his oilskins. "Gorm—" he stared at Hesper—"I'd never've known ye." He chuckled and gave her shoulder a resounding thwack—"M' hearty young fisherman!" But catching Susan's minatory eye he went on quickly—"They've gone, all right. Old man stumpin' along up Circle Street an' the slave-catcher creepin' through the shadows a few rods behind. Wind's slackenin' some—praise be—but tide's comin' in fast."

Susan pulled the window curtains tighter and opened the closet door. "Call 'em, Hes!"

The girl manipulated the panel and ascended the narrow steps, her creaking clumsy oilskins catching against the chimney's rough stone. "Come down," she called gently into the darkness. "It's safe now."

There was a soft movement in the hidey-hole, and Hesper backed down the steps. The mulatto girl followed at once. She stood crouching over the baby, and trembling. Her black eyes slid from one to the other of them, her golden-brown face was a mask of fear.

"Here now—" said Susan, "stop shaking. You're almost free. These two'll get you to the ship." She doused the candle and opened the back door.

Johnnie went first, then the slave girl, then Hesper. The moonless night was overcast with heavy dark clouds, yet was not too dark for Hesper and Johnnie's keen young eyes. They followed the familiar path between the vegetable and herb patches past the apple trees and around the great elm tree that marked the eastern boundary of the Honeywood lot. They crept in the shadow of Pitman's fish warehouse, and Johnnie paused to inspect the cove. All the fish flakes had been covered with tarpaulin for the night, all dories beached and made fast. Their peering eyes could discern no movement in the darkness. There was no noise but the lap and suck of the water on the shingle, and then the crunch of their heavy fishing boots as Johnnie led the way over the shore pebbles to the strip of land which at low tide connected the mainland and Gerry's Island. The slave girl glided silent as a forest doe between them. As they reached the island the rising waters wet her feet and she gasped from the sudden cold, but made no other sound.

They crossed the bare little island to the ocean side where Johnnie had hidden his new green dory between two sheltering rocks. Johnnie tugged until it floated, then guided the two girls while they clambered in. He placed the slave girl in the stern, and as she settled herself the baby woke up and gave a fretful cry. She crouched lower over it, a dark shape against the darker rocks behind, and they heard her crooning—"Hush—Hush—Hush." Johnnie put Hesper on the forward thwart, and himself amidships. He fitted in the oars. He had set the tholepins earlier, then wrapped them round with sacking. "All set—Hes," he whispered. "Pull slow and steady. Don't get winded and don't get skeered."

" 'Course not," she answered scornfully, for they were still in the lee of Peach's Point, and the rowing easy. She had never rowed this mile-and-a-half stretch to Cat Island before, but she had sailed it several times. Of late years since the Salem Steamboat Company had bought the island and built there a large summer hotel, it had been rechristened Lowell's Island, and become a favorite sailing goal for Marblehead children, who amused themselves gaping at the fashionably dressed excursionists the steamer deposited at the wharf. In the last century the island had had still another name—Hospital Island, from the smallpox pesthouse situated upon it, but Marbleheaders, ever indifferent to ephemeral fancies, continued to call it by its original name.

Hesper and Johnnie rowed steadily towards the east and the four heavy eight-foot oars dipped together in a smooth rotating rhythm, until gradually they drew abreast of the lighthouse on the Point of the Neck to the south.

This was easy, thought Hesper, not near as bad as Johnnie seemed to think. But in another moment they reached the open channel, and the brisk north wind hit them full force. The waves, at first merely choppy, grew bigger until their tumbling white crests slid by at eye-level in the darkness. The staunch little dory shuddered and twisted and climbed and slipped down again into the troughs. Hesper lost her stroke, and found that over and over she was beating her oars on empty air. Spray showered on her back and ran down the oilskins.

The slave girl began to cry softly—"Oh lawdy, lawdy, save us—" and they heard her retching.

"Steady on—Hes!" cried Johnnie twisting his head. "Ship your port oar, bear all you've got to starboard, we're bein' blown off course."

She obeyed, pulling now with both hands at the leeward oar, trying to time it with Johnnie's powerful strokes. The dory swung slowly back into the wind. Sweat poured down her face and neck and between her breasts, her arms and shoulders began to ache with a fiery pain. The grayish white-tipped masses rocked beneath them, the bilges sloshed with deepening water.

Hesper clenched her teeth and pulled, watching the lighthouse creep inch by inch astern. She heard Johnnie's unconscious grunts as he exerted all his strength on each down pull. I can't go on—she thought once, as her oar twisted and buried itself in a mountain of water. Her hands were raw inside the leather fishing mittens, a knife was twisting in her shoulder blades. But she clung to the oar, yanked it out, and went on. Forward—pull—back. Forward—pull—back. Mechanical and mindless. There was no room for fear, nor pity for the poor drenched seasick creature on the stern seat, no room for anything but tough jaw-clenching struggle. On and on through the night and the wind and the savage tossing sea.

She was even unaware of Johnnie, and his triumphant shout took a moment to rouse her. "Well done, Hes. Here's the island. Ye can rest a bit now." After a moment she turned her stiff neck and saw the dark mound rising up before them, and the shape of the hotel, now closed, on the northwest tip. Johnnie pulled them in close to the shore and the water suddenly grew calm. She slumped forward on her oar, panting.

Johnnie reached back and patted her on the knee. "Get your breath, Hessie. I couldn't a asked for better help. It'll be easier goin' home with the tide, poor lass."

She couldn't answer, but she heard the new note in his voice as he spoke to her, and the pounding of her heart and the pain in her back subsided a little.

Johnnie rowed almost noiselessly around the southern point. He knew the island was deserted at this season, the hotel wouldn't be open for another three months, but there might be a caretaker.

"Yonder's the brig—sure enough—" he cried triumphantly, as they glided to seaward of the island. "Chirk up—slave girl, you're purty nigh safe!"

The dark figure raised her head, they all three stared through the gloom at a silent black hull that loomed against the grayer sky. The brig rocked quietly at anchor two hundred yards off shore, and not a light showed on her, but as they drifted nearer, the clouds lifted and a few stars pricked out between the masts.

Johnnie rowed up close amidships, and the brig's broad white strip below her square ports glowed like a ghostly ribbon above their heads. "Ahoy there! Brig ahoy!" he shouted through his cupped hands. There was a footfall on deck, a head peered over the rail and vanished, but there was no answering hail.

The slave girl spoke then for the first time. "Dey mus' want de password, massa—" she said softly. "Tell 'em 'cat.' "

Johnnie cupped his hands again. "Brig ahoy—Cat! Have ye a cat on board to quell your rats? But anyway I bring ye a cat, a cat and a kitten! That ought to be enough cats to ease their minds," he chuckled to Hesper.

Apparently it was. A head reappeared at the rail, and a dark lantern cast its wavering beam down on the dory. "Ahoy there!" called a man's voice. "Ye've been long enough deliverin' your cats, I'd near given ye up." The voice had an intonation like that of the men off the Nova Scotian coalers.

"Aye, well we'd a bit o' trouble, here'n there—" answered Johnnie cheerfully. "Will ye take 'em aboard now? My mate and me must get back."

"Stand by for the ladder," responded the voice and the head disappeared.

Suddenly the slave girl came to life. She leaned forward from the stern and spoke with harsh breathlessness. "Ah doan know how ter thank you-all, yo buckra been maughty good ter me up No'th. Cain' take it een ah'll get to mah husban' in Halifax now. He runned off a year gone, he been waitin' fo' me."

"Aye—" said Johnnie soothingly. "You don't have to thank us."

The girl went on unheeding, the words spurting from her. "Massa he beat me, he lash me wid th' bull whip, but Ah wouldn' tell him where Cato he run ter. Then Massa, he seed Ah'm yaller gal, not bad lookin'—he quit beatin', an' he use me—" She stopped.

There were voices on deck and the outline of a ladder appeared over the rail aft of them. Johnnie let the dory drift to position, and Hesper, startled by bewildered pity, said the first thing that came into her head. "How glad your husband'll be to see the baby too!"

"Ah doan know," answered the voice from the stern, and now it was weighted with a stony resignation. "Ah reckon so—but Ah doan rightly know effen hit's Cato's chile or de massa's."

Hesper stiffened. What did that mean? How could it be she didn't know? Something ugly—something disgusting and frightening like a bloated dead snake she had found beside the kitchen step.

"Trim ship—Hes," ordered Johnnie sharply. He was standing on the floor boards, holding the wooden ladder with one hand and supporting the slave girl with the other. Hesper slid hastily along the thwart to the gunnel. The slave girl knotted her shawl tight about the baby, and climbed to the waiting hands reached down to help her.

They lifted her over the rail, and at the same moment a voice boomed, "Avast heaving there! Lay aft to the jib halliards!" followed by running footsteps and the creak of windlass.

Johnnie shoved off and began to row. The slave girl leaned over the rail. "Good-bye—" she called. "De Lawd bless you—Buckra."

"Good luck—" shouted Johnnie, and Hesper whispered "Good-bye." She watched the three jibs spring like white triangles from the bowsprit. She heard the thud of the anchor on deck—the long thrilling call —"All hands make sai-il-l-l . . ." The square sails burgeoned one after another up the two high masts. The brig veered slowly off the wind, the sails slatted and filled. She gained headway, and glided eastward into the starlit night.

We did it, thought Hesper, we did it! She was suddenly caught up outside her tired body by a golden spring of joy. And in this moment of exaltation while she watched the brig vanish, she apprehended the rare purity of accomplishment which brought no personal gain. They had all of them, her mother and Johnnie and the old man, submitted themselves to worry and actual danger in behalf of an ideal, nothing more. Maybe the slave girl wouldn't be happy after she achieved freedom, maybe the obscure ugly things she had suffered would not let her really be free. But it didn't matter to those who helped her. It was not the past or the future but the cat itself that counted, the act of liberation.

"Matter, Hes?" asked Johnnie, rowing past the rocks at the tip of the island. "D'you feel bad?"

"No—" she said, stirring. She tightened her grasp of the oars and she began to row. "I feel good. Kind of windswept and clean. Like sometimes at meeting, when we sing 'Jerusalem the Golden.'" She didn't care if Johnnie laughed at her. She no longer minded the pain in her back muscles or the raw sores in her hands. They were good clean pains.

Johnnie didn't laugh. He said "Aye—" in a thoughtful voice, and nothing more.

They emerged from Cat Island's lee into open water again, but the wind had slacked off, and the sea flattened to lazy billows. The tide flowed shoreward beneath their keel, and the lighthouse on the Neck danced fleetly past them. The sleeping town lay huddled amongst her rocky ledges, scarce visible even as they crossed the mouth of the Great Harbor except that here and there, in Barnegat or high on Training Field Hill, a mother tended a sick child, and a window glimmered yellow in the darkness.

As they sped once more between Fort Sewall Point and Gerry's Island the church bells chimed twice.

Johnnie beached his dory in her usual place, near the path that led up to his home in Barnegat. Hesper neatly shipped her oars and pulled out the tholepins, but when she tried to jump ashore as Johnnie had, she found that her legs were numb and would not move.

"Criminy!" she dropped back on the thwart, with a small embarrassed laugh. "I'm stiff as a frozen herring."

"It'll soon pass," said Johnnie still in the grave, tender voice that was so unlike him. He waded into the water, scooped her out of the boat and carried her, oilskins and all, high up on the beach.

She swayed as he set her down, and he kept his arm about her. She looked up and she could see his face a little higher than hers dim beneath the sou'wester in the starlight.

He reached up and unfastening the chinstrap on her sou'wester, threw the hat to the beach. Her hair fell about her ears and her face shone white as milk against the sky.

"Hes—" he said and stopped. She heard him swallow. Rough and off-hand, he went on, "Would ye like I name the dory after you?"

Her heart bounded, then raced harder than it ever had in the moments of fear tonight. A boat named for a real woman meant only one thing.

She nodded her head, inarticulate as he was.

His arm tightened around her. "It'll be a long time, Hes. A matter o' two, three years, afore I can ask you to be anything but sweetheart."

"I know—" she whispered. What money Johnnie made from the trip on which he sailed tomorrow must go to help his mother and the brood of children, for the shoe shop could not support them alone. Not tomorrow—*today* he was sailing.

"Johnnie, you'll be careful on the Banks. You'll do nothing rash?"

He had to smile at this but he answered quite sharply. "Gorm, Hes. Ye talk like a landlubber, like those chits in silks and laces off the excursion boats—'Oh do be careful, Harold, you might wet your feet!' The sea's a job like any other—"

She stared at him, feeling in her heart for the first time the gnaw of aching worry that fretted the fishermen's women, and one must not voice it. Already she had broken the code.

"I'll be waiting at the wharf when you sail back to the harbor—" she said, trying to smile. "Look for the brightest dinner pail, it'll be mine for you, and filled with a savory pork brew, the best in Marblehead."

Johnnie chuckled. "I'll dream on't, when I'm tossin' in the fo'c'sle and smellin' little Sandy's cautch o' stinkin' garney—Aye, Hes—it'll be good to know you're waitin'."

He pulled her close, and pressed his young beardless lips to her mouth. She returned it shyly, and they drew apart. Neither of them felt the need for more. They understood each other and were content.

They turned and walked together up the path, past Pitman's fish warehouse and the fish flakes, under the elm and the apple trees to Hesper's home.

CHAPTER 5

HESPER awoke late on the morning of her nineteenth birthday, the fifteenth of April, 1861. She yawned and nestled deeper into the feather bed. Ma'd let her dawdle a while on this one morning of the year. A slanting ray of sunshine fell across the ladder-back chair where she had flung her underclothes last night. It would be a good day for her junket with Johnnie.

She held up her left hand and looked at the ring Johnnie had given her three days ago; two gold wires twisted into a true lover's knot, a tiny diamond chip in the center. "Cupid's tear trembling in a golden chalice—" Hesper whispered tentatively. Would Pa think that a pretty phrase? Anyway, Johnnie'd think it silly. She smiled tenderly at the ring. Johnnie'd gone all the way to a jewelry shop in Lynn to buy it, and he'd used the money he'd saved for a new dory-roding. Spliced up the old one somehow. Johnnie was smart, all right. Ablest young fisherman in Marblehead. A "high-liner."

On last fall's fare to the Banks, Cap'n Trefry said Johnnie'd outfished them all. Twenty hours a day when they had a spirt, lashed himself to the mainmast so he wouldn't fall overboard if he dozed. His share had been big, near a hundred dollars. And he was just as skilled at the mackereling, as he was at catching cod. Cast and burnished his own jigs, some heavy and blunt for rough spirty days, some sharp and delicate as fly hooks to tempt the most finicky of mackerel. He'd worked so hard, never skipping a fare to the Banks, and mackerel and Bay fishing in between too. But it was only this past year he'd begun to get ahead a little.

There'd been a long spell of bad luck, after that night on the beach when he had bespoken her. The *Diana* stayed out till November that summer, and she did very badly. Came home with only half her salt wet, and but four hundred quintals of cod in her hold. And the next fare was far worse, for she sprang a leak and foundered in a storm off Cape Breton, and though all her crew had been rescued by the *Ceres* and eventually conveyed by steamer from Halifax to Boston, nine hundred quintals—the fruit of their summer's work, had sunk with the *Diana* to the bottom of the sea.

Yes, those were bad times, Hesper thought. They'd seen so little of each other, a week here and a week there, before Johnnie'd sail off again. But when Johnnie sailed next time it would be as master of his own pinkie. He had his eye on a right trig one in Salem. A good banker she'd be, tender but fast, and when he got the bounty money, there'd be enough to buy her—after the wedding in June. Wedding.

Hesper sat up in bed, drawing her breath and looking down at her pillow. A delicious apprehension tightened the muscles of her stomach, and flowed along her back. Imagine, Johnnie's head there on her pillow. The curly black hair, stubborn and crisp as hedge grass, the square brown face, shadowed blue all over the jaws, his powerful red neck, weathered by the sun and salt. And then what? Her body flushed all over and she jumped out of bed. Ma'd think it awful to have such thoughts before she was married. Anyway, whatever it was exactly took place between man and woman, would be beautiful with Johnnie.

She slipped off her long flannel nightgown, poured water from the dented pewter pitcher. The room was chilly and she shivered, but on a birthday morning one must wash all over. Start the year right, Ma said. Spanking clean underclothes too; best frilled drawers and petticoat, hemstitched bodice, new white stockings. While she put them on she sang blithely, a hauling chantey Johnnie was fond of.

> Oh a yankee ship came down the river
> Blow boys, blow boys, blow!
> Oh how do you know she's a yankee ship?
> WHY—By the cut of her jib and the list of her skipper—
> Blow, my bully boys, Blow!

She finished dressing, bundled her hair into a black crocheted net that was more becoming to her than any of her earlier efforts at dealing with her despised hair, and she went downstairs humming the last verse of the chantey, changing the words to suit herself.

> Oh her masts and yards they shine like silver
> Blow my bully boys, Blow!
> And who do you think was the captain of her?
> *Why*—Johnnie Peach was the Captain of her
> Blow boys, Blow boys, Blow!

Susan was in the taproom setting it to rights before the day's business commenced. Her tight mouth softened as she surveyed her daughter, but her eyes were grave. "Morning, Hes. Happy birthday. Kettle's on. I fried you up some fishcakes."

"Thanks, Ma. Isn't it a grand day!"

"You aiming to go out junketing with Johnnie?"

"He said he'd take the day off, maybe we'd go sailing in back of the Neck."

Susan turned and began straightening the beer mugs. The girl was happy at last for sure, never had heard just that lilt to her voice before, but she should have some warning. Susan banged a beer mug onto the shelf.

"News is bad, Hes. When Benjie brought the flour he said there was a big crowd hanging around the Town House waiting for the proclamation. Might come any minute over the telegraph."

A tremor shook the girl's mouth, she compressed her lips. "What if it does. Johnnie wouldn't go. He's not in the militia. They want to fight down there-along—let 'em."

Susan shook her head, her heavy face showed a kindling. "Marbleheaders've been the first to fight in every war we've had. You could hardly call 'em stay-at-homes even without the wars, always off to the Banks or someplace. Excepting your pa—of course."

Hesper ignored this familiar jibe. "Well let the *shoemakers* go fight then," she said with angry contempt. The Peaches had had plenty of trouble with that Porterman and the other shoemen. The strike last year had come to nothing, and then Lem Peach had taken ill and died of the consumption all on account of trying to work too hard.

Susan shrugged and hung up her dishcloth. "Not a bit o' use scorning the shoe manufacturies, my girl. Like it or not we'd be in a bad way here without 'em, now our fishing fleet's so small. No—have done, child—" she checked Hesper's retort with more sadness than asperity. "Someone's got to face facts around here, you're a lot like your pa with your romantical fancies. Go eat your breakfast."

Hesper sighed and turned into the old kitchen, determined, however not to let her mother dim the radiance of her day.

Her father had left his study door ajar, and he came out into the kitchen when he heard Hesper. His narrow stooping shoulders hunched beneath the alpaca jacket, his graying hair hung nearly to the velveteen collar, he had grown even thinner of late, and his recent nickname amongst the small fry of Marblehead was "Scare-crow," but Hesper saw only his eyes beaming through the spectacles with undisguised affection.

"Blessed be thy natal morn, fair daughter of the Western Star—" he said kissing her cheek—and quoting from the birthday ode he had written for her. "Do you feel much older?"

"Well, I do—Pa," she answered laughing, and happy again. "Have some coffee with me."

He pulled up a Windsor chair and sat beside her at the heavy oak plank table. It was covered by a shiny oilcloth square, patterned with sulphurous yellow roses. Roger with sudden irritation lifted a corner and threw it back. "I wish your mother wouldn't cover the table with this thing!"

She smiled at him, wondering how soon she might expect Johnnie. "But, Pa, the table's so dreadful old and scarred. I guess it's all right in the kitchen, but I wish we had a new one."

"Ah, but Hesper—if this oaken board could talk. Look child—" He pointed to a dent, long since filled level by applications of beeswax. "The mark made by the dagger Davy Quelch the pirate threw the night they captured him here. In 1714 that was. And look at this—"

Hesper had heard it all before and many times, but she bent over indulgently. A name had been carved on the trestle beneath the table. *"Izak Hunywood, 1642."* "That was young Isaac, born right here in this house shortly after they settled. He must've been about eleven years old and I wager he got a larruping from his mother for marking the table. His mother was Phebe, you know."

She nodded and poured out more coffee. She was not much interested in tales of the old house, and she listened vaguely to her father as she had listened to Gran long ago; today it was an especially pallid pastime, and she glanced at the banjo clock and then toward the window.

"Speaking of Phebe—" continued Roger, oblivious as always to lack of interest from a hearer when he was riding his twin hobby horses: Marblehead and Honeywood history—"This'd be a good day for you to hear the Lady Arbella's letter about Phebe, again. I'll get it now."

"No, Pa. Not now," she said decidedly. Poor Pa, he acted as though that letter about people dead two hundred years was a sort of talisman, or a magic incantation. "Maybe later—" she added because he looked so disappointed.

He sighed and accepted that, finished his coffee. "Lafayette drank a glass of punch at this table in '84. My father remembered it," he said at last, a trifle sulkily.

"I know, Pa," She touched him on the shoulder while she stacked the plates. She knew too how it saddened him that there were no more male Honeywoods and that the name would die out with him. That was one reason he set such store by the house itself. It would go on if the name didn't.

She was glad that she didn't have to leave him—and Ma, of course. Johnnie and she were going to live in the big yellow bedroom in Moses' wing after they were married, until they had enough money to buy a cottage. That way they didn't have to wait as long as many bespoken couples. Poor Clara Messervey had been waiting six years for her Jacob.

Hesper began to hum again as she tossed the Staffordshire cups and plates into the stone sink, barely avoiding nicks. She pumped water over them hastily. She was never one to linger over the household chores and certainly not this morning.

"How's the work coming, Pa?" she asked, as he still lingered. Only Hesper referred to the hours he spent in his study composing the "Memorabilia" as work.

"Pretty well—" he said brightening. "I'm working on the canto that treats of Elbridge Gerry's birth—I feel he was a veritable Solon, and shall draw that comparison later." Roger frowned, thinking of the proper presentation of Elbridge Gerry, one of Marblehead's most famous citizens, vice-president, "signer," and of course the "gerrymander," it would take several cantos to do Gerry justice. Might tie him in with Captain Mugford's daring exploit when the "Memorabilia" eventually reached to the Revolution. . . .

"Oh, Pa—do move!" cried Hesper laughing. "You're standing on the sweepings. You know I've got to leave the kitchen clean or Ma'll never let me out with Johnnie."

Roger nodded and shambled back to his refuge. Hesper heard the tinkle of the door bell, and waited, her fingers tight on the broom handle. But it was only little Snagtooth Foster come to fetch a mug of ale for his granny.

When Johnnie did come she did not hear him, having decided to work off her impatience by getting ahead with the chores. She stood by the west window grinding the next twenty-four hours' supply of coffee.

The rattling coffee beans and the rickety old grinder drowned out Johnnie's footsteps. He put his arms around her waist and kissed her on the neck. Hesper jumped and dropped the coffee bag.

"John-ee—you scared me."

He grinned, showing his blunt teeth. He bent over and picking up one of the scattered coffee beans, held it out to her. "Found the red one—" he said. "Means I should do it again."

"Nonsense—" she backed off blushing, always this wave of delicious embarrassment when Johnnie looked at her like that. "That's only for corn-husking and you know it. Johnnie—Ma might come in!"

He put his hands on her shoulders, pulled her toward him, and kissed her hard and long on the mouth. "That's for your birthday, sweetheart."

She whispered "Thank you—" confused and blissful, knelt quickly to gather up the coffee beans. They'd never been much of a couple for kissing or spooning. That was only for low-life easy girls, Ma said, plenty of time for that after marriage. And it was true, when you saw each other so seldom and had so much to talk about, and plan, just being together was enough.

Johnnie helped her get the beans back in the bag; then he said, "Boat's over by the town dock. Wind's fair south. Ought to have a good sail." Johnnie had a small fishing sloop now, as well as his dory. "Get your jacket, Hes—" he continued, "and we'll be off. Have you the lunch?"

"Fishcakes and gingerbread and a bottle of ale."

He nodded. "Where would you like goin'? I must be back early but we could make Baker's Island or Cat. I've much to say and I want no interruption."

Johnnie's keen young eyes darkened and slid from her happy face. She pushed down the fear. It's not that. I know it isn't. And if it is—I can make him see—coax him out of it.

"Let's go to Castle Rock—" she said softly. "Can you land at this tide?" Castle Rock, on the ocean side of the Neck, favorite meeting place for lovers since the earliest days of the settlement.

"I can beach the *Fire-top* anywhere—" said Johnnie laughing again. "*She'll* do my biddin'." The little sloop was also named for Hesper, but as the dory had duly become the *"Hessie H."* Johnnie had adopted the girl's childhood nickname for the newer boat, nor had Hesper minded; any link with his seafaring life was precious.

Johnnie picked up the wicker lunch basket. Hesper put on the blue pea jacket he had given her and started off beside him.

As they reached Front Street they both paused and took instinctive summary of sky and water. Breeze still south but veering a little to the east, so the Great Harbor was calm, the dozens of bare masts hardly swaying. Tide on the turn, slack just past, all the bows and bowsprits pointed out to sea again as they would for six hours. Overhead the thin blue sky was brushed with scattered mare's tails, but the Cape Ann shore, four miles away, showed neither too clear nor too misty. The fair weather would hold for today at least.

They walked up Front Street past the line of tight-wedged silver-gray houses, neither of them conscious of passers-by until, at the corner of State Street, they were checked by the Widow Cubby who was hurrying along the tiny sidewalk. Leah Cubby stopped in front of the young couple and her magnificent dark eyes, which had been peering into the shops and the little waterfront tavern, focused on them slowly.

"Oh"—she said— "Have you seen aught of Nat—or Mr. Porterman?"

"Why no, ma'am—" said Johnnie, while Hesper shook her head, staring curiously. It was seldom that Leah left home nowadays, and she was a striking figure. Slender and handsome in her black draperies. She looks younger than she possibly could be—thought Hesper, startled out of her own absorption. Leah's pale oval face was totally unlined, her full lips redder than ever, her dark wings of hair untouched by gray.

"I can't think where they'd be—" said the widow in her soft, hurried voice. "They left the house before breakfast and never a word to me. 'Tis not like them to go together. You know Nat's wrong about Mr. Porterman. He doesn't see what a wonderful man Mr. Porterman is. I have to beg and coax or Nat'd turn him from the house, but Mr. Porterman's no trouble at all, and he pays us so much money for his board. His wife's worse, you know." The widow leaned nearer, and her lips curved in a gentle smile. "I saw her once—she's not very pretty."

Hesper gave the beautiful face a startled glance, and yet she thought at once, Leah hadn't actually said anything out of the way, no more than any landlady gossip, and Ma said it was cruel to remember the fit of madness Leah had once had. Grief drove many to temporary distraction, that time healed completely.

"You'd better go home, ma'am—" said Johnnie very kindly. "I reckon they're at the Town House waiting for the proclamation. I wouldn't fret." Even Johnnie showed a protective admiration toward Leah, Hesper thought, ashamed of a twinge of jealousy.

"Oh—" said the widow, nodding, and she clasped her long white hands that were scarcely reddened at all by the housework. "Thank you—maybe that's it. Nat's all for the South, you know."

Johnnie compressed his mouth. "Come, Hes," he said abruptly, and turning, they left the widow.

Blast Leah! thought Hesper, trying by main strength to recapture the gaiety of the morning. Nat Cubby, Amos Porterman, and the proclamation—all disagreeable subjects. To hell I pitch it—she whispered, and her anger was much relieved.

They reached the Town Dock at the foot of Water Street and were forcibly projected into a new mood, for the ground around the entrance to the dock seethed with a tangle of yelling, pummeling small boys.

"Squael him—squael him good—" shrilled a voice, and a stone flew out of the mêlée in Hesper's direction.

"Down bucket, Hes!" cried Johnnie, and she ducked.

"What in Hell d'ye think you're doin'!" Johnnie reached to the ground and brought up a struggling red-faced urchin, held him securely by the ear. The victim pointed at a larger youth who picked himself from the ground. "He was kickin' my cat. He's from Salem."

"Oh if that's the right of it—" Johnnie released the ear. "I thought it was you wharf rats fighting the Barnegats again, and I'm a Barnegatter m'self, remember."

"Sure, Jigger," said the small boy humbly. "Jigger" Peach was a hero to the small fry, and so nicknamed because of his famous skill with the mackerel jig.

Johnnie turned to the foreigner. "What're you doin' in Marblehead?"

"Come to live with me aunt on Pearl Street. Me brother's been called to his company awready, and I've no place to stay in Salem."

"Ah—" said Johnnie. "To my thinkin' there's no place *fit* to stay in Salem. Ye're better off now, m' lad, but not if you go a kickin' our cats, or ye'll be rocked out o' town for sure."

"Yes, sir—" said the youth and walked sulkily away.

"Ye want to toss me the painter once we're aboard?" said Johnnie to the small Marbleheader, whose nose was dripping blood that mingled with two dirty tears.

Johnnie's order was obeyed with gratitude after Hesper jumped into the boat. Johnnie followed, shoved off, and hoisted the sail. "Keep the tiller, Hes," he said. "There's still gurry in the bilges, for all I swabbed this morning. Mind you leave that Gloucester ketch to windward," he added sternly, as he went to work with scoop and sponge.

"Yes, sir," said Hesper smiling, mimicking the small boy's adoration. She cleared the harbor and all its craft nearly as well as Johnnie would have, and after they rounded the Point of the Neck off the lighthouse and the *Fire-top* swished along on the port tack, she relaxed into a dreamy content, watching Johnnie. He'd cleaned out the last of the gurry, an ancient composite of fish remnants, chopped bait, and sea slime, still faintly odorous but not disagreeable to Hesper whose nose was accustomed to all kinds of fish smells. And now he squatted on the floor boards tinkering with a splitting knife, his head bent, the muscles in his shoulders moving beneath his dark blue jersey, while he whistled softly through his teeth. She watched his brown hands, spotted with healed scars from the hissing line and the fish spines.

And she thought his hands wonderful in their deftness and strength, for all the scars and the black hairs that grew on the backs.

"What are you thinking of, Johnnie?" she asked at last, for he had repaired the knife and was now fussing over his tackle box, re-allocating lines, hooks, and sinkers already neatly stowed. She knew that he was avoiding talk.

He shut the tackle box with a snap. "I was thinkin' of you, Hes."

The tenderness in his voice, and the underlying note of portent, distracted her. Johnnie moved aft. "Watch it—you're losin' headway!"

She let her hand fall from the tiller as Johnnie took over, and she leaned her head against his shoulder. If we could only stay like this. The crisp sunlight, the salt smell of the long Atlantic rollers, the little *Fire-top* gliding over them so smoothly. Alone on the wide blue sea, with the feel of Johnnie's arm around her and the warmth of his body coming through the heavy jacket to her own flesh.

Johnnie did not speak again, nor did she wish to. He steered the sloop to the cove south of Castle Rock and beached her on the shingle. Hesper jumped out, wetting her feet.

"I suppose I might a carried you," said Johnnie, laughing at her, "but even a landsman should know enough to wait for the wave to suck back."

They clambered up the "Castle"—piled masses of porphyritic rock, tawny yellow, rose, and pale green squared into gigantic blocks and cleft at the base by deep fissures. Into these the Atlantic crashed and foamed throwing up jets of spray. They scrambled to the top to a cuplike depression protected from the wind and covered with sparse earth and sparser beach grass.

"Take off your shoes and stockin's, Hes—" said Johnnie. "You don't want to feel crimmy."

Hesper obeyed, tucking her bare feet modestly beneath her long woolen skirts, setting the shoes and stockings to dry in the sun.

Johnnie stood with his back to her gazing down the Neck. "Old Churn's beginnin' to spout, wind's about right," he observed. "Want to look? Much better show than Rafe's Chasm, Cape Anners're so boastful of."

Hesper knew and Johnnie knew that they had both seen "The Churn" at work a dozen times, throwing spray a hundred feet in the air and booming like a cannon. Johnnie was making conversation.

"Sit down, do—" she said. He turned, and giving her a look half of appeal, half of decision, threw himself on the coarse beach grass beside her. He picked up a pebble and shied it out over the rim of sheltering rock. "Proclamation's in, Hes. The Postmaster let me read it head o' the official announcement. It's War."

Hesper gathered herself up tight, not looking at his upturned face. "Well, we expected it. The militia'll go I suppose. It's nothing to do with us—nothing at all!"

He sat up straight. "Hes! How can you talk like that! Have ye forgot the night we rescued the slave girl? You were concerned enough in that!"

She frowned, searching for the right words, remembering the emotions of that long ago night. There had been pity and excitement and fear, and exultation, but all tepid now in memory, irrelevant to the joy of what came later when Johnnie bespoke her on the beach.

"Slavery's bad, of course"—she said; she paused to control the shake in her voice, went on with cool reason—"but there's no need for war. They could settle it without fighting if they'd only try. Even if they do fight, it's nothing to do with you Johnnie. You're a Marbleheader and a fisherman."

He sighed. Women, he thought—even Hes, and his mother'd been as bad. They'd argue, they'd forget in a moment the things they'd always believed in. As if it wasn't hard enough without their tears and pleadings.

He took Hesper's hand and held it in both of his. "I'm goin', sweetheart. It may be wrong, but I'm goin'."

The bright sky darkened, the sun-warmed rocks pressed down on Hesper, sharp and threatening. Her fingers clutched at his hand. "But why? Why? Why? There's plenty of others to go. You'll never make a soldier. You're no landsman. And what about us—our wedding?"

She hadn't meant to say that. Hot tears started to her eyes. She turned from him, staring at a seagull that dipped and vanished and rose again.

"I know, Hes." That Johnnie should speak so patiently gave her fresh fear. "I'll not be a soldier, bufflehead. You're right it'd be hardly to my likin'. The sea's to my likin' and it's on the sea I'll fight. I've joined up with Cap'n Cressy on the *Ino.* I've to report at Boston tomorrow."

"You've already done it," she whispered. She took her hand from his.

She leaned her cheek against the rock. Down below them a wave crashed into the fissure and sucked back to sea with a long sigh.

"I had to while I had the courage, Hes. I know you'd talk me around, else. I don't want to leave you, sweetheart. I needn't tell you that, but it'll not be for long. Those Rebs're soft, and I'll wager there's not a seaman knows larboard from starboard in the lot of 'em. It'll be over soon, and we can be wed as we'd planned."

She was silent, her head bowed, her gaze fixed now on a tuft of salt-rimed grass. He loved her, yes—but despite that you couldn't get around something else. He wanted to go. He didn't have to, he just wanted to.

"Use reason, Hes." He put his hand over hers where she held it clenched in her lap. "It's no different than if I was off to the Banks for a fare."

She stirred then. "It is, Johnnie. It's very different. I've no fear for you at sea anymore. You understand the sea. But what could you do against shot and shell?"

"Why, I must take my chances like the rest," he said crisply. "Come, Hes. No long face. Give me a smile, Lass. I'll be back safe and sound afore you know it. You should be proud, not grouty. Marblehead men are ever the first to fight for their country, no matter we keep ourselves to ourselves between whiles. And your own stock as forward as any of them."

Yes, thought Hesper, and they got killed too. A cold wind blew through her veins; she could not smile, though Johnnie had his arm around her waist, and murmured love words which she did not hear. Instead she heard Gran's long-forgotten voice, high and quavering. "Richard never come back. He said he would but he never come back. Crazy to go he was, standin' right there on the rug I hooked in his fine new uniform. . . .

She turned to him at last, throwing her arms wildly around his neck. "Johnnie—I love you so—don't leave me—" but her cry was silenced by his mouth.

The breeze freshened as they clung together, and the distant booming of the churn mingled with the hastening crashes of the waves on the base of Castle Rock. The spray flew up into their sheltered summit to drift down and mingle with her tears. Unknowing and unscheming, she wooed him with the warmth of her young body until she looked into his face and saw the grim mask of desire, then she drew from him with a sobbing cry.

He shut his eyes and his demanding arms dropped. "Aye—you're right—" he said very low. "We'll not have long to wait—I swear it. I'll be back by snowfall, Hesper." He drew her head down to his shoulder, and her fear vanished before his calm certainty. They sat together talking a little of their future until the shadows deepened on the wall of encircling rock, and rising wind blew chill from off the ocean.

When they climbed back in the boat for the sail home she was calm and comforted. She'd been a fool to make such a fuss. Why then should she suddenly see Aunt 'Crese's black face plain against the sail as it bellied taut and hear the rocking waves whisper "Heartbreak. Heartbreak—yo'll think it won't mend, but life's got a hull lot up her sleeve foh you. De heart's tough, honey."

Rubbish, she cried, as she had in the smoky little tavern three years ago, the old woman was crazy. There'd be the familiar heartbreak of waiting for news, and the joy of reunion. That was what Aunt 'Crese meant if she meant anything.

She looked up at Johnnie's dear profile, rugged and sure against the darkening sky.

Johnnie was killed in a skirmish at Gibraltar in April of the next year. Killed by a random shot on the deck of the *Ino* after she had blockaded the confederate steamer *Sumter*.

The news reached Marblehead in June and was conveyed to Johnnie's family. His mother, Tamsen, herself distracted with grief, did not at once think of breaking the news to Hesper, and when she did ask the Reverend Allen, Pastor of the Old North, to tell poor Hes Honeywood, it was too late. The town crier had preceded him.

That afternoon, Hesper was in the taproom drawing ale for a couple of Marblehead privates who were home on furlough, George Jones and Bushy Chapman. Hesper knew both young men well, and having listened to their account of the capture of Roanoke Island was now indulgently turning a blind eye to their present amusement of matching pennies. This Susan would never have allowed, nor any form of gambling in her Inn. But Susan had gone over to the Neck, to Brown's farm for chickens. Provisions for the Inn were getting hard to come by on account of the war.

"You any news o' Johnnie, Hes?" asked Bushy Chapman, pocketing six pennies. "His ship still over to Gibraltar?"

"Don't know. Haven't heard since Christmas."

Bushy who was not observant thought she spoke sharply, and thought her unmannerly to turn her back like that. He shrugged and drank from his mug. Nice enough girl, not bad looking if you didn't mind 'em big and all that red hair, but not his cup of tea. This reminded him of something, and he bent across the table to murmur to George. Hesper, checking the account book, heard fragments. "Mighty tempting pair of ankles—Second house on Training Field Hill—"

Hesper smiled a trifle acidly. That would be Charity. All the boys were after her, but she hadn't settled on anyone yet.

The jangle of an approaching bell and a sort of whining shout cut across the taproom. Hesper and the two men turned around.

"What now?" said Bushy. "Bad news by the oily way he mouths it."

The jangle and whine grew louder as the crier turned the corner of Franklin Street. Hesper distinguished the words "Peach" and "In action."

Hesper stood up resting her hands on the counter, her eyes fixed on the window. The crier stopped in front of the Inn.

"Hear Ye! Hear Ye! Another of our brave young men gone to glory. Young John Peach killed in action. God rest his brave soul."

The two young men stared at each other "Poor Johnnie's got his—" then Bushy jumped—"Down bucket, George! she's going to keel over!"

But Hesper pushed them away. She ran to the door and called the crier back. "What did you say?" She listened, her face glistening white in the doorway. "You're sure there's no mistake—"

"There's none, miss." The crier looked at her curiously and waited. Mrs. Honeywood often gave him a sip of port to wet his gullet, no matter the news, but it seemed the girl wasn't going to. He moved on toward Front Street, jangling the bell. "Hear Ye, Hear Ye—"

Hesper walked back into the taproom and sat down at the table. She put her left hand flat on the beer-stained wet top and stared at Johnnie's ring. She didn't say anything, or move, even her eyelids didn't blink.

George and Bushy stood nervously across the table. "Wish her ma was here—" whispered George, "Gorm—she's white as a flounder's belly."

He cleared his throat. "Hes—we're motal sorry about Johnnie. He was a good lad."

Hesper did not move. Her head with its heavy weight of red braids held rigid as if she was sitting for a tintype.

"Let's get her some brandy—" said Bushy, and poured out a nogginful from a bottle he found under the counter. But Hesper would not touch the brandy; she shook her head and continued to stare at the little gold ring with the diamond chip in its center. Bushy drank the brandy himself.

George picked up his peaked blue cap. "We'd best let her be. Though I wonder if her pa—"

The door bell tinkled and both boys sighed with relief, for the Pastor came in.

"She's heard the news about Johnnie Peach, sir—she won't speak—" The young men sidled past the Reverend Allen and escaped.

The minister was himself at a loss, in the face of the girl's immobility. He touched her on the shoulder. "Hesper, I've come to bring you God's words of comfort." He spoke sternly, knowing that best in shock. "Stand up and come with me to your parlor. This is no suitable place."

She raised her gaze from the ring and let it rest on the black frock coat in front of her, her eyes moved upward over the white stock to the bland middle-aged face above it.

She put the hand with the ring in her lap, and turned her head away.

"Child, you must rouse yourself!" The minister sat down staring with distaste at the stained table. "You're a good Christian. You know that death is but the gateway to a more beautiful life—life everlasting. And those that die gloriously for their country, like young John Peach, I'm sure that the Gentle Shepherd gathers those lambs very quickly to his loving bosom."

Hesper's lips quivered and the minister leaned forward.

"Johnnie wouldn't like that, being a lamb," she said. "He'd want to be on the sea."

The minister swallowed. These Marbleheaders, Especially the old stock. You never knew where you were with them. Trouble ever since he'd come here from his quiet Maine town.

"I make allowances for your grief," he said coldly. "But you must bow your head to the will of God, and you'll find solace. Your church and Holy Writ alone can give you comfort. And if you cannot accept this yet, rest in the memory of all those who have suffered in the past and found help in Jesus. Your own forefathers—"

Hesper raised her head and her eyes rested again on his face. "My forefathers didn't come to Marblehead for religion. They came for fish."

"Really, my dear Miss Honeywood!" His face flushed and he stood up. "I believe you have no feelings at all. I'm wasting my time. I'm amazed, that you—a regular communicant, should receive me like this —I don't know what to think."

Hesper seemed to listen to him, and as he stopped she nodded. "You see, I don't care what you or anybody thinks. With Johnnie—" she paused, went on in the same measured voice, "With Johnnie killed, it doesn't matter."

"There child—" said the minister, slightly mollified. "Try not to think about it. I shall pray for you, and return in a day or so, when you're more yourself."

Hesper rose. She was as tall as the minister, and he involuntarily stepped back from her, startled by the chalk white of her face, the forehead glistening with tiny beads of moisture, and above it the burnished red hair—like a patch of blood against the pine wall.

"Don't come back—" she said.

The Reverend Allen picked up his round black hat and went out with no further word.

Hesper wadded the corner of her apron and wiped her forehead. She walked through the parlor to the front staircase. Since the war, months went by without foreigners in town. There was nobody in the house, even Roger had gone to the stationer's.

Hesper mounted the staircase and opened the door to the Yellow Room. It was in here that she and Johnnie had thought to start married life. It received her with the listening stillness peculiar to long-shut rooms.

She parted the frayed yellow damask curtains and looked out of the east window, toward Little Harbor. The Harbor was nearly deserted since the war, the fish flakes empty.

Across the shipyard she could see the monument on Burial Hill, and below on Orne Street the brownish roof that was Johnnie's house.

Hesper let the curtain fall. She walked across the room to the great four postered bed and threw herself on it. She lay on her back looking up at the frayed golden canopy.

Susan found her there in the dark, hours later, and was frightened. The girl wouldn't answer or move. She just lay there staring up, and she looked like death, her cheeks fallen in and her eyes sunk back.

But she started when her mother touched her, and allowed Susan to coax her off the bed and downstairs. She ate a little chowder for supper, but she didn't mention Johnnie's name, or speak except to ask Susan if she'd had a good trip to the farm, and her voice was tiny and polite like a talking doll.

All over Marblehead they said that poor Hes Honeywood was acting awful strange.

The passing fishermen would see her sitting on the rocks at the tip of Peach's Point staring out to sea. One day little Snag-tooth Foster went over on the Neck to hunt for Indian arrowheads, and he saw her on Castle Rock, hunched up on a big stone right down by high-water mark where the spray blew over her. He said she didn't hear when he called to her, and she seemed to be writing something in a book she had on her lap. Once she tried to borrow Johnnie's dory from the Peaches, but Johnnie's younger brother had taken it out flounder fishing, and the Peaches would never have let her go out alone in it, as she seemed to want to. " 'Twouldn't be safe, my pore gur-rl—" said Tamsen Peach. Her own eyes were reddened with weeping for her son, but in them there was a look of patience and resignation. "Go home, Hes," she added, "and try for rest. Yore lookin' mighty peaked."

Hesper nodded to Mrs. Peach, without saying anything more, and walked back down Orne Street. Later that day she borrowed a skiff in the Little Harbor and set to rowing out towards Cat Island.

Fortunately Susan who was cleaning an upstairs room at the Inn saw her go. She came down to Roger and found him out of his study for once and prowling uneasily around the kitchen.

"That girl's rowing out to sea like the Old Nick was after her," she said. "I don't like it. I've kept hands off, like you wanted me to with all her pixillated comings and goings, but I think someone should keep an eye on her. Wind's blowing up."

"She knows the water roundabouts well as anybody—" said Roger, "let her be, she's working it out her own way." But his voice lacked conviction; he went to the window and stared through it.

Susan made a sharp sound, and turned her back. The door bell jangled and she welcomed the customer with relief. "Cap'n Ireson, you got your dory handy? Our girl's rowing purty far out to be alone, might have trouble getting back 'gainst the tide."

The old skipper nodded, replaced his tarred canvas hat, and re-buttoned his oilskins.

"Wait—" said Roger, "I'll go with you."

His wife's mouth fell open. *"You,* what hasn't set foot in a dory over thirty years!"

Roger's nostrils indented. He reached to a peg behind the door for his great coat. "I believe I can still row."

Susan said nothing. She went to the cupboard and bringing out his muffler put it around his neck. Her rough, fat hand lingered for an instant on his shoulder.

The men went out the back through the garden patch and along the weedy path to Little Harbor.

They found Hesper an eighth of a mile outside of Gerry's Island fighting her way back. The little skiff bobbed over the mounting waves and disappeared in the troughs, and against the racing ebb tide she was making no headway.

Captain Ireson grunted, came alongside, and both men pulled the girl over the gunnel into the dory. She was trembling with fear and exhaustion, but she had properly shipped the oars and she had the skiff's painter tight in her hand. Roger made it fast for towing.

"Glad to see you've sense enough not to lose Davie's skiff for him anyhow," said Captain Ireson severely. "Fool gur-rl, puttin' out so far. Women don't belong on water—"

Hesper did not hear him. She lay flat on the floor boards. "Pa—?" she said wondering—"*you* came—"

"Worried about you—"

Neither Honeywood spoke again until they rounded the island and came to calm water in the harbor. By then Hesper had recovered, and she helped her father from the boat, for his muscles, long unused, were trembling, and his face grown moist and green from nausea.

"I'm sorry—Pa—" she whispered. "I didn't mean to—" But she didn't know what she had meant in that frantic escape toward Cat Island. A groping, a yearning for that other night so long ago. . . . Johnnie, where are you—ah, it had been easy gliding out, easy as the ride out had been hard that night. Easy to go on, on and on past the island to the open sea, and forget, find Johnnie there. And then halfway across the channel her dreamy apathy had been shattered by a bolt of terror, I must get back. Oh, you fool, you fool—Johnnie isn't out there. He isn't any place. Turn back. She had struggled, panting, with the light oars, and the tiny skiff that twisted and trembled in the wind's clutch.

She clung to her father as they entered the house.

Susan's worry, and relief at seeing them, resulted naturally in anger. She seized Hesper's shoulders and administered a good shaking. "You crazy loon, what do you mean by such daft behavior! Troubling Cap'n Ireson here to go out for you, and look what you've done to your pa, his death o' chill most likely, and him green with the seasickness. You know he could never abide a boat."

Hesper bowed her head and said nothing. Susan poured a glass of grog for the two men and whipped up an eggnog for Hesper. Captain Ireson said "Thankee mum" and withdrew to the taproom where Susan followed him.

Hesper and Roger were left in the kitchen. He sat down in the Windsor armchair, before the fireplace. "You want to rest, Hesper?" She shook her head. "Then I want to talk to you."

She fetched a log from the back porch and threw it across the andirons, above the smoldering embers. "You don't feel crimmy, Pa?"

"No, not now—Sit down child."

She sank to the little stool which had been the favorite seat of her childhood. Just within the great ten-foot fireplace. She leaned her head against the bricks and watched the new log catch.

"I want you to stop fretting for Johnnie, Hesper."

She lifted her hand and let it fall to her lap. "I can't."

He leaned forward and spoke with a sharpness she had never heard from him. "Do you think you're the first to feel sorrow? Right here in this house, how many times do you think sorrow's been met, and bravely."

"I don't know—" she said and there was sharpness in her tone too. "Thinking of the past's no good to me. All the Honeywoods that were killed or drowned. What good's that?"

"You're to think of those that were left and lived and went on; that's why we're here."

She was silent, turning her head from him so that he saw only the fire reflected on the fire of her hair.

"Perhaps—" he said slowly, "you think I'm not one to talk. I've been a failure. Yes—I have. I've not met life fair and square. But I want you to. The rest of them did."

The rest of them, she thought, and a sullen resistence rose in her. All the memories of Honeywoods imprisoned in this house. They were gone, but their possessions were not. Phebe's andirons, Isaac's table, Gran's hooked rug, and in the new part, Moses' staircase, Moses' foreign wallpaper. The new part—a hundred years old. And what did they ever do anyway? Those dead Honeywoods. Fishing, innkeeping, making a little money, losing it again. Racing off to war if there was one, getting killed. Going off to the Banks and getting drowned. In either case the women staying home and suffering. No sense to it. Nothing to be proud of.

Roger got up and came over to the fire so that he could see her face. He sighed, went back to his chair and sat down.

"You've been writing some poetry, lately, Hesper?"

She moved her shoulders. "A little, it helps some."

"Of course it helps," he said. "Let me see some of it, won't you?"

"Maybe, Pa. Sometime."

For an instant the bitter yearning lifted. She saw herself sitting with the ladies of the Arbutus Club, saw them look up from their sewing and bandage-making, eyeing her respectfully, whispering—"Hes Honeywood has had a poem printed. Of course talent runs in the family, her father . . ."

The banjo clock whirred and jangled out the first of six notes. Hesper released her breath. She got off the stool, and went to the peg behind the back door for her apron. She dumped water off peeled potatoes, and began to chop them on the sink board with vicious little jabs. She knew what they said at the Arbutus Club. "That Roger Honeywood—never did a lick of honest work in his life . . . and that queer gawk of a girl, never could see what poor Johnnie saw in her. . . ."

Roger shambled across the kitchen. "You've cut your finger, Hesper." She nodded impatiently, pumped cold water from the spigot over the welling blood.

He touched her shoulder. She gave him a quick, blind smile and moved away. She shook down the little pot-bellied stove, set a greased frying pan and a battered coffeepot on top of it. She went to the great fireplace, swung the crane and its dangling iron pot over the fire.

Roger cleared his throat. "What are we having for supper, my dear?"

She turned, startled for a moment. Pa never cared what he ate, then she saw his anxious eyes trying to reach through to her, pleading with her, and she answered.

"Fried potatoes and fish brew, same as dinner, same as yesterday, Ma can't seem to get anything else." She took an iron ladle and stirred up the mixture of salty codfish, beets, and dried peas.

"Guess I'll do a little work, till supper's ready."

"Yes, do—Pa. I'll call you." She scooped the sliced potatoes from the drainboard into the frying pan, set them back on the stove. He took a step towards his study door and paused. "Hesper, you won't go off like that alone again—on the water?"

She stiffened, bending over the stove. He saw her hand with Johnnie's ring, clench on the handle of the frying pan. "No, Pa." She bent lower, and added in a whisper, "Thank you for coming out there to me."

When Susan came into the kitchen twenty minutes later, she found it deserted. She frowned. An acrid smoke rose from the potatoes, and the boiling coffee water made great hissing spats on the stove. "That girl"—she muttered snatching off the potatoes—"With all I have to do —and the worry . . ." She swung the crane and its bubbling load of fish brew back from the fire, threw an angry look at Roger's shut door, and called "Hesper-r-!"

She opened the back door, and called again into the damp windy twilight. The branches were creaking on the old chestnut, and the nor-'easter swirled past her as she stood on the step. Behind in the Great Harbor the breakers pounded.

Susan drew back and shut the door. "She'll not be out in this. She has *some* sense. She's mine too, despite all you hear is of Honeywoods."

Susan thrust a spill into the fire and lit a candle. Her fat hands shook and the freckles on them stood out like brown flies. She mounted the narrow stairs meaning to go through the second landing to the new part. The girl often shut herself into the Yellow Room. But outside Hesper's own door, she stopped. The scowl cleared from her face, and she listened to the sound from within.

She nodded slowly. "Thank God, she's broke down at last. She'll stop fighting it now." Susan rested the candle on the square hand-hewn newel post, leaned against the wall, looking at Hesper's door with a tenderness the girl had never seen. "You get noplace by fighting it, Hes. The Good Lord knows I've had to learn that."

She picked up the candle and descended the stairs.

CHAPTER 6

THROUGHOUT the war years Marblehead seethed with patriotism. In July of 1862, President Lincoln issued a call for additional volunteers, and sixty-nine men responded. The Marblehead band played, the church bells rang, fourteen of the town's prettiest young ladies dressed themselves in red, white, and blue bunting and waved flags.

Fort Sewall on the south point of Little Harbor had been in ruins since the War of 1812 and the town voted four thousand dollars to add to the Government appropriation for its repair. The Government also built two new forts, one at Rivershead Beach, the other on Naugus Head, the promontory towards Salem where two hundred years before, the first settlers had had their Derby Fort and the memory of a similar promontory in England.

All three forts were garrisoned by foreigners from other parts of Massachusetts, and the Marbleheaders curbed their normal antipathy toward the outlanders and endured them as patiently as possible. This was not easy. These companies were mostly composed of homesick farm boys, distrustful of the water which surrounded them, and bored by inactive duty.

They brawled in the narrow streets, tried to seduce Marblehead girls, and made constant fun of the Marblehead speech. There were therefore reprisals.

One night in the Hearth and Eagle taproom there was a bloody fight between two old Barnegat fishermen and two Pittsfield boys who were stationed at Fort Sewall.

It began because one of the Pittsfield boys was suddenly inspired to recite Whittier's "Skipper Ireson's Ride"—sure spark to any Marbleheader's tinder.

" 'Here's Flud Oirson, fur his hor-rd hor-rt' " cried the young corporal, striking an attitude and declaiming in a taunting voice:

Torr'd and furtherr'd an' corr'd in a corrt
By the women o' Morble'ead!

"That's a Gawd-dom lie!" shouted one of the fishermen, jumping up.

The corporal was delighted; things were mighty dull around this God-forsaken place, and it was seldom you could get a rise out of any of these fishy men.

Small pity for him! He sailed away
From a leaking ship in Chaleur Bay—
Sailed away from a sinking wreck
With his own townspeople on her deck—

continued the corporal, encouraged by the applause of his friend.

"I tell ye—" cried the fisherman, shaking his fist, "that's a stinkin' whoreson lie!"

"Have done—Ned—" said Susan emerging from behind the counter, "I'll deal with him. Look, my young cockerel—" she turned to the elocutionist. "There may be some that think that Whittier's a poet, but I'm not one. Years ago he courted a Marblehead girl; her parents had sense enough not to let her take him, by-the-bye—because it's evident he'd no regard for fact. Benjamin Ireson was a fine man, his trouble no fault of his own, and his family much respected here. I'll thank ye to shut your mouth."

But the young corporal was exhilarated by Susan's rum, and barely waited for her voice to stop before he began to chant—

" 'Here's Flud Oirson fur his hor-r-rd hor-rt—' " The old fisherman promptly knocked him down. The other fisherman and the remaining Pittsfield boy jumped forward, and Susan stood by grimly until they had battered and knocked each other into quiet, and broken four of her earthenware mugs as well.

After that she denied the use of her taproom to any of the garrison, and times for the Honeywoods grew hard. Prices were rocketing and with the decline of fishing the business center of town moved back from the waterfront. Only the shoe manufacturers were prosperous.

By the fall of 1864, Susan was frightened and she showed it by sharper temper and hours of glum silence. The larder was empty, her credit had run out, the last keg of beer was nearly dry. If they were not to starve there was but one thing to do. For days she had been mulling it over, but had said nothing to Roger or Hesper.

Roger had been bed-ridden, with a grippy cold and it was hopeless to talk to him anyway; there'd be nothing of help from him but a spate of poetry, and a reminder that the Honeywoods had never done such a thing.

She had not wanted to worry Hesper until it was imperative. The girl was slowly recovering, her figure had filled out a little, and she had begun to take an interest in war work. She went regularly to sew with the ladies of the Soldiers Aid Society, and she had recently been over on the Neck to a husking bee with other young people. She had unfortunately no special admirers, but then Hes had never been the type for beaux, and anyway there were mighty few young men left in town.

On the crisp October afternoon when Susan made her decision Hesper had been to the druggist's to buy cough medicine for her father. She came into the kitchen, took off her bonnet and shawl, and counted out the change, four pennies, into Susan's hand.

"How's Pa?"

"Not coughing so much. Give a look in the bean pot, Hes."

Hesper opened the brick oven at the side of the fireplace. "They're browning but I don't see the salt pork."

"Isn't any. That's the end of the m'lasses too."

Hesper threw a puzzled look at her mother's back. "Didn't you order more?"

Susan did not answer. She took a pot of thin gruel off the cook-stove and poured some of it into a pewter bowl for Roger. "When I popped over to see how poor Nellie's doing this afternoon, I ran into Amos Porterman on State Street," she said.

"Did you?" Hesper answered indifferently. "I never could abide that man."

"And why not? I'd like to know." Susan whirled and advanced on her daughter. "He's not bad looking, he does a lot for the town an' our soldiers, an' he speaks real civil."

"Shoe man," said Hesper with a lift of her lip. "Foreigner. Johnnie—Johnnie always said those shoe factories ruined the town, ruined the fishing.

Susan's green eyes snapped, but she controlled herself. "Shoemaking *saved* the town. We'd 've starved without it. The Embargo, back in my pa's time ruined the fishing. Gale of '46 that took Tom and Willy and most of our fleet ruined the fishing. This war's ruined the fishing —not shoes."

Hesper, startled not by her mother's vehemence, but by the length of her rebuttal, tossed her head. "Well, anyhow—I don't like Amos Porterman."

"That's too bad," said Susan turning her back again and picking up the gruel, "because he's coming here this afternoon."

"Whatever for—Ma? You mean to the taproom?"

"Taproom's closed and not likely to open. Mr. Porterman's coming here to tea because I asked him to." She paused at the door of the kitchen bedroom where Roger lay temporarily. "If we want to eat, Hes, I reckon we'll have to learn how to make shoes." She shut the door behind her.

Hesper collapsed on the settle, staring at the shut door. Irritation at her mother eclipsed everything else. How like Ma to spring a thing like that without warning. Bossy she was, always deciding things in herself and then telling people what they were supposed to do.

Things couldn't be as bad as all that. Money was tight, was for everybody. But the Inn had always brought in enough. Would still if Ma hadn't been so persnickety about the garrison boys.

But Hesper's resentment, as always, was tempered by her strong sense of justice, for Ma *was* a good manager, and she had doubtless done the best she could. Hesper frowned and thought back. The taproom doorbell hardly ever tinkled lately, and long ago they'd stopped serving the beans and fishcakes or flapjacks customers used to ask for. Hesper hadn't paid much attention, except for a vague recognition that here was another evidence of this hateful war. Lately nothing had seemed very important except keeping busy. She'd been out a good deal. Meetings at the Soldiers Aid, sewing with the older women at the Arbutus Club, even a little church work, because all the other girls did it. The Reverend Allen had been nice enough and welcomed her to Wednesday prayer meeting, never referring to the way she'd acted that day he came to comfort her. It made her hot now to think of it. But she didn't want to think of it or anything about Johnnie. That seemed a long time ago, and only sometimes at night when she listened to the wind and the rhythmic crash of the waves on Front Street did the old intolerable pain rush at her.

The bell jangled and Hesper jumped. Susan came out of the kitchen bedroom. "That'll be Mr. Porterman. Take off your apron and let him in. I've laid a fire in the parlor. Mind your manners," Susan added, seeing resistance in the girl's face.

Hesper compressed her lips. "You might have told me sooner. You always treat me like a child."

Amos Porterman was a very large man, six foot two and proportionately heavy, and in his fawn-colored greatcoat he filled the little entry. Hesper stepped back into the taproom, feeling dwarfed for all her own height and resenting this, as she was prepared to resent everything about him.

"Good afternoon, Miss Honeywood—" he said, bowing. His gray-blue eyes expressed a courteous interest, but in his deep voice she detected a note of patronage.

She stood stiffly by the door. "Afternoon. Ma's expecting you. We'll go through to the parlor."

In the empty taproom, she waited, unsmiling, for him to take off his outer things and place them on a chair, while she noted the ruby-eyed owl stickpin in his glossy satin cravat, the newness of his gray broadcloth suit, the massive gold watch chain which glinted across his striped waistcoat. The *shoemen* had plenty of money.

She led the way to the chilly parlor, reached to the mantel for a match.

"Permit me—" said Amos, taking the match from her. She drew back, watching him bend his bulk down to the small fireplace. There was something lumbering about him, she thought with satisfaction. Before the war a man had come to Marblehead with trained animals, little dogs in ruffs, and a bear that shuffled in time to his master's jew's harp. Mr. Porterman was like that bear dressed up, except his face. That was oblong, squared at the jaw, and again on the high forehead where it met his flaxen hair. He was clean-shaven, and when he raised his face, flushed from bending over, it occurred to her that he was not as old as she had thought. She had never, since the day they'd helped the slave girl and he came to inquire for rooms, had a good look at him without his hat. She had thought his hair grayish, but she saw now that it was a pale and ashy blond.

The fire crackled and glinted off Susan's brass andirons. "Thanks," said Hesper dryly and sat down on one of the knobby crewel-work chairs. Amos took the other and it creaked as he settled himself. He cleared his throat but did not speak. He was astonished by the hostility he saw in the girl whom he barely remembered. She seemed unwilling to talk or even look at him; instead she held her head turned and seemed to be contemplating the story of Jonah and the whale which ran in blue and white tiles around the fireplace. The long-unused parlor was dank, it smelled of mustiness and the camphor Susan kept under the cabbage rose carpeting.

Amos cleared his throat again and crossed his legs. "Is your mother coming soon?" He spoke with a mixture of amusement and irritation. This visit had been none of his doing. Mrs. Honeywood had shown such urgency in inviting him that he had canceled his late afternoon appointments at the factory. He respected Mrs. Honeywood, knew her to be a worthy woman, and was quite willing to help her out, since she had indicated a desire for work. But the girl made him feel like a clumsy intruder.

Hesper stood up again in answer to his question. "I'll go see. I guess she's fixing the tea things." She went out.

Amos raised his bushy blond eyebrows, and reached in his pocket for a cigar. Couldn't light it in a parlor, but he held it between his teeth, chewing pleasurably. Queer girl, that. Bad disposition that was supposed to go with red hair too, apparently. But he didn't understand her being so uncordial. He had a forthright and orderly mind, and he cast about for a reason. Suddenly he remembered meeting her with that young Peach boy a couple of years ago. They'd been walking down Front Street hand in hand, and he had thought how young and happy they looked.

Amos nodded to himself, and spat into the fire. Maybe that explained it. Young John Peach's father had been one of the strike leaders in the trouble of 1860. He remembered the black-browed vehement little man, swinging a placard and protesting the wage cut. That had been a bad time for all the shoe manufacturers in Marblehead and the thing had spread to Lynn. But we had to cut costs, Amos thought, couldn't help ourselves.

After a while most of the strikers had seen reason and gone back to work in their little shoe shops, skiving and slicking the soles at home before delivering them at the factory to be fitted to the uppers.

But Peach had held a grudge. That was the worst of those old Marbleheaders, always balky, no matter how badly they needed money.

Amos thought again of Hesper and this time with some sympathy. Poor girl, no doubt she'd loved that tousle-headed young fisherman. Love and lose— His thoughts turned to his own loss. It had been some time since he thought of Lily Rose, and he could no longer see her face. In memory she appeared as a series of luminous concepts, white and pink and flowery like her name, pale gold and blurred at the edges. The smell of lilies on her coffin, the lavender scent of her frilly pillows, but mingled with those scents too, the thin, bitter odor of the medicine she used to take. Her smile that was piteous and appealing, brave in the midst of her suffering; yet it had often chilled him.

She had guarded herself with that brave smile, holding him away from her fragile body. He had loved her very much at first and indulged and petted her, proud of her delicacy, and willing to restrain his own grossness, and yet he had not always believed in her sufferings.

And then, almost a year ago, she suddenly died. And he had felt sharp remorse, regretting each time he had been impatient with her, each time when he had stalked from the house and taken a train for Boston to visit a certain discreet brownstone house on lower Boylston Street.

Well, but a man needed a woman at times, he thought, sighing, and he was only thirty-two now. Lately he'd been thinking of marrying again, when it was decent to. Maybe some lively pretty girl like Charity Trevercombe, good family, and a hot little thing by the look of her, not like poor Lily Rose. Charity had a parcel of followers, but he'd walked her home from a lecture at the Lyceum and her big eyes had been inviting; she cuddled all the way against his arm.

At any rate, he thought, frowning, marriage or not, maybe he'd have to move from Leah Cubby's. There'd been a change since Lily Rose died. It was a nuisance, because Leah'd always made him comfortable, and he didn't want to move until he had the house built he was planning on Pleasant Street. But lately he had been much more aware of her—the graceful indolence of her movements and the slumberous, troubling lights in her huge dark eyes. Then there was that strange incident two nights ago. He moved uneasily—remembering it.

He'd been asleep when a sound in his room startled him broad awake. In the darkness he couldn't see, and he'd lit a candle. Leah was standing silent and motionless in the middle of the floor, wearing a thin white nightgown, and a white veil bound around her head and falling down her shoulders beneath two long black braids.

She looked extraordinarily beautiful, and uncanny, standing there without moving, her wide-open eyes fixed to a point just above his head.

"What d'you want, Leah!" he had cried, feeling his flesh creep, and yet he had not been able to help staring at the lovely outline of her breasts and hips through the gown, and he realized that he had never called her by her first name before.

She had not answered. Her eyes lowered and fixed themselves on him with an expression of puzzled yearning, and her full red lips trembled. Then suddenly she turned and glided from the room, shutting the door which he jumped up and locked. She'd been sleepwalking, of course, but the whole business was disturbing. That had looked mighty like a bridal veil on her head, and one might laugh at the episode, except that there was a dignity about Leah which precluded laughter.

The next morning she had been much as usual, quiet and self-contained. Nat, that precious son of hers, had sat at breakfast watching his mother with the peculiar inscrutable look he often gave her. But to

Amos, Nat had been unusually amiable. Had actually asked for a job in the factory, which Amos had been glad to arrange. Nat was an intelligent man for all his grouchy silences, and he couldn't make much out of fishing, any more. So it was a natural enough request and Amos had started him right off in the stock room, where he caught on fast, the foreman said. Nat was sensible, anyway, Amos thought with approval, closing his mind to the thought of Leah. Thing to do was forget that episode, blot out the disturbing memory of her as a voluptuous woman, re-establish the old relationship when she had been merely Mrs. Cubby. My Lord, thought Amos, suddenly impatient with himself, the woman has a grown son, and the whole thing is ridiculous.

He heard approaching footsteps, at last, and put his chewed cigar back in his pocket.

The parlor door was flung wide and Susan bustled in carrying a tin tray loaded with the best tea set of creamy Liverpool ware. It had belonged to Roger's mother, Mary Ellis, and since her death had been kept in the china closet and used but a dozen times.

Hesper followed her mother, bearing Moses Honeywood's gilded Sèvres platter heaped with the flaky doughnuts Susan had been frying.

All this fuss for Mr. Porterman! The best tea cloth, the six rat-tail silver spoons, exhumed from their plush case in the attic, the last of the India tea. And indeed Susan could not have put into words the two reasons for doing Mr. Porterman extreme honor. The first was pride, Susan had never asked a favor in her life, this tea ceremony was for advance payment, propitiation, and self-respect. The other reason was maternal and not quite recognized. Mr. Porterman was now a wealthy widower.

As they seated themselves around the tea table, Susan darted her daughter a look of exasperation. The girl wouldn't talk, she was clumsy about passing the cups, her hands on the cream-colored ware looked large and red.

Amos quite shared her opinion. He thought Hesper unattractive. Her brown cashmere dress was shabby, a wisp of that unfortunate red hair had strayed from her net, and her feet—scuffed black brogans, size six at least, not from us—Harris & Sons "Boy's special," probably, he thought with distaste.

He brought his eyes quickly back to Susan. "Fine doughnuts, Mrs. Honeywood. Delicious tea." He was not much of a one for small talk but he was sorry for Mrs. Honeywood, who looked anxious, her fat cheeks as flushed as her daughter's were pale.

"Maybe you'd 've liked something stronger than tea, Mr. Porterman," said Susan, poking the doughnuts at him again with a nervous smile, "but the truth is I've nothing left but some cider that's worked too far. Seems funny for a tavern."

Amos accepted another doughnut which he did not want. "Yes ma'am, times're mighty hard."

Hesper, who had seen Amos' disapproving appraisal of her, suddenly turned her head. "Not for you shoemen," she said acidly, "and those who aren't fighting."

Her mother's nostrils flared, and she dropped the lid of the sugar bowl on the carpet. "Hesper!"

Amos flushed, he leaned over and picked up the lid. This was a completely unfair attack. He had responded lavishly to every patriotic appeal for funds, and none of the other shoe manufacturers had enlisted, nor were they desired to. "I have many government contracts to fulfill, Miss Honeywood. Our army needs shoes," he said with restrained anger.

Hesper murmured an apology and subsided, ashamed of herself. Ma wouldn't be catering to this man if she didn't have to. Lord, I wish *I* was a man, she thought. A dull misery weighted her stomach. She put the half-eaten doughnut on her plate. Ma and Mr. Porterman were talking.

Her eyes wandered to the east window of the parlor; through the looped lace curtains she could just catch a glimpse of the lighthouse and the ocean beyond. If I was a man I'd be out there, war or no war—I'd own my own schooner and skipper her myself. I'd wrest a living from the sea, the way Marbleheaders always used to, the way they were meant to from the beginning. Pa knew that though he hadn't practiced it. That was the way his "Memorabilia" began:

> Marblehead denizens ever must be
> Nurtured and soothed by their Mother, the Sea.

But I'm not a man, and I'm too old for foolish daydreams. Twenty-two. Day by day goes by and nothing changes, nothing but we get poorer—and the war. I guess I should read the Bible more. Get more comfort out of religion. If you really find God they say you don't hanker for anything else.

"Stop wool-gathering, Hes! Listen to Mr. Porterman."

Hesper came back with a jump. "Sorry, what did you say?"

Amos looked grimly patient. He had forgiven the girl's rudeness, for while he had been talking with the mother, he had glanced at Hesper's averted face and caught on it an unguarded expression of wistful unhappiness. But his mouth was set and his blue eyes were grave. For this was business, and of no great advantage to him either. To be sure, the war had taken the best factory hands, and he needed more, but unskilled women were a dubious asset.

"I was explaining to your mother that I'm putting in the new McKay machines, so we've mighty little work to give out at home any more. I might find some special orders for Mrs. Honeywood to hand-finish, but if you want a job, you'd best work in the factory. In the stitching room."

Certainly he had caught Hesper's attention at last, and she stared at him with horrified dismay.

She had never imagined factory work. That was only for foreign women who'd moved to Marblehead and settled in the new cottages the shoemen had built way up town on Reed's Hill.

Marblehead women who worked on shoes had always done it at home, stitching and binding the uppers while the men gathered sociably in the little backyard shoe shops to last and finish.

But the factory! She thought of the Porterman building on School Street, past the depot in the new part of town. A dingy four-story frame building. She'd passed it the other day and looked in the windows. It was dark inside except for the smoky flare of a few kerosene oil lamps. There was a rasping clatter and whir of machinery, and she had seen a couple of pasty-faced girls listlessly stepping on treadles. She had felt for them a pitying contempt, caged in there over twelve hours every day but Sunday. No air, no sun, and no freedom.

"I *couldn't* work in the factory, Mr. Porterman," she said very low, adding in a choked voice, "Ma—please. I didn't know we were as bad off as all that, I'll do anything else."

Amos was dumbfounded to see that the hazel eyes shimmered with tears, and that the strong, clear-boned face had crumpled into frightened appeal. Dammit, he thought, what *is* the matter with the girl? I can't stand tears. They all know that, damn 'em.

He rose hastily. "My dear young lady, don't distress yourself. I guess I can find work for you both to do at home. Report to my foreman Monday morning. Thanks for the tea, Mrs. Honeywood."

He got out as fast as possible and swung down Franklin Street in great exasperated strides. That girl acted as though working in his factory was tantamount to a jail sentence. If I hadn't been sorry for the mother I'd have washed my hands of them then and there. Snob, that's what that Hesper is, thinks she's too good to be a factory hand. Lot more aristocratic to run an Inn, I suppose—starving in a tumbledown old shack. "Shoemen," she said, the way you'd say "cockroaches." He gave an angry laugh. Of course that's a very lowly occupation compared to rolling around in the bilges with a lot of dead fish.

He plunged on up Washington Street and his annoyance cooled. Well, he'd give her a chance, never get any thanks for it, of course, but she'd see even a shoeman from Danvers could be generous.

Too bad about that Lem Peach, he thought. I didn't know he was dying of consumption. I'd 've been generous to him too, if he'd given me the chance. Cantankerous old loon. But you can't run a business like a Ladies' Aid picnic. I'll do what I can for those Honeywoods, but I'll not inflict my presence on that girl again.

As he passed the yellow clapboard Town House, Steve Hathaway, one of the selectmen, came down the steps, and bowed quite cordially. That had the effect of restoring Amos' equanimity. I'll lick this town yet, he thought, expand the factory, buy that ropewalk over by the shipyard. Be a selectman myself some day. You'll see. I'll make 'em accept me.

He started up Pleasant Street, intending to stop at the factory and then walk a couple of miles out the Salem road to inspect the house site he had bought for himself. But he changed his mind, and reversing his steps continued on Washington Street up to the Common, which the natives called Training Field Hill. On the grass in the center, several children rolled hoops, while others clustered around an old peddler who had spread a few cheap toys on a bandanna, and was hawking them in a hoarse, urgent voice. Amos paused to watch the children, his intent eyes softening. He noted one dirty little boy who gazed with yearning at a painted yellow monkey on a stick. Amos bought the monkey and presented it to the small boy, whose face lit with a cherubic smile.

Yes, thought Amos, pinching the small cheek, and turning towards a large house across the common, I want a youngster like that. I want someone to love.

He hesitated a moment on the sidewalk, then mounted three wooden steps to a white-painted and fan-lighted door. He rang the Trevercombe bell.

Charity herself opened the door in a flutter of ribbons and curls. "Oh, Mr. Porterman—this is a delightful surprise—" her little fingers curled around his big hand and clung.

She's glad to see me, at any rate, he thought, allowing himself to be led into the parlor. He accepted a second tea, since Charity insisted so prettily, and he leaned back comfortably watching her. Admiring her tiny red shoes and exquisite ankles, the rose-pink of her round cheeks;

listening to her tinkling chatter about the Bazaar at the Rechabite Hall next week, for our poor darling soldiers—"And, Mr. Porterman, I've crocheted some antimacassars and daisy tea cosies—you'll buy them, won't you? I'll be *so* provoked if you don't."

"What would a poor lone widower do with tea cosies?" said Amos smiling and accepting the opening. Yes, pretty soon maybe I'll ask her, he thought. Too soon yet—wouldn't look right.

He allowed Charity to flirt with him and enjoyed it, untroubled by callow doubts over her exact reactions. He knew himself to be attractive to women but if the girl was making up to him more on account of his possessions than himself, that was all right too. He'd had one love match and a dismal failure it had turned out. He longed for someone to cherish, but he no longer believed in the reality of romantic love. He looked now for a pretty, healthy woman to grace his home and give him children. Charity would probably do.

But no hurry, he thought, with a twinge of inner alarm. If she won't wait till I get ready, I'll find somebody else. Lots of pretty, well-bred girls in the world.

Charity, dimpling and cooing, unfolded her fancy work and laid it out for his inspection, at the same time shaking her lilac-scented curls almost in his face. He admired the fancy work, and compliantly touched the glossy hair—murmuring "Beautiful—"

She's a mite obvious, he thought, as Charity jumped away in blushing confusion, but I'll soon change all this flutter after the thing's settled. At least she's no ill-tempered redheaded gawk.

He left right after tea, and Charity watched him through the window as he swung down the hill headed for State Street, and that queer Leah Cubby's where he boarded. She felt very hopeful. Of course he wasn't just the husband she and her mother had dreamed of. But I'm twenty-two—she thought, suddenly frightened. So many beaux, always, and yet the years were passing, and somehow the right one hadn't shown up. I don't care if he is a "foreigner," and a lot of people don't like him. I'll make him take Ma and me traveling, Boston, New York. . . . I'd have a sealskin coat, and keep my own carriage. At the Rechabite Bazaar, she squared her chin, turning from the window—I'll make him commit himself. I can do it.

But Amos did not go to the Rechabite Bazaar, though he had promised to. He spent that night of the Bazaar back in Danvers, negotiating the sale of his tannery, a highly profitable transaction. And he forgot all about the Bazaar.

CHAPTER 7

THERE NOW BEGAN for Hesper a period of plodding and vacuous existence, undignified by anguish, unrelieved by expectancy.

Amos Porterman kept his word, and at some inconvenience to himself. He consulted with his foreman, Mr. Johnson, and arranged that the kid uppers for a certain fancy line of young girl's slippers should be cut at the factory as usual, then reserved for hand-stitching and binding at the Honeywoods.

Johnson naturally protested. "The new machines'll do 'em in half the time and better, sir."

Amos shrugged. "I know, but I've made the arrangements. And I want you to pay well—say a dollar a dozen."

Sam Johnson had come from Danvers with Amos, and he was devoted to his chief, but he protested vehemently. "That's terrible high pay—crazy I call it—grumblin' enough in the makin' room as it is—if the other hands learn—"

"They won't," Amos interrupted. "The Honeywoods are not the type to gab. Anyway I expect to get it back. Boscombe's on Tremont Street 'll take the stuff, I'm sure. We'll point out the advantages. Special jobs, custom made just like the old days. Their Beacon Hill clientele'll fall for that; we'll charge more and so can Boscombe's."

Johnson's face cleared a trifle. "I see, sir. But are these women skilled? Suppose they make a botch out of the work?"

Amos shrugged again, pulled a mass of orders to the front of his desk. "They maybe will at first. You'll have to show 'em. I'll leave it all to you, don't bother me about it." He picked up his pen and dipped it. "How's Nat Cubby getting on?"

Johnson frowned. "Well enough—" he said grudgingly. "Startin' to learn cuttin' now. But I don't know how it is, because I never see him open his trap, yet the men near him 're ever the worst grumblers. Old Schmitty, our master cutter, sassed me back t'other day. Never done such a thing in all these years. I docked his pay, o' course."

Amos was not interested. He nodded and signed another order. "Schmidt's maybe getting a mite old for his job, I wouldn't blame it on Nat. By the way, the Honeywood girl's to report Monday. Have the uppers ready."

The foreman grunted and went out muttering dolefully. More green hands, and Marbleheaders to boot. Mr. Porterman don't rightly appreciate how much trouble I got all the time here, he thought with sour pride. Wish we was back in Danvers, despite we're making money hand over fist.

When Hesper reported Monday morning Johnson duly gave out thirty-six pairs of uppers, and in the ensuing weeks found his worst fears justified. Half the work came back botched. The stitches were uneven, the tape bindings wavered and bulged. He had to scrap several pairs, send others back. To his angry, disgusted comments, each Monday morning when he inspected completed work and gave out new, the redheaded Honeywood girl answered almost nothing. She always stood just inside the door of the foreman's little office, holding the wicker basket full of uppers stiff-armed straight out in front of her until he took it and placed it on his desk. Her face flushed a dull red, while he pointed out mistakes; each time she said "I'm sorry—I'll do it over—" and nothing else. It was always her work that was criticized, Susan's hands obeyed her will. She had tried to help her daughter, but this Hesper, forcing her swollen pricked fingers to a task they abhorred, was ashamed to allow. Ma had more than plenty to do as it was, besides the house management and feeding them on three dollars a week, and home sewing too, turning and ripping and making their old clothes do. Even Roger was working now that they couldn't afford to feed "Looney." He had, as Susan expected, been bewildered and horrified at the idea of his women folk taking in piecework. Susan had shaken him out of his dim, enchanted country into the reality of their destitution by means of a bitter and violent scene, suggested he help out for once and outlined his duties.

Roger was moved, not by Susan's diatribe, but by an uneasy sense of guilt at the spectacle of Hesper, pale and silent, struggling with tough limp shoe leather. So he complied with his wife's orders, took over the care of the pig and the garden. The pig he frequently forgot, and his wife or daughter supplemented his spasmodic memory, but he discovered satisfaction in the raising of vegetables. The plot was small, but since it was part of his land and his kingdom he became attached to it, and was not unhappy.

Nor was Susan unhappy for she had plans and a definite goal. The war couldn't last forever. When it was over she would reopen the Inn, and to finance this she would request a loan from Mr. Porterman. Why not? she thought, she'd made a go of the Inn before and she could again, it would be a good investment for him, and having once asked a favor of him, it'd be easier.

But for Hesper's soul there was no nourishment more sustaining than pride and a mounting, hopeless longing for escape.

On the fourth Monday after the arrangement started, she delivered the completed batch of uppers to Mr. Johnson, and waited silently, as usual, for his verdict. He breathed hard as he sorted out twenty-one pairs and piled them in a box, then flung the remaining fifteen pairs in front of him on the desk. She fastened her eyes on a sign above his head that said in large black letters, "Employees are expected to be punctual. Those taking more than half an hour at noon will have their pay docked accordingly. A. Porterman."

"My dear young woman—" cried Johnson, slapping the fifteen pairs with the flat of his hand—"d'you really think I can send these off to Boscombe's with the others?"

Hesper dragged her eyes down from the sign. "Aren't they any better?" she said dully. "I tried."

The foreman shook his head. Time for plain speaking. Lord knows he'd been patient, like the chief said—but Mr. Porterman had also said, "I'll leave it up to you."

"These uppers ain't good for nothin' but to sell as seconds to the peddlers. They ain't worth two bits a dozen, that's what. Yore ma's 're okay, I guess, but I wouldn't be doin' my duty as overseer if I didn't point out these here uppers're a dead loss for Mr. Porterman."

The girl looked kind of white and puny, standing there leaning against the door, opening her mouth and then shutting it. Of course the chief could afford to lose a dollar or so a week, but it wasn't business and he hadn't said anything about charity. Ruining good goat skin, and the price of hides sky-high since the war.

"Look, young woman—you need *honest* money, don't you?"

Hesper shut her eyes. Failure, humiliation, beholden to that Porterman. Wny can't I go away? Find a job somewhere—anywhere—send money home. Run away—there must be something I can do.

"There's only one thing to do—" continued Johnson. "You can't get the hang of handwork, that's sure. Come into the factory. Any idiot can run the stitchin' machine."

Her face flushed geranium-red, and he saw that his choice of words had not been tactful. "You'd make more too—" he added. "Maybe fifty cents a day. That'd help out at home, now wouldn't it?"

He felt a trifle sorry for her. Sort of a fish out of water she was. Poor as dirt, obviously, but not like the few other Marblehead girls who'd come to the factory. More of a lady, and she didn't talk that thick hot-potato lingo. On the other hand she was worse-dressed than any of them, he thought, studying her. Same old brown knitted shawl she'd worn every time, not a ribbon or gew-gaw anywhere.

"Well?" he said impatiently, for she just stood there, staring down at a fine litter of leather shavings on the dusty floor. "You want to try the stitchin' room? There's a vacancy."

Hesper stirred and raised her head. "I might as well—" she said.

Susan received the news with approval, and quelled Roger's objections. Of course a Honeywood had never done such a thing, but no Honeywood had ever been so poor either. The girl was strong, could earn good money, and even Hes ought to be able to step on a treadle and slide a piece of leather around. Beside it wouldn't be forever, and it should liven her up—keep her from mooning around alone, reading and scribbling every chance she got.

The next morning at six, Hesper went into the factory. Through the uncertain dawn she walked the mile and a half from home and the waterfront to the new part of town and found herself one of a crowd of men and a few women, none of whom she recognized. In the business district which clustered around the depot, there were a dozen shoe factories and the hurrying stream of workers divided into rivulets at each door. Hesper joined the branch that trickled into Porterman's.

It was dark inside the narrow corridor, and Mr. Johnson stood beneath the flicker of a kerosene lamp, watching the hands sign the time sheet. He motioned Hesper aside while a hundred and twenty-four employees filed by, and disappeared down the dark hallway. Then he greeted Hesper without enthusiasm. "So you're here. I'll take you to your forelady. Mind you do exactly like she tells you and obey the rules."

"Yes," said Hesper.

"Stock room's in the basement—" explained Johnson hurriedly, "shippin' and soles on this floor, through that door. Cuttin', lastin', and finishin' upstairs. You go in here." He opened a door at the extreme end of the ill-lit hall and shoved Hesper ahead of him into a rectangular room furnished with a long table, ten sewing machines, and ten stools and one high three-legged chair. This was for the forelady, who rustled toward them.

The forelady had a quantity of brassy yellow hair, skewered to the back of her head with rhinestone-tipped hairpins. She wore paper arm cuffs, and a black taffeta apron. Her chilly smile disclosed a dazzle of bluish china teeth, and her gimlet eyes were puckered at the corners by sharp crows'-feet.

"Here's the new hand, Miss Simpkins—" said Johnson. "Name's Honeywood. Green as grass."

"Oh, indeed," said Miss Simpkins in refined accents. She came from Boston where she had made a precarious living as a seamstress, until driven by near starvation to the disgraceful plunge into factory work. "We'll soon, soon alter that, won't we, dear?" The china teeth flashed, and Hesper's heart sank. Inexperienced as she was, she saw that Miss Simpkins would be petty and tyrannical.

The nine other stitchers had raised their heads to watch the new arrival. Their ages ranged from fourteen to thirty and they all looked apathetic. As the door closed on Johnson and Miss Simpkins turned, the heads were all lowered again. The treadles rattled and hissed, the needles went plop, plop, plop as they plunged through the leather. The stitching room had two small north windows which looked out across School Street to the depot. The light was poor, and the women kept their heads bent close to the machines.

"Hang your shawl there—" snapped Miss Simpkins pointing to a wooden knob behind the door. "That apron won't do. You'll wear black bombazine like the others. Get one. Now read the rules out loud to me, I wish to be quite sure you understand them." She pointed to a placard between the windows, and stood behind Hesper, jerking the pyramid of brassy hair as the girl finished each sentence.

1. No talking except to forelady.
2. No loitering anywhere on the premises.
3. The female employees may not hold converse anywhere at any time with the male employees.
4. You may not absent yourself for more than five minutes.
5. You may not leave the stitching room at night until the day's quota has been checked out by the forelady.

"That clear?" said Miss Simpkins sharply.

"Yes," said Hesper with no particular interest.

"Yes, ma'am," said the forelady, scowling.

"Yes, ma'am." Hesper sat down on the vacant stool between an undersized girl who looked about fifteen and a stout woman of thirty.

She bent all her concentration to understanding the forelady's grudging and curt instructions. The process was not difficult, once you learned how to thread the needle, for the thread had a tendency to keep breaking. You stitched the tape binding along the inside of the top on the piece of leather, snipped the thread, turned it over and stitched the outside. The forelady walked back and forth behind the stools, pouncing and criticizing. Sometimes she sat in her own chair and sucked peppermint lozenges in an alert and disagreeable manner.

The hours wore by. Hesper's shoulders ached from hunching over the machine; she was too tall for the height of her stool. Her eyes blurred from constant watching of the needle in the dim light.

At twelve o'clock, the nooning bells jangled through all the factories. Amos had not put steam in yet, though he was planning to.

The women got off their stools and fetched brown paper parcels from a row on the floor under the shawls. Hesper had two codfish sandwiches in her pocket. She pulled them out and began to eat them. "Can't we talk now?" she said to the stout woman on her right.

The woman shook her head glancing at the forelady, who's head was bowed over her own lunch.

"Why not?" whispered Hesper.

The woman answered out of the corner of her mouth. "Old bitch's rules. She does what she likes in here."

"What could she do?"

"Dock your pay—fire you."

Miss Simpkins raised her head, peering in Hesper's direction. "If you're through eating, get back to work," she said.

"Why, I only stopped a few minutes ago," answered Hesper crisply. "The sign in Mr. Johnson's office says half an hour for lunch."

The forelady stood up, her lips drew tight over the china teeth. "You'll do as I say or out you go, miss. I run the stitching room."

Her fellow workers all stared at Hesper with mild interest, hopeful of a scene. The new girl was green all right—talking back to Simp. She'd soon learn—that is if she lasted out the day.

Hesper gave a small shrug, and pulled the waiting pile of uppers onto her machine. What was the use? She had expected nothing agreeable from factory work. I won't let the old bitch fire me, and I won't quit until I'm good and ready to, she thought. And underneath there was another thought. I'll show that Porterman. Turn out more uppers than anyone in the room, then tell him what I think of his precious factory. When I quit it won't be to Simpkins or Mr. Johnson—it'll be direct to him. For she had a confused picture of Amos jeering at her bungled handwork, with the foreman, but directing that she be paid anyway—out of charity, as Mr. Johnson had suggested—then of Amos' incredulous surprise when he heard she was working in the factory after all.

None of this picture was true. Amos had dismissed the matter of the Honeywoods after turning it over to his foreman; all his attention was centered on obtaining a better royalty basis for the lease of McKay machines, and for this purpose he had been on a business trip to Farmington, New Hampshire, to interview Gordon McKay. It was not until the middle of November that Hesper was recalled to his mind at all.

Once a month as a matter of policy, Amos made a tour of the factory. His walnut-veneer and snugly carpeted office was on the ground floor and had a separate entrance from the street, so that in general he saw little of the hands. That was Johnson's business. And he did an excellent job. Still, it seemed to please the workers and give them more incentive if the owner occasionally appeared, and Amos enjoyed the respectful bows and smiles which greeted him.

This November tour progressed even more pleasantly than usual since Amos had an agreeable announcement to make. On the Wednesday evening before Thanksgiving there would be free beer in the stock room. The news was greeted with subdued cheers—and the various sub-foremen expressed respectful thanks on behalf of their men.

Amos, attended by Mr. Johnson, reached the stitching room last. His visits were always unannounced, and for a moment after he opened the door nobody knew that he was standing there. Miss Simpkins had her back turned and was counting out the new batches of uppers, while the workers were all hunched over their machines. The treadles clattered and the cords hissed on the wheels.

Amos ran his eyes perfunctorily over the bowed heads, and was brought up short by an auburn one, bright against the dingy wooden wall behind. He was startled to feel a distinct and not unpleasant shock. Why, she's not bad-looking at all—he thought, staring at the bent profile. The low forehead, straight nose, and square chin were clear-cut as a cream medallion. What's she doing here? he thought, in the moment that Miss Simpkins turned with a little shriek of embarrassment —"Why, Mr. Porterman! This *is* an honor, I'm sure. Girls—girls—stand up!"

The stitchers braked their wheels with their hands and stood up. Hesper was taller than any of them. She tilted her chin, and gave Amos a long level stare, not quite insolent. He noted that under the heavy, almost black eyebrows, her eyes were not green as he had vaguely thought, but a brownish gold with a dark circle around the irises.

"All together now—" prompted Miss Simpkins. "Good morning, Mr. Porterman." There was an obedient chorus. Hesper said nothing.

Amos collected himself and bowed. "Good morning, ladies. Everything going all right?" Miss Simpkins rustled and nodded enthusiastically.

"You quite warm enough?" continued Amos, looking at the potbellied little stove in the corner. The room was not warm, for cold air seeped continually through the thin wooden walls and around the rickety window frames. He noted that Hesper and the other stitchers wore their shawls, and Miss Simpkins a gray knitted hug-me-tight. "I'll have more wood sent up—keep a good fire," he said.

Miss Simpkins rustled again. "So very kind and thoughtful. But our girls don't expect pampering, sir." She herself kept comfortable since she had moved her chair next the stove, and always sat with her feet on the ledge.

"Machines running all right?" continued Amos. "Don't hesitate to report any trouble." Moved by a sudden impulse he walked over to Hesper's machine. She stepped back, proud of the neat pile of bound uppers ticketed for delivery to the making room. Let him find fault with those—she thought watching him sardonically.

Miss Simpkins followed, divided between gratification that Mr. Porterman was spending so much time in here for once, and annoyance that he should choose that Honeywood girl's work for inspection.

But Amos' keen eyes did not see the uppers. He saw the girl's long shapely hand resting on her wheel, the tips of the fingers were red and rough.

"How do you like the work?" he said stiffly, feeling her hostility hit him in a palpable wave.

"It serves to earn *honest* money," she answered. "At least I don't make a froach of *these*."

He was puzzled, uncertain of the Marblehead word, and ignorant of the circumstances, which he intended immediately to find out from Johnson. He passed on and bent over someone else's machine for the look of the thing, murmured commendation, then suddenly remembered his announcement.

"There's to be free beer Wednesday night for the men—" he said smiling, "but as that will hardly suit you ladies, you may all go home early instead. You can leave at six." This was generosity indeed, and he accepted the ripple of gratitude with complacence. The other factories were all keeping the hands overtime on Wednesday to make up for the holiday next day. His eyes slid to Hesper, but her expression had not changed.

Ah yes—you're the grand Bashaw all right, aren't you! she thought, smirking and bowing and conferring favors when you feel like it. She watched him turn and leave—the massive back in the pearl-gray broadcloth suit, the fair wavy hair that shone like silver and augmented the impression of smug prosperity. I wonder how *he'd* like to work in here under Miss Simpkins.

By now she had learned the meaning of the forelady's rules. Miss Simpkins ran the stitching room like a reform school. It was impossible to go to the toilet without explanation, grudging permission sometimes withheld, and then timing. Five minutes by Miss Simpkins' silver-plated watch. There was a fine of a penny a minute for infraction. The ladies' W.C. was in the opposite end of the building in the basement behind a stock pile of tanned hides over which one usually had to clamber. Miss Simpkins' earnings were therefore supplemented by many pennies a day which she pocketed.

Rules numbers 2 and 3, "no loitering, and no converse with male employees" were thus redundant. The women had no opportunity to see the men, except for an occasional sniggering stock-room boy. In the morning when they checked in, Miss Simpkins stood beside Mr. Johnson until the last of her inmates had been herded to the stitching room, and at night rule number five turned out to mean that the stitchers were usually the last to leave the building at seven-thirty or eight o'clock—after a fourteen-hour day—while Miss Simpkins, who received a percentage of the output, and had scant interest in returning to her own bleak lodging on Reed Street, demanded one more batch completed.

Hesper had settled to dogged endurance. The work became automatic, and despite fines, she earned from two-fifty to three dollars a week, gratefully received by Susan, who allowed her to keep fifty cents for pocket money, sorry that the girl was working so hard and home only long enough to eat a bite of supper and fall into bed exhausted. But everyone was working hard; life *was* hard just now and no amount of pity would soften it.

Throughout that winter only one incident was vivified for Hesper by any emotion more compelling than endurance. This was a meeting with Nat Cubby.

It happened on a January evening, when Miss Simpkins had been routed by a blinding headache. Despite desperate efforts she had been unable to write out the day's work slip, and had turned it over to Hesper with the worst possible grace. She disliked Hesper, but she knew her to be the most intelligent and honest of the workers.

Hesper struggled on alone in the chilly, dark stitching room, tabulating Miss Simpkins' cramped figures, until after the church bells rang eight. Then she blew on her fingers, stamped her numb feet, and turning off the two kerosene lamps, went out into the dark corridor and dropped the work sheet into a slotted box which was nailed on Mr. Johnson's door, before signing out on the time sheet.

As she turned and wrapped her shawl tighter, and put on her mittens, a voice from the shadows said "Ahoy there—Fire-top!"

She jumped, and peering by aid of the one night lamp, perceived that the slight man in overalls was Nat Cubby.

"Hello—" she said, smiling a little. She had seen him at a distance and knew he worked in the cutting room, but in all these years since the night he acted so strangely and brought the slave-catcher to the Inn, she had not spoken to him. Now, however, she felt a faint pleasure. No matter his personal peculiarities he was a link with the past—with Johnnie.

"You're late too—" she said, glancing nervously around. But there was nobody to spy and report. Johnson had left some time ago, and the night watchman must be in some other part of the building.

Nat shrugged. "I've got my reasons. I like to keep an eye on things."

Hesper was puzzled, for it seemed to her that he glanced towards the closed door which led to Mr. Porterman's private office.

"Don't you miss the sea?" she asked, after a moment, beginning to walk down the hall. "This is a mighty different kind of life."

"More money," said Nat. "Besides I don't care to leave—home so much. I like to keep an eye on things." He repeated those words with a peculiar intonation.

Now what does he mean by that? she thought, sighing. The moment of pleasure at seeing him had passed. There had never been any real contact with Nat. It was time to hurry home, eat, get to bed. Her bones ached and she felt lightheaded and faint.

"Wait 'till I get my coat, I'll walk down-along with you," said Nat.

She assented indifferently. Anybody seeing them would be astonished to see her walking with a young man, she thought bitterly. But then Nat didn't seem like a "young man," really. And he was so ugly, poor soul, with that twist to his lip, and his yellow lynx eyes and skinniness.

They walked down Pleasant Street to Washington, their boots crunching over a light fall of snow.

"How's your ma?" she asked presently to make conversation.

Nat said nothing for so long that she thought he was not going to answer, then he muttered—"At least that bostard's out o' the house."

Hesper jerked around, staring at him. "D'you mean Mr. Porterman?" she asked with a startled laugh. "Isn't he boarding with you now?"

"No, he went to the Marblehead Hotel."

"But what made him leave?" persisted Hesper.

Nat jerked his head, shuffling his feet through the snow. "I don't rightly know. If I did—"

He had not raised his voice, but the last words grated with leashed violence. She stared at him again. His head was bent and he gazed down at the snow. Oh well, she thought, they had some kind of a row. It's no business of mine.

They walked silently along together until they passed the Town House, then Nat said suddenly—"Come home and see her for a minute. She'd be glad to see you."

Hesper, whose mind had been concentrated on getting to her own home and resting, took a moment to understand him. It's queer he never calls her "Ma," she thought.

"Oh no, Nat. I'm tired. I've got to get back."

He stopped and looked straight at Hesper. "She'll give you some supper with me." The yellow lamplight from an unshaded window fell on his face, and Hesper was again startled. The sardonic malevolence had softened into unmistakable appeal. Why, he isn't really dangerous or sinister, she thought. Maybe he's lonely. Johnnie said that once. "No use expectin' Nat to be like other folks because he isn't. But that's a mighty lonesome way to be." God knows I'm lonely too, she thought.

"I'll come for a little while, Nat."

He nodded, and she followed him down the narrow snowy sidewalk to the center of State Street, and between the carved wooden pilasters of the Cubby doorway.

Leah had been sitting in the parlor by the window, waiting. She came out in the hall to greet them, a sinuous figure in flowing black. Her soft hair was gathered into a loose knot at the back of her neck, and the hair shone like black satin against the duller black of her gown. Her red lips smiled their tender sleepy smile.

"You're so late—" she murmured to Nat, and her eyes slid past him to the door as if she looked for someone else.

Nat shut the door sharply. "Had to work late. I brought Hes Honeywood for supper."

"Welcome, I'm sure—" said Leah in vague greeting, scarcely looking at the girl. "It's all hotted up on the kitchen table." She walked ahead of them down the narrow hall to the kitchen, and Hesper noticed a whiff of spicy fragrance trailing after her. Sandalwood, thought the girl, identifying the perfume with a carved fan they had at home in the curio chest, and this puzzled her. Marblehead housewives did not perfume themselves, but then none of them looked like Leah either.

As they ate her discomfort grew. Leah's fishballs and Johnnycake were even lighter than Susan's. Her dried-apple pie had a delicious tang of lemon and fresh dairy butter, but Hesper's initial appetite dwindled.

Whatever impulse had caused Nat to want her there tonight seemed to have vanished. And she felt herself an intruder. Soon she had the disagreeable sensation of not being there at all, so tangible was their preoccupation with each other. Nothing very definite. Only once did Nat look at his mother, but during that brief glance his eyes held a hungry, brooding intentness—and Leah, meeting the glance obliquely, turned her head away and lowered her lids.

"It was cold out today—" said Hesper, nervously at random. "Maybe the harbor'll freeze over again."

Leah turned her dark head, seeming to come back from a great distance. "Why yes, it was cold out," she said. "Very cold."

Nat's body jerked upright from the table, his fork clattered on his plate. "You didn't go out! I told you not to!"

A tremor and a delicate flush passed over the lovely face. "Only to the wharf—" she said. "Just for some air—dear."

"Anywhere else?" He spoke with the same controlled violence Hesper had heard earlier. "You didn't go up Pleasant Street?"

There was a pause, and Hesper, uncomprehending, yet felt a swirl of dark emotions sweep like wind through the kitchen.

Leah shook her head. "I wouldn't do what you didn't want."

"You're not to leave the house unless I'm with you! If I can't be sure, you know what I must do."

Leah bowed her white neck, her dark eyes stared at the tablecloth. "Cruel—" she whispered, her lips barely moving—"Ah, Nat, let me go—" Her head bent lower, and then she added in a loud voice as though she spoke of someone else. "Let Leah go! She can be cruel too!" and she smiled a strange, secret smile.

Hesper felt a creep of primitive terror. She jumped up from the table, scraping her chair and stammering—"I must get back."

The two who had forgotten her turned their heads and looked at the girl. Leah emerged again from the fringes of that other scarlet-shadowed world into which she was being once more driven by the intolerable pain of longing and of shame.

She rose from the table, and held her hand out with so much naturalness that Hesper was abashed. "Good-bye—" Leah said. "It was kind of you to come. Nat and I are much—alone."

Nat had risen too, and moved close beside Leah. He did not touch her, and yet it seemed to Hesper that the two were meshed together by a mysterious bond, and that they stood alone together on the other side of a chasm looking across at her.

Oh, I wish I hadn't gone, Hesper thought, hurrying out into the cold. The moments in the Cubby kitchen held the eeriness of half-conscious fantasy—not devoid of pity or shock, but incomprehensible as a nightmare. The dark words and emotions, sliding past her furtively, only half apprehended. "You didn't go up Pleasant Street—" I shall forget the whole thing, she thought in sudden disgust. They have nothing to do with me. I needn't ever see them again—ever. And she hurried faster, beginning to run along the dim street.

Ahead of her she saw looming the outline of her home, dark in the wintry sky, though there was a light in the kitchen window. And her footsteps slowed. She stood in the darkness and looked out across the water. The black waves dappled with ice heaved and sighed amongst the rocks, and she felt for them a fascinated revulsion, continuance of the fear which she had denied. My life is like that—she thought with panic—back and forth like the waves, trapped here amongst the rocks, never really changing. She shivered but she did not know it. She stared into the blackness, and for the first time in years she had a vision of old Aunt 'Crese, long since dead. "Heartbreak, fire—the bitter taste of death. Three men—three kinds of love—always a hankering too hard. But at the end you'll know. . . ."

Hesper raised her arm in a savage gesture—and let it fall. "At the end—when there isn't even a beginning! God . . ." she whispered in prayer and in hatred. She turned and walked up the path and into the house.

CHAPTER 8

It was not until the June of 1866, when Hesper had at last achieved a sort of resignation towards what she believed to be her drab destiny, that she was suddenly released from it. But before release came there had been minor changes.

The year before, a month after Lee's surrender, Susan obtained the loan of a thousand dollars from Amos, who had asked no security but her written promise to pay. This was not from sentiment, though he was conscious of unusual warmth towards Mrs. Honeywood which he did not analyze. He thought the Inn was a good investment. In business matters he was usually right, and he was right in this.

The Hearth and Eagle reopened that August, and the taproom under Susan's competent management quickly regained most of its old standing.

And at the same time Hesper left the factory. In quitting she denied herself the scene with Mr. Porterman which she had pictured so pleasurably. Her mother's loan had squashed that indulgence. You couldn't be rude to a benefactor. So she informed only Miss Simpkins and Mr. Johnson who were equally indifferent. She had been a good stitcher but now that the war was over, there were plenty to replace her. Yet she did see Amos after all, for on her last Saturday as she went to collect her pay, Johnson told her she was to report to Mr. Porterman's office.

Hesper raised her eyebrows, and knocked on Amos's door. He rose from his mahogany roll-top desk as she entered, and said, "Good afternoon, Miss Honeywood," in a formal voice.

The office was large and comfortable. It was carpeted in red lozenges. The two armchairs were of mohair and walnut veneer, and there were three framed chromos hanging against the green and yellow roses of the wallpaper. The windows were draped in brown plush fringed with woolly brown balls and excluded much daylight. So the lamps were lit—

female draped figures made of plaster of Paris whose raised arms supported the frosted lamp globes.

He does himself well, Hesper thought, and said "Good afternoon."

Amos indicated a chair and sat down. He wasn't very sure why he had summoned her, nor did he know what to say, now that she was here.

"Johnson tells me you're leaving us—" he said abruptly. "Too bad, you've made quite a good record." He hadn't meant to strike that tone at all—condescending, owner to factory hand. But it was her own attitude that embarrassed him. Always remote, when it wasn't actually hostile.

"Yes. I'm going home to help Ma with the Inn," she said. "We're grateful for the loan." Her hazel eyes passed over his face and rested on a snow-scene paper weight on his desk.

"Purely a matter of business—" he said, more ungraciously than he meant to.

"Oh, I've no doubt of that—" she answered with faint sarcasm. "But thanks anyhow."

She wasn't as handsome as he had sometimes thought, and he had been very conscious of her during his inspections of the stitching room. She sat awkwardly in the armchair, she was too pale, and thin, her cheekbones and jaw too prominent. And yet, he couldn't take his eyes off her.

I didn't ask her here to be thanked, damn it, he thought, annoyed. He crossed his legs, and leaned back in the swivel chair. "Factory work wasn't as bad as you expected, was it!" he said on a hearty, rallying note.

Hesper turned her head. Her mouth curved. "Quite as bad," she said. "There's never been a moment of these ten months when I haven't loathed it."

Amos's chair squeaked stridently. He jumped to his feet, flushing—"My dear Miss Honeywood! What d'you mean by that! My factory's as well run as any in the country! I do a great deal for my hands. You can't say you haven't had fair treatment."

Hesper got up too. "I didn't mean to make you angry, Mr. Porterman. You asked me and I told you. It's doubtless that I'm not suited to the work." And not another word will I say. I'm quit of the place, thank heaven. I never thought he had such a sharp temper, he doesn't look it, being so fair and big. She waited coolly.

Amos controlled himself, ashamed that she had roused him to a disproportionate fury. She was under no compulsion to like his factory, yet for a second he had wanted to slap her.

"Good-bye—" she said, as he didn't speak. She smiled again. She had the strange and pleasant sensation of having the upper hand. I wonder if Charity knows how to manage him, she thought. Everyone knew that Charity and Mr. Porterman were keeping company, though there'd been no announcement.

"Well, good-bye," he said through stiff lips, suddenly wishing that she wouldn't go, that she would look at him with friendliness. "I daresay you'll be happier at home. I—" he had meant to give her a bonus, with a few cordial words of commendation. He had the five-dollar gold piece all ready in an envelope on his desk, but the gift was unthinkable now. "I may run down some day, and see how your mother's getting on—" he said. "Unless, of course, I'd be unwelcome."

"Oh no—Mr. Porterman. Ma'd admire to see you, I'm sure."

After she left, Amos sat on in his office, brooding. The girl disliked him, and he disliked her; at least she aroused in him feelings of embarrassment and inadequacy. Too trivial to think about except that her attitude seemed to typify the general one of Marblehead. He'd tried to be kind to her, as he'd been generous toward his adopted town. Both accepted his generosity, expressed tepid thanks, and continued to exclude him. Except Charity, of course. He slipped his bulbous gold watch out of his vest pocket. Due right now at the Trevercombes for supper. He'd be late again, and she'd be archly reproving—"Naughty man—working so hard at that horrid old factory—forgetting all about poor little Charity—" fluttering, tense and anxious underneath. Her mother too, watching—waiting as Charity was, for him really to declare himself. Poor little devil, he thought. I'll do it tonight. He had used respect for the memory of Lily Rose as long as he decently could.

He sighed and got up, going behind the fretwork screen to fetch his gloves and beaver hat. Well, at any rate, he thought, the Trevercombes would make him comfortable and give him a good supper, much better than the Marblehead Hotel.

He walked along School Street from his factory and crossed Pleasant Street, passing rival shoe factories, but none as big as his, he thought complacently, except Harris & Sons with their new plant on Elm Street, and he had every intention of surpassing them soon.

He turned down Washington and his pleasant thoughts were cut short by a dark shadow that moved behind a maple tree. He smothered an exclamation and stopped, but it was not a woman. It was only a trick of the waning light.

Besides, Leah had not been out of her house since January, he knew through the discreet inquiries he had had Johnson make. They said in the town she had had a recurrence of the madness she once suffered from, and her son was caring for her, as he had before.

But I didn't know she wasn't—wasn't normal—and even if I had— His face and neck grew hot, and he tried not to think of what had happened, but the scene took shape inexorably in his mind. This thing had happened before supper. He had come home early to attend to some personal correspondence, and Nat wasn't due for a couple of hours yet. He had been sitting at the table in his bedroom, when Leah walked in dressed again in that white nightgown, or whatever it was. He had jumped up—and suddenly before he knew what was happening, she had twined her arms around his neck, and was pressing the length of her body against him, murmuring "Love Leah—love Leah—you know you want to—" her head thrown back and her great dark eyes burning. He had felt her full breasts pressing against his chest, from the warmth of her body there rose a compelling perfume, and her face seemed to shimmer in a flame. And he had lost his head. There had been strange unreal moments, gilded with a bizarre beauty, and then he had returned to himself, appalled. He had shoved her away, shouting at her, telling her to hurry out of there lest Nat should come back. She had stared at him piteously, seeming not to understand—"Don't tell Nat—" she whispered. "You must never tell him, love—oh, you don't know . . ."

"No. No—" he'd said more gently. "We'll both forget this forever. I'll leave here in the morning, of course."

"Leave—?" she said in a small bewildered voice like a child. "You want to leave Leah, alone?"

"I must. Be reasonable. I can't stay now." He spoke very sharply, because he felt a quiver of fear. And he took her arm and led her across the threshold. She went quietly, but as she stood by the door of her own room, she raised her head and looked at him with a clouded and poignant yearning. "Leah'll be watching and waiting for you always—" she whispered.

She had stayed in her room the rest of that evening, locking her door, and not answering Nat when he knocked and tried to find out what was the matter. The two men ate their cold supper in silence, both conscious of faint, stifled sobbing upstairs from Leah's room. After supper Amos had made the bald announcement that he was leaving the next day, and had seen the lightning flash of relief in Nat's eyes. Nat might connect this with his mother's distress, but thank God he could guess nothing of what had happened.

The next morning, Leah had seemed to be her normal self again, though her motions and the few words she spoke were very slow, as though they proceeded from conscious effort. When his luggage was all piled in the van, the awkward moment of farewell had not been difficult. She had stood beside Nat in her doorway, and said "Good-bye" quite naturally, though her great dark eyes had not looked at Amos.

He had seen her but once since then, about a month later, when she had suddenly emerged from the shadow of a porch on Pleasant Street as he walked home from the factory. Her hands were outstretched toward him, her eyes alight, and there was a joyous beseeching smile on her lips. He had seen at once that she was in the other phase, the one in which she spoke of herself in the third person, in strange disassociation from the passionate and tortured beauty which possessed her. There were many passers-by on Pleasant Street, and he had been seized with a furious embarrassment. "Go home!" he shouted at her and turning his back had crossed to the other side of the street. He had not seen her again.

What else could I have done? thought Amos walking faster up the hill on Washington Street towards the Trevercombes. Her son knows how to take care of her. This damn town. Lots of them are queer, it seems to me. Inbred. Never leaving the place for as much as an hour. Moss-backs, die-hards, got to do everything the way their "grandsir" did it. Got to use words the rest of the world never heard of—show how exclusive they are, I guess. Planchment, grouty, froach, crimmy, gormy, clitch, cautch—lot of gibberish. Some of the old-timers you couldn't understand at all, and they were proud of it, he thought with sharpening irritation. He stumbled against an abutment of rocky ledge and looked down at his boots. Their sleek, polished blackness was gray with clinging dust. Look at that—wouldn't you think they'd pave their streets, at least! He entered Charity's house in a lowering mood.

Hesper slipped back quietly into her normal rôle of helping her mother at the Inn.

The Marblehead matrons said that she had settled down and become an excellent daughter. Usually this remark was directed in reproach at one of their Annies or Bessies who were sulking under parental discipline. Most of Hesper's own contemporaries had married long ago, except, of course, Charity.

Sometimes Hesper, urged by her mother, went to take a cup of tea with one of her married friends—Nellie Higgins who had married Willy Bowen, or Agatha Bray, now Mrs. Woodfin. From these expeditions she usually returned with a dull headache and a feeling of constriction around her heart. Marblehead had always been known for its fecundity, and the new young matrons rapidly contributed to the tradition. Hesper had to endure a good-natured patronage, and she was always called upon to admire a clutch of round-cheeked infants, trotted out in pinafores or swaddling clothes for the admiration of Miss Hesper. Now be good, dear, Miss Hessie won't eat you, she just loves babies.

Hesper increasingly avoided these visits. She helped her mother at the Inn, she did a little church work, she still occasionally wrote little verses in her Pansy Album, and once unsuccessfully submitted one of her poems to the *Atlantic,* then *Leslie's,* then *Godey's.* She did not try again.

She knew that nobody had the slightest expectation that she would ever marry. There weren't enough men to go around in Marblehead. Hesper had had a chance and been unlucky. Well, there were plenty of useful spinsters, and always room for more. Hesper consciously shared this view, but she suffered from strange unhappy dreams full of yearnings and unknown faces, from which she sometimes woke up crying.

The fifteenth of June was a beautiful day and a quiet one at the Inn. The fishing fleet lay off the Georges Banks for the summer fare, because now only a couple of the sturdiest old jiggers ventured as far as the Grand Banks. For the first time since before the war the town had tried to give its fleet the traditional sendoff. On the Monday morning of their departure each freshly painted schooner had sailed up and down the harbor, and the drone of chanteys from their decks competed with the spasmodic ringing of church bells and the honk of fish horns blown by excited small boys. Hesper and Susan had stolen time from the taproom to climb Fort Sewall and watch. But the celebration had rung hollow. Susan had shaken her head, sighing. "It isn't like before the war is it—Hes—and you should've seen it in my young days. The harbor so thick you could've walked across on the decks, an' the whole town dressed to kill and singing too. Those days there wasn't one of us but had a man on board, and we sent 'em off to man's work. It's a niminy-piminy business now with the dory fishing and the trawling and the seines."

Still, there were over a hundred men gone with the fleet, and the Inn was nearly empty. On this June day Hesper served fishballs and ale to two old sail-makers who had come over on business from Salem by dory, and to a seedy youngish drummer from Boston who was trying with little hope to interest the new Emporium in a line of ladies' cloth gaiters. He had wandered in to the Hearth and Eagle because someone had told him it was a cheap place to board. Seeing that Hesper was young he volunteered a few listless sallies. These small-town girls always expected to be sparked a bit by the traveling men. But as Hesper returned no answer at all, and served him in chill silence, he pushed back his pie plate, pulled out his gold-plated toothpick, and relapsed into nervous gloom.

Hesper stacked the dinner dishes and carried them into the kitchen where they clattered into the old stone sink.

"Have a care—" said Susan automatically. She was kneading bread in an enormous wooden bowl, and her stout freckled arms and one cheek were dabbed with flour. A gauze of flour dust swirled in the ray of June sunlight that fell across the sink, the scarred oak table, and the glossy wide-planked floor. A soft breeze fluttered through the open door and stirred a tiny cobweb high against the smoke-blackened summer beam. The kitchen sharpened to the scent of Atlantic salt and wild roses.

"It's a fine day," said Susan, plunging her fingers again into the viscous gray dough.

Hesper nodded. She pulled the wooden stopper from under the cleansed dishes. The dirty water gurgled through the pipe in the wall and dispersed itself on the grass beside the back step.

"Did you get 'em real clean?" asked Susan sharply. "I was mortified at that egg spot yesterday on Judge Salter's plate."

Hesper nodded again, not answering. She stacked the dried plates on a lower shelf of the oak dresser.

One of her black spells, thought Susan with annoyance and pity. "Go out an' help your pa in the garden, child, breath of air'll do you good."

The girl shook her head. "I've got to shred the cod and the potatoes aren't peeled yet. Besides I don't fancy fussing in the garden."

Susan's irritation flared. "Rather go back to stitching uppers at Porterman's I guess—" and she would have said more, but something in the dulled look of Hesper's face stopped her. "Never mind the garden," she said more gently. "It'll wait. And the fishcakes too. Get your shawl and go out for a walk. Over to the Neck, mebbe. You used to like that."

Hesper glanced toward the south window, toward the bare slopes and green tufted outline of the Neck. "I don't feel like it, Ma."

Susan looked again at her daughter, then she rolled pellets of dough from her fingers, wiped her hands on her apron. "Domnation—Hes! I'm not asking you how you feel, I'm telling you to go. Here's your shawl. Now scat. And don't come back 'till suppertime."

Hesper gave her mother a dreary little smile. I wish I never had to come back, she thought, but there was no actual urge or conviction. She took the shawl and went out the back door.

She wandered along Front Street glancing without interest into the open windows which ran along beside her at shoulder level. Blinds were never drawn in Marblehead, even at night. Old Gee Haw and Mrs. Bessom were sitting in their parlor entertaining the stylish young niece from Beverley. They nodded at Hesper, who nodded back, seeing in that one quick glance that the niece was very pretty and smartly dressed and her saucer-blue eyes held a coquettish assurance.

Hesper quickened her step and her gaze after that remained on the waterfront side with its string of docks, sail lofts, ship's chandleries, and boat yards. The smell of tar and oakum and paint mingled with the smell of roses across the way. Beside each house a meager plot sprawled over the cliff and flamed with lusty pink cabbage roses.

At the town dock, Hesper paused. The ferry was about to cross over to the Neck. Well, why not? It had been two years since she had gone there. "Budgeo" Watson the ferryman was a frequent customer at the Inn, and greeted her amiably. "Ye goin' over to Ham's far-rm fur yore ma?—Business is been mighty brisk terday. Took three furriners over this mar-rnin'. Young couple from Par-rtsmouth was goin' to board a week with Mor-rtin Ham. They was screechin' about how ro-mantic the Neck was. I liked to 've bust a gut laughin'." He chuckled and rested on his oars. "But they warn't the queerest. Was a paintin' feller went over too. Leastways said he was, when the young folk axed him. Had a tin box with him an' a package an' his vittles in a red kerchief. They axed him what he was goin' to paint, an he said, 'Anything worth the paintin'—' Just like that. Gruff an' grouty. An' then they kep' at him and axed where did he come from and he give 'em a smile sharp as a splittin' knife, an' said 'From here an' there along the coast.' That shet 'em up."

Budgeo chuckled again. "He warn't as gabby as most furriners," he said, approvingly. Hesper smiled, warmed by the sun. Budgeo pulled hard against the incoming tide. The wherry rocked gently. Except for a few dories the great harbor was empty. Far ahead of them in the South Channel, an East Indiaman sailed past, bound for Salem.

Budgeo tied up at the rickety Neck dock. Hesper jumped out.

"You goin' to walk back by the Beach or comin' home with me in about two hour?" asked Budgeo.

"I don't know," said Hesper, and with the voicing of it she was engulfed by the futility of this expedition. What use was it coming over to the Neck? What use to go to Castle Rock, or to look at the sea? She trudged up the path that led toward Martin Ham's farm, but before she reached it she branched off through scrub pine and sand, heading for the ocean on the other side. Her steps dragged. It was hot here in the middle of the Neck. Might go and look at the Churn, she thought listlessly, but even that mild excitement would be unavailable today. The wind and the tide were wrong. I might wade, she thought.

Behind Castle Rock there was a cove and a strip of shingle called Ballast Beach, because the ballast lighters often put in here to gather the heavy round stones. She scrambled down the bank and stood at the line of foam breathing deeply. It was just about here Johnnie and I landed that day war was declared, she thought, but it was only a faint, bitter memory. It was good to be alone with the ocean and the sun, and no living thing in sight except a square-rigger out beyond Halfway Rock.

Hesper stared through the dazzling blue at the Halfway Rock. The outgoing fishing fleet always tossed pennies at it with prayers for a full fare and a safe return. Fathoms deep in the blackness the ocean bed must be spangled with pennies, she thought. That might make a poem; indestructible pennies, indestructible wishes glinting through the darkness of time.

She sat down on a chunk of driftwood, wadding her brown merino skirt up under her, and thought about it. But there was no rhyme for wishes except fishes, which might be appropriate but not elegant, and none at all for pennies.

She sighed and gave it up. There was a small breeze but it was still hot. She took off her heavy shoes and darned cotton stockings, laying them carefully above high-water mark. She kilted her skirt up around her thighs, showing the hemstitching on her cambric drawers, and pulled the coarse net off her hair. Her loosened hair fell across her shoulders and down her back like a rippling red-gold shawl. It made her hotter than ever, but she had loosened it because of an earlier and happier memory of Johnnie. Twelve years ago when they were children they had sailed to the Neck one summer afternoon and gone wading like this. Now, when she felt the cold water on her feet and the salt breeze in her hair, it brought back a little of the magic of that earlier afternoon.

She waded deeper into the water, waiting for the slow waves to break around her ankles, running out as far as she dared, following the suck-back to sea, counting for the seventh or the eighth big one.

I should be ashamed at my age, she thought, playing silly games like this. Thank heaven there's nobody to know. She gave a quick guilty look around her and was transfixed by the sight of a man leaning against an abutment of Castle Rock staring in her direction and apparently sketching.

She clutched at her sodden skirts trying frantically to loosen them from under the belt where she had tucked the bunched hems.

She had forgotten the ocean behind her; the great wave swept up in its own rhythm and swirling at her knees knocked her down.

Her mouth and nose filled with choking green water, her fingers clawed at the shifting pebbles, and for a moment of gasping fear she felt the bottom drop away beneath her and the backwash suck her outward. Then her neck snapped back; even through her terror she felt sharp pain in her head, and then under her hands again the tumbling gritty shingle. Another yank at her head, reinforced by one at her waist, and she lay panting on the beach.

She lay raised on one elbow coughing and spitting out the sea water, while a hand thumped her forcefully between the shoulder blades.

In a moment she sat up and looked at her rescuer. Wet to the waist, his blue trousers plastered to his legs, he seemed very tall and thin. His dark, narrow face was tanned as any fisherman's. And he was looking down at her with an expression so new to her experience—a blend of speculative interest and amusement—that the shock of it counterbalanced the physical shock of her escape.

"Thank you—" she panted, still coughing. "I don't know how I could 've been so stupid, I'm bred to the water, but I didn't expect to see anyone—"

She pulled her wet skirts closer about her bare legs and blushed.

He nodded. "Lucky you've got so much hair. Handy to grab on to. It streamed through the water in back of you." He looked down at his hands. Several of her long bright hairs still clung to his wrists. He plucked them off, twisting them together, and frowning down at them. "Strange color. Hard to get," he said thoughtfully.

Hesper scrambled to her feet, hurt to encounter here again a taunt about her hair, and hurt too, by a sensation of anticlimax. He was young, and in an odd way attractive, he had just fished her out of the sea and probable drowning, now surely there should be drama of some sort. Or at least, gratitude and chivalrous declaimer.

She made another attempt. "You saved my life, sir. I don't know how to thank you. I'm Hesper Honeywood, I live in the town. If there's anything—"

"Yes, there is." He spoke decisively. "Stand right there as you are now, and let me sketch you. I'd started while you were paddling around in the water, but this is better. Now your clothes are wet I can see your body structure."

Again the color flamed to her face and anger with it, when suddenly he smiled and added, "You've a fine body. Good bones. You're really a beautiful woman."

Hesper felt her mouth fall open. She stared at him suspiciously. He was smiling but there was, surely, no mockery in the smile. Instead there was warmth and friendliness. He had short teeth, white as corn milk, dazzling against his dark skin. The smile vanished; he turned to the rock where he had laid his sketching things. The pad, the pencils, the square box. She noted with surprise, that though he must have run to rescue her, yet he must also have taken time to lay all these down first.

"Just look out to sea, toward that rock out there, turn towards me just a trifle," he called, assuming her consent. "Oh, and tuck your skirt up again, the way it was. I want your legs and feet."

"No!" she cried. "I'll not indeed." Otherwise standing as he wished her to. He shrugged and said nothing, picked up a long piece of charcoal and began to sketch.

She stood turned in profile to him, staring out toward Halfway Rock and two strong and conflicting emotions possessed her. It didn't occur to him that she was soaked through, and in need of warmth and rest after such an experience; on the other hand he was wet too, the sun was hot and he had saved her life. She thought of Budgeo the ferryman's reference to the artist feller, "Gruff and grouty." Well, he was that sure enough, but there was more. "Beautiful," he'd said. The syllables sang in her head like a melody. A beautiful woman. She held her shoulders back, raising her bosom proudly.

The sun dipped behind the trees on the Neck, purple and rose lights streaked across the ocean. The breeze freshened and she shivered. She turned her head and looked toward him appealingly.

She saw him nod and put down the pad. He walked toward her. "That was fine. You're a good model. You'll pose again tomorrow? I want to do a water color."

"Oh, I couldn't. I've work to do at home." She began to twist up her still damp hair, bundling it into the drab net. "Please to turn your back while I put on my shoes and stockings."

He gave a grunt of laughter, went back to the rock where he assembled his paraphernalia. When she was ready she joined him. "Can I see the picture?" He pulled back the cover and showed her the drawing. She stared at it, disappointed, and embarrassed. The figure of a woman, certainly, and all in curves, breasts, hips and swirling hair, but he'd drawn the sea in curves too so you could hardly tell the woman from the waves. And he'd drawn her with bare legs anyway.

"You don't like it?" he said flipping back the cover. But she saw that he had not the slightest interest in her opinion, and again she had the feeling of anticlimax.

"Well, I'll be going," she said dully. "Good-bye."

"Wait!"

She looked up at him and saw a change in his face. Up to now though he had been staring at her, and all the time he had been drawing her it was as though he had wrapped himself in a veil. The recognition had been oblique and at one remove. He smiled now again, that penetrating smile, and she felt herself become focused for him.

"Look, Hesper—" he said, putting his long brown hand on her arm, "Was that your name? Mine's Evan Redlake. Why—your sleeve's still wet. I'm a thoughtless beast. Here." He opened the red kerchief and took out a small flask of wine. "Drink some."

She obeyed, finding the red liquid nasty and sour. Ma'd never have served a wine like that in the taproom. He finished the bottle himself and threw it far out to sea. "Now come on—we'll run and warm you up." He flung his left arm around her waist and rushed her up the slope.

"Oh please—" she cried. "Let me go—" but he paid no attention, and the two of them pursued a headlong scramble over and around the sumach, the scrub pine, and the furry mullein stalks.

He stopped at last when they reached the ferry path. And Hesper found herself laughing, her cheeks hot, her heart pounding, and yielding to that pressure around her waist, the first intimate masculine touch—since Johnnie.

"Now you've come to life," said Evan. He took his hand from her waist and pressing it behind her head kissed her deliberately on the mouth.

Hesper gasped. She raised her fists and gave him a violent reflex shove on the chest. But he had already released her, and the shove was meaningless.

"Ungraceful," he observed. "Hesper, you need teaching. You have beauty and strength and probably passion, but you don't know it, or at least you don't act it. Hold your head up and stop slouching. How old are you anyway?"

"Twenty-four," she said sulkily, turning her back on him and beginning to walk down the path. Stinging tears filled her eyes. He walked along beside her swinging his red kerchief and the tin box.

"Then you're a grown woman," he said, "and should act like one."

"You're not the one to teach me," she said, quickening her step. Evan did not answer. They walked in silence until they reached the top of the harbor slope.

"Would you know—" said Evan suddenly, "of any place in town I could board for a few days? Marblehead suits me well."

Yes, thought Hesper with violence. He can go to Martin Ham's or the Marblehead Hotel or to Mrs. Cap'n Barney's at Redstone Cove. Far away as possible.

"Hesper—" he said softly, and again he put a detaining hand on her arm. Through her sleeve she felt its warmth and she looked down at it quickly, sidewise.

"We keep an inn," she said, her eyes on the row of houses across the harbor. "Likely Ma'd find room for you."

"Good," he said.

CHAPTER 9

EVAN REDLAKE was born in Amherst in 1838. His parents were well to do. His father, Thaddeus Redlake, owned a small paper mill on the north branch of the Fort River, and the Redlakes lived on College Avenue in a new and comfortable yellow frame building adorned with elegant white pilasters and a mansard roof topped by a white-railinged "captain's walk." This feature had no functional purpose on a house in a small inland town, but Mrs. Redlake had been a New Bedford girl, and strongly attached to her home. She was a woman of decided views on all subjects, and five of her six children had been impressed by a formidable stamping iron. The four girls and young Simon yielded without undue rebellion to the maternal pressure.

The girls were accomplished and demure. Mary played the pianoforte while Bessie sang plaintive ballads in a small fluting voice, Lucy was skilled at hair embroidery, and Harriet painted charming woodland scenes upon china. Mrs. Redlake herself had a talent for water colors, the faithful petal-by-petal reproduction of floral arrangements, and the Redlake artistic causeries accompanied by light wine and cakes were an esteemed feature of Amherst life.

Evan, however, had never taken part in the artistic causeries. This was all the more disappointing to Mrs. Redlake, since he appeared to show marked interest in drawing from the moment he could hold a pencil.

His mother encouraged him and set herself to giving him drawing lessons. These were a failure. Evan would not make a delicate shading chart. Evan would not copy the elaborate designs presented in *Mrs. Stebbins' First Steps in Art.*

In fact, as long as his mother insisted on the bi-weekly drawing lessons, and sat purposefully across the table loaded with pencils, water colors, and sheets of paper, Evan would not draw at all. He was not sulky or verbally resistant—those traits Mrs. Redlake could have handled with dispatch—he simply fixed upon his mother the candid stare of polite boredom and waited until she had finished.

"But, Evan, you like to draw, look at all those pretty little pictures you did of kitty. Of course they didn't look much like kitty because you have a lot to learn, but they were very good for a little boy."

"They weren't supposed to be kitty," said Evan calmly. "They were what a cat makes me think of, and they weren't no good at all."

"Any good," said Mrs. Redlake. "Well, my dear, I see what you mean, that's quite a deep thought, and that's what I try to do myself, see the inner truth of objects; all artists do, I guess—"

Here she smiled companionably at Evan, but his eyes had wandered, they rested on the rustling green elm branch across the window. His expression was one of complete and unselfconscious detachment.

"Evan!" Her voice was sharp, and he brought his gaze back. He had long dark eyes; the lids were heavy and gave him at times an oddly un-Anglo-Saxon look disconcerting to Mrs. Redlake. None of the other children had it, nor the curved mouth suggesting a sensuous softness that his square and jutting chin denied. She reassured herself by attributing these features to the Welsh blood in her own family.

"Evan, I insist that you start shading that square at once. Start here, very faint, in the upper corner."

Evan allowed the pencil to be put in his hand and made a few inept scrabbling marks.

"Pay attention, you're not keeping in the lines. Evan! You can do better than that. Stop that stupid messing. I shall have to punish you."

Evan put down the pencil, folded his flexible little hands together, and waited. His gaze wandered back to the elm branch.

In this and all other matters in which her will ran counter to Evan's Mrs. Redlake suffered defeat. Gradually as he grew through adolescence into manhood, she resigned herself and took outward pride in his nonconformity. "He's quite a mystery to us, I must admit. He seems to have no interest in the usual boyhood pursuits. Of course he has inherited my own interest in art, but he does nothing about it. It's quite tiresome."

Nor did Thaddeus understand his son, but he was a calm man, unburdened by subtlety. The girls were marrying well, one to an Amherst Classic professor, another to a Boston merchant.

The younger ones had plenty of beaux; Simon the baby was as normal a boy as a father could wish, in and out of trivial scrapes and already intelligent about the workings of the paper mill. If Evan was a disappointment with his long silences, his disappearances for days at a time when he apparently did nothing more sinister than take solitary walking trips, his absolute refusal to attend college—well, at least the boy gave no trouble, and it might be worse.

In 1857, when he was nineteen, Evan left home for good. He announced his decision one morning at the breakfast table, and he prefaced it by his rare and attractive smile.

"I've had enough of Amherst," he said. "It's too pretty. You'll not be sorry to have me go, Mother. I know I've been a trial to you."

To Mrs. Redlake's indignant protests he listened with his polite air of detachment and he looked at her not unkindly.

"But what are you aiming to do, Evan?" asked his father.

Evan lavishly buttered a slab of fried johnnycake. "I shall paint." He bit into the johnnycake and chewed it lingeringly, savoring the buttery crispness. His mother watching him knew a familiar annoyance. He always seemed to capture a sharp, almost sensual pleasure from eating.

And from other bodily sensations too. Sometimes he would lie for hours in the one stationary bathtub, floating dreamily in the tepid water, selfishly excluding all who wished to enter the bathroom. And he had a really indecent passion for odors. Once she had found on his pillow a decaying fungus edged with blue mold, and to her outraged question he had answered that he liked to smell it because it had a sharp gray clean smell.

"You can't support yourself with painting, my boy," said his father heavily. "And what makes you think you can? You've done no drawing for years."

"I know I can," said Evan placidly munching. His bright dark eyes turned to his mother and away quickly. He thought of the shack in the woods a hundred feet from the bank of the Connecticut. He had built the shack himself when he was twelve, and here he had lived his real life. The walls were papered with drawings, in pencil, in charcoal, and lately, though most of them fed the fire in the small smoky fireplace, there had been water colors of the rocks and the chestnut trees along the riverbank. And now he was sick of the shack, and the trees and the river. They had served their purpose.

"I mean to travel," he said. "And I mean to paint." He buttered another piece of johnnycake, poured maple syrup over it.

"And how will you eat?" snapped his mother. "You like to eat, you know."

Evan inclined his head. "I do. If Father will lend me or give me some money, I'll be delighted. If he doesn't, I'll manage."

In the end Evan's father gave him twelve hundred dollars and the confidential information that the paper mill was not doing so well, "and I'd be hard put to it to find more money for you, Evan. But I must say you've never been a trouble to me and if you're set on going out into the world . . ." He sighed. But Evan's desire was in the best Yankee tradition, and there were no particular objections.

So Evan set out on his wanderings. He had no regrets and no special goal. He had one consuming interest, and that was a search for the best ways to express the essence of sensation, the moment of rightness when harmonious thrilling of the nerves heightened his sensitive perceptions. This harmonious thrill sped to him along the paths of taste or touch or smell. These however led to a dead end, and there was no way of capturing or reproducing the essence. Nor, for him, did the gate of release lie beyond sound, as he had no instinctive understanding of music. He had, therefore, never doubted his medium, nor until he reached New York had he had any doubts about technique, or seen the work of other artists.

He rented a small room off Broadway and haunted the exhibitions, the auction sales, and the National Academy, and he found very little to admire. He disliked the sugary romanzas of the landscape painters. Had any of them ever really *seen* a tree or a rock? He was bored by the tedious competency, or the flat prettiness of the historical painters, and the portraits of pretty women and wealthy merchants displeased him most of all. Flabby, he thought contemptuously, tea-and-toast painters.

But he was disquieted all the same and much as he disliked the treatment and subjects of the paintings the public admired, he was forced to admit that the artists showed a knowledge of technique of which he was entirely ignorant.

Throughout the winter Evan attended a night class at the Academy. In this class he caused never a ripple. The teacher found him attentive and competent enough at following instructions, but he also thought him lazy, since Evan produced nothing for criticism if he could possibly avoid it. In those sketches he did turn in, the teacher invariably pointed out a lack of fidelity to the subject, an element of exaggeration and lack of discipline.

Evan would compress his mouth and his eyes would take on the glaze of boredom which he had used to combat his mother. But he was not happy, and inevitably since he saw neither life nor painting in the way the others did, he was lonely.

The following June he had had enough. He shipped as steward on an old windjammer bound for Martinique and in that island for a while found delight and release.

He had always known himself appealing to women, but until his visit to the West Indies he had been too fiercely concentrated on realizing his ambition to be interested. In Fort-de-France he fell in love with a lush Creole dancer named Tini, and she, being flattered by the sketches he made of her, and responsive to his assured and imaginative love-making, soon established him in a room of her pink stucco villa.

During their association he broadened and became a man and they pleased each other. To be sure Tini was often disconcerted that he never showed the faintest jealousy.

"If you want someone else, Tini—" he would say, and use her own frequent phrase, "*Vas-y, ma petite*. You take nothing from me in sharing yourself with others."

Then Tini would storm and cry, reminded again that he loved her only as a vehicle for his own twofold release, that of his body and of his art. And it took her a long time to realize that he had lost interest in her, since search as she might she could discover no other woman. But his love-making gradually became perfunctory, and as for his painting he ceased using her as a model. Instead, to her acute boredom, he drew squalid street scenes, bougainvillea or palm trees which bore scant resemblance to the originals, and he spent hours squatting on the filthy docks painting the Negro conch divers and stevedores.

In the fall of 1860 they parted amicably; Tini established herself with a rich planter and Evan returned to New York. He had a portfolio filled with water colors, and a desire at last for recognition. For recompense too. His money was nearly gone.

Evan retired again to a room on Broadway and considered the situation. If he were to attract any attention he must exhibit, preferably an oil. He leafed through his sketches and chose one of two naked Negro children sprawling on a beach; this he enlarged and reproduced in oils. He painted directly onto the canvas without underpainting or glaze, and he painted as he had seen, in vivid tonal masses, eliminating all details, and flooding the beach, the palms, and the brown bodies in a harsh tropical glare.

When he had finished he knew that it was good, and he sent it to the Academy with perfect confidence. It was promptly rejected. Evan was first stunned and then angry. He brushed his one good suit, clipped his waving dark hair which had grown too long in the tropics, and went straight to the Academy.

Here he encountered two members of the jury and some very unpleasant criticism. They remembered the entry well, and thought it was against policy to explain a rejection; both gentlemen were annoyed by Evan's truculence, and they enlightened him without mercy.

"One would have thought that canvas the work of a child, Mr. Redlake. Except that fortunately no child would choose to portray so ugly and unrefined a subject. Nudity where it has place at all can only be excused by classic beauty. Besides, the canvas shows no evidence of composition, and the coloring is beyond belief raw and crude."

"Have you ever been to Martinique, sir?" asked Evan.

"I suggest, Mr. Redlake," said the gentleman with an exasperated side glance to his confrère, "that you give up this odious dabbling in an art that you are quite unfitted for. You're young, we all make mistakes."

Evan bowed, picked up his shabby hat, turned on his heel, and went out. Fury sustained him on the walk back to his dismal room. But when he had locked his door, he threw himself on his cot and found that his heart was pounding, his mouth dry, and that there was a pricking at the base of his nose and under his eyelids.

He lay on the cot until the rumble of drays and the clop-clop of carriage horses thinned to silence on the street, and the wavering light of the gas lamp outside the window faded into dawn.

Then he got up and opened a dusty flask of Chianti which he had been saving. While he drank and munched on a stale baker's roll, he stared at the canvas "Martinique."

After a while he got up and turned the canvas to the wall. He opened his carpet bag, rummaged under a pile of dirty socks, and fished out a cardboard box. He opened it and counted his money. Thirty-two dollars. He stuffed it back in the carpet bag, went to a book seller's and bought magazines which he studied intently. Then he picked up pencil and drawing block and walked up to Central Park.

He went past the Mall toward the Refectory and sat down under a rustic arbor to wait. Very soon he was rewarded. Two pretty young school misses approached from the Sixty-fifth Street entrance. They were stylishly dressed, one in mauve, one in bottle green barège. Their hoops swayed above their small kid slippers, they held identical round seal muffs against their waists like small shields, and their steps were at once mincing and provocative.

Evan jumped up and accosted them, smiling. Would they pose right there under the arbor for just an instant? He was courteous and determined. They recognized in his voice the unmistakable accents of education, and after the requisite amount of blushing, giggling, and protest they did as he wished, whispering to each other that he looked romantic but awfully shabby, poor thing, and deciding that while this would be a wonderful tale to tell the other girls, it need not be mentioned to Mama.

Evan kept them there rather longer than was exciting, but they were delighted with the result. He had made them as pretty as the fashion-plate ladies in *Godey's* by conferring a chiseled piquancy on their noses, cupid's bows on their pouting lips, and greater luxuriance to their flowing ringlets. "Capital," they cried, "utterly charming. How talented you are, sir! But what is that we have in our hands?" For Evan had eliminated the muffs.

"Croquet mallets I think," said Evan politely. "Don't you play croquet? Or maybe it's a shepherdess' crook. Not sure yet."

They giggled again and plied him with questions but Evan had lost interest. He thanked them and departed, leaving them to cast disappointed glances at his retreating back.

Once again in his room he made two finished drawings from the sketch. The first one was of the young ladies holding croquet mallets delicately balanced in tapering fingers and behind them the piazzas and porticos of a shore hotel. Underneath in flowing script he wrote "Summer Pastime."

Then he did the young ladies all over again substituting ribbons in their hair for the pork-pie hats, removing the hoops, shortening the skirts a trifle, and sketching in crooks, showers of roses, and a distant sheep, the latter copied from a farmers' almanac he had bought.

This one he titled "Yankee Pastoral." He worked on the sketches two days, achieving a glossy neatness in every line. When he had finished he stared at them with loathing, mixed however with a bitter triumph.

The next morning he braved his first editorial offices. *Godey's Lady's Book* took the shepherdesses, and *Hearthside* the croquet.

He was now the richer by twenty-five dollars. Throughout the early spring he produced and sold a drawing a week for these markets.

Then in April war was declared. Evan, whose knowledge of Negroes was confined to those in Martinique, was not kindled by the cause of abolition, nor by any deep regional patriotism. But he did feel a compulsive curiosity. In his grate he burned all the lady's magazines and all the sketches of pretty girls. He stored his Martinique water colors with his landlady and volunteered.

During the war he was promoted to a lieutenancy, and was slightly wounded at the Battle of Shiloh. The sights and sounds and smells of war excited him at first and he reproduced many in his sketch book. Later they disgusted him and he began to long for the strength and serenity of nature; particularly he longed for the sea. After Shiloh, he saw no fighting and the constant pressure of many men about him rasped on his nerves. He made a few friends, but when peace came at last, he found that he cared little about them. He paid a brief and unsatisfactory visit to his parents and returned to New York. It was then that he painted his one battle picture. A startling conception of two privates in torn and bloodied uniforms, one Confederate and one Union, fishing amicably together on the ruins of a bridge.

This painting had force and fidelity, the faces were clearly drawn, and the subject was sentimentally apt to the first reactions of peace.

He sent it to the Academy and it was accepted by a jury who knew nothing of his earlier rejection. Its subject caused a mild flurry and some public approval. The critics were not impressed. They scolded him in terms with which he was to become increasingly familiar. "Garish use of color," "lack of taste in selection," "incomprehensible distortion."

But the picture was bought by an art collector, a quiet French Jew called Durand who paid Evan's price of five hundred dollars without protest, saying only, "I like the way you paint, my young friend. You have a new vision. Do not let them discourage you."

"I don't," said Evan, who banked most of the money and set out up the New England coast, sketching as he went. The Long Island Sound and later the flat sandy coast below Boston did not greatly appeal to him.

He sought for a more rugged sea, for turbulence and grandeur; for bleakness too, an outer severity enclosing a subtlety of emotion more seductive, because more elusive, than the sea scapes he had attempted in Martinique.

He knew at once upon his arrival in Marblehead that he was approaching his object. And from his first glimpse of Hesper playing in the waves, he had seen that she might interpret it. He had felt on their first afternoon no particular wish to make love to her; indeed, since she so obviously insisted on eliciting the personal, like all women, he had been somewhat repelled. And in her ugly clothes, with her rich hair hidden, a clumsy self-consciousness enveloped her. The Lorelei of the rocks and ocean vanished. However, the insight which never failed him on any subject connected with his art showed him that to win back his first vision he must, however reluctantly, give her something of himself.

His brain, that first night at the Hearth and Eagle, teemed with pictures. He saw the thick, shimmering green of the advancing wave and Hesper's body flattened beneath it. He saw her standing sturdily on the beach, her shoulders drooped a little, her head uplifted while she seemed to search the horizon with the age-long patience of the fisher wives. Someday he would interpret the sea in itself alone without human accent, but not yet. He lay in the yellow bedroom of the new wing at the Inn, sleepless because of a rich excitement.

Hesper, too, could not sleep. She relived each moment of their afternoon, and each section was informed with strong emotion. Fear, relief, pleasure, mortification. But at least they *were* emotions, better, even the worse ones, than the aridity of these last years.

He had indicated that he would stay some time at the Inn if Hesper posed for him, and he had vanquished Susan's strenuous objections by the same imperviousness which had daunted his own forceful mother. He had also found an unexpected ally in Roger.

"Let the girl go, my dear. The fresh air'll do her good, and you can get somebody to help out in the taproom."

Hesper had seen at once that Roger liked Evan. He had hailed him as a fellow creative artist. After supper, and Evan had not failed to praise the fishcakes and gingerbread, Roger had even fetched the ink-stained pages of the "Memorabilia" from his study and shyly read passages aloud.

The verses celebrating the launching of the ship *Desire* in 1636 and the tragic attendant accident to Mark, the first Honeywood.

Evan had listened, and made appreciative comments, but Hesper, watching him covertly as she moved around the kitchen putting away the supper dishes, had wondered if he were bored.

His slanting heavy lids had fallen across his eyes, hiding their brightness, his narrow face, turned to the older man in the Windsor chair, held a sleepy look.

But as the summer days went by, and each afternoon Hesper posed for him by Castle Rock, she discovered that she could seldom read Evan's inner feelings from his face. There was but one expression of which she could be sure, the one she came to call the "painting look." In this his dark eyes burned with a cold concentration, his mouth thinned and became immobile; and for hours at a time he saw and heard nothing that was not relevant to the canvas on his easel.

He was sketching her in oils now, and she understood the results no better than the original drawing, but during those afternoons she was happy, because once the light changed he stopped painting, and on the walks across the Neck back to the landing he became hers. He talked little about himself, because the subject of his past life or experiences did not interest him. Nor did he talk about his future, for of its general pattern he had no doubt. But he asked her many questions and soon knew the scanty facts of her own life. These did not interest him either, but she found that her background and surroundings did. He enjoyed every bit of Marblehead folklore she could tell him. He listened avidly to Roger's tales of the old house and eight generations of Honeywoods, and he pumped Susan for legends of the sea and fisher folk.

"I don't see what you like about that old stuff," said Hesper one day, as they walked back across the Neck. "It's so silly and all past."

Evan gave her remark unusual attention. "Because—" he said thoughtfully, "it makes a richness. I need it to get the painting right."

"Oh," she said. "The painting." And what about me? she thought. I'm in the painting too. A pain went through her heart, and the contentment vanished. Since the first day he had not tried to kiss her again. At first she had been wary, on the defensive. Then relieved. Now the relief had gone too, leaving dissatisfaction.

Evan gave her a quick look. "Sit down a minute." He pointed to a pine log.

She hesitated, though to this new gentle tone she responded with a secret hope. "Tide'll soon be running out," she said. "It'll be harder rowing." After the first day Evan had hired a skiff, and they rowed themselves back and forth across the harbor.

Evan ignored this remark and drew her down beside him on the pine log. He put his arm around her and after a moment she leaned her head against his shoulder.

He felt her tremble and looked down at the radiant head against his faded blue shirt. Her hair shone like tiny copper wires, and it smelled of the sea mist.

"Why are you discontented, Hesper?" he said.

She stirred uneasily. That was not what she hoped to hear. "I hate Marblehead," she said. "Hate it." Though until that moment she had not realized this.

"But why? You're part of it and it of you. That old house of yours and the sea and the rocks, you're woven into them. You belong to them."

"I don't," she snapped. "Just because Phebe and Mark Honeywood happened to settle here two hundred and whatever years ago. What's that got to do with me?"

"It makes a quite beautiful pattern," he said after a moment.

"Well I don't think it makes any pattern at all. And I don't see why you think so. You left your own birthplace."

"True. But I wasn't rooted there. Mother came from New Bedford, and my father from Pennsylvania. Besides, I'm cut out to be a wanderer."

She felt the warning in his stress on the last word, and she straightened her shoulders, drawing away from him.

"Like all men—" she said coldly. "Marbleheaders wander as much as anybody. Not only to the Banks and further, but let anyone blow a bugle or wave a flag and off they rush to war." She moved still further from him, thinking of Johnnie, and the dull old pain merged to this present aching.

Evan laughed. "You're hard on the men. It takes both to make full life. The rushing out, and the coming back to something steady and warm and sure that's been waiting."

She turned her head and looked up at him. "Is that what you want, Evan?"

Her soft question startled him, and the sudden clear beauty of her upturned face white against the fronds of her burning hair.

"Sometimes," he said below his breath. She lifted her open hands to him in a small submissive gesture. It moved him to compunction and pierced his guard. He pulled her to him again and kissed her. Soon he was astonished to feel the depths of passion which her response began to stir in him. The thick cream whiteness of her skin through the loosened bodice, the pulsing hollows at the base of her neck intoxicated him, yet even as he kissed her and savored the faint aromatic perfume of her skin, the watcher within made note. The shadows of her flesh were not violet as he had thought, they were bistre, and in her eyes upraised to his in half-frightened appeal, the moss-green irises were speckled with brown.

"Ah, Evan I love you—" she whispered and at her own words, breath strangled in her throat. She shook her head and pushed him away, not clumsily as she had the first day, but with a decision that surprised him. She got up off the log and looked down at him.

"What is it, Hesper?" He stood up at once.

"When you've finished the pictures of me—" she said, "what then?"

His face darkened. He reached an impatient hand to an overhanging pine branch and snapped it off. He ran his fingers down the sharp needles.

"When I've done what I want in Marblehead, I'll leave, no doubt."

She swallowed, gazing at his shut, averted face. The thin jutting nose, the long chin, the full lips curved in now on themselves.

She picked up the wicker basket and started silently down the path. After a moment in which he watched her retreating figure, he loaded himself with his paraphernalia and followed her.

When he reached the boat, she was already seated on the center thwart, her hands on the oars. Neither of them spoke as she rowed across the harbor.

She landed them in Lovis Cove by Thatcher's Sail Loft, and as they walked down the wharf one behind the other she was vaguely aware of two men standing in the doorway of Thatcher's building. As she passed one of them stepped forward and said, " 'Evening, Miss Honeywood."

Hesper started and blinked, collecting herself. Amos Porterman, gravely bowing, his keen blue eyes startled and disapproving as they glanced at Evan and back to Hesper.

" 'Evening, Mr. Porterman," she said, and would have passed on, but Amos did not step aside. He continued to stand, large and immovable in the path. Hesper was forced to introduce Evan.

"This is Mr. Redlake, boarding at the Inn. He's an artist."

Amos bowed again, drawing his bushy blond eyebrows together in a frown. "I've heard you were in town, sir," he said to Evan. "Is the painting good on the Neck?"

Hesper felt herself grow hot. Mr. Porterman and his polite question had managed to convey the fact that it was well after sunset, and that he did not like Evan's looks.

"Why, tolerably good," said Evan pleasantly.

Amos stared again at Hesper's vivid indignant face. He drew in his breath, and stepped back in the doorway. The two went past him and he watched them turn down Front Street. After a moment he resumed negotiation with Mr. Thatcher for the purchase of the sail loft, but found that he had lost interest in the transaction. He made another appointment, and walked off, leaving a startled Mr. Thatcher behind him.

CHAPTER 10

AMOS SPENT a troubled night tossing on his knobby bed at the Marblehead Hotel. At six o'clock he leaned out of the window and watched the swelling procession of shoe workers turn off onto School Street, bound for his factory in back of the hotel. This sight gave him none of the pleasure it usually did.

Nor did the hitherto interesting appointments he had scheduled for the day. Final negotiations with the Boston firm of engineers for the conversion to steam. Introduction of compo work in a corner of the Making room; an experiment, but they were doing well with it in Lynn. Dinner at the Hotel with Macullar's buyer, talk him into doubling his order. Ticklish interview with Josh Harris, find out if possible exactly what volume Harris & Sons were actually doing.

Amos went through his day, fighting a black depression that ruined his appetite and even spoiled the taste of cigars. By four o'clock he decided to pay the Hearth and Eagle a call and found several reasons for doing so. It was only natural that he should take a friendly interest in the Inn and commend Mrs. Honeywood for the promptness with which she was paying back his loan. And then it was only friendly to warn her that there might be talk about Hesper and that long-legged painter. Girl had no business to be traipsing off alone to the Neck with a fellow like that. It shocked him to find that sensible Mrs. Honeywood permitted it. Very likely she'll thank me for pointing it out.

Amos left the factory and strolled down Pleasant Street, and his depression lifted. Action was always the answer to discomfort. He hastened his steps, and found himself caught by the charm of his adopted town, seeing it with an indulgent eye.

The spell of fair June weather still held. As he walked beneath the maples and the wine-glass elms, the sun flickered from a vibrant blue sky, and he sniffed the scent of ocean salt and flowers. There were roses and petunias in the rocky back yards, geraniums and heliotrope in the window boxes. He approved fresh coats of dazzling yellow paint on scattered houses in Franklin Street. He approved too the majestic horse chestnut which shadowed the Hearth and Eagle yard, its white blossoms shining proud as candles amongst the glossy green leaves.

But there as he viewed the old house itself his approval ceased. He shook his head, staring at it with a pitying exasperation.

The silver-gray clapboards were as innocent of paint as on the day they were cut. The steep ridgepole on the original ell, and the gambrel roof on Moses Honeywood's larger addition, showed a rakish irregularity of line that offended him. And why in time couldn't they have placed the windows fair and square to begin with? Must have had level and plumbline even in those days. He stood for a moment, his hands on the crumbling picket gate, and modernized the house. Raise the roof on the oldest part, cut new windows, top it off with a nice fretwork cupola, run a verandah across the front, with rocking chairs where the guests could sit and enjoy the view across the harbor. Put in a couple of bathrooms, attract the best class of people instead of riff-raff. Like that painter fellow.

He tightened his lips, walked up the path, and entered by the taproom door. The low smoky room held four customers who looked up as the bell jangled. At the table below the casement window old Pinney Coit played checkers with his brother. At the center table, Cap'n Brown, master of an antiquated "heel-tapper," sat morosely drinking grog and listening to a spate of political conjecture from "Gabby" Woodfin, who was as expert at cod-splitting and salting as he was a tedious talker.

They knew Amos by sight, and greeted him with perfunctory grunts. The checker players continued their game. None of these men felt for him any particular animosity. They were all seamen and had remained so, stubbornly clinging to the dwindling trade into which they had been born, and they were entirely indifferent to a shoeman who was also a foreigner.

Amos, quite accustomed to this attitude by now, nevertheless saw a good opportunity to ingratiate himself. He still cherished political ambitions—town selectman at least, even the legislature. He was well aware that so far he had made no progress, but it might be helpful to show these old Marbleheaders that he understood their interests.

Mrs. Honeywood was not in sight, her place behind the counter being filled by a frowsy girl in a spotted apron. Amos decided to postpone the object of his visit for a few minutes, sat down at the center table between

"Gabby" and Cap'n Brown, ordered drinks and plunged into appropriate questions.

Was it true the fleet'd soon be in from the Banks, and that they'd caught full fare? That a big mackerel spirt had headed right into them? What a damn shame it was the government had voted to rescind the fisherman's bounty. Times were bad enough without that, and you'd think even that parcel of fools in Congress'd have more sense. And how was Cap'n Brown's old "heel-tapper?" Still laid up on the ways for repairs? Was there hope she'd sail again soon?

The seamen drank Amos' grog and thawed a trifle. Cap'n Brown delivered himself of monosyllables, but "Gabby" brightened into response as Amos complimented him on his loaded fish flakes. "I was over to Dolliber's Cove yesterday—" said Amos, "and noted your cod was curing faster than anybody's."

Gabby nodded complacently, running his scarred fingers through his lank gray hair. "Aye, Oi've the best dun-fish. They'll be brown as a nut, fetch high in Par-rtygal. Oi tend them splits loike they was babies, keep headin' 'em into the sun, swaddle 'em at night, an' afore they ever reach the flakes, Oi press 'em in the foinest oaken kenches to pint up the flavor. Oi send clear to Provinceto'n fur me salt; was a toime Oi reckoned Beverley salt'd do, but it's a queer thing about thot salt, don't seem to give out brine as quick. Now you wouldn't think there'd be difference twixt salts, nor difference twixt cod, neither, yet it's well known that a fish cotched Newfoundland side o' the Gr-rond Banks tastes different to them as is cotched eastwor-rd. Oncet when Oi was a leetle lod, cut-tail Oi was, on the *Hannah,* she was Chebacco-built at Ipswich, twenty tons burden, an' as seawar-rthy a croft as you'd find from Nahant to Newbury, the skipper was a Tom Cheever an' Oi remember—"

Like a turgid brook burbling over stones, Gabby's flow continued. The checker players had resumed their game. Cap'n Brown hunched himself over his mug, his bleary eyes glazed by interior mediation.

Amos sighed, got up and paid the frowsy barmaid. Nobody noticed. Gabby's monologue continued unchecked. Amos went in search of Mrs. Honeywood.

He found her in the buttery off the kitchen skimming milk, and much disconcerted at the sight of him.

"Why, Mr. Porterman!" she cried, throwing down the tin skimmer. "You're heartily welcome, but I'm flustered to receive you like this. I'd no idea— Come through to the parlor, do." She rolled down her sleeves, and untied her calico apron.

"Please don't trouble, ma'am—" said Amos, "I just came to see how you were, can't stay long. Can't we sit here?"

He glanced around the kitchen, and upon Susan's reluctantly seating herself on the settle, he wedged himself into the only armchair, the Windsor comb-back. It had been made in Boston two hundred years ago for Isaac Honeywood and Amos, surprised to find that it did not even creak beneath his weight, nevertheless thought that it should have been chopped for kindling long ago, like most things in this house. Look at those worm-eaten beams, and that rough-hewn lintel over the fireplace. Not even a decent mantelpiece.

"With your head for business, ma'am," he said to Susan, "I'm sure you'll soon be making enough to refurbish the place a bit."

Susan nodded, agreeing with the implication. "Nothing I'd like better, but Roger he won't hear of it. Wouldn't even let me cover them old planks with some of that new oilcloth, would've brightened us up here. I had a fight to get the little cookstove, then I wanted to board up the fireplace summers. Roger, he jawed at me something fierce, till I had to let be. He likes to look at those old black fire-dogs. You'd think them made of gold."

Amos glanced at the andirons, and he made a sympathetic noise. He crossed his legs and cleared his throat, "Does Miss-uh-Hesper share her father's views?"

Susan snorted. "That girl, she's no views of any kind, right now, excepting on that painter feller. I wish I'd never been so addle-pated as to give him house room."

"I thought as much—" said Amos under his breath, relieved to have the subject well launched, and to find that Mrs. Honeywood's good sense had not failed her.

"What's he doing in Marblehead, anyway?" asked Amos.

"Painting pictures." Susan got up and went to the dresser. "Have a sup of my blackberry cordial," she said over her shoulder, "unless you'd rather have something from the tap-room?"

"No, thanks—" said Amos, "the cordial'd be fine," and he waited, for Susan was clashing the decanter with a simmering vehemence. She put a pewter plate and glass beside Amos and sat down again. "Hesper's in love with him," she said starkly. "She's daft about him, the poor buffle-headed girl."

Amos gulped a mouthful of fiery purple liquid. "He's not suited to her!" he cried. He added more quietly, "Do you know anything about him?"

Susan sighed, glad to be able to share her worry with a man whose opinion she respected. "Unsuited indeed for a match, though he claims Massachusetts birth and seems to have some means." She shook her head, drawing her sandy brows together. "Still, I'd not fret so much for that, Mr. Porterman," she said slowly. "The girl's not been happy ever since Johnnie Peach was killed. She's seemed to fit in no place. She'd never make a contented spinster, but it seemed 'twould be her lot. Now she's found somebody, and niminy-piminy furriner that he is, I'd not stop her only—" she compressed her pale mouth and looked down at her lap. "That's not the nub of the matter."

"What is, then?" asked Amos, leaning forward.

"I doubt he'll ever marry her," said Susan. She turned her head and looked into the empty fireplace. "But she's that daft about him, I'm afraid . . ." The dull red rose up her neck and cheeks and into the sandy gray-streaked hair.

"But that's outrageous—" shouted Amos, springing to his feet. "Get Mr. Honeywood to throw him out of the house."

Susan gave a curt laugh. "Roger's no use. He's daft about him too. Roger won't ever see what he don't want to."

"Then *you* must do something." He strode over by Susan and stood beside the settle glaring down at her.

"I'd do plenty if I knew what," she answered tartly. "Hesper's a woman grown, I can't lock her in her room."

"Talk to that, what's his name—Redlake."

"Nothing to talk about. There's no getting hold of him. He's a good listener, I'll say that for him, but you try to get anything out of him and he's close as a poked clam. Only one thing I know, excepting what I can read of him with my own two eyes is"—she paused, added with an ironic pride—"he thinks Hesper's mighty handsome."

Amos opened his mouth and shut it again. Frowning he went back to the Windsor chair and sat down. "Well, I guess she is," he said weakly. His depression returned to him, bearing with it a type of unhappiness he had not felt since he was a boy in Danvers and his puppy had fallen through the river ice and drowned. The same feeling of helpless loss, and rage and loneliness. Even Lily Rose's death had not felt like this.

"I ought to go," he said, but his deep voice so lacked its usual incisiveness that Susan looked at him sharply. A fine figure of a man, she thought. Big and dependable. Looked like a sea-faring man, though he wasn't. Steady far-seeing blue eyes under the tow-colored brows. Thick hair, so light you'd think it frosted with brine. And a skipper's mouth, tight-clamped, made to give orders but upped at the corners a bit so there'd never be petty meanness.

Why'd that fool girl have to treat him so stupid, why'd she have to throw herself at this gangling dolt of a painter instead!

"I'd admire to have you stay on a spell, Mr. Porterman," she said.

Amos shook his head, half rising. "I must go, ma'am, I really must—"

He stopped and they both turned their heads toward the back door. From outside on the stoop there had come a light clear laugh, tinged with excitement. I never heard her laugh before, thought Amos.

Hesper came into the kitchen followed by Evan. Her shining hair was loosely bundled into the net and curled around her smiling face. She had an astonishing air of assurance and coquetry, though the smile faded as she saw Amos and her mother staring at her. She said "Oh—" and turning put her basket on the table. Evan gave the two in the kitchen a semi-ironic bow. He looked harried and sulky. Carrying his easel and paints he disappeared through the buttery and back passage toward his room in the new wing.

"At least—" snapped Susan to her daughter, "you're a mite earlier than usual. You've not greeted Mr. Porterman."

"G'd afternoon," said Hesper lightly in Amos's direction. "Yes, we're early because Evan couldn't seem to get the hang of the painting today. He gave it up."

Her eyes sparkled as she said this, and she moved to the drainboard, and unpacked the basket with an air of secret triumph.

"You mean he's all through, and he's going to leave Marblehead?" asked Susan, but without hope.

"Oh I don't know about that," said Hesper. This time she gave them both a vague and tolerant smile.

Amos clenched his hands on the chair arms. Emotions he had never suspected seemed to rush into his hands. He wanted to shake Hesper, he wanted to strangle Redlake. In a moment his hands unclenched and the violence rushed upwards into his tongue.

"What's going on between you two!" he shouted in a thunderous voice.

Hesper started as though an actual clap of thunder had rent the kitchen. She turned on Amos a look of pure amazement, seeing him simply as a man—instead of intrusive foreigner and factory owner, for the first time in their relationship.

Her heart began to beat with a nervous disquiet. She put her hand to her throat. "I can't think that you've the right—"

"No, I haven't." Amos had hold of himself now. "And I apologize. But I respect your mother, and I don't like to see her worried."

He stood up, towering above Hesper, and even in her bewilderment she felt the change in his attitude towards her.

She stepped back and turned her head towards Susan who stood watching. "You can stop fretting then, Ma—" she said. "Mr. Redlake has asked me to marry him," and she marched out of the room.

Hesper's triumphant announcement in the Hearth and Eagle kitchen was not strictly true. Evan had not asked her to marry him on that sunlit afternoon by Castle Rock. He had said that he loved her and he had asked her to go away with him, but the assumption of marriage had been Hesper's, after which he had been silent for a long time, staring out over the ocean.

Then he had said, "Yes. I suppose so. You must have marriage. You're not the kind of woman for anything else, are you, my dear?"

He took her hand in his looking down at the long slender fingers. They were roughened by housework but their fineness of line to the slightly tapered tips and the oval nails always gave him pleasure. They were the hands of a voluptuous and forceful woman yet they had a clinging quality. The fingers closed around his own hand now with childish trustfulness.

Evan sighed and turned again to contemplation of the sea. "Hesper, there's something I want to make you understand—if I can. I love you—your body. I'm a man and I want you. But there's nothing in the world I can be sure of still wanting a week, a month, a year from now—save my work. It's the only thing can hold me."

"Oh I understand that—" she cried. "And I'll help you. I'll go anywhere with you, I'll never complain. I'll keep out of the way when you don't want me, I'll pose for you—"

Evan shook his head, as he kissed her eager upturned face, his eyes over her shoulder rested on the easel. Ever since his desire for her had got in the way, the painting had been bad. Today he had not been able to work at all. The unfinished picture glared at him with accusation. Hesper's figure had gone wooden like an oversized puppet. The flesh tones were pasty. The oncoming wave behind her had thinned to a curl of green tissue paper. She saw his expression and for a frightened moment thought it directed at her, then she understood a little.

"It'll come right when we're married, darling—" she cried. "I know it will. Though I think it's fine now. The colors are so pretty."

Evan wrenched his eyes from the canvas, his nostrils tightened and a harsh look came into his eyes, then suddenly he laughed, pulled her over against him, burying his face in her full rounded throat.

The wedding was set for the following week in the parlor of the Hearth and Eagle. The Reverend Allen, their pastor from the Old North, was to officiate, and there were to be no guests except Peg-Leg and Aunt Mattie Dolliber.

"Hole and corner" business, Susan thought angrily many times during that week. Hesper seemed to have no mind or wishes of her own, and showed nothing but an indecent desire for haste. Susan's dislike of her future son-in-law mounted daily.

He had refused to summon his family or even acquaint them with the news. He had objected to a church wedding, saying that he had no use for churches and even less for community gatherings.

"No use for weddings either, I'll be bound," Susan had snapped, and Evan had smilingly agreed, with the silky insolence which she found impossible to answer. "You understand me quite well, Mrs. Honeywood. The marriage is entirely to please Hesper. I doubt—" he added, "that I'll be able to do much else to please her, poor girl."

"Aye—you never spoke truer. I'll be blosted if I know what she wants with you! You've nothing in your heart but your brushes and your tubes and your grummets of charcoal."

The derisive light faded from Evan's face. "Perhaps," he said. "I wish Hesper saw as clear as you." Suddenly he looked worried and boyish.

"*I'm* not in love with you," Susan muttered, but in that moment she liked him better than at any other time.

Roger was pleased with the marriage, except for the pain it gave him to lose Hesper. But he was moved by her obvious blooming—and he approved of Evan. He discharged his paternal responsibilities by catechizing Evan on his family, then writing to the minister at Amherst. The combined information was satisfactory.

Mrs. Redlake had been a New Bedford Robinson, daughter of a whaling captain and descendant of well-known Welsh and Lincolnshire lines. Mr. Redlake, though an outlander from Pennsylvania, came from good Quaker stock, was well to do and highly respected in Amherst.

A Marbleheader would have been better, of course, but there was excellent precedent for this match.

"It's not unlike the romance of Agnes Surriage," said Roger at supper on the wedding eve, pushing back his plate and beaming at Hesper and Evan with gentle benevolence.

The two young people looked up, Hesper smiling and happy as she always was now, and Evan interested. Susan flared up at once. "No more like than a mackerel and a lobster. Sir Henry was a lord, and Agnes was a maidservant, and to her everlasting shame she run away with him without a wedding."

"Well, they got married in the end, my dear—" said Roger. "And it all began at an inn. The Fountain Inn, over by Bailey's Head off Orne Street," he explained to Evan, certain of his attention to any bit of Marblehead lore, "it burned down years ago, but back when Sir Henry Frankland fell in love with little Agnes it was the chiefest inn here. Our place was closed at the time. That was in 1742, and my great-grandfather, Moses, was prospering."

"A real love story?" asked Evan smiling.

Hesper looked across at him quickly, her heart contracting. Had she imagined a faint stressing of "real"? I mustn't be a fretting fool, she thought. We're being married tomorrow. He loves me. He said so. He's different from other people. But I don't know much about men. Only Father and Johnnie— A warm soft pain washed through her and receded. If this had been her wedding eve with Johnnie. We'd have been dancing, she thought, with astonishment, there'd have been people everywhere, bunches of flowers and maybe white streamers. There'd be a fiddler in the taproom. Half of Marblehead would be here. Johnnie had so many friends. We'd 've danced most the night and been married in church in the morning. Then we'd have danced some more, and afterwards we'd have sailed off to Boston on Johnnie's ship, like we planned so many times. Then after a while we'd have come back here—

She looked around the kitchen in sudden revulsion. Thank God I won't be coming back here. I hate it.

She and Evan were going away. Not by boat; by train. And going to New York right after the ceremony. This was Evan's decision, he wished to return to New York. He didn't want to finish her picture by Castle Rock, he didn't want to go on painting the sea. He wouldn't talk about the picture at all. And that was wonderful, because all week he'd been entirely hers.

She sent Evan across the table a look of passionate love and gratitude. He responded to it, meeting her eyes with a somber intentness that made her heart beat fast and a shiver run through her flesh.

Tomorrow night, she thought, and so strong was the delicious panic that she murmured an excuse and left the table. She went out into the summer night hoping that Evan would follow her. But she waited under the chestnut tree for a while and he did not, so she walked slowly through the gate and down the street. It was soothing to be in motion outdoors and she had a desire to take final leave of Marblehead. Maybe, she thought with triumph, I'll never see it again. Ma and Pa can visit me. And she walked past the houses on Orne Street looking through the unshaded windows at those inside and feeling sorry for them. Nellie Bowen with her parcel of brats and her stupid bewhiskered husband. Damaris Orne, swollen with her first baby, anxiously hotting up coffee against Tom's return from the fire house where he spent most of his time. Did I ever really envy them? thought Hesper.

The streets were deserted, everyone was at supper, she walked rapidly up the hill by "The Old Brig" and the site of the Fountain Inn, feeling weightless and unreal. Ahead of her against the paling greenish sky loomed the Burial Hill and its surmounting shaft. How many times had she been dragged up those steep steps to bend her young unwilling gaze on the family tombstones and the Memorial shaft?

Now that she was leaving them, Hesper felt at last an interest. They must be included in the farewell.

She went first to the monument for drowned seamen, who had been lost off the Grand Banks in the great gale of 1846. Tom and Willy amongst them. She stood looking at the monument in the waning light and trying to remember her brothers. But she could not.

She wandered down the slope on a familiar path to a cluster of slate stones. The Honeywood plot. Isaac, John, Moses, Thomas, and their wives. All lavishly decorated with skulls and scythes and angels. Her father had told her that Mark and Phebe must be there too, near by, but their softer stones had long since crumbled. The latest stone of all was of granite adorned with a weeping willow. Sarah Hathaway Honeywood 1754–1848. That was Gran. What a one she was for telling me stories of the past, thought Hesper. She knelt down beside a richly carved tombstone, one which she had spelled out often as a child.

"Melissa Honeywood, wife of Moses Honeywood. Died July 6, 1732, aged 17 years," and the epitaph.

O Careless youth, as you pass by
As you are now, so once was I.
As I am now, so you must be
Prepare for Death and follow me.

This had used to frighten Hesper, but now Melissa and the three-day-old baby buried with her intensified the joy of deep, singing life.

I'm through with all of you, she whispered to them. I'm going out, free, away from you, with Evan. The slender gray stones seemed to gather themselves into an acquiescent stillness. The night breeze was rising and blew across Gerry's Island to the Burial Hill. Hesper stretched tall, leaning against the wind. Across the harbor on the Neck the lighthouse took up its measured blinking. Below her in the town the huddled houses sprang one by one into an amber glow. Two skiffs rowed homeward into Little Harbor, she heard the clinking of the row-locks and smelled the pungent odor of cod from the fish flakes on shore.

She turned toward the south and straining her eyes in the dusk made out the high-hipped and peaked roof line, the two jutting chimneys of the Hearth and Eagle. Was Evan still inside listening to her father's ramblings, sparring with her mother? Why didn't he follow me? she thought. She walked more soberly down the lower slope of the hill and back along Orne Street. As she turned the corner onto Franklin, she saw a very tall figure walking ahead of her.

Mr. Porterman again. Once she would have avoided him, but since his last visit her hostility had vanished. Amos Porterman, and indeed everybody in Marblehead, had receded to shadowy unimportance.

She came up beside him, smiling and saying "Why, hello—were you coming to call?"

Amos stopped dead, tongue-tied as a boy, at the sudden sight of her, close beside him and smiling and friendly as she had never been.

He nodded, and snatched off his hat, holding it clumsily against his broad chest.

She put her head on one side, looking up at him through her lashes. "I do believe you're sweet on Ma—calling so often!"

"Hesper!" He gaped at her unbelieving. After a moment he gave a grunt of laughter. "You're a mighty different girl from what I thought."

Her smile faded. "I *am* different," she said. "I'm happy."

He dropped his lids for a moment, and turned his head away. She began to walk and he kept step with her.

"Are you really going to marry that—going to marry Redlake to-morrow?"

"Yes."

"I wish you wouldn't," he said very low. "You ought to marry a different kind of man—one who'd take care of you—who'd understand you—"

"Fiddle—" she said quickly and flippantly, straining to see through the windows of the Inn—no light upstairs in his room, he must be waiting in the kitchen—"Besides, no kind of man has asked me till Evan."

Amos drew a sharp breath and stopped again, by the picket fence in the shadow of the horse chestnut tree. He put his hand on her arm.

"There's one asking you now—Hesper."

Her head jerked back and her mouth dropped open. "What?" she cried—choking on a hysterical laugh. The light flickered through the leaves onto his big square face, and the flaxen white hair above it, and his eyes were looking down at her with a yearning and bitter sadness.

"Yes, I suppose it's funny—but I mean it—" he said harshly, and he put his hands behind his back. She shut her mouth and swallowed, sorry that she had hurt him, and still dumbfounded.

"But what about Charity—?" she said, picking the most obvious of the many questions. She was excited and flattered and extremely curious. Underneath there was a beat of triumph. She'd tell Evan—no one else, that wouldn't be kind—but Evan—he'd see—not come to him valueless. . . .

"I can't marry Charity," said Amos. "I've known that quite a while." He did not want to think of Charity—the increasing boredom, shame that he'd let her dangle so long—

"I love you—" he said with difficulty, twisting his hat in his hand like any gawky yokel, feeling like a fool. "I don't wonder you laughed. I guess I didn't know it myself—until—" Until when? The night she'd come in sparkling with that Redlake? The night he'd met them on the wharf? but it seemed to him now he'd always loved her.

"I didn't really laugh—Mr. Porterman," she said gently, "it's just I was so surprised, I never thought of you that—"

"Oh, I know," he interrupted—"You never liked me even." He put his hand on the gate and pushed it open for her. "Don't look so worried. I know unwanted love's a damn nuisance. Forget it, Hesper. I didn't mean to speak."

She gave him an uncertain apologetic smile. The scene, the sudden shift of relationship, seemed to her unreal. Impossible to believe in Mr. Porterman as a lover—or in anyone but Evan. At the thought of him a dark and tender fire ran through her veins, she walked quickly through the gate and up the path to the kitchen door. Amos followed because he couldn't help himself. Only a few more minutes. Tomorrow she'd be gone.

There was nobody in the kitchen except Susan, who stood at the table stirring the bride cake in a huge wooden bowl.

Hesper said, "Here's Mr. Porterman—" in a thickened voice, and waited until her mother had greeted him, then she edged up close to Susan and said very low—"Where's Evan?"

Susan compressed her lips, glancing toward the visitor. She beat at the cake with vicious stabs, but pity for her daughter subdued the sharpness of her answer. "He's gone up to his room, and locked himself in with a bottle of my best Medford rum."

The girl winced, the faint rose whipped by the breeze and Amos's startling proposal drained from her cheeks. Her eyes slid unseeing over her mother and Amos, who turned and looked out of the window pretending that he had not heard. She moved across the boards to the stair door. "I guess I'll go to bed too—" she said. "It's sensible. We've a long journey tomorrow." The door shut behind her.

Amos and Susan heard the slow ascending footsteps as the stairs creaked. Their eyes met for a moment, and Susan saw plain the meaning of his expression. So that's how it is, she thought—that poor fool girl, but she's made her bed now, she'll have to lie in it. She poured another cupful of floured raisins into the bride cake, moistened the batter with rum.

There was a moment's silence in the old kitchen, filled by the banjo clock's unhurried tick, then Amos rushed into speech. "I stopped by to leave a wedding gift for the bride. Nothing fancy, though it might be useful." He fished a bundle from his pocket and put it on the table beside the mixing bowl. He ripped open the wrapping to disclose a pair of thin sateen slippers, and a pair of black kid button shoes.

"That's mortal kind of you, Mr. Porterman. She needs 'em."

"I think they'll fit her—" he said tonelessly. "I'm a pretty good judge of size."

"You're a good judge of everything." She tilted the bowl. The muscles in her stout forearm lumped as she beat the heavy batter.

"Well—good-bye," said Amos, moving past the table toward the door. "I hope she'll—she'll be happy."

"Happy," repeated Susan with contempt. "A woman can do without happiness. But she can't get along without two other things. Not a woman like Hes. She must have self-respect, and she must belong somewheres."

Amos gave a tired sigh—entirely unconscious, nor had he any idea how well Susan understood him, until she looked up from the bowl, with sympathy plain in her eyes. She shook her head, and hunched her shoulders. "I'm right sorry—Mr. Porterman," she said. "There's naught so blind as a desiring woman." She went to the oak dresser to find the big cake tin, while Amos flushed and muttered something. He went out to walk heavily back to the Marblehead Hotel.

CHAPTER 11

HESPER AND EVAN spent their wedding night in Boston at the Parker House. The brief wedding itself, the hurried farewells, the strangeness of the train trip to Boston, the incredible bustle and noise of the city, the magnificence of the hotel lobby, and then the first sight of their cheap attic room—all these were blurred for Hesper by nervous excitement. It sustained her on the surface of the crowding new impressions, and enabled her to minimize Evan's attitude.

He was, throughout the wedding day, charming and detached. He made no reference to his disappearance the night before, nor did he show any overt effects from the bottle of rum which Susan had found empty on his dresser. During the services he gave his responses promptly and rather in the manner of an adult reciting nursery rhymes for children.

On the train this had also been his attitude as he pointed out to Hesper the sights along the way.

When the disdainful bellboy had shut the door on them in their hotel bedroom, Hesper looked at the sticky yellow varnished door, the single hissing gas jet, the lumpy brass bed and her excitement left her, to be replaced by a dreary dismay.

What am I doing here so far from home with this man who is a stranger? she thought, thus echoing the initial honeymoon panic of most brides through the ages.

Evan lowered the gas jet and sat down on the bed. "This room is ugly and smells abominable," he said. "Sorry I can't afford a better one." But he said it without much interest.

"It's all right," she answered, not looking at him.

He leaned back against the knobbly brass head rails and crossed his legs. "Take your bonnet off, Hesper, so I can see your hair. Take that hideous dress off too, for that matter. We're married now and it's quite proper."

She looked at him then. The narrow dark face, the heavy-lidded eyes, the full mouth with its ironic half-smile. He wasn't like this at Castle Rock.

She turned quickly away. She took off her bonnet, a dish-shaped yellow chip straw bought by Susan at Miss Hattie's little shop near the Town House. It was trimmed with buff ribbons to match the heavy brown moiré dress hastily run up from a length Susan had been saving for years in the lumber room.

Hesper hung the bonnet on a wooden knob behind the door and sat down on the slippery mohair chair by the only window. She held herself tight, staring through the dusty window out over the city. It was hot here under the roof. Two flies buzzed around her head and, wheeling, settled on the cracked marble washstand.

Evan looked at her profile against the window. The straight nose and firm chin overbalanced at the nape of her neck by the waterfall of bunched red hair. He looked at the brown dress buttoned up to her throat, bunched at the sleeves and bunched out by horsehair over the hips. It encased and distorted her like a coat of armor, and the color of the dress—of swampwood, of imitation walnut—threw muddy light onto her white skin.

He looked more intently, savoring his revulsion, using it as a shield against her who would come too close, and he saw tears shining on her cheek.

He shot out his breath in mingled annoyance and contrition. "Good God, my dear—don't cry." He knelt down beside her chair and began to kiss her. At first she would not respond, but he was patient and gentle. He unloosened her hair. His deft fingers unbuttoned her collar and removed the disfiguring dress. Gradually, as the sense of her beauty returned to him, he made love to her with compelling passion and she followed him blindly into the timeless moments where there is no space for doubt.

For three weeks Evan was a fervent and intuitive lover. The days and the nights to Hesper swam together. Outer discomforts, though many, became negligible or even interesting, infused as each was with the spirit of shared adventure. The day after the wedding they took the cars to New York, a day-long trip of racketing wheels, glaring heat, and soot from the engine stack.

In the city they went to Evan's old room in the boarding-house; then

Evan rented a skylighted loft on Fourth Street near Broadway, paid two months rent in advance, and spent the remainder of his capital for a few pieces of second-hand furniture.

They set up the bedstead, and the washstand, hung a curtain across the sleeping corner of the loft, stacked canvases and easel in the other corner, placed a table, two chairs, and a cupboard near the rusty little wood-burning stove, and left the rest of the moving in for later, intent only on their physical concentration with each other.

When they became hungry they went to a small German saloon on the Bowery where for a few pennies they found beer, sausage, and strong rye bread. In the evenings they wandered around the city, down Broadway to the Battery to sit and feed the pigeons near the cylindrical bulk of Castle Garden, or up Fifth Avenue to Central Park, where they sat on a rustic bench near the Mall.

They talked very little. Hesper tried once or twice to speak to him about his painting, and always he eluded her, cutting through her tentative questions with the weapon of physical contact, pulling her close to him, his hand on her breast while her swift-answering blood pounded, and she forgot her question. She had his whole mind and attention during those three weeks, and she glowed into a new loveliness. Evan had bought her a green silk dress, a bargain from Stewart's basement, marked down because the style was dated. Evan made her wear it without the crinoline. Neither of them cared that it was unfashionable, since the delicate moss green was extremely becoming.

The first time she had worn the dress she had posed proudly against the baize curtain, arms outstretched. The clinging silk made her slender as a fern, and her hair was loose as he liked it, streaming in red-gold strands down her shoulders.

"Ah, Hesper—" he said, half whimsically—"you're like a fountain of fire on a jasper column."

"Am I, darling—" she whispered, throwing her arms around his neck —"Don't you want to paint me like this, then? Don't you?"

"Someday," he said lightly, kissing her.

She persisted, baffled again by his withdrawal. For what else had first brought them together except his wish to paint her? "Or—the other way. Without my clothes, if you never let anyone see it." Color ran up her face, and yet it was amazing how soon she had become accustomed to nakedness, when at first she had been miserably self-conscious.

"You're very nice, either way—my Marblehead beauty," said Evan and she heard again an echo of the ironic detachment which he had used on their wedding day.

Her arms fell to her sides, she turned from him, and at once he wooed her back, laughing at her, rumpling and tumbling her at last onto the bed.

The change came abruptly. One evening, it was now late July, they walked further afield than usual for their supper. Evan, who had seemed as indifferent to food as she, suddenly suggested that he was tired of beer and they might try a little French café on Broome Street. Hesper was pleased and later surprised when they entered a tiny tile-floored room to find that the proprietor greeted Evan as an old friend and an epicure.

"So long we have not seen you, Monsieur Redlake—" he cried, bowing, his hands massaging his spotted apron, his moon face beaming. "And we have *rognons en brochette* tonight, just how you like them."

"Good," said Evan, flashing his quick charming smile. "Yes. I've been away. This is—" he stopped for a full second, "my wife."

Hesper forgave his hesitation which had looked almost as though she weren't, in the shock of hearing the phrase for the first time. They had so far talked to nobody but each other.

"*Enchanté*, madame—" said the proprietor, and added familiarly to Evan, who had picked up a good deal of French in Martinique, "*Elle est vraiment belle.*"

Evan nodded, and did not translate. He plunged into an intensive survey of the menu. Hesper sat back and tried to look interested.

The dishes when they arrived were very queer indeed. Imagine serving kidneys, not hidden in a stew to piece out the honest meat, but baldly in their natural shape. Ma would've died of shame before she'd serve such a thing to a customer. And here was that sour red wine again, something like the stuff Evan had given her the first day they met, when he pulled her out of the ocean.

"This reminds me—" she began softly, putting down her glass, and looking across the table with loving eyes—"Oh, Evan, do you remember—"

But he was not listening, he was looking at two young men who came through the door, and as they neared his table he rose. "Hello, La Farge—" he said. "I was hoping to find you here."

The men returned the greeting and at Evan's invitation pulled up the next table and sat down beside them. Hesper was introduced, accorded a dual stare of interest, a polite sentence, and then forgotten.

The men were artists, it seemed, called John La Farge and Homer Martin, both around thirty, a couple of years older than Evan.

Their talk at once became nearly incomprehensible to Hesper.

Mr. Martin had been to a place called the Adirondacks, where he thought he had succeeded in catching a crispness of tonal quality. He then spoke of someone called Corot whom he admired, someone in France. Mr. La Farge also said a great deal about France, which he seemed to know well, and he mentioned ateliers and schools and the "Quarter."

Evan listened mostly, but with an expression of thoughtful interest. Sometimes he asked a question, and these involved more obscure words. "Gouache," "Under-glaze," and "stretchers."

They finished eating and all sat sipping with apparent enjoyment some nasty thickish fluid in no way resembling the coffee served at the Hearth and Eagle. In tiny cups too, so it hardly seemed worth while.

Now they were discussing art galleries in the city, and Evan said, "I haven't much ready, but I hope to hold a sale at Leeds and Miner's, I need some money." He smiled, and for the first time since the others had joined them his glance included Hesper. The other men smiled too, and Mr. La Farge turned to Hesper with courtly gallantry. "I'm afraid this painter talk has been very dull for you, Mrs. Redlake. Unless of course you're used to it?"

"No—" she said and blushed, feeling ungracious. "That is, I don't mind." She shoved the tiny coffee cup nervously away from her and some of the black fluid sloshed into the saucer. Her pleading eyes flew to Evan.

"Hesper's a Marblehead girl," he said. "Never been away from there before. The kind of talk she knows is fish, and innkeeping and the sea."

He had not failed her, and his tone was one of affectionate amusement, but she knew a dull hurt all the same, for neither had he been with her. He had the air of stating facts in whose reception he had no personal involvement.

"But that's most interesting," said La Farge warmly, "a charming town, I've heard," and Mr. Martin chimed in, in his rougher twangier voice and said he wasn't any good at marines but he'd always admired the sea coast.

Hesper could think of nothing to say. Was Marblehead a "charming town"? The two words repeated themselves meaninglessly in her head. Dingle Dong, like a bell buoy. She gave a tentative half-smile and looked down at the tablecloth.

La Farge was kind and sensitive and his perceptions were heightened just now by persistent ill health. He saw the girl's discomfiture. "Forgive me for being personal, Mrs. Redlake, but your hair is pure Venetion. It reminds me of Titian."

Hesper felt the kindness and she looked up gratefully, but what answer was there to that, either? "Ma had red hair—" she said after a moment. "All her branch of the Dollibers have. I—I used to hate it—but then Evan—" She stopped, feeling that she was being too childish, too confiding.

Evan cut in, "As a matter of fact I married her for her hair." And the men laughed. La Farge said, "I doubt if even you can reproduce just that tone," and went on easily to talk of some Japanese prints he had imported.

Hesper crept into herself as the talk washed by her. There was a cold place around her heart. Yet how could he say to those two strange artist friends of his, "I married her because I love her." Bufflehead, she said to herself in Susan's astringent voice, you've not got the sense of a flounder. She had an instant vision of home, made up of little whirling colored bits like a kaleidoscope. Susan's grim, capable face bent over the wooden mixing bowl, Roger standing backed up to the bright fireplace and the andirons behind him. Gran's ship and sunset hooked rug vivid on the floor, though she hadn't really noticed it in ages, the smell of fog and burning cedar, the lap of water in the cove, the feel of wet salty spray on her face. All these little bits whirled, then went gray. I'm so glad I'm here, she thought, here with my husband. I wasn't a bit happy at home.

But would they never have done talking? She ached to be back alone with him in the wide bed, Evan's arms around her and the baize curtain shutting out the day shine and the star shine through the skylight.

Still, when at last they left the stuffy café and said good night to Mr. La Farge and Mr. Martin, she found that she was not to be alone with Evan. He left her at the foot of the brownstone steps of their building.

"Go to bed, Hesper. I'm going for a long walk."

He waited for neither acquiescence or protest, put the key in her hand, and turning on his heel strode east along Fourth Street.

She stood on the sidewalk clutching the key. He walked fast, his body bent forward a little as though he were breasting the wind, though there was no wind. At the corner he passed under a street lamp and she saw the gleam of his wavy dark hair. In the parts of the city where it would not excite comment he always went hatless, but his dress was not eccentric. He wore a dark blue suit which he kept neatly brushed. She watched him until his figure dwindled to a shadow amongst other shadows, then she mounted the four flights of stairs to their studio loft.

He had returned in the very early morning, and she, broad awake at once, turned on her side in the bed, and held her breath waiting for him to come to her. But Evan did not kiss her, he did not even touch her. He stretched himself out on the edge of his side of the bed. In a moment she heard the even, deep breathing of sleep.

When she awoke again, Evan was already up, shaved, and dressed in shirt and pants. She raised herself on her elbow and smiled at him. He did not respond. He was crouching on a three-legged stool, holding a large palette on his knees and rubbing at it with a rag. His lips were tight and indrawn. The room was filled with the pungent smell of turpentine. "Oh, you're awake," he said. "Hesper, get up and do something about this place. It's a pigsty."

She swallowed, pulling the coarse cambric sheet around her naked shoulders. She looked about the loft. For nearly three weeks it had been their bower and lovers' retreat. None of its details had come through to her conscious attention.

Now she saw that the loft was cluttered and dirty, the drawers in the deal bureau which they shared were bulging with miscellaneous articles of clothing, and her small cowhide trunk was but half unpacked.

Hesper got out of bed and pulled on her calico wrapper. "I'm sorry," she said faintly. "I'm not much of a housewife, I guess."

He gave a short laugh, stacked the cleansed palette against the pile of canvases. "Well, you ought to be, with all that staunch Yankee tradition. I've got to have room for my work. I'm not used to living with anyone—" he added in a blend of apology and irritation.

Hesper was dressing rapidly. "I know. I'll try not to be in the way. I'll get us properly settled here today."

"Be quick about it. I'm going to get out some more paints. Then as soon as I get my easel set up, I want you to pose."

"Oh, darling—" she said, the worried frown clearing from her face. "You know I'd love to."

That morning began a new régime. She carried up pails of water from the next-floor landing and attacked the loft with remorseful energy. She unpacked and allocated their belongings, washed the accumulated laundry in a basement tub, and learned the vagaries of the tiny wood-burning stove. In an hour, it produced acceptable coffee, and by keeping the pot pushed away back and resting against the stovepipe there was room for one more saucepan. In this Hesper cooked pot roasts, stews, and fricasseed chickens. She discovered that through the years of watching and helping Susan she had become a capable cook.

Evan abstractedly ate what she gave him, for now he refused to go out at all. She knew that his money was nearly spent, but that was not the only reason. His existence had narrowed to an interior preoccupation. He ate, he slept, he painted, and he spent a good deal of time hunched on a chair and brooding. When she spoke to him he answered her with masked annoyance, or did not answer at all. He did not make love to her. At night he went to sleep. It was as though he had withdrawn behind a nearly opaque curtain, through which Hesper and their life together in the loft appeared blurred and meaningless.

Nor was it better when she posed for him. She had expected him to go back to the Marblehead canvas, but he did not. She sat on the high stool until her muscles twitched and her head throbbed while he made sketch after sketch in charcoal, in water color, in oil. And each one he discarded, saying nothing, giving no reason.

One August afternoon, she at last rebelled. The loft was stifling; through the open skylight the sun glared down on them. Pearls of moisture gathered on Hesper's upper lip and ran salt into her mouth. Evan was working on a large study, full length, and she was wearing the green dress. Wet patches had soaked through under her arms and across her shoulder blades. Her back ached. Their supper simmered on the stove which added its smoky heat to the room. Kidney stew, since Evan loved kidneys stewed in red wine, and they were cheap. The heavy smell of kidneys and onions mixed with the ever present odor of turpentine.

She broke her pose to look at him. His face too was dripping with sweat which he wiped off with a painting rag.

"Evan," she said sharply, "how is it going?"

He made the quick impatient noise through his nostrils and stuck his brush in the crockery mug. "Rotten. I can't paint inside four walls. Lighting's all wrong. It's all stale and set."

"Well, I can't pose any more either. It's too hot." She came down off the overturned box which served as platform, and stood beside him looking at the half-filled canvas. "Why, it's real pretty, Evan, I think it's wonderful," she cried, astonished. Usually he tore up or painted over the studies before she saw them at all.

"Bah—" said Evan ripping it loose from the easel. "A cheap chromo, might as well be china painting. Can't you see there's no truth to it?" he added angrily.

He picked up another canvas from the wall stack and put it on the easel. This was a small oil of a schooner in Boston Harbor. He had painted it before reaching Marblehead. He squinted at it, took his palette knife, and began to scrape very carefully at a blob of Chinese white in the ship's wake.

Hesper watched him a minute. Her throat closed and she clasped her hands tight together. "Evan, for the love of God, can't you leave that stuff alone for a moment. I—" Her voice thickened and broke. "Don't you love me at all any more—" she whispered. She ran behind the baize curtain and flung herself face down on the bed. Sobs tore at her, and she tried to control them, until suddenly she did not wish to control them.

She felt him sit down on the bed beside her, and a touch on her shoulder. She kept her face buried in the pillow. The grasp on her shoulder dug into her flesh. "Stop it—" he said roughly. "Turn around."

She obeyed slowly.

He looked down at her blotched and swollen face. "I told you how it would be. You've no cause to act like this."

No cause, she thought, meeting his cold appraisal. Never a word of love since the day we went to that café. Nothing but the cooking and the cleaning and the posing, shut into this stifling loft with a stranger.

"I told you how it would be," he repeated. "I like this no better than you do. I've need to be alone."

"You *are* alone. You might as well be." She put her hand to her mouth. Don't! cried a tiny voice in her head. Don't speak again. And she saw them both as little figures teetering on the edge of a cliff, wrestling together. She looked at his dark face, shut against her, the curve of the muscles on his arm, the sweat-matted hairs on his chest. She shuddered and hid her face again in the pillow.

The kidney stew bubbled and sighed. In the stove a log fell apart with a shower of small cracklings. Down through the open skylight came the distant rumble of a horse car and the sharp clop of hooves on the Broadway cobblestones. Somewhere a baby wailed.

"Hesper—" he said, his voice cool and round. "You know as well as I do, my money's about gone. I've got to get some things in shape for exhibition. Maybe some dolt will buy, though I've done nothing decent this summer."

She pressed her eyelids against the blackness. "It's not my fault, is it? I've tried to help."

She heard him get off the bed and walk to the washstand and pour himself a drink of water. "It's not a question of fault, or blame."

She pushed against the pillow and sat up. He stood by the washstand holding the dented tin pitcher. They had bought it and the tin bowl off a pushcart for ten cents. Her eyes slid down to a glued curlicue on the corner leg of the washstand. The glue had dried out and the curlicue of yellow birdseye maple dangled from a nail someone had tacked to it. Her eyes followed the bulbous little whorls back and forth.

"Why do you shut me out so?" she said very low.

He put the pitcher down and turned to her violently. "Because I can't help it. Because nobody is very important to me for long. Because inside me there's a core, no, it's like a glass ball that mustn't be touched or it'll shatter. Do you understand that?"

"I don't know—" she said. "I don't know. But at first it was so different. You loved me. We were happy. Then you left me high and dry. Ah—don't look at me as though you hated me—don't."

Her head drooped. She crumpled up a corner of the sheet in her hand, and smoothed it out.

He walked over to the bed and sat down beside her. "Look, Hesper. I'm not a monster. I don't want to make you miserable. I was afraid it would be like this, that's why I didn't want—"

She winced, still pleating the sheet corner. "You wanted me just to sleep with a few times—and to paint. Only now neither of them is any good?"

He was silent, shocked and released by her perception. A rush of pity came to him. He looked at the curve of her down-bent head, and the beautiful hands, and she slid back into focus for him.

"No—that's not true. There's more than that—" he cried. "What love I have is for you."

She held her breath, looking up at him. When he kissed her, she yielded to him silently. There must be no more time for thoughts. But now her thoughts would not still, they leaped and darted even through the passion, and underneath the dartings, like a black river, ran bitterness.

The first week in September, Goupil's Art Gallery at the corner of Broadway and Ninth Street, held an exhibition of Evan Redlake's paintings. These included a dozen water colors of the Connecticut and Massachusetts seacoast and half a dozen oils. One of the latter was a picture of the Hearth and Eagle, expanded from a sketch. There were no portraits of Hesper.

Very few people came to the gallery on Opening Day. Most of those interested in art had not yet returned to the city from their summer homes at Newport and Long Branch, nor was Evan a popular or well-known painter.

He and Hesper arrived at three. She wore the green dress, rather wilted now for all her anxious cleaning and pressing, and the yellow chip straw bonnet, since she had no other. Evan wore his dark blue suit, and he was in a savage mood. Nothing that he was exhibiting except two minor water colors pleased him. The gallery was badly lit and stuffy, Leeds and Miner's far more attractive place had been unavailable.

Upon their arrival Evan retired to a corner and gloomy consultation with Mr. Goupil, the owner. Hesper wandered around, feeling nervous and self-conscious. She edged up behind the only other couple in the gallery and tried to overhear their comments. This couple were honeymooners from Cincinnati who had been sauntering up Broadway and dropped in out of curiosity. Their remarks were not cheering.

"Mercy on us, Harry!" cried the bride, giggling and poking at her husband. "What a thing to paint."

She pointed to one of the largest oils. It showed a red country schoolhouse, set in a meadow. In the foreground a group of boys pummeled each other, while four little girls played ring-around-a-rosy. In the background to the left of the school there was a small privy. It was nearly hidden by the shadow of a vast elm, but it was to this building that the bride referred. "And what dirty children," she added, "and maybe that school is supposed to be red, but I call it purple."

"Yeah—" agreed her husband placidly. "Terrible. Look at that crazy lopsided house over there. The fellow can't draw."

The lopsided house was the Hearth and Eagle. Hesper followed their critical stares and a sharp pain went through her chest. Don't you dare say anything about my home! she thought, and she glared at the bride's unconscious face. She waited until the couple had gone out, then went over and stood by the painting. She had never until that moment taken any interest in it. Evan had painted on it mornings while she had been busy inside with Susan before the afternoons at Castle Rock. She remembered wondering rather impatiently what in the world he found to interest him about the shabby old house, and thinking as did most first beholders of Evan's painting that the colors were very queer. Then she had forgotten all about it until he unearthed it for the exhibition.

She looked at it now in the hot New York gallery and a strange unknown sadness came into her heart. Evan had painted by the morning sun and crisp golden light bathed the high-gambreled eastern half of the house and sparkled on the waters of the Little Harbor behind it. But the rest of the house was in shadow, violent purple and green shadows under the black horse chestnut. The two divergent roofs and their wavering ridgepoles, their uncertainty much exaggerated by Evan, the rusty chimneys, the small-paned windows, and the sloping lean-to were all unified into one dominant emotion—a defiant and rugged endurance. With astonishment she saw this in the painting, although she had never seen it in the actual house.

A handful of people had drifted into the gallery and Evan went to greet them. But Hesper could not leave the painting.

It seemed to her as she stood in the hot gallery, gazing at Evan's picture of her home, that she heard her father's voice, not high and plaintive as it really was, but reading with a golden sonority the words about Phebe in the Lady Arbella's letter—"A most sturdy courage to surmount any disaster—to follow her man anywhere—found a lasting home."

"Yes—" Hesper whispered, answering her father, answering the house.

Evan's voice, cool and defensive, cut in behind her. "And that—is a queer old inn, in Marblehead, Massachusetts. My wife's home as a matter of fact."

The living house flattened on the canvas into blobs of garish paint. During the instant in which she turned to Evan and the group, her exaltation became ridiculous. She faced the polite stares in bitter silence from which she could not at once arouse herself.

There were two ladies in billowing taffetas and lace shawls, a supercilious gentleman with Dundreary whiskers and a single eyeglass in his left eye, and another gentleman, short, fat, and quite bald except for a black fringe above his ears and along the back of his white collar. She heard none of their names as Evan introduced them. The ladies and the eyeglassed gentleman barely touched her finger-tips, but the fat little man bent over and kissed her hand, which she snatched back in startled reflex.

Evan laughed curtly and said to her, "Mr. Durand is the discerning gentleman who bought my 'Two Soldiers.' " She heard the note of warning, and forced a smile. It was on the sale of the "Two Soldiers" that they had been living.

"I admire your husband's work, madame," said Mr. Durand, revealing a flashing set of teeth. "I believe he has a great future."

The supercilious gentleman looked bored and adjusted his eyeglass. The ladies made cooing non-committal sounds and arching their necks gazed up at Evan. "My friends, perhaps, do not agree with me," went on Mr. Durand imperturbably.

"Most people don't," said Evan on another acid laugh.

"My dear Redlake—" said the eyeglassed gentleman, languidly, "I would suggest a study of the masters, don't you know. There've been none in America, of course. I mean the French masters: David, Bouguereau, Cabanel. They could teach you a great deal."

Evan's face set into the sulky contempt Hesper knew so well. "Well, you're wrong. If a man wants to be an artist, he should never look at other people's pictures."

Oh, why does he have to act like this, thought Hesper. The gentleman shrugged his shoulders, swept the gallery with his eyeglass, and gathering up the ladies with a cool smile moved toward the door.

Mr. Durand shook his head though his eyes twinkled. "Ah, my friend, you should not so treat our leading art critic. I had trouble enough to bring him. He will blast your little show with explosions of distaste."

Evan's mouth twisted, he raised his hand and let it drop again. "I can always go back to my croquet girls and dairy maids. They'll sell if I put in enough roses and ringlets and doves."

Mr. Durand smiled. "Oh, come, it's not so bad as that. Your painting is Avant-Garde, I think. You paint impressions of reality as you see it, not what you think you should see or what others have seen. There is a very young man in Paris, Claude Monet, does the same. But unlike our departed critic, I do not say, study the French or study anyone. I like that you paint simple things. I like that you use brutal color and even that you distort line if you see it like that.

"Now that we have the photograph, there is no more need for exact representation in painting, and we may forget all but art's two functions. These, interpretation and true emotion, I feel in your works."

There was a silence, and Hesper looked up at her husband wonderingly. His lips were parted, and his breath came fast. "Thank you," he said in a low humble voice. "You've said it all for me."

I've never seen him like that, thought Hesper—defenseless, happy—Never has he been like that with me.

She shut her eyes and walked away. In the center of the gallery there was a circular red plush seat. She sank onto it leaning her head against the high tufted back. A cold tide rose and lapped at her heart. Nothing I can ever give him will make him look like that. She thought of the last weeks, since the afternoon when she had forced an issue between them. She had believed them to be closer since, the tension less. They had gone out a few times together, and sometimes they had made love. She had silenced the inner doubts, chiding herself for expecting too much, for feeling that their partially renewed intimacy of mind and body cost him laborious effort. But he had done no more creative painting, nothing except varnishing and minor changes and spot-work on the pictures already finished.

She turned her head to find him. He was circling the gallery with Mr. Durand, pausing before each picture and talking with an eager animation. Near them at that end of the gallery, there was a handful of people. She saw a young dark-haired girl in violent silk walk up to the art collector and be introduced to Evan, who gave her his warm quick smile. She saw pleased response in every line of the girl's slight figure, saw her laugh and touch Evan's arm with a pretty gesture.

That won't get you anywhere, my lass, thought Hesper, whatever you may think, unless he wants to paint you. And even then—

She withdrew her eyes from the group, a threesome now, and a spasm of nausea twisted at her stomach, sending bitter fluid into her throat. The gallery and its colored paintings swam around her in a sickening spiral. She held her breath, and her stomach settled. She licked her lips, holding her handkerchief tight against her mouth.

In her head she heard a peal of derisive laughter. Oh yes, and there's *that* too, she thought. I suppose it's that.

She turned her head to the left and looked again at the picture of the Hearth and Eagle. "Sturdy courage—to follow her man anywhere?" But supposing he doesn't want me to follow? What then? What would you do then, Phebe? Fight? Clutch at what you never really had?

From Evan's picture there was no answer.

CHAPTER 12

MR. DURAND bought a water color of marsh grass and the oil of the schoolhouse and children. For these Evan received three hundred dollars, which was fortunate, since nobody else bought anything. The supercilious art critic duly lambasted Evan Redlake in his paper, and no other critics bothered to come.

The unsold canvases returned to the studio loft, and Evan disappeared for an entire night, returning the next morning at eleven quite sober but smelling strongly of whiskey. As on the similar occasion of their wedding eve, he gave no explanation, but Hesper saw that he was in a good mood. He kissed her, when she met him silently on the landing, and he had bought her a present. A brooch oddly shaped in a triangle of beaten silver which enclosed a large cat's-eye. Hesper thanked him with delighted astonishment, privately thinking the thing very queer, but he pinned it on her work apron and admired the effect.

"Suits you, my dear—" he said, "silvers and browns and greens like your own Marblehead."

"Marblehead seems a long way off," she said without meaning to. He pushed the baize curtain back and threw himself down on the bed.

"Homesick?" he asked lazily.

"No—" she snapped, but the question disturbed her. That night and morning waiting for him to come back, wondering once, in the cowardly hour at dawn, if he would indeed come back, she had pictured herself in her cool passionless chamber at home, felt the south wind pouring off the sea through her windows. And this morning, when she had dragged herself from bed and been sick in the slop pail, she had thought of her mother in an entirely new way, longing for the practiced fingers on her hot head, longing even for the tart, guttural speech.

"Evan—" she said, coming to stand over by the bed and looking down at him. "I guess I'm going to have a baby."

Ah, I knew it—she thought bitterly, watching his face change.

"Are you sure?" The icicle voice, cold and smooth and sharp.

"I think so. All the signs." She walked over to the bureau and began to straighten their brushes and combs. "I don't like it any better than you do." But I guess I would if you did, she added silently.

He got up and began to walk back and forth across the creaking floor.

"I'm sorry, Evan," she said. She heard her own pleading voice, and suddenly anger possessed her. She jerked her head up and stood squarely in front of him. "I know you feel trapped, you needn't pace back and forth to show it. I know you feel me a millstone, though I've done all you wanted. I know you had no wish to marry me. But you did. I don't know why, I doubt you rightly know yourself. But you did."

Evan was startled. They stood looking at each other and a dull red stained his face. His hands opened and shut. "You're quite right," he said. "Forgive me, Hesper."

"Oh Evan—oh darling—I didn't mean—" The tears that came so quickly nowadays burst from her. He put his arm around her, and she clung to him, hiding her face on his shoulder. He stroked her arm gently.

She stopped crying. She reached up and kissed his cheek. "I guess I've got the shogs—" she said with a small laugh, making use of her mother's expression for nervous outburst. "Likely it's the—the baby." She went to the wash bowl and washed her face.

Evan said nothing. After a moment he set a sketching block on his easel, and began to draw on it in pencil. She came back and stood behind him, emboldened by their new understanding.

"What are you starting?" she asked, seeing a girl's face emerge. He added extravagant eyelashes, erased the mouth and drew the upper lip more pouting. "Shepherdess, I should think," he said. "A lapful of violets for a change. I'll have to get a *Farm Journal* for the lambs."

She stood rooted to the floor behind him. He rapidly sketched in the curly head, and above it two birds on a branch. "Everybody likes doves," he said.

"Evan, don't. Please don't. I know how you hate them—" She twisted her hands together. "I heard how you spoke of them to Mr. Durand."

"Spoke of what?"

"The—the croquet girls and shepherdesses—"

"True, my dear, but may I point out that three hundred dollars, two hundred and seventy actually, after Goupil's commission, won't last very long. We both need clothes, the winter is coming and also your confinement, and after that the little pledge of our love must be provided for. One must be practical."

"There could be some other way—" Her voice dropped. "Evan—we might go home, to Marblehead. Ma'd take us in, until the baby's born—"

"No." He blocked in a lamb with short vicious strokes. "I'm through with Marblehead. And you—you were wild to get away from there. Your suggestion astonishes me."

"I was," she said. "Yes, I was. But—" She looked at the back of his head, the set of his shoulders under the loose painting shirt, his right hand moving so rapidly over the white paper.

"I want to be wherever you are, Evan."

His mouth curved in the courteous smile of one interrupted by a casual compliment. He slanted his pencil and began the shading under the plump, dimpled chin.

She turned away and went to the bed corner. Dear Lord, she thought, what am I doing to you, Evan? But what *can* we do—either of us, but make the best—she clenched her hands and looked down at her belly with disgust. It seemed to her that already under the apron there was a tautness. She stared at the loft. The bed corner here, the washstand and bureau. The stove, table and shelf above it. The painting corner, with Evan silent at the easel, hunched close to it because of the crowding stacked canvases behind him. Everything crowded and shoddy. If only there was a window, something through which to look out and away. Instead of that pitiless skylight.

She took off her apron yanking at the entangled strings until one tore off. She flung her little crocheted shawl over her shoulders. "I'm going out—" she said. "I want to walk." She waited a minute.

But Evan merely grunted. She saw relief on his intent face. She went out quickly. The streets were dusty and noisy, Broadway was crowded with jostling strangers. There were fashionable matrons bound for shopping at Lord and Taylor's or Stewart's. There were frock-coated men hurrying uptown for lunch at Delmonico's, there were tradesmen and clerks and tourists, all intent and purposeful. She found herself peering into the faces as they passed, seeking for recognition. But there was none. The indifferent eyes flowed past her in an implacable stream. If I only had someone to talk to, she thought. She stopped and stared, unseeing, into a window filled with clocks and bric-à-brac. Suddenly she was exhausted. Weariness fell over her like a dense black veil. Her knees trembled. She turned down Broadway, and dragging each foot forward in painful effort, she plodded back to the loft.

During the fall and winter months Evan sold illustrations to the magazines, *Our Young Folks, Hearth and Home, Appleton's Journal,* and two New York scenes of girls skating on the pond in Central Park to *Harper's,* which paid better. He received from ten to forty-five dollars for his drawings, and on these proceeds they lived, reserving two hundred and fifty in the bank for emergencies.

The loft ceased to be hot and stuffy, it became cold and draughty. In November the snows began, and lay thick on the skylight, consigning them to a gray half-world until Evan climbed up the ladder to the roof and brushed off the clinging flakes. The little stove which had seemed so cruelly hot in August now barely warmed its half of the room, and along the floor there ran an icy draught.

Hesper was used to cold winter rooms, but at home they were only in use at night, and the rush from warm bed to the huge crackling fire in the kitchen downstairs had never taken more than a momentary fortitude.

But the months went by, they wore heavy clothes, wool stockings and stout shoes, Evan warmed numb fingers over the stove, and sketched doggedly. He was neither ill-tempered now, nor gay. He treated Hesper with kindness, sparing her all the heavy tasks, and more and more he avoided looking at her as her face grew pinched, the thick white skin lost its translucence, and her body swelled, blurring into grotesque lines. Often he went out on trips to editorial offices, or sometimes to see La Farge, Homer Martin, or Mr. Durand. Once or twice he suggested that Hesper accompany him, but she refused, unequal, during this malaise and lethargy of advancing pregnancy, to making any unnecessary effort, and knowing that he would be happier without her.

Hesper read a great deal, huddled close to the smoky kerosene lamp. She read the magazines in which Evan's drawings appeared, because they usually got free copies. And she read romances that he brought her from a small circulating library on Astor Place. Sometimes these stories were about artists, and these puzzled and surprised her.

One December night as they sat at dinner she mentioned this. The weather had turned warmer, and the loft was more comfortable. She had made a rich chowder, having trudged through the slushy streets all the way to the Washington Market for the clams and haddock and salt pork. She used the famous Hearth and Eagle recipe which incorporated the fish and pork with plenty of potatoes, fried onions, milk, and cream. Susan added a sprinkle of nutmeg, but nutmegs were expensive and Hesper had no grater. All day the chowder had been resting against the stovepipe to blend, and the result pleased Evan.

He leaned back in the creaking chair and crossed his legs. "You're a good cook, my dear," he said. "It's smart what you can do on that miserable stove."

She smiled, savoring the moment of warmth and digestive pleasure. Strange that two people could live so close, and yet it was as though their lives ran in two parallel grooves. She saw the grooves deep and sharp like twin channels, chiseled on an infinite wood plank. Evan and she were two tiny wood ticks, caught in these grooves. What a fancy, she thought. I never used to think ugly things like that when I was writing poetry back home. Ah, but then what fancies had she not had! Of romance, of gold and silver castles and princes.

"Evan—" she said, "I read a story in *Appleton's Journal* about an artist's life, and then the novel by Mrs. Rhoda Broughton, the things they say—it isn't a bit like our life, or even, I guess, like that of those other artists you know."

"How do you mean?" Evan was diverted. The wavering lamplight cast a kindly shadow over her. Her hair, which lately had seemed to lack all life, glowed bronze.

"Why, those artists I read about always seem so gay, even if they're poor. They sing and have parties with models and drink wine out of slippers, and their studios are hung with vivid brocades and they always have a Moorish divan loaded with carelessly tossed pillows."

Evan laughed. "Do they do any work?"

She laughed too, after a moment's hesitation. "I guess so. They starve and struggle and their hearts break, they're in despair, then suddenly—"

"They smuggle a painting past the judges, who've turned it down, hang it on the line, in the Salon of course. The public is enraptured, the critics swoon, jostling each other for the privilege of touching the artist's hand. All Paris is at his feet. After that he doesn't have a care, but he doesn't let his fame and riches spoil him. He marries the sweet little girl from the provinces who has been patiently waiting, or he marries the little model, virtuous as a snowdrop, despite the giddy life, and the Moorish divan."

"Why, you read 'Heart of an Artist,'" she cried, half laughing.

"No. But I can even finish the story. Our hero becomes a superb family man, dandling the little ones on his velvet-clad knee, and he continues to paint masterpieces with one hand while he dandles with the other. Everybody is very happy, especially the sweet little wife who is now dripping with diamonds."

"But doesn't it ever happen like that?" she asked after a moment. "At least I mean the gaiety, and living for the moment. Artists are supposed to be impractical and—"

"Bohemian is the word they use in Paris, I believe," said Evan. "You find me disappointing in the artistic rôle. Perhaps you should remember my solid, middle-class Yankee background, not unlike your own." His chair scraped across the varnished boards, and he got up. "At least I'm becoming a good family man." There was no mistaking the sudden venom in his tone.

Hesper sighed, the moment of intimacy had curdled as it always did nor did this hurt her, as it used to.

Evan was struggling into his greatcoat and muffler. She watched him apathetically. It was an effort to feel or think these days. At the slightest cause the black weariness descended. Her head began to throb and the chowder which had tasted so delicious lay heavy in her stomach.

"I'll be back later," Evan said, his voice once more controlled. "You look very tired, Hesper. Go to bed, I'll fix the stove when I come in."

Christmas and New Year's passed with no celebration except letters from home and a box full of cookies and wool socks from Susan. The letters were unexpressive in the case of Susan, and uninformative in the case of Roger who covered four pages with spidery writing to tell her that he had taken up the study of Arabic, and found it engrossing, even to the point of still further retarding work on the "Memorabilia." He assumed that she was enjoying the "busy marts and stimulating society of the great city with her talented husband," and he thought of her often with deepest affection.

Susan's letter was more objective.

Dear Hes—

How are you keeping? Mind you don't reach up much, it twists the cord. A grummet of dry crust soaked in brandy mostly stops a queasy stummick if you're still bothered. Can't you fix it so's to come here in March? It ud be mighty hard for me to leave the Inn, without that I've no relish for travel. Let me know, there's plenty of time. There was a big fire on Front Street. Brown and Ledger's wharfs both went. They broke out the new engine, the "M. A. Pickett" but she didn't help none. The wind was westerly, and we fretted some here, but Glory be, it shifted.

I served one hundred seventy-one dinners last month, making a tidy profit. Twice had to use the parlor. Mr. Porterman was in yesterday. He's bought a new buggy and a pair of bays. He looks fine and is building a great house up Pleasant Street. Well I guess I'll close now, haveing no more news. Your Pa and me keep pretty good. Remembrance to Mr. Redlake.

Your affectionate—Ma.
SUSAN DOLLIBER HONEYWOOD.

Hesper reread both letters many times. The scenes they evoked would not come vivid, yet an unhappy compulsion continually forced her to try. She lay on the bed shivering beneath the cheap quilts, and pictured the fire on Front Street, the shouts, the church bells clanging, the running feet, the hiss and bang of the pump on the new engine, the excitement and fear in the smoky air. But she could not picture Front Street without Brown and Ledger's wharves.

Nor could she picture such a press of customers as would force Susan to serve them in the sacred parlor. She had been gone six months and already there were changes at home which had seemed unchanging, and this hurt her like a deliberate and callous desertion. She knew it to be unreasonable. Yet the sense of loss persisted.

She thought too about Amos Porterman, the new carriage, and the new house. Likely he was going courting, maybe he and Charity had settled it after all.

I didn't want him, why shouldn't he? she told the hurt resistance in her heart. And she lay hour after hour, not fully awake but staring at the ceiling—the planchment, they called it in Marblehead.

It became increasingly hard to drag herself from bed. Her ankles and feet were puffed like white pincushions, and when the blood ran into them they throbbed painfully. Her head throbbed too, and giddiness swirled in it like water; sometimes black spots swam across her vision and the implacable outlines of the stove, the easel or Evan dissolved into grayish blur. Early in January she fainted on the stairs on a trip down to the water closet on the lower landing. Evan, fortunately at home, soon found her and helped her back to bed.

He was deeply concerned, forbade her to move, and rushing out to Mercer Street summoned a doctor, whose brass plate he had noticed. "Arthur M. Stone, M.D." The young doctor opened the door himself. He had fresh rosy cheeks and a hopeful smile, and he had been graduated two months from the Bellevue Medical College.

"I don't know anything about this kind of thing, of course," said Evan as they hurried along together. "She didn't have much of a fall, but she's been looking very bad. Still, maybe that's natural."

"Oh, certainly. I think so. Quite, quite," said the young doctor nervously. He had had very few obstetrical cases, and those had all been husky Irish girls who did the business themselves in an hour or two.

He was disappointed in the shabby loft after he had climbed all those flights. Mr. Redlake's speech had been cultivated and he had hoped for a rich patient. Still, one would do one's best.

At the end of his quick self-conscious examination, he was not at all sure what his best should be. The girl didn't look right, that was certain, her color was bad, her heart beat irregularly and there certainly seemed to be a lot of edema, even her hands were swollen.

Still she seemed to be in no particular pain, and smiled at him feebly before she again shut her eyes.

He decided to go home and look in his textbooks. Before leaving he opened his bag and poured out a placebo, of colored peppermint water, told Evan in a loud confident voice to keep her in bed and not to worry, said he would return in the evening, and departed.

Hesper opened her eyes and turned her head on the pillow. "Evan—" she whispered—"I'm an awful bother to you. I'm sorry."

He pulled the stool over to the bedside and took her hand. "You're going to be all right, Hesper," he said levelly. "I'll take care of you."

She lay looking up at his averted face. She saw how thin it had grown; the bones of his cheeks and jaws pushed out the dark skin. There were lines she had never noticed before on either side of his mouth and between his eyebrows. His brooding gaze was fixed on the wall beyond the bed.

She made no sound, but the tears ran from her eyes and down her cheeks. Tears of pity for Evan, for the feeble thing that fluttered inside her, and for herself.

That day and the next, he tended her, bringing food from the outside, performing the most intimate duties with a matter-of-fact efficiency. By the next evening, and the undecided young doctor's third visit, the need for diagnosis had passed since Hesper had gone into active labor. Doctor Stone watched her for a few minutes, then with a sensation of relief sent Evan for a midwife.

The woman was fat, she arrived wheezing and panting from the climb, flung her bonnet in the corner, examined Hesper, vouchsafed the young doctor a glance of utter contempt, and rolled back her sleeves.

"You'd best bestir yourself, me fine young cub, and lend me a 'and 'ere, if you don't want to lose 'em both."

Doctor Stone started and flushed. "Labor appears to me quite normal," he said stiffly. "Unfortunately it has come on so early, of course. But she had a slight fall."

"Fall, me foot. It's 'er kidneys 'as backed up, as anyone without a fine medical degree 'ld know. She'll go into fits next, lessen me luck is in. 'Ave you no chloroform in that shiny new bag?"

Doctor Stone threw Evan a miserable look, and followed the midwife behind the baize curtain.

Evan stood in the painting corner by his easel. On the rack there was a half-finished sketch of three young ladies in a rowboat, ordered by *Hearth and Home* for their May issue. He stood looking at the sketch in the dim light. From behind the baize curtain by the bed there came dreadful sounds; the figure of the doctor and midwife hunched like monstrous dwarfs passed and repassed through the lamplight.

Evan's face contorted. He kicked the easel. It swayed and fell sideways against the wall. He turned and ran, coatless, down the stairs into the bitter January night.

The baby was a girl, and it never breathed at all, nor did the doctor and midwife pay much attention to it. A seven-months baby had little chance at best. They had their hands full with Hesper, and when it appeared that she was out of danger, both claimed the credit, credit really due to the sturdy young body, strengthened by years of healthy living and healthy ancestors.

Hesper recovered rapidly, the midwife sent a daily woman in to nurse and cook for three weeks, and at the end of this period Hesper's body felt normal. The binding had come off the breasts, which had been agonizingly distended with milk for which there was no use. Her face and hands and feet returned to their natural fine-boned thinness, her white skin and flaming hair regained their brilliance.

During the weeks of the daily nurse's reign, Evan kept away during the daytime, returning late at night and lying carefully on his side of the bed so as not to disturb her. At seven in the morning, he was already dressed and waiting. The instant the nurse came he went out. The half-finished sketch for *Hearth and Home* remained untouched on the easel.

Since the morning after the birth they had made no reference to the baby. At that time, Doctor Stone had met him on the landing with the tragic news, and had been shocked to have Mr. Redlake interrupt his laborious preamble.

"You mean the baby's dead?" said Evan and at the doctor's reluctant nod, he had added something under his breath that sounded like "Thank God." He had gone to his wife, and kissed her on the forehead. She had raised weighted lids, looking up at him steadily. "There isn't any baby, Evan."

"I know. You've had a bad time, Hesper. Try not to worry about anything."

Doctor Stone, hovering in the background, was puzzled. The words and sentiment were adequate for the circumstances, but somewhere there was a lack. It occurred to him that Mr. Redlake's attitude toward the girl might have been that of any sympathetic friend. You'd never think him part of an intimate mutual tragedy. He's a queer duck. No-account artist, thought Doctor Stone, staring at the cluttered loft and wondering about his fee. Then the obvious explanations for all that puzzled him flew into his mind, and he flushed at his own lack of sophistication. Of course, they aren't married. What a fool I am, he thought, and adopted toward Evan a cold truculence. He presented his bill to date at once, and was somewhat disgruntled to have it paid at once and in cash. Apparently the artistic temperament and irregular morals did not extend to money matters. So Doctor Stone felt disapproving pity for Hesper, congratulated her on her complete recovery, and disappeared forever from the Fourth Street loft. Twenty years later, when Doctor Stone had become a fashionable doctor, he told the story quite differently, and with it bedewed lovely eyes and brought lumps to manly throats at many a Gramercy Park dinner party.

To Hesper, neither doctor, midwife nor daily nurse ever emerged sharply from the gray blur. She followed their commands and allowed them to do what they liked to her body while her spirit withdrew itself to a small shut room and waited.

On Thursday the fourteenth of February a brilliant sun sparkled off the snow and through the skylight which had become a rectangle of blue. Hesper got up early, made coffee and fried bacon, finding zest in these tasks so long suspended. Evan too seemed to share the buoyancy of the day. He ate his breakfast leisurely and showed no signs of going out as usual.

"You look well," he said, wiping his mouth and smiling at Hesper. "Do you feel all right now?"

She nodded. "Never better." She straightened, throwing back her head and shoulders. The sunlight touched her hair to fire and her body, more slender than it had ever been, seemed to glow through the faded calico wrapper. "I'd forgotten what it felt like to be healthy," she said, laughing. Her eyes met Evan's enigmatic gaze. She took a step toward him. Of their own accord her arms lifted, palms outstretched, and her heart began to beat fast.

"Would you like to go out?" he said, still sitting at the table. "I believe there's a minstrel show over at the Olympic today. Poor girl, you've had a thin time of it in New York."

Her arms dropped, the quick rose spread through her cheeks and died.

"Why, of course I would. But, Evan, we couldn't afford it, could we?"

"I'll manage," he said. From somewhere far off she heard the warning bell, and she silenced it angrily. I've no cause for sick fancies now, she thought. Why must I forever be fretting when he doesn't act as I expect? He's been good to me, and now he's planned this outing to give me pleasure.

She dressed herself in the warm blue serge gown he had bought for her in October, thinking what joy it was to have it fit again. She filled her mind with small satisfactions. The blue plush bonnet was becoming, the snow-packed streets were gay with sleigh bells, and in some shop windows there were racks of gawdy valentines.

They lunched at a small café to which neither had been before. She finished everything and a second helping which Evan indulgently ordered for her. She tried not to notice that he ate almost nothing.

The minstrel show was a delight; the end men in absurd pink and blue checked costumes, their enormous mouths left white on the blackened faces, cracked very funny jokes. Pretty broad too. Even Evan laughed at the one about the red-skinned man whose mother had been frightened by an Indian. And most of the songs were funny too, and of a rhythm that set your feet tapping. Until just before the end, when the lights faded on the stage and all the minstrels disappeared except a quartette who put their heads close together and began to sing in murmuring harmony.

At first Hesper, caught by the slow melody, did not understand the words. She leaned back in her seat, conscious of the nearness of Evan's arm, and still buoyed by the gaiety which had gone before and the laugh she and Evan had shared.

But the quartette continued and the audience grew very quiet. And now the words came through to her borne on the mournful tune.

> Look down, look down, that Lonesome Road,
> Hang down your head and sigh.
> The best of friends must part some day
> And why not you and I?

She turned her head and looked up at Evan's dark profile beside her in the dim theater. He seemed to be watching the stage.

"What a stupid song!" cried Hesper suddenly.

"You think so?" said Evan. "Then let's go," and he rose. They pushed their way to the aisle, and out onto Broadway.

He offered her his arm and she took it silently. They walked back to the lodging house. She preceded him up the stairs and waited for him to unlock the door. She took off her bonnet and shawl, hung them up on the peg, then she put some sticks of wood into the stove.

When she had finished and the stove gave out warmth and crackle, she stood beside it, leaning her back against the wall.

"Evan—" she said. He had been washing his hands. At the tone of her voice, he hung the towel on the washstand and came over to her.

"*You* don't think that's a stupid song, do you?" she said. "You think it's true."

"You mean that last thing, Lonesome Road? Must I have an opinion about it?"

She made an impatient gesture. "I'm well now. You can stop trying to spare me. It's all over between us, isn't it? I think you gave me a treat today, the way Ma used to make me a special gingerbread man before she took me to the toothpuller."

"My dear—" He took a step toward her and stopped. "Don't be bitter, Hesper."

"But it's true, isn't it?" she persisted. "The Lonesome Road is what you want. What you've always wanted."

He opened his mouth and shut it again, shrugging his shoulders. He walked over to the chair by the table and sat down.

"Look, Hesper, you're no happier than I am. I can't be a husband. I can't even be a lover for long. I knew damn well it wouldn't work—"

"Then why did you—" her voice thickened, she turned her back to him.

He sighed. "Oh, I suppose because the delusion was beautiful."

"While it lasted."

"While it lasted." His eyes became cold. "I think, whatever my shortcomings, I've not earned reproaches."

No, she thought, he had not earned reproaches. He had warned her first, though she would not listen. And after they knew of the baby's coming he had forced himself to work he loathed. She thought of the days he had nursed her.

She went and sat in the other chair across the table from him, exactly as they had sat for so many meals here in the loft. "What are you planning, Evan?" she asked very low.

In the moment before he answered she felt a new numbness wrap around her heart. Now there was no more pain. The words of the song began a measured beating in her head. "The best of friends must part some day and why not you and I." And we weren't even the best of friends, she thought. Not friends at all.

"I'm going to sail for England, next Thursday, on the *Cedric.*"

"Indeed," she said. "And are you taking someone along to pose for you?"

She raised her head and looked at him. Her hazel eyes steady on his face.

"I am not," he retorted. "Nor will I ever be tied again—in any way. I shall go to Scotland to paint. Then to France probably."

"Paris?" she said. "The Bohemian life you mentioned?"

"Perhaps."

"And what is to become of me?"

"You can't doubt that I've made provision for you. You shall have all I have in the bank, and I'll send you more when I can. Durand has advanced me money for my trip."

She said nothing.

Suddenly he put his hand across the table and touched hers. "Don't look like that, Hesper. You'll go back to Marblehead. You're part of it, and it of you, don't you know that yet?"

She took her hand from under his. The touch had seemed to send fire up her arm and into her breast. The fire consumed the cold numbness. "Why did you touch me, then?" she whispered.

She held herself tight against the chair. Her upturned eyes, no longer steady, searched for his. But they were shuttered against her.

"No, Hesper," he said. "I'll not be caught that way again. You saw what happened, though you never rightly understood. I couldn't paint. My strength went, and all the sureness—the inknowing. I can't travel two roads at once. Maybe the road I've chosen won't lead anyplace. So be it. I've got to follow it."

The loft gathered itself into silence. "Yes," she said. "I see."

He got up and stood beside her, looking down at her. "You'll be much happier, my dear, believe me."

Yes, she thought. I too will be much happier, away from this place of ugliness and pain and failure. Go home, discarded wife. Home to the house that has seen a thousand heartaches before yours. Home where the dozens of Honeywoods will welcome you back into the waiting clan and shelter you from this stranger for whom you deserted them.

She rose and went behind the baize curtain to the bureau where she found pen, ink, and paper.

Evan followed her. "What are you doing, Hesper?"

"I'm going to send Ma a telegram. She'll want some warning."

"There's no hurry," he said uncomfortably. "We have some arrangements to make, and I don't sail for a week."

Hesper gave a brief laugh. "Oh, I'll stay on here a day or two. After all it'll be no different from what it has been these six months." Her pen scratched across the cheap lined paper.

He watched her bent head, the firmly compressed lips. He saw the lovely fluid line of shoulder, bust, and hips, the whiteness of her thin arm and hand as she held the pen, and against her long neck, caught loosely by the black net she had worn for their expedition, the coil of hair, a trifle darker than it used to be, the color of sunlit madeira. It might be possible to paint her now that he was released from her, he thought with sadness. In her face now there was a harshness, a stony resignation that symbolized the spirit of the fisher girl he had been trying to paint in Marblehead. In her face then there had been nothing but youthful excitement and desire to please.

Although for so long he had been eager to leave her whenever he could, he now lingered, hovering near her, himself held by pain different from, but as inexorable as, hers.

It was she who dismissed him. She folded the paper across, and held it out to him.

"Be so kind as to send this message for me, Evan. And you can find some other place to spend the night, no doubt."

He bowed his head, and took the paper silently. For a moment they confronted each other across the shiny square of oil cloth on the floor. The fire in the stove had died down, the kerosene lamp sputtered and spurted smoke against its cracked glass chimney. Above them night lay black against the skylight.

"I'm sorry—" said Evan. He turned and went out, closing the door carefully behind him.

He had returned in the morning with two hundred dollars, and he had bought her a ticket to Boston. They had been very polite with each other. She accepted the money and ticket calmly, and then told him that she wished nothing more, from him. "I'll get along at home as I always did," she said in a thin, formal voice. It was he who mentioned divorce, a word she scarcely knew. "Not that I care," said Evan, "but in time you may wish to be quite free. I'll do whatever's necessary, of course, you have but to write me." To this she had answered nothing at all, for the subject seemed to her unimportant. She had no tears now, nor inclination towards them. She observed herself and Evan with detachment.

Evan tried to be generous, to share with her his few possessions, his paintings too. She would accept nothing.

When their discussion had ended, she held out her hand and said,

"I guess that's everything." Her hand was cool and steady, her eyes were cool and green as the sea. Her speech was clipped.

"Good-bye," she said. "Now that you're rid of the anchor drag, I hope you'll be a very great painter."

"Hesper—don't— Maybe I'm no artist at all, it's just that—"

"Good-bye, Evan," she said.

At seven that evening she sat alone in the loft. Her box and trunk were packed, ready for the morning train to Boston. She had drunk a glass of milk, and now she sat by the table staring at an old copy of Harper's which she had read two months ago. The lamp sputtered as it always did and smelled of kerosene. But the smell of paint and turpentine was gone. The painting corner was empty of easel and canvas, instead it contained her strapped cowhide trunk.

One more night to spend on that bed. She looked at it with loathing. The cheap speckled brass, and two knobs missing from the top whorls. The lumpy flock mattress, the sagging springs that grated and quivered. On that bed she had known passion and laughter, on this bed she had brought forth her stillborn child, but in these memories there was no reality. They had happened to someone else, like Corinna, this heroine in Harper's. She leafed through the pages, rereading a snatch of the story here and there.

Evan had drawn the tailpiece which showed Corinna in her bridal dress with a coronet on her head.

Hesper shoved the magazine across the table. I'll have to get out very early to find a hackney that'll take the trunk, she thought. I must allow plenty of time. The shore-line train started from Twenty-seventh Street and Fourth Avenue. Wasn't there a stop for food at New London, or should she take some sandwiches? How long would she have to stay in Boston before catching a Marblehead train? Would the trunk go with her, or was there some way it could be sent afterwards? Of the details of the trip down she remembered almost nothing. I wish I had a watch, she thought. Evan had had one, but she had never owned any timepiece. She would have to judge the hour of getting up by the skylight, then listen for the Grace Church chimes. I wish I could go tonight, she thought, but there wasn't a night train. Perhaps it wasn't too early to try to sleep.

She lifted the stovelid, and poked at the sulky embers. Suddenly she heard steps on the stairs outside; the fourth tread from the top squeaked as it always did. Her hand fell from the poker, and her heart gave a leap. But he wouldn't come back now. It was finished. Why should he come back?

The door resounded under a determined knock. She expelled her breath sharply, staring at the peeling wooden panels. "Evan?" she called, her voice high and shaking. There was a low indistinct murmur.

She unlocked the door and opened it an inch. A very large man, much taller than Evan, stood on the landing, indistinct in the gloom.

"What do you want?" she whispered, holding the door against her body.

The figure bent near. "Don't be afraid, Hesper. It's Amos Porterman. Let me in."

She moved slowly back, pulling the knob with her. Amos came in stamping the snow from his boots. His startled gaze swept the cold miserable loft, and Hesper, thin and white, shrinking to the wall by the stove, and staring at him.

"My poor child," he said. "I've come to take you home."

The black wash of hope and disappointment receded from her. She moved from the wall toward him. "It's good of you to come, Mr. Porterman. Let me have your coat and muffler. Did Ma send you?"

"No. But she showed me your telegram, and I wanted to come, and she was glad of that. Where's Redlake, my dear?"

My dear. Evan had called her that so often and always the two words had been tinged with irony.

She shrugged her shoulders. "I don't know. He's gone."

Amos's lower lip jutted out. Under the bushy blond eyebrows his eyes narrowed to slits. "The yellow-bellied bastard. I'll find him and—"

"No, no—" she whispered on a note of weary exasperation. "Please. Let be. I don't want to talk about it."

Amos sat down heavily on the other chair, Evan's chair. His powerful hands rested on his thighs. "Well—" he said. "Well—" His breath came like smoke in the chill room. "I've not changed. I don't want to displease you."

She looked at him and smiled a little. His big comforting presence warmed the room. Is he then still fond of me? she thought, vaguely. "How are Ma and Pa?" she said. "And the Inn, and your factory?"

Amos shook his head. He saw the exhaustion in the drop of her body, heard the effort in her voice. She'd been through even worse than he'd known about, it seemed, though what Mrs. Honeywood had told him of the stillbirth, and her husband sending her home, was bad enough. Bastard, he thought again. He wanted to take her in his arms and hold her like a child, letting that tired head rest on his shoulder.

"The questions 'll all wait, Hes," he said quietly. "You look fit to drop in your tracks. Get some rest, and I'll be back with a cab in the morning, eight sharp, in case you're sleeping, there'll be time to rouse you."

"Thank you—" she said. "I was wondering how to manage." He stood up, and she went over to him, laying her hand on his arm. With him there was no self-consciousness, no uncertainty or fear of rebuff. Because it didn't matter. With Evan she had always been the heavy, the serious one, but Amos made her feel weightless, fluid as quicksilver.

"Mind you don't get pixilated in this great blaring city—" she said with faint humor. "Oh, I forgot you're not a Marbleheader."

He covered her hand with his. "Did you forget that, Hesper? Did you really?"

She slipped away from him, but Amos was happy. Happier than ever before in his life. The brief spring-time love for Lily Rose had not been like this. There'd been never a day since Hesper married that he hadn't thought of her with bitter yearning. And now at last he had hope. It would be bad. A long time before she got over that fellow. And then a mess. Divorce. He quailed at this, but there was no help for it. It could be done quietly. But if she'll have me, we'll face 'em all down. He had a vision of her dressed in velvet and lace, a decent dress for once in her life, standing in the gilt and rosewood hall of his new house, waiting for him to come home. And she would be smiling as she was now—gently, gratefully.

He wrapped his muffler around his neck, and picked up his hat.

"Ah, my dear—" he said, "I'll be well content to bring you home, where you belong."

"And I to go—" she answered—her shadowed eyes resting on the empty corner where Evan's canvases had once stood.

CHAPTER 13

On the new year's morning of 1877, Hesper awoke to a placid contentment. It seemed to be sleeting outside, she could hear the faint crackle on the window panes behind the drawn plush curtains, but here in the great mansion on Pleasant Street, weather never seemed important.

She yawned and stretched, burying her head deeper into the soft frilled pillow. It must be nearly nine o'clock. Soon Annie would knock and come in with coffee, draw back the portières, and light the fire. Though you really did not need a fire when the hot-air registers kept the whole house warm as summer.

Amos, beside her in the huge double bed, snorted a little and flopped over. She raised herself on her elbow and looked down at him with amused affection. Since their marriage he had grown sideburns; they were soft and wavy, a shade darker than his flaxen hair, and he was very proud of them. But despite his bearded cheeks and his size, when he was asleep and the pucker lines smoothed from his forehead, he was the image of little Henry.

I do hope there *is* going to be another, she thought. Lately she had been almost certain, but there had been false alarms before, and Henry was already seven. Dear Amos—she had never imagined he could show such feeling as he had on the night that Henry was born. Amos wasn't much of a one for showing emotion, even in their most intimate moments. That part of marriage was moderate and tender and pleasantly satisfying.

And I'm glad it's that way, she thought. I had enough of the other thing with Evan. She lay back on the pillow again, deliberately remembering—as she had not been willing to do in years—those strange ecstatic, and then miserable, eight months with Evan. The memory no longer brought much pain and it was hard to believe they ever happened.

She had heard no word from or about him in the nine years since the final divorce decree came through. He had been in London then, and he had sent a cable that said, "Better luck—Redlake." It had angered her very much at the time and she had burned it up at once in the great fireplace at home between Phebe's andirons, saying to her, "Take that, you and your wifely virtues and your enduring courage!" And she had been very impatient with her father's fumbling attempts at comfort, and resentful of her mother's "I told you so's." Yet her parents had been good to her during that difficult time of waiting. They had borne with her prickly defensive moods, and shielded her from Marblehead's gossip. There hadn't been as much scandal as they had feared. Amos had seen to it that the divorce on grounds of desertion was discreetly handled in Boston. Only a few of the old Marbleheaders knew the facts—the Dolliber connection and the Peaches—and they rallied around to protect their own. Poor Hes had had a dreadful time with some worthless furriner, and had had to get shet of him. Well, it served her right—but least said soonest mended.

Her marriage to Amos was quite another matter. She and Amos had driven back from Salem and the magistrate's ceremony to face virtual ostracism from the old Marbleheaders, and a chill indifference from the newer industrial society. The first group felt that Hesper had forfeited all indulgence by this demented new alliance with another furriner, one, moreover, whose aggressive business tactics, ornate new mansion, and continual exhortations in town meeting towards expansion and progression made him increasingly unpopular. The shoemen and their wives had simpler motives. Amos was taking business away from many older firms, and that redheaded Honeywood woman he'd suddenly married had some sort of an unsavory past. Some said widow, some said not. There was a rumor that she had at best actually been a factory hand herself once, and came from that dilapidated old fishing inn down by the wharves. Not the sort of person you'd call on. And they did not call.

Charity Trevercombe, whose motives were simplest of all, since Hesper had captured the man Charity had marked for her own, did her best to keep the animosity hot against them for a while. But then suddenly, after her mother had died, Charity had experienced a kind of conversion and lost her resentment, so that now relations were friendly enough.

Ah, well, thought Hesper, it's a stupid little town anyway. I've grown beyond it. I wish we didn't have to have Ma and Pa for dinner tonight. For the Portermans were planning a dinner party in honor of the Hay-Bottses, an English couple they had met the summer before at Franconia Notch. Charity had been invited and Eben Dorch, a middle-aged bachelor, to escort her, and it was a pity that the elder Honeywoods must also be included. You never could tell what Ma might say, and you knew all too well what Pa would, but they always came to New Year's dinner. Ma closed the Inn and planned for it weeks ahead, and it was the only time Pa would leave home. It had been a terrible struggle to get him out the first New Year's Day after their marriage, but now he looked forward to it eagerly. The annual dinner had become tradition.

Hesper sighed and smiled a little. Poor Pa and tradition. . . .

There was a loud knock at the door and Annie stamped in with the coffee. Her white morning apron and the streamers on her cap were freshly starched for the New Year, but scarcely mitigated her crumpled uniform and frowsy stack of hair. She said, "Happy New Year to yez, mum, I'm sure—" put the tray down with a clatter, flung back the heavy mustard plush curtains, and put a match to the waiting fire, managing to knock over the brass fire tongs as she did so.

Amos waited until the girl had gone out, then he said with unusual querulousness, "Dammit—can't you get something better than Annie—or train her better?"

Hesper sat up, shaking back the thick braids, and staring at him surprised. "Why—what's the matter with her? She gives good service, and she and Bridget get on well, and she's good to Henry. Oh, Amos, stop scowling. I never thought you'd wake up cross. It's New Year's Day and I've just been thinking how nice our life is."

Amos gave a mollified grunt, swallowing his coffee. He'd learned by now that Hes wasn't much of a one for noticing little things, but she was a mighty good wife for all that, loyal and responsive and usually sweet-tempered. And she set a good table—if she didn't always keep the hired girls up to the mark.

He stood up beside the bed, sliding his feet into his carpet slippers. A fine figure of a man, she thought, even in his night shirt, that showed the golden hairs on his chest and massive legs. A heavy man, but she didn't mind that. Solid, dependable. And just as he'd looked older when he was in his twenties, now in the middle forties he looked younger.

"What are you fretting about, dear?" she asked gently. "You haven't even wished me a Happy New Year."

He put on his quilted maroon bathrobe, pulled the tasseled cord tight, came around the great bed and kissed her. She put her arms about his neck, and kissed him back, but Amos was preoccupied. He gave her a pat on the buttocks and went over to the fireplace, to warm the back of his legs in the age-old masculine manner.

He *was* fretting, but he had no intention of sharing his worries with Hesper. Protecting her from worry, coddling her with ease and luxury had been one of the pleasantest parts of a satisfactory marriage. It hadn't been possible to dazzle Lily Rose, who came from a wealthy home, but Hes from the very beginning had received her new way of life with astonishment and gratitude. The elegant mansion, the carriage, the two hired girls, and the coachman, the wardrobe full of new clothes, the trips, to Portsmouth and Boston, and the White Mountains, the bathroom with its huge zinc tub edged with mahogany in which he could hear her splashing right now.

Amos pulled a cigar from the humidor on the marble mantel and lit it. He thought about tonight's party. Bit of luck, meeting Hay-Botts at the Franconia House in New Hampshire last August. Wealthy Englishman from Bristol, boot and shoe manufacturer, and interested in the industry here. If he could only be persuaded to invest in the factory.

Thing to do was to keep him away from Lynn if possible, convince him Marblehead was still the foremost shoe center. And it is too, Amos thought, this is only a temporary recession. He frowned at the veined marble hearth and spat into the fire.

No denying money was tight since the panic of '73. Got to get the bank to grant an extension. Got to get O'Malley's order out fast. God damn those lasters. Threatening strike again. And we've only held up their pay checks three weeks. Some of the other factories are a month behind.

He walked over to his wardrobe and extracted a letter and a clipping from the vest pocket of the suit he had worn yesterday.

The letter was unsigned, printed in penciled capitals on cheap paper. It opened without salutation and said:

"Amos Porterman! What right have you to do business on money belonging to others without paying a rate of interest for hired money? How dare you hold up our pay again, to further your own selfish interests? Has it come to this that Marblehead Americans must submit to the lash of Boss, because they ask for what they earned? Think not we are hapless slaves! We know what to do."

And the attached clipping was from the *Marblehead Messenger,* and began, "The Grand Scribe of the Knights of Saint Crispin addressed all shoemakers at Lyceum Hall last night, on 'the grievous wrongs of Labour.' "

Amos wadded the two pieces of paper and threw them into the fire. Damn fools—I haven't the *money* to pay them until we ship O'Malley's order and get the check. They know that, they know I've always treated them right. He thought with indignation of their ingratitude. What about the pension he paid out of his own pocket to old Smitty the retired cutter? The milk he was buying for Bodfin's sick child? The bottle of rum the factory donated to each honorably discharged hand? The free beer on holidays?

I wonder could Nat Cubby be at the bottom of this new agitation, thought Amos suddenly, and felt a spasm of disquiet.

Hesper came out of the bathroom, glowing above a frilled muslin negligée, her damp hair curling around her face.

"Heavens, Amos—" she cried. "You still standing there and scowling. Whatever *is* the matter?"

"Oh nothing—" he began, following his usual pattern. But he paused, she looked fresh and strong and handsome, her wide mouth smiling, her level eyebrows like composed black wings above her questioning eyes. His steady affection heightened to awareness, and an unusual impulse made him speak. He laughed casually.

"As a matter of fact, Hes, I was thinking of Nat Cubby. There's a bit of trouble at the factory."

"Nat Cubby?" she repeated, puzzled. "Why, I thought he'd settled down long ago, and was doing fine. He's head laster, isn't he?" She hadn't thought of Nat in years. She could hardly remember the story, but sometime during Hesper's absence in New York, Leah had had pneumonia and nearly died. After her difficult recovery she had become an invalid, never left the house. And Nat had changed at the same time, acted more contented—people said. Paid attention to his work, and quit grumbling. Never went anywhere except straight home from the factory, but then he'd always done that anyway.

Hesper's nightmare fancies, and the panic she had felt at supper that night with the Cubbys so long ago, now seemed to her ridiculous. Indeed most memories of her Marblehead life before Evan seemed vague and distorted.

"Yes—" said Amos. "He's a good laster. I guess I'm crazy. No reason to think it's Nat. Everybody's having labor troubles." As a matter of fact the letter had not sounded like Nat, words too fancy. More like these Knights of Saint Crispin agitators.

But Nat had been acting queer lately. Drinking a lot more than he used to, and muttering to himself. And one day last week, after hearing Johnson's report, Amos had made a special trip up to the making room, just to say a word to Nat, and ask him how his mother was. All through these years since that regrettable episode with Leah, he had shown Nat unusual consideration, and at Christmas he always told Johnson to send the Cubbys an expensive hamper of hothouse fruit, for which Nat often expressed terse thanks. There'd been no trouble at all. Nat's attitude last week had, therefore, been perplexing.

Instead of answering Amos' civil inquiry, Nat had given him a peculiar sideways look, of a tigerish furtiveness, spat out a mouthful of tacks and hunched his narrow shoulders over the last.

Amos had still lingered. He watched Nat's expert motions as he seized another wet upper from the bin beside him, pulling and shaping it in his skinny brown hands before tacking it to the prepared sole, molding it onto the numbered wooden last and then flinging it on a rack to dry. Of the thirty-six operations required to make a shoe, this was the most important. It was the shoe's actual birth, the climax when all the amorphous pieces of leather were fused into a recognizable entity, and the sight always gave Amos gratification, not unmixed with regret that at this moment of midwifery none of the new machinery was of the slightest use.

"You're a skilled laster, Nat—" he said, looking over the many gleaming tools on the edge of Nat's bench. The pinchers, the tack pullers, the toe bone and knives, and the hot iron for smoothing which rested on the tiny oil stove. "I like to see a man buy good tools and keep them neat."

The hands always provided their own tools, though Amos was more generous than the other factory owners in supplying wax. And yet that infernal union of Saint Crispin had the gall to demand that the owners buy the tools.

As Amos stood there, Nat pushed rudely past him to hold a sole into the light, squinting at some flecks of glue. It was then that Amos noticed three long angry marks on the laster's cheek. Marks like scratches; one of them had turned a lumpy purple and showed a thin yellow line of pus.

"Why, what've you done to your face, Nat? Not an accident here, I hope."

Nat put the sole down on the bench, picked up the hot smoothing iron, and rubbed along the channeled edge. "No, you bostard, but you're the cause of it, all the same."

Amos, stiffening, could not believe he had heard aright. Nat's voice was very low and mumbling, and he smelled strongly of rum. He replaced the hot iron on the stove, and picked up another sole without pausing. The other lasters, too, had settled into routine after the momentary flurry at the boss's appearance. The making room presented its normal medley of purposeful action, in the tap of the hammers, the hiss of the smoothing irons, the smell of wet leather and glue.

Amos glanced again at Nat, cleared his throat, and walked downstairs to his office.

It couldn't be Leah. Not after all these years of quiet. Everybody knew that her critical illness had cured her of the crazy spells and left her a feeble invalid entirely dependent on Nat's care. It was a pity about that—that unfortunate incident that evening long ago, but that's all it was, an incident. And I couldn't help it—after all I'm a man, and she— Amos had banged up the lid of his roll-top desk, sat down, and irritably yanked toward him a sheaf of unopened bills. Anyway, nobody ever knew, or would have believed her if she had said anything.

I must have heard Nat wrong, thought Amos, or else he was just drunk and rambling. He had put the matter out of his mind, and he did so again, now, in favor of the more immediate problems of the Hay-Botts' entertainment.

"Hes, I'd like everything to run very smooth while they're here. Like 'em to stay over a few days, get Hay-Botts to invest in the factory."

"Yes, dear, I understand—" answered Hesper blithely. "Don't worry. Everything'll be fine." But she had not the faintest idea of the extent of Amos's worries. He was and always had been the miraculous provider of comfort. He seldom mentioned the factory, and discouraged her from doing so. She understood very well that he preferred to forget that she had ever been one of his stitching hands, and she was quite willing to forget it.

There was a precise double knock on the door, and Henry entered. "Good morning, Mama and Papa—" he said submitting to Hesper's hug. Annie had dressed him in his best velvet jacket and plaid kilts, his pale taffy hair was slicked into sausage curls on his large head. He had a clear, high voice, read exceptionally well for seven, and caused no trouble at all, unless he was subjected to a breach in routine or expectation. This he disliked, and combated by obstinate silences.

Amos patted his son on the shoulder and said, "Well, my boy—have you learned the verses you're going to speak for the company this evening?"

Henry nodded, and began. "What does little birdie say—"

His parents listened proudly, Hesper ready to prompt. But Henry needed no prompting.

I hope the new baby will be a girl, she thought, and she had an instant vision of it, dark and tiny and helpless. A baby that cooed and clung as Henry never had. Not that Henry wasn't a darling.

He finished his rehearsal and the family went down to breakfast.

The sleet had changed to light snow and a gray uncertain light wavered through the large dining room. Amos pulled down the center gasolier and lit the burners. The harsh white glare funneled down on the white table cloth, and sharply illuminated the woodwork trim—grained to imitate marble, the brown-plaster copy of "The Ragged Urchin" which stood on a pedestal in the bay window between two rubber plants, the fireplace which was never used and was filled by a fan-shaped pink paper frill, renewed twice a year.

Annie clumped around the table flanking Amos with platters of griddle cakes and sausages, pies and a fried steak. Hesper served the scrambled eggs and poured the coffee, smiling at her two menfolk.

During the minutes of listening to Henry recite, she had suddenly been sure, instead of guessing, that she was indeed to have another baby. And she was happy. A new baby would make up for everything. Make up for what? she thought, laughing at herself, I've got everything.

The morning progressed pleasantly. She inspected the spare room which Annie had already prepared for the Hay-Bottses. She descended to the basement kitchen and ran over the dinner menu with Bridget, and she was relieved to find that both activities seemed to be superfluous. The spare room was presentable, and under Annie's resentful eye she did not investigate very closely. In Bridget's department, the fish chowder was already simmering on the stove, the squash and apple pies cooling in the pantry, and the ice cream waiting in its bucket of rock salt to be churned.

Dinner was to be at seven instead of midday, in deference to the Hay-Bottses who were not arriving until three, and had moreover mentioned at Franconia Notch that they were accustomed to evening dinner, so after lunch Amos departed in the big sleigh with Tim, the coachman, to meet the guests at Salem. There were no direct trains to Marblehead on holidays.

Hesper went upstairs and dressed herself in her best afternoon gown. It was a dark blue moiré, lavishly trimmed with shiny black bugles and scrollwork braid, and gathered into a large bustle in back. She put on the coral necklace, brooch, and earrings which Amos had given her, wound her heavy auburn braids into a coil around her head, dusted her face with rice powder, and went downstairs to the drawing room to wait in perfect confidence.

She no longer worried about her appearance. The doubts and uncertainties of her first youth were far behind. And though she knew that Amos did not find her beautiful—as Evan had sometimes—she knew that he was pleased with her appearance, particularly when she was dressed as she was now, in an elaborate Boston-made gown, for which he never begrudged the high price.

She sat down in the bay window in the drawing room, where she could look out under the porte-cochère and watch the approaching curve of the drive as it mounted the steep little rise on which their tall mustard-colored mansion was situated.

Her eyes wandered and rested on the cast-iron stag in the center of the lawn. The stag was powdered now with fine snow along its back and antlers, and seemed very lifelike. Amos had paid nearly two hundred dollars for the stag and he was extremely proud of it.

Around the margin of the window there ran strips of colored glass, red, yellow, blue, and purple, and Hesper moved her head up and down so that she might see the stag reflected in shifting tinted worlds. A pink stag on rosy snow, and then a yellow, or a purple. A childish game invented for Henry who had shown no interest in it. "But Mama—" he had protested, "it's only make-believe. The lawn isn't really pink or blue, and it isn't a real deer anyhow."

Maybe the new baby—

Hesper started forward with a slight exclamation, and peered through the clear glass. Against the bare forsythia bushes behind the stag, she had caught sight of motion. As she stared a small man in a peaked cap stepped out onto the open snow, turning his head slowly from side to side as though he searched for something.

Her muscles tensed, ready to run to the front door and ask his business there, when he raised his head and looked straight up at the house.

Why, it's Nat Cubby—she thought, her movement checked by astonishment. The snow had stopped, and a thin watery sunlight fell on his pallid face; the scar above his lip and three livid marks on his left cheek stood out sharply. She could see the breath vapor from his mouth and the yellowish glint of his puckered eyes.

What's he doing here? What's he looking for?—she thought in confusion, and for a moment she shrank back, hiding behind the portière. Then her common sense returned. Lord, she said to herself, don't be a fool. Go ask him!

She raised her chin and walking through the hall to the front door, flung it open. But Nat had disappeared, doubtless back through the bushes and down to the street, as he had come.

She returned to the drawing room. Probably he had just come from curiosity, wanted to see what the house looked like since they'd re-painted and put the fretwork around the cupola. Maybe they'd been talking about it in the town. The most elegant mansion in Marblehead, that's what it was, even if they wouldn't admit it. Only why hadn't he rung the bell? She would have been glad to have him come in—for old times' sake. It had been a long while since she had talked to any-body from down-town, except of course Ma and Pa.

She walked restlessly about the drawing room, her earlier contented mood shattered, and conscious of a desire for companionship.

The large house seemed very still and empty. Bridget was inaudible in the basement kitchen, and Henry had gone out with Annie for his usual afternoon walk.

She tried to distract herself by a conscious appraisal of the drawing room's elegant furnishings. The Gothic peaked walnut and mohair chairs Amos had bought in Portsmouth. The bouquet of wax roses under glass. The lithograph of a Spanish galleon sailing on a sea made of thin slabs of mother of pearl.

There was a red brocaded throw over the round center table, and in the exact middle there lay a plush and gilt album like the one in her mother's parlor. But this was not really an album; the gilded leaves were made of china, and when the plush cover was lifted it disclosed a candy box.

"Make-believe?" Hesper said half in anger, half in question. What nonsense. Their possessions were new and fashionable and she was as proud of them as Amos was.

She heard the tinkle of the sleigh bells, and the swishing thud of the horses' feet as the sleigh drew up under the porte-cochère, and she hurried to open the door. But the Hay-Bottses arrival did little to re-store her tranquillity.

They followed Amos silently into the house. They were muffled in greatcoats, fur caps and tippets. They stood a moment before they both murmured, "How d'you do—" in tepid tones, then waited like twin cocoons, immobile by the hat rack.

George Hay-Botts was a round bullet of a man with a booming voice, and normally jovial. Emmeline Hay was the daughter of a Wiltshire squire who considered that she had lowered herself to marry George Botts, the son of a wine merchant. But George had agreeably repaid the condescension by making a fortune, first through the sale of the sherry called "Bristol Milk" and then by expansion into boot manufacturing and tanneries. The addition of his wife's name to his own, the purchase of a country seat, and the probability of being returned for Parliament in the next elections, all contributed to Emmeline's complacence with herself and her choice.

The trip to America, moderately entertaining at first, had long since degenerated into tedious discomfort. George had business interests to sustain him; Emmeline, after a disappointing visit to cousins in Toronto, had no interests. Nothing but a consuming desire to board the ship for England which was to sail from Boston on the sixth of January. It was this geographical nearness to Marblehead which had led George to take up the fervent invitation issued them last summer by the Portermans.

One did things like that in this excessive country, it appeared. Americans thought nothing of impounding strangers, and enthusiastically plying them with unconsidered hospitality.

Well, Emmeline thought, standing motionless in the front hall, the tip of her nose purple from the frigid drive, here we are.

"Do take off your things—" said Hesper, nervously plucking at Emmeline's sealskin cape. "We can hang them in the closet."

Emmeline stepped back, and carefully unfastened the hook and eye. Not even a parlor maid. One had thought the Portermans people of wealth and refinement last summer at that mountain hotel. But last summer, just after landing, one had been inclined to view Americans with a more charitable eye.

"Perishing cold, what!" said George, suddenly coming to life, and stamping his feet. The veins gleamed like red threads in his ruddy cheeks.

"Not in here—" said his wife, with a thin smile. "You Americans keep your houses extraordin'r'ly warm. It is, as I wrote my dear brother, the vicar of Whitchurch, a land of violent contrasts."

She allowed Hesper to take the cape, and divested herself of her long furry tippet. She followed Hesper into the drawing room, and they sat down. Emmeline wore a shapeless gray wool dress, and her sealskin cap perched like a doughnut atop her faded blond hair. She folded her hands in her lap, thereby quite unconsciously exhibiting several magnificent diamond rings. She fixed a remote eye on the lithograph of the Spanish galleon, and waited.

The men sat down in two of the Gothic walnut chairs by the empty fireplace. Amos asked a question about the use of the American buffer in the Hay-Botts boot manufactury, and Hesper saw with relief that at least the men were talking.

"Would you like to go to your room, maybe?" said Hesper desperately. "Tim, the coachman, took the bags up."

Emmeline detached her gaze from the galleon, and let it rest on Hesper's flushed face. Extraordin'ry lookin' woman, she thought. All that ginger-colored hair, and black eyebrows, rather poor form, overdressed like all Americans.

"Why, no—" she said. "I believe I'll not retire to our rooms until after tea."

Tea. Hesper swallowed. Tea was a meal in England, wasn't it? And there was no tea in the house unless Bridget had some for herself.

Emmeline saw the consternation, and having met the situation before read its meaning. She waited, not maliciously but implacably. If one must endure overheated houses, outlandish hours and food, and in this case inadequate service, apparently, one must at least have tea.

Hesper rose, excused herself, and went down to the kitchen. Bridget had tea and further proffered the information that "them English" would probably want it at four o'clock, and it would raise the very devil with the dinner preparations, since Annie was needed in the kitchen. Hesper soothed her as best she could, ordered tea, and returned to the drawing room.

Emmeline, appeased by the news, now thawed a trifle. She observed signs in George which meant he was interested in Mr. Porterman's conversation, or to be explicit, a certain eagerness that meant George saw the gleam of still more money to be amassed.

She arranged herself more comfortably on the slippery mohair sofa and prepared to chat.

"Y'know, I'm quite hopeless about American geography, but I rather got the impression before we arrived that this town—uh—Marblehead, was on the seacoast."

These chance and passionless words gave Hesper a shock.

"It *is* on the seacoast," she answered hotly. "It's—it was the foremost fishing port in New England. We have a very fine harbor."

"Indeed? I don't remember seeing the sea."

"Well, of course you couldn't from here. We're two miles out of town. You get no idea of the town from here."

"Indeed?" said Emmeline again, mildly astonished at the woman's sudden vehemence.

"I was born right by the sea, in an old house, the oldest in Marblehead."

"Ah, really?" said Emmeline, varying the formula. "How old would that be?" In Buffalo she had been urged to admire the antiquity of a preposterous frame shack built fifty years ago.

"It was started in 1630 and many rooms added on at different times."

Emmeline was interested. Even for England that was a respectable date, and the phrase "many rooms" suggested a manorial spaciousness.

"Does your family still live there?" she asked.

"My mother and father, yes. You'll meet them at dinner later."

"Your father is in business here too, like Mr. Porterman?"

"Oh, no—" said Hesper, bored with this catechism and preoccupied with an inner disquiet. "He doesn't do anything. He—he writes a little."

Emmeline now readjusted all her ideas. Her mouth lost its condescension, and she looked upon Hesper as almost an equal, seeing here a marriage like her own, the daughter of gentry and a prospering business man—reduced, of course, to American terms, but still most reassuring.

"I should so much like to see your little town and your old home," said Emmeline with what amounted to warmth.

"Well, I'll drive you around tomorrow," answered Hesper unenthusiastically and rose as Annie came bustling in with the tea tray. She found that she did not want to drive Mrs. Hay-Botts around Marblehead.

It was not that she feared to expose the town to critical eyes. Emmeline's approval had during the last few minutes become unimportant. It was rather that she had had a sudden vision of the town as a hostile entity. She saw it crouching there two miles away, huddled beneath the snow, girdled by greenish-black water and black snow-capped rocks. She felt it accusing her, and central to it all, the nub of the accusation, she saw the shabby old, old house on the waterfront, from which she had been so glad to move with Amos. She saw it with the clarity and meaning it had had on Evan's painted canvas, in the New York picture gallery, but now she felt an impact of warning, of brooding enmity.

What is the matter with me? she thought, am I making all this to-do just from seeing Nat? It's not like me to have fancies. There's no reason for guilt. We've done our best by Ma and Pa, all they'd let us. I haven't neglected them. And we improved the house, put gas in despite Pa. And as for the town, it's nothing but a narrow-minded hard-bitten little village. If it wasn't for the shoemen like Amos they'd all starve. I wonder if he couldn't maybe sell the shoe factory and move away altogether. And she knew that this thought was the first sharp upthrust of what had long lain beneath the surface.

Emmeline, seeing her hostess grown grave and unresponsive, very different from the gauche eagerness to please she had shown upon the Hay-Bottses' arrival, was still further reassured. She drank her tea, and felt that if the visit should progress along these lines of cool reserve, it might be quite endurable after all.

She said as much to her husband when they had gone upstairs to rest and dress for dinner. "Really quite decent for Americans. . . . Mrs. Porterman quite a lady, superior background. I freely admit, George, that I misjudged her. But one has met so many odd people while racketing around this extraord'n'ry country, one hardly knows how to judge any more. Their customs and their speech, so different from ours, but I quite realize one must be broad-minded."

To these observations George replied with a grunt. "Porterman seems a sound enough feller. Sound business man. I'll 'ave a look at 'is fact'ry tomorrow. Shouldn't wonder if it wouldn't be a good place to leave a spot of cash."

In the Porterman bedroom across the hall, Amos and Hesper were also talking. As soon as the door was shut, he pulled her to him and gave her a hearty jubilant kiss. "It's in the bag, Puss. I think."

Hesper returned the kiss gently, emerging with an effort from her own depression.

"What's in the bag, dear?"

"Hay-Botts and his pounds sterling, a couple of thousand of 'em I hope."

She looked up at him wondering. He looked elated, almost boyish.

"Is it so important, Amos? You didn't tell me. Isn't the factory doing well?"

"Why, of course it is. Just a little temporary pinch, that's all. Nothing for you to worry about. Just you keep on being nice to Emmeline, and we'll try to make 'em enjoy their visit. George is a great one for what he calls 'sound home life.' Says he judges everything by a man's home life."

He smiled at her. "We've got a good home life, haven't we, Hessie?" He reached in the humidor and pulled out a cigar.

"Yes," she said. "We've been happy."

Something in her intonation checked him. "Why'd you say it like that, like a question?"

"I don't know. I didn't mean to." She moved to the window, and parting the curtains, stared out. It was snowing again, snowing quite hard, but through the dusk and the softly falling flakes she could see the outline of the iron stag. She had no impulse to tell him of Nat's appearance. There was nothing Amos could do about it and no use in worrying him.

Behind her in the room she could hear Amos slamming bureau drawers, opening the door of the wardrobe and whistling cheerfully through his teeth. Her answer had satisfied him, and his thought had reverted to the successful progress of negotiations with Hay-Botts. He looked forward to the dinner party. He enjoyed entertaining, and it was a pity they had so little opportunity.

Hesper still by the window watched their sleigh glide from the stable along the drive and disappear over the sharp rise down to Pleasant Street. That was Tim, following orders to fetch the Honeywoods from the Inn to the party. I wish Ma and Pa weren't coming, she thought, not with the rueful amusement of that thought in the morning, but with violence.

She turned from the window and began to rearrange her hair. Her hands and feet seemed weighted with lethargy, but she took unusual pains. Everything must be right for Amos at the dinner party.

CHAPTER 14

EBEN DORCH arrived first at the Porterman mansion that New Year's night. He came in a sleigh hired from the livery stable. He was a spruce little bachelor who lived on Washington Street above his drug-store. He was a town selectman, a member of the Samaritan Tent of the Rechabites, a Freemason, and just now campaigning for election to the state legislature on the temperance and reform ticket. Marblehead was in the grip of a great temperance revival, and Eben's affiliation with it was dictated by policy rather than conviction.

So, indeed, was his acquaintance with the Portermans. Amos Porterman might be unpopular, but he was one of the town's heaviest tax-payers. Besides, Eben went anywhere he was invited and enjoyed a good dinner.

As Hesper hurried down the stairs to greet him, Charity Trevercombe rang the bell, and was ushered in by a spruced-up and nervous Annie.

Charity had changed amazingly since her bitter disappointment in Amos. Some months after his marriage to Hesper, Charity's mother died leaving more money than had been expected, and shortly after that Charity discovered Divine Healing and the joys of independence, simultaneously. She lived alone in her handsome house on Washington Square, except for an old German woman who was an expert cook. She kept a pug dog and three canaries, she was the leader of a Divine Healing group, which had members from as far away as Lynn. She was the rich Miss Trevercombe and she did as she pleased.

She was no longer jealous of Hesper; in fact she pitied her, poor thing, stuck in that dreadful house way outside of town, and of course nobody ever calls on her. So she thought thoughts of love and harmony for Hesper, and came to see her sometimes.

Tonight she kissed Hesper on the cheek, said, "How well you look, dear—such a pretty gown," and tripped cheerily into the drawing room. Charity had grown very plump during these latter years of contentment, but she still wore her hair in clustered ringlets about her ears and dressed in the bright colors of her youth. Tonight she wore yellow satin, and several tinkling gold bracelets, but she no longer assumed the coquetries of dress from a desire to please anyone but herself.

She sat down by Eben Dorch, brushed off his gallantries, and began to talk to him about the noise the workmen made in the construction of Abbot Hall, a municipal building which was being erected on the common in front of her house. "I wish you to take the matter up in town meeting—" said Charity in a tone of calm command. "There's no excuse for the language the men use, the oaths and the shouting. I spoke to the foreman personally in the most loving spirit, but I got no results. Of course," she added forbearingly, "he was a foreigner, from Boston, I believe."

Eben nodded gravely and said he would take the matter up in town meeting.

Amos and the Hay-Bottses entered the drawing room together, and Charity was momentarily silenced by the English couple's magnificence. They were in full evening dress, George in a black claw-hammer coat, wearing ruby studs and a watered-silk vest, and Emmeline in a dowdy gray cashmere, but it was cut far lower than the dresses of the two American women, disclosing a great deal of scrawny chest, and a necklace of large pendant diamonds.

Oh dear, thought Hesper, they must expect a very grand dinner party. She hurriedly introduced them to Charity and Eben. Emmeline cast an astonished glance over Charity's yellow satin and ringlets, but she was determined to be tolerant. They all sat down.

Hesper said, "I wonder what can be keeping Ma and Pa—Tim left for them ages ago. I hope nothing's wrong."

Charity withdrew her gaze from the Englishwoman's decolleté and diamonds. "Naughty Hesper—" she said shaking her head and smiling. "Never give reality to evil, by voicing fear. Of course nothing's wrong. God constantly works for good."

"Well, I guess so—" said Hesper absently. She was accustomed to Charity's spiritual interpretations, and her ears heard the approaching jingle of sleigh bells. "Here they are." She rose to greet her parents.

Emmeline turned to Charity and murmured, "Do you do much church work, Miss Trevercombe? At least—ah—do you have a Church of England here? Americans seem to have so many denominations."

"Yes," said Charity complacently. "Saint Michael's is Episcopalian and there are half a dozen other churches in Marblehead. But I no longer attend any of them. I find no need. Truth flows direct from the Divine Soul into my heart."

"Oh, really," said Emmeline faintly.

Charity continued to expound her doctrine.

"Yes, I see what you mean—" murmured Emmeline, and got up with relief. Mrs. Porterman's parents at last.

The relief was short-lived. Mr. and Mrs. Honeywood were not at all what she had been led to expect. His appearance was gentlemanly enough, though his old-fashioned coat was shabby, his sparse hair much too long, and his fingers ink-stained.

Still, he had a sweet smile and a pleasant voice and one might forgive the rest in a gentleman scholar. Not, however, by any stretch of imagination could one consider Mrs. Honeywood a lady. A heavy freckle-faced old woman in cheap black alpaca too tight under the arms. Black laced boots like a man's. And her speech! A thick, heavy burr, and really most uneducated. She cut through all the polite trickles of greeting.

"Domn dirty weather out," she said, acknowledging her introduction to the Hay-Bottses with a nod. "We'd a time getting here. There's a drift across Franklin Street high as the horse. And more snow to come. Wind's backing in again up the harbor."

"Oh dear—" said Hesper, "I should have sent for you earlier, I didn't know."

Her mother regarded her with a certain calm amusement. "You don't know much about what's going on in town, Hes—"

It was a statement and not a criticism, but Hesper flushed. I wish Ma wouldn't speak so loud and rough, she thought. She threw a nervous glance toward Amos, but he and Dorch and George Hay-Botts had drawn together by the empty fireplace and were talking volubly of business conditions.

Roger did not join the other men; he pulled a chair up close to Emmeline, and said with a rather touching shyness—"It's a privilege to meet English people, ma'am. We're proud of our English ancestry, you know. The first Honeywoods to come to Marblehead, they came from Dorset, they weren't Pilgrims, of course, they were Puritans and landed with Winthrop's fleet. Their flagship was the *Arbella* as, of course, you know? . . ." He had grown very deaf in the last years, and he leaned forward eagerly cupping his hand behind his ear for Emmeline's response.

She stared at him blankly, drawing back a little, and Susan gave her characteristic snort.

"Good God, Roger!" she cried. "Don't start that rigmarole now. Your precious Honeywoods left England because they wanted something different, I guess, and what's there in that to interest Mrs. Botts!"

"Hay-Botts," said Emmeline coldly. Her broadmindedness and feeling of kinship with Hesper were slipping.

During the first course at dinner—a fish soup, of all extraordinary things—they slipped further. Mr. Honeywood on her right bored her with exploits which had taken place in Marblehead, while Mr. Porterman on her left treated her to a spasmodic geniality, but obviously preferred talking across his mother-in-law at George.

The wine was poor and half the company did not touch it. That little Mr. Dorch was "temperance," it seemed, and felt it necessary to say so. And this brought out a further revelation. Mrs. Honeywood kept an inn. Emmeline asked a startled question, and from the answer discovered her earlier mistake. The large old house referred to by Mrs. Porterman was nothing but a country inn. Emmeline froze into unhappy silence, genuinely shocked. Her hostess was the daughter of a tavern keeper. Her mother ran a pub. She cast an appealing look at her husband. Had he also heard? Apparently not. He was eating steadily, and drinking the indifferent wine. George was not perceptive, except in business matters.

Hesper, sitting at the other end of the table, saw the sudden cloud settle over Emmeline and was troubled, though she had not the slightest clue to its appearance, except for a vague suspicion that it had something to do with Ma, or Pa.

I must try harder, she thought, be a good hostess for Amos's sake. She smiled at Hay-Botts and asked him a question about their coming voyage. She turned to Eben and mentioned the disputed election. Did he think Tilden or Rutherford B. Hayes would eventually win out? Eben, like most Marbleheaders, was a Democrat and hoped for Tilden. He laid down his fork and launched into speech. Hesper tried to listen and could not. She had the sensation of pushing a tremendous burden uphill before her, a dream sensation of futile effort. The fumed-oak dining room, the table damask swathed and laden with dozens of small dishes and platters containing half-eaten food, the faces of her guests, were all blurred and diminished by opaque malaise. She could eat nothing.

The heavy dinner progressed and finished at last in a welter of melting ice cream.

The women got up and left the dining room. Hesper murmured the conventional question. Charity did not wish to go upstairs, she would wait for them in the drawing room. Emmeline said, "Yes. I shall retire to my room for a few minutes," in a pinched voice.

Susan followed her daughter up to the Porterman bedroom. "What's the matter, Hes?" she said as soon as the door had closed. "You in the family way again?"

Hesper made a distracted motion with her hand, and sank down on the pink ruffled ottoman by her bureau. "I don't know. I think so. It isn't that."

Susan planted herself in the middle of the rug, and folded her arms; her shrewd eyes appraised the drooping figure. The dense skin was too white, not its normal ivory tone—but greenish. And Hesper's lips were trembling.

"You ought to get out more, house too hot anyway," said Susan briskly—"and take a good dose of salts. You wasn't built to be a niminy-piminy fine lady."

Hesper's head jerked up. "Oh, Ma—for the Lord's sake—" she cried. "There's nothing wrong with my health! You always make everything seem so—"

"What *is* wrong, then?" cut in Susan.

Leave me alone, thought Hesper. I don't know what's wrong, except nobody fits here tonight. I don't fit. Go back to your tumbledown old house by the sea. You and Pa. You don't belong here.

"Answer me, Hes. Stop acting moon-struck."

Hesper's mouth tightened. "Amos is worried about the factory," she said sulkily. "He's counting on Mr. Hay-Botts to invest some money."

Susan gave a grim nod. "Aye—things a'nt going so well for Amos, I know. But I'm surprised you do. If ever a woman was coddled and kept clear of worry—you're her. You put me in mind of those wax flowers under glass."

"Ma, that's mean! It's not true. Amos loves me and cherishes— I had so much trouble before with Evan, he wants to make up . . ."

"Oh, quit babbling, child." Susan put her fat mottled hand on her daughter's shoulder. "I didn't say it was your fault exactly. Or that it *was* a fault. You've a good marriage, I guess. Now—you better go down to your company, or that long-nosed Englishwoman'll get even groutier than she is."

They all gathered again in the drawing room, sitting along the edges of the wall on the mohair sofa and the Gothic chairs. Annie had turned the gas up, and the gasolier shed on them a bleak white light from its seven hissing mantles.

Outside the snow had stopped falling and a watery moon cast a glow over the Porterman mansion, on the snow piled on the mansard roof, the fretwork curlicues that edged the porch, and on the high cupola, shaped a little like a Chinese pagoda, to which no stairs led. A thin strip of light from the drawing room filtered through the heavy portières onto the snow. In the basement kitchen where Annie and Bridget were washing dishes, they had not bothered to draw the blinds.

"Moon's out—" said Annie, slopping a rag around the soup tureen and glancing idly at the window. "Funny—" she said, peering closer. "I thought I saw a shadow-like, over by the stable. But it's gone."

"You 'ad a nip too much o' the master's cookin' brandy, that's wot yer shadow is—" answered Bridget, crossly. She was very tired, mountains of dishes still to be washed, and that Englishwoman hadn't hardly touched all the good food. Acted like it was poisoned, Annie said.

"I've a mind to give notice, I have, lessen they'll get me a kitchen maid. Too much work, and the madam bone lazy—if ye ax me."

"Not so much lazy as indifferent-like," said Annie, judicially. "She don't notice things."

The bell above the kitchen door jangled. "That'll be her wanting Master Henry to say his piece," said Annie, putting down the soup tureen. She went up the back stairs to the nursery, found Henry cutting out pieces of lead foil to use for money, in a game of store he played incessantly by himself. He needed no slicking up, his sausage curls, velveteen jacket, and kilts were all as tidy as they had been in the morning. He accompanied Annie downstairs, entered the drawing room, and walked toward his mother.

The group welcomed him as a distraction. They were all weighed down by post-prandial torpor. Amos and George Hay-Botts had no more to say to each other for the present. They were going to tour the factory tomorrow morning, and their thoughts were compounded of the hope of mutual benefits, but they had run out of conversation. Eben Dorch was struggling against a gnawing pain beneath his breast bone, which had been plaguing him lately after meals. Susan and Roger were both afflicted by the sudden overwhelming sleepiness of age, and Roger succumbed, his head fell forward on his chest and he drowsed. Emmeline sat withdrawn from the group, her eyes once more fixed on the Spanish galleon with an expression of stony endurance.

They all listened to Charity, who was never troubled by physical discomforts, or averse from talking. She slid imperceptibly from general remarks on Divine Healing, and her own miraculous demonstrations of it, into the lecture she had prepared for the Thursday meeting of her disciples.

Her audience had been listening and waiting with varying intensity for the hour of release.

Henry paused a moment by Hesper's knee, smiled at his grandmother, whom he rather liked, particularly since she never tried to kiss him, saw at once that his grandfather was sleeping and not to be disturbed, said "How do you do" to everybody else, walked to the center of the carpet, and folded his hands behind his back. He began at once in his clear, precise treble.

> What does little birdie say, In her nest at peep of day?
> Let me fly, says little birdie, Mother, let me fly away.
> Birdie rest a little longer, Till the little wings are stronger.
> So she rests a little longer, Then she flies away.
> What does little baby say in her bed at peep of day? . . .

Hesper, watching him with loving pride, nevertheless was seized with revulsion. Why did I teach him that thing? she thought—it's so silly. There's so many other things—what things? She thought of the sea chanteys and ballads of her own childhood. "Blow the man down, blast you—Blow the man down—" Impossible to imagine Henry reciting that, nor would I want him to. It's vulgar.

Henry reached the end of the poem and stopped. He received the applauding murmurs with composure. Even Emmeline unbent, for she was fond of children, and said "Well done, little man," in the practiced tone she reserved for the small cottagers in the village at home.

Henry said good night and disappeared upstairs. He put himself to bed, and usually fell asleep before Hesper came up for the good-night kiss.

Relief rippled through the company. They all rose. They're glad to go, thought Hesper and I'm glad to have them go. The thing is, I've nothing in common with Marbleheaders. Just because I happened to be born here. And of course Amos isn't one. We must get away. I'll make him sell the factory and this house.

She said good-bye to her father. Poor old darling, maundering about the past. Her good-bye to her mother was tinged with resentment. "Wax flowers under glass—" what did Ma know anyway? Never been out of Marblehead, but always acted like she had the wisdom of Solomon.

She said good night to Eben Dorch, and Charity, who was driving him home. To think I ever envied Charity. Old maid, no matter how she sugarcoats it with her Divine Love and her independence.

She shut the door behind them, and with a sudden rush of tenderness smiled up at Amos who stood beside her. Safe and protected, of course. What happier rôle for a woman?

"Well, Hes—" he said, smiling back. "Went pretty well, don't you think?"

"Oh yes, dear," she whispered fervently. "Fine." And in saying it her spirits rose. The earlier guilt and forebodings and disquiet now seemed ridiculous. They had had a good dinner and Hay-Botts would invest in the factory tomorrow. Emmeline's thoughts, whatever they were, did not matter. She walked back to the English couple in the drawing room, and said cordially—"Wouldn't you like something to drink before we retire?"

Hay-Botts nodded, Emmeline said nothing.

"I'll ring for Annie—" Hesper moved to the carpet bell pull. Her fingers touched the strip of carpeting and then closed on it convulsively, her breath expelled itself from her opened mouth in a smothered cry.

She swung around, staring toward the curtained window. The noise she had heard from outside grew louder, a succession of disjointed sounds—soft yet penetrating, like sobbing laughter.

"My God, Porterman—what's that!" cried Hay-Botts jumping to his feet.

"I don't know," said Amos. He moistened his lips and moved protectively towards Hesper. The four of them stood staring toward the window.

The sounds began again, a little further off—a crescendo of soft soulless laughter.

"It don't sound human—" whispered Hay-Botts. "You got animals make a noise like that?"

Amos shook his head. He took a step towards the portières by the window. "Don't—" whispered Hesper and she clutched at his arm.

They waited, listening, held by an atavistic fear of the unknown terror by night.

"It's stopped—" said Amos after a moment. "It was boys playing a prank, I guess."

Emmeline gave a nervous titter.

Then a new disturbance reached them. Annie's unmistakable shriek, tearing up from the basement. "Holy Mother! Come back here—you! Stop her!" and then the sound of light running footsteps on the stairs.

The group in the drawing room stood motionless. The steps ran toward them down the hall. A woman in black appeared between the double doors at the entrance to the drawing room. A shawl covered her face and shoulders and behind the sheltering folds her face floated white and shapeless—around the dilated blackness of her eyes.

They heard her quick breathing, and she swayed a little, leaning against the edge of the door. Melting snow lay in the ridges of her shawl, and her thin kid slippers were caked with snow.

"Leah—" whispered Hesper; she took a quick step toward the black figure. "You poor thing—what? . . ."

"Careful—" Amos's arm shot out in front of Hesper. He shoved her behind him.

A tremor ran through the figure by the door. She straightened and stood tall. The shawl slipped from her head. A magnificent head still. The gray in her loosely bound hair seemed as fortuitous as the snow on her shawl. Her cheeks were no longer rounded, but behind the planes and hollows of her unlined face there lived a weird and ageless beauty.

When Amos spoke the huge dark eyes cleared from their bewilderment, they focused on him, and she smiled.

"There you are—love," she said with delight. "Leah's been searching for you so long. She saw you through the window, and she laughed —for joy."

"She's mad—" whispered Hay-Botts. "Get up behind her and—"

Leah turned her head slowly in his direction. Her lids fell and she seemed to contemplate him with a reflective sadness. He recoiled against the wall. "Leah has a knife," she said in the same soft coaxing voice.

Emmeline gave a moan, and shrank further behind a chair.

Has she really a knife? thought Hesper. Leah's hands were hidden beneath the black shawl. Hesper felt no fear. Her mind seemed to be working with a blinding clarity.

She saw Amos pulling himself together, the increased tension of his muscles. He put his hand out palm upward. "Give me the knife, Leah." His voice was admirably calm and forceful. But why doesn't he look straight at her? thought Hesper.

Leah shook her head, backing off and gazing up at him earnestly. "No, love. Lcah might need it. Against Nat, you know. Nat's bad. He keeps Leah locked in so she couldn't find you. Sometimes he ties her down with ropes."

Amos swallowed, his hand dropped. He turned his head toward Hay-Botts, who stood ten feet away at the other side of the fireplace, trying to signal a plan.

Hesper saw this and was sickened. Leah might get violent, she might have a knife, but she wasn't violent now. There was dignity and pathos about her. Surely there was no need to assault her physically. "And," said a clear voice in Hesper's brain, "why has she been searching for Amos, why does she call him 'Love'? She's crazy, of course, but . . ."

Hesper stepped out from behind her husband, eluding his quick motion to stop her. "Leah—" she said, "what do you want here? You haven't come to do harm, have you?"

The cavernous brilliant gaze moved from Amos's face to Hesper's. The huge eyes clouded with the bewilderment she had shown at first. Tears came into them. "Leah wants her love—" she said. "Wants him to hold her in his arms and love her, the way he used to."

Hesper heard a stifled gasp from the Hay-Bottses. Amos heard it too. He pushed his wife roughly aside. "For God's sake, Hesper! The woman's crazy. You know she doesn't know what she's saying. Here, you—I've had enough of this!" He lunged toward Leah, his great hands clenched, and she eluded him in one lithe motion. Her shawl fell off her shoulders to the floor, and in her right hand she held a long, sharp splitting knife. But she made no attempt to raise it, she held it point down, tight against her chest. The tears glistened on her cheeks and she threw her head back, looking up at Amos piteously.

"You're angry at Leah?" she whispered. "You want to hurt?"

Amos hesitated. And suddenly Leah turned and stared at Hesper with full recognition. "Hessie?" she said in a groping voice. Her mouth twisted. "Was it you took him away from Leah? Does he love you too?" Her hand closed convulsively, but without intent, on the handle of the splitting knife. And Amos sprang, pinioning her arms. The splitting knife fell from her lax hand as he grabbed her, and she overbalanced and pitched headlong. Her head hit a glancing blow on the seat corner of one of the Gothic chairs. She gave a little sighing moan, then she lay still on the flowered carpet.

Amos stared down at her, breathing hard, his powerful hands still clenching. His ruddy complexion had gone gray.

Hesper knelt beside the unconscious woman. Her brain continued to work with precision. She felt the blue-veined pulse in the limp wrist. She pushed aside the lustrous silver-black hair, and examined the small wound made by the chair corner. Then she got up. "She's only stunned, I think," Hesper said not looking at any of them. "Let her rest there awhile."

"But Good God—" cried Hay-Botts, emerging from the paralysis of disbelief, outrage and shock. "Get some rope, or sheets, and bind 'er whilst you can. She was going for you with that knife, Mrs. Porterman, wasn't she?"

"I don't think so," said Hesper dully. She picked up the splitting knife and looked down at it. One of the long sharp knives used to split cod or mackerel. Leah must have found it amongst Nat's old gear from his sea-going days. Hesper put it out of sight behind a blizzard paper-weight on the what-not.

"Amos, take your handkerchief and bind her ankles," said Hesper. "That'll be enough." She did not look at him, but she felt his revulsion. He doesn't want to touch her, she thought.

"Well, get on with it!" shouted Hay-Botts, nudging Amos. "What's the matter with you people! Or maybe the woman isn't so mad—is that it? Maybe she was speaking the truth about all that loving." His little gray eyes had narrowed to slits.

"Don't be a fool!" Amos jerked a large evening handkerchief from his tail pocket, bent over, and wound it around Leah's ankles. Slender ankles in black stockings soaked with snow water.

The front door burst open in a blast of frigid air. Amos, still tying the knot, raised his head and turned with the others. Nat ran into the midst of them, his head outstretched from his hunched shoulders. He paused a second staring at the group. "What are you doing to her, you bostard!" He raised his foot, and with one powerful jerk of his heavy boot kicked Amos's hands from his mother's ankles.

Amos straightened and got up; his face turned purple. His left hand, which had received the full force of Nat's kick, tingled and then throbbed with a violent pain. "Nat—" he said, "Nat—" in a dazed voice.

Hesper stepped between them, speaking fast. "Nat, your poor mother came here and acted very strange—she had a knife with her, and she fell down hitting her head. But I'm sure she's all right."

Amos turned on his heel and walked out to the front door which he shut. He stayed in the hall a few minutes.

Nat gave Hesper a long inscrutable look, his nostrils flaring above the scar on his lip. Then he knelt down beside Leah. He touched her cheek and she stirred and sighed, softly, like a girl. Her quiet face seemed luminous, the low forehead, straight nose, pale lips, and round chin purged now of all passions. Only Hesper saw Nat's expression as he bent over his mother. The corners of his mouth drew down in a grin of anguish, and behind his yellow eyes there was fierce yearning.

Hesper had felt no fear before. All during the scene with Leah there had been impersonal clarity, but now she knew a moment of terror as naked as the look in Nat's eyes.

He's mad too, she thought; more than madness. Why does he never call her Mother— And then it was as though a wall sprang ready-built across her mind which shrank behind it. The poor woman's mind is clouded sometimes, everybody in Marblehead knows that. It's dreadful and unfortunate but no deeper than that. And of course that wasn't true about Amos.

"Come, Nat," she said briskly. "Leah's coming to. I know you can manage her. We better carry her upstairs to bed. You can't go home on a night like this."

Nat unwound the handkerchief from his mother's ankles and threw it on the floor. "We'll go home," he said. "I've a sleigh outside. I've been hunting for her all day. She slipped out this morning. I knew she'd come here. This is one of her bad times."

See, thought Hesper, how reasonable he is. His face showed no more than it's usual sullenness. His speech was clipped and controlled.

Leah sighed again and opened her eyes. Their gaze wandered, then rested vaguely on the ceiling.

"She must go to an asylum, Nat," said Amos suddenly. He had returned to the drawing room and stood by the center table. He held up his injured hand cupped by the other, but except for that he was his normal self. Forceful and kindly. A man of authority. "The new state asylum at Danvers. They'll treat her well. I'll make all arrangements for you."

Along the figure on the floor there ran a shiver. She lifted her head, then let it sink back on the carpet.

"No, you won't," said Nat. He stood up, his hands in the pockets of his greasy workman's jacket. "She'll stay with me, as she always has." His head thrust forward from his shoulders, seeming to flatten into a serpentine weaving. "You know why she seeks for you in the bad times—" he said through his teeth.

"Indeed I don't, Nat—unless she's somehow confused me with her drowned husband."

Relief flooded over Hesper. Of course, that was the explanation, and she saw a flicker of uncertainty in Nat's face. It touched a memory of nineteen years ago. The night they hid the slaves. Nat had stood like this filled with malevolence that nobody understood, poised for harm, and then when Johnnie had spoken there had been the same uncertainty, and he had done nothing after all but slip away into the darkness.

"You walked down State Street to the wharves last week, and she saw you from the window. That's what set her off again—" said Nat slowly, and it was almost as though he begged for reassurance.

"Why, good lord, man. I can't help that. She has delusions, I suppose. Really—" said Amos on a note of exasperated patience, "I don't know what you mean by these ridiculous— After all, Nat. You know very well she's nothing but a crazy old woman."

"Oh hush . . ." whispered Hesper, for Leah had pulled herself up onto one elbow; her movements were slow and thick as though she dragged herself through water. Hesper and Nat bent quickly together to help Leah rise, and beneath her own hand Hesper felt the thin body in sharp recoil away from Nat.

Leah stood alone, her head bowed. No beauty or light now in her down-bent face. The muscles of her mouth sagged, the skin that covered the sharp bones had grown limp at chin and throat.

"I heard you—" she whispered in a voice that came from bleak distance. "I heard what you said." She did not look at Amos; the haggard eyes stared down at the flowered carpet by his feet.

Amos's lips tightened, but he did not move.

She's sane now, thought Hesper; she says "I," not "Leah."

But Nat put his hand on his mother's arm. "Come home now," he muttered.

Leah moved her arm so that Nat's hand dropped from it. She raised her head and looked into Amos's face. He met the long gaze of the sunken eyes without flinching. His blond eyebrows drawn together, his mouth firm. Hesper watching could see no emotion but the exasperated patience. "For your own sake, Mrs. Cubby," he said reasonably, "you should have professional care."

Her eyelids lowered and she turned her head aside.

"Come now—" said Nat again, putting his arm around her and pulling her shawl over her hair. "Pay no heed to the stupid bostard. I'll give you the care you need."

Hesper heard the sharp indrawn breath, and Leah's eyes sought her face. For an instant they held an agonized appeal.

But what can I do? thought Hesper. "You'd best go with Nat now—" she said gently.

Leah pulled herself up to her full height. "Aye." Her voice was like a bitter wind. "Him and me as it ever was. There's naught else, is there?" She walked from the room ahead of her son.

They heard the front door open and close. The drawing room returned to quivering silence.

Then Amos cleared his throat. His injured hand was swelling rapidly and turning bluish. He looked down at it, then thrusting it in his pocket, advanced on the English guests who were by the fireplace. "I'm sorry, folks—" he said heartily, with a nearly natural laugh. "Dreadful scene. Wouldn't 've had it happen for the world, but you get some queer characters in these old seacoast towns, you know. Now how about a nightcap before we go to bed?"

Emmeline stirred at last. After Nat had run into the room, she had collapsed on a chair, and had watched from then on in a rigid and horrified silence. She now rose and spoke through stiff lips.

"Nothing whatsoever would induce me to spend another minute under this roof. Kindly order your coachman to bring up the carriage."

Amos swallowed. "But, ma'am. There's nothing to be afraid of now —you can't leave at this hour—there's no train . . . and . . ."

"Then we will spend the night at a hotel in Salem. Never in all my life have I been subjected to such a—" Her lips quivered, and there were frightened tears in her eyes.

"B-but surely—" stammered Amos, turning to Hay-Botts. "Tell her it was just an unfortunate happening, we regret it deeply, but there's no danger, you know."

George Hay-Botts shrugged his chunky shoulders. Suspicion and a cold distaste had hardened his ruddy face. "I quite agree with me wife," he said. "We'll leave at once."

Oh dear, thought Hesper. She saw that it was hopeless, but she knew that she must make the effort. "You've had a shock—we all have—" she said, trying to smile into the two tight faces, "but please don't leave like this. It isn't anybody's *fault.*"

"As to that—" said Hay-Botts, "I wouldn't know. Wot I do know is, this isn't the kind of a 'ousehold I care to have me wife stop in, nor me neither. And as for our little deal—" he said turning to Amos, "it's off. Where there's muddle in personal life, there'll be muddle in business, I say. And that's the sum of it."

And within half an hour, the Hay-Bottses left.

Hesper and Amos undressed silently, except that when she tried to treat his wounded hand with arnica and bandages, he turned away from her muttering "Let me alone." He clambered into his side of the bed, and she heard his uneven breathing and felt the restless motions which he tried to control.

"Please don't fret, dear—" she ventured at last, into the darkness. "You can make money without Hay-Botts. You always have."

Amos said nothing, but presently he slid his arm around her, and drew her head down to his shoulder. In this accustomed position she felt immediate warmth and comfort. The fears and ugliness and disappointment of the evening dwindled to unimportance. Forget it all, she thought drowsily. The Hay-Bottses don't really matter. And as for the scene with Leah, that was just what Amos said—an unfortunate happening. She turned her head a little on his shoulder and fell asleep.

The next morning, the milkman brought news when he made his routine trip from town to the Porterman mansion. Hesper was called down to the kitchen by a wildly excited Annie. "That woman—mum, that woman what forced her way in here last night . . ." Annie became incoherent, but the milkman repeated his story with grim relish.

Leah Cubby had stabbed herself with a splitting knife. She had done this on top of her house in the scuttle or widow's walk. Tom Gawden, the apprentice blacksmith, had been going down State Street on his way to work, when he happened to look up and see the body. All dressed in black it was, hanging half over the railing. And even from the street you could see the blood dripping down onto the roof. Tom had rushed into the house and found Nat Cubby still asleep. It seemed his mother'd made him think she'd gone to bed. She'd locked her door from the inside, they had to break it down to get in. Then she had climbed up the ladder to the scuttle.

It was an awful thing. Tom had had to yell for help in quieting Nat. He seemed to go right out of his head for a while, but you couldn't hardly blame him.

Hesper sank down on a kitchen chair. Her face was as white and shocked as even the excited servants could wish. "That's terrible—" she whispered. "Terrible. But the poor woman wasn't right, you know—never was."

"What was she doin' here last night, mum?" asked Annie eagerly, her eyes glittering. "Me and Bridget was that skeered we dassn't move for our lives!"

The milkman crowded forward too, waiting for the answer.

"Why, Mrs. Cubby's coming here had nothing really to do with us—" said Hesper. "Her mind was clouded and she happened to wander this way—oh, I suppose she remembered that Nat works for Mr. Porterman, it must have been something like that she had in mind. Nothing to do with what—what happened later." She spoke with growing firmness, and she saw that, disappointed as the servants were, she had convinced them, and the milkman, who would carry no new lurid story back to town.

She rose and walked steadily from the kitchen and up two flights of stairs to the bathroom where she suffered a violent and prolonged attack of nausea. When it at last abated, she crouched on the shiny, checkered oilcloth floor, and leaned her head against the mahogany rim of the tub. Her eyes fixed themselves on the gleaming brass faucet. Instead of the faucet she saw Leah's limp black-covered body, hanging across the scuttle rail and the blood dripping down onto the roof as the milkman had described it, and superimposed on that she saw Leah as she had stood last night in the drawing room, her head thrown proudly back, her great brilliant tear-filled eyes fixed on Amos in entreaty, in an agony of bewildered longing.

"Yes," said Hesper, aloud. "It was true." She shut her eyes, and the sickness heaved again in her stomach. Ugly. Ugly. How could he—how could he pretend last night . . . lying and without pity. . . . Oh, Amos, how could you. . . . I can't stand it. . . .

When Amos came home to midday lunch, he burst into the bathroom crying, "Hesper, for heaven's sake, I've been looking everywhere for you. What is it, dear—are you sick?" He picked her up off the floor and laid her on the bed.

She lay very still, looking up into his worried face. "Amos," she said, "do you know about Leah?"

"Yes, I know. It's a terrible thing. But don't let it upset you like this. I'm afraid it was what I said about the asylum."

"No," she said, sitting up and regarding him steadily. "It wasn't what you said about the asylum. She knew Nat would never let her go. It was what you said about a crazy old woman. It was knowing at last that you'd never loved her, in spite of—of what had been between you."

"Hesper—" He glared at her in anger, in blind unbelief. "Have you gone crazy too? How can you believe that clap-trap, that balderdash the poor woman was babbling!"

"Amos! Listen to me." He had never heard that note in her voice. "I'm not a toy. I'm not a child. I'm not a wax flower under glass to be protected from the slightest jar. I guess I've let you treat me like that, because it was easy and pleasant for both of us. But in this thing with Leah, I won't be put aside with evasions, I won't let it slide by until I've forgotten it. I know you were—were Leah's lover. But I want to hear the truth from you."

Amos stood up so abruptly that she fell back against the pillows. He stared down at her and his face was as set and hard as her own.

"Why?" he said with cold fury. "What difference does it make?"

She felt a pain like a dull blow on her heart. In all their marriage she had never suspected that he could look at her like this. An enemy. They had never quarreled, never had there been a locking of wills. A good marriage, Ma had said, and it was, it had been. And now she saw the danger of disturbing his image of her. And yet she could not turn back.

"It's because of our love—" she said, groping for words. "It's because, though you lied last night—and maybe you had to then, I can't bear it if you lie to me."

"Very well," he said in the same furious and bitter tone. "I was with Leah once, twelve years ago. I don't expect you to understand how it happened, nor do I feel any need to explain. It was the trifling sort of thing that happens to most men."

"Not trifling for Leah—" she said faintly. "She thought you loved her. She's killed herself because of it."

She heard the sharp rasp of breath through his nostrils. She saw the sharp clench of his right, uninjured hand. "Leah was mad—you little fool! By God, Hesper. I never thought you'd act like this."

There was no sound in the room but Amos' angry breathing. Suddenly the strength that had buoyed her ebbed away leaving her flat and vanquished. Her desire to force admission from him now seemed to her ignoble. The moral issues were clouded and uncertain. For was there not deeper evil in Leah's pathetic life, than her deluded love for Amos? What of that other alliance, the sinister bond from which her soul had struggled frantically, in fantasy, in violence to escape? Oh I don't *know* what's right, she thought.

She lifted her head and tears filled her eyes. "I'm sorry. Don't look so black at me, Amos. The whole thing's been an awful shock."

But his anger did not abate. Making scenes, he thought, sitting up in bed looking wan and tearful and prying into things no wife should want to know—unpleasantly like Lily Rose. Adding to the stupendous humiliation of last night, instead of soothing it. Good God, haven't I suffered enough for that stupid hour with Leah years ago? Thank God the woman's dead.

"Amos—" said Hesper very low. "Don't shut me out. I'll never mention the thing again. Except—" She stopped.

"Except what?" cried Amos violently.

She did not want to voice it. She was exhausted, drained of emotion, and longing only for the return of their understanding, of the tenderness and content in which she had floated for years.

"I'm afraid of Nat," she said. "Afraid for you."

"Nonsense!" But her appeal had reached him. He spoke more quietly. "Nat'll be all right. After he gets over the tragedy, of course, it'll be a relief to him. Must have been terrible trying to restrain his mother in her bad times. Why, she'd even turn on him—those welts on his cheeks."

Yes, thought Hesper, sickened. And perhaps she had cause.

"Nat's evil," she said. "He's different from other people."

"Nonsense," repeated Amos. "He's sulky and mean at times, I'll grant you. But he never really does anything. It's more of an attitude."

"He's never really done anything bad, because of Leah, or the thought of Leah. But now she's gone."

"Hesper, for God's sake, stop exaggerating and harping on this thing. Nat'll be back at his bench in a day or two, doing skilled lasting and grumbling about his pay check as usual."

"Oh, my dear—" she whispered, twisting her hands. "Don't you know he hates you? He's always hated you. I think it was to watch you he stayed in the factory. And now with Leah doing this thing—he'll think you responsible. I don't understand Nat—but—" Her voice dropped.

But I understand him better than you do, she thought. Her thoughts ran together in confusion like the tossing of a stormy ocean. She heard the menacing pound of rising waves battering on the rocks, as she had not actually heard them in years. It was the town—the good and evil and the violence and the richness—it was a heritage apart—apart from Amos who had blundered in, unknowing. Who had never known.

"Go wash your face," he snapped with renewed anger. "It's a sight. Then may I be permitted to have my lunch in peace? You're talking rubbish." He stalked to the shaving stand and ran a comb through his thick fair hair.

Maybe I am, she thought wearily, pulling herself off the bed. I'm all tuckered out and overwrought. Maybe it's the baby. Tell him, she thought, tell him now. So he won't be angry any more.

She walked up in front of him, reached up her hands to his shoulders. "Amos, I'm going to have another baby."

She watched the sullen anger melt from his face, and then the incredulous blaze of delight. Ah, it was good to see the indulgence return to his blue eyes. Good to have him kiss and pet her as she had known he would.

"So that's why you've been so upset this morning, my poor girl. I'd never have spoken so sharp if I'd known. You should have told me sooner, Pussie."

Hesper leaned against his sheltering arm. They descended the stairs together and she let him support her as though she had become too weak to walk alone.

CHAPTER 15

THE WINTER MONTHS passed, and the memory of New Year's night faded from Hesper's consciousness. It seemed that Amos had been right and her fear of Nat baseless. Though Nat had never returned to the factory. This much Amos had told her, but no more. The topic was closed between them. It was from the milkman that she had heard how Nat had disappeared the day after Leah's burial. Locked up his house and vanished like smoke, said the milkman, and not a mortal soul knew for sure what had become of him. Though one of the Tucker boys swore he had seen him trudging up the highway to Swampscott. Had recognized him by the way he had of slouching along with his head poked forward. So doubtless he'd left town.

Hesper was reassured. Her life settled back into effortless routine, hazed by the discomforts and the lethargy of advancing pregnancy. The veins in the back of her left leg swelled a little, and vagrant pains attacked her body. With Amos's hearty approval she took to having Annie serve her breakfast in bed. Gradually she spent more and more time in bed, arising only to have supper with Amos. There was no need to get up. The two Irish women ran the house well enough, and Bridget was a good cook. Once a week, Tim drove to Salem and brought back a laundress. Annie did most of the mending. Only Henry really required his mother's time and attention. The nearest grammar school was in town near Amos's factory and to it Henry would eventually have to go—if they remained in Marblehead—but in the meantime Hesper preferred to teach him herself.

Henry was an apt if unenthusiastic pupil; he did as he was told and in arithmetic he progressed so fast that it was only by anxious pre-study of the arithmetic book that Hesper could keep ahead of him.

Sometimes she worried because Henry had no companions of his own age. Then she bundled him up and sent him out to go skating on the ice pond near their home. Many children walked out from town or the near-by village of Devereux to skate there, but amongst them Henry made no friends. But Hesper's solicitous questions elicited no pathetic picture of ostracism, nor of the rough bullying which she well knew to be characteristic of Marblehead youth.

Henry skated so proficiently that he commanded respect even from his elders. He participated in snow fights, and had an unerring aim. When tripped up by an outstretched foot, or hit by a snowball, he picked himself up again and proceeded calmly with whatever he had been doing. He evoked neither friendship nor hostility, and the other boys soon let him alone. But Henry was not colorless. Now and again, Hesper was conscious of strength and purpose in her son's burgeoning personality.

One morning after lessons, Hesper lay propped up in bed, and Henry sat beside her on a stool, sponging his slate. She looked at him with a sudden surge of warmth, seeing the down-bent flaxen head, the straight nose and firm little chin. He'll be a handsome man like his father, she thought.

"I wonder what you'll be when you grow up—" she murmured fondly half to herself.

Henry raised his head. "I'll be rich," he said. "Very rich."

"Why, Henry!" she laughed. "You mean like Papa?" she added indulgently.

Henry shook his head. "I don't mean rich in Marblehead. I mean rich in the whole world." He gave her a kindly smile, and resumed sponging his slate.

Now how in the name of heaven did he get an idea like that—she wondered, a little shocked at Henry's cavalier estimate of Amos's means. "Papa's very well off. He keeps us very comfortable," she said crisply.

Henry piled his spelling and arithmetic books on the cleansed slate. "I guess so. But he isn't real rich. Gramma said so. I ast her."

"Gramma said so!" Hesper sat up straight, staring at her son with annoyance. How like Ma to say a thing like that. No business of hers, and she didn't know anything about it anyway. Things were looking up again at the factory, Amos said. Oh, he'd had strike trouble—in the middle of January the lasters had walked out, and the cutters too. But he'd soon handled that, brought in a trainload of workers from Danvers. There'd been a lot of fuss and threats and grumblings. She'd read about it in the *Marblehead Messenger,* but Amos hadn't seemed much perturbed. And all the other shoemen had trouble too. Anyway, the Marbleheaders hadn't held out long. Couldn't bear to see Danvers men

swiping jobs from them, and had slunk back one by one with their tails between their legs, Amos said. Hesper thought he'd been mighty decent to take them back, after the trouble they'd made. He fired the Danvers substitutes right away and let bygones be bygones. And Amos had managed without Hay-Botts's money. "Arrangement with the bank—" he had told her briefly, "not the slightest cause for worry." Nor did she dream of insisting that he talk of matters he didn't wish to. Never that again.

"Where did you see Gramma?" she asked, frowning.

"In Dorch's drugstore, when I went down-town with Annie, Friday," replied Henry, edging toward the door. "She was buying peppermint oil for Grandpa's cough."

"Why didn't you tell me?" Hesper snapped. "No, come back here. What did Gramma say—is Grandpa really sick?"

Henry sighed but returned to the bedside. "I forgot. I guess he's not so sick. I dunno. She ast how you were feeling. She said you might as well be living in China for all she ever saw you."

Quick color ran up Hesper's face. She sank back on the massed pillows. "She knows I'm not well enough to go out. And she won't come here on account of that dratted Inn. If she'd let your papa help her, she could close the Inn and she wouldn't have to work so hard."

Henry looked bored, perfectly aware that Mama was talking at rather than to him. "Can I go now?"

As his mother said nothing, but seemed to be staring at the footboard, he departed, shutting the door carefully behind him.

Hesper lay quiet, and forced herself to a few minutes of uncomfortable analysis. But there was no reason for the stab of guilt. She sent Tim to the Hearth and Eagle to inquire for her parents, whenever he drove to town, and he never went empty-handed; he took gifts from the Porterman larder, or sometimes a dress length for Susan, socks or handkerchiefs for Roger. Gifts, it might be added, accepted matter-of-factly, without enthusiasm. He also bore little notes from Hesper, inviting her parents to come and see her. Susan had come once since New Year's, and the visit had not been a success. There was nothing to talk about.

"I ant at ease here, Hes, and that's a fact," Susan said. "There's a heap to do at home, and it's not as if you needed me. Why'nt you come and see us? Do you good to get out—quiddling around all day in one room, or are you ashamed of your old home?"

"No, Ma—of course not," Hesper had cried indignantly. "But Doctor Flagg won't let me go carriage riding, just now, and you know I couldn't walk with this leg, even if it wasn't so far."

No, she wasn't exactly ashamed of the old Inn by the sea, no emotion so simple. It was more of an intensification of the hostility she had felt to it and from it, on New Year's Day. When she thought of the town she knew a painful repugnance, not unmixed with fear. Buried too deep for complete recognition lay the feeling that it had struck at her in revenge through Leah, on New Year's night—but revenge for what nebulous betrayal? There was none. Morbid, she thought—rubbish. She rang for Annie, directed her to tell Tim to set off down-town at once, to ask after Mr. Honeywood's health, and take some of those hothouse peaches Mr. Porterman had had sent in from Boston.

While Annie was still in the room, Hesper made a sudden effort, throwing back the bedclothes, and sliding to her feet on the carpet beside the bed. At once her head grew giddy, the room swam in sickening coils. Her left leg began to ache. She clutched the bedpost and let Annie help her back into bed. "I guess I've got to be careful—" she said with an apologetic little laugh.

"Yessum," agreed Annie, who enjoyed running the house to suit herself. "The master he's give orders you're not to strain yerself in any way. You jest lay quiet till I fetch up your dinner."

It's funny—thought Hesper, lying back on the pillows, I had no trouble at all carrying Henry. Felt fine and of course we traveled quite a bit. But—what about the first time—what about Evan's baby? Everything went wrong then. That's why I've *got* to coddle myself, no matter what Ma thinks.

Ah, I wish we could leave this place, leave it for good. If Amos could only get a good price for the factory—I'd live anywhere, anywhere else. In August after the baby's born and I'm all right again, we can begin to look around. She picked up the novel she had been reading, *The Maiden Widow,* by E. D. E. N. Southworth, closing her mind to everything but its romantic story.

Spring came with a flurry. There were no trees near the Porterman mansion, which had been erected on a bare and stony slope. But the carefully tended lawn flushed green, and the forsythia hedge, which protected the house from observation by passers-by on the Salem road, became tipped with yellow buds, and then burst into flower.

A pair of foolhardy robins started to built a nest at the base of the cast-iron stag's antlers, and were summarily dispossessed by Amos, who directed the daily gardener to freshen up the stag with a coat of lifelike brown paint.

Amos made, however, no other spring improvements this year. The repainting of the mustard-colored trim around the windows, the renewal of gravel on the drive, the addition of a cupola on the stables to match the new one on the house—these must wait a bit. Money was very tight, tighter than it ever had been in January when he had hoped for Hay-Botts's investment. Well, he'd weathered that storm, and he'd weather this one.

There was but one person to whom he sometimes exposed some of his fears, hopes, and maneuverings. This was Sam Johnson, his foreman and faithful employee of twenty years.

On Friday morning, the twenty-second of June, Amos called Johnson into his office at the factory. More than ever Johnson had grown to resemble a grizzled old watch dog. His Airedale face was alert as he cocked his head and stood in the doorway, waiting for his chief to stop reading a letter and recognize him.

"Oh, hello—Sam—sit down—I want to talk to you," said Amos, looking up.

Sam sat down, grumbling a little from habit. "That new channel turner ain't workin' so good. Got to go upstairs and put the fear of God in all them sole cutters. They're slowin' up the whole line."

"Yes, I know. But wouldn't you say things are going smoother now, since the strike?"

"If you ain't sensitive to black looks, and unsigned cards full o' dirty name-callin' bein' shoved under your door, I'd say things was goin' pretty smooth," answered Johnson with a wintry smile. "They're all back at work anyways. You sure scared hell out of 'em when you brought in them Danvers boys. Took the wind right out of their sails, that did. Didn't take 'em long to see they'd have to eat humble pie, or starve." Johnson gave a mordant chuckle.

Amos nodded. "Well, I had to. Don't mind telling you now. I'd have been wiped out if we'd shut down. I've had to do a tightrope walk as it is. Credit's run out. Got all the extension from the bank I could possibly hope for. You know what a time I've had to meet the pay roll. I've had to sell most everything I own, except my house and this factory, and they're both mortgaged to the hilt."

Johnson expressed his dismay in a long whistle. "I didn't know it was as bad as that."

"I wouldn't tell you now, except here's a piece of mighty good news for a change. Thing I've been hoping for."

He shoved the contract he had been reading across the table to Johnson, who picked it up and holding it at arm's length squinted at it painfully. "Jesus—" he whispered. "Hunt and Slocombe of Cincinnati? Ain't they the biggest jobbers in the West?" Amos grunted, and Johnson read on to the end, when he emitted another whistle this time of ungrudging elation.

"Ten thousand pair of Ladies three-button Morocco, as a starter! Holy mackerel, that's far and away the best order we've ever had, nor anybody else around here, I reckon. Top price too. How in the name of God did you do it, sir?"

Amos smiled. "Bit of luck, I guess, at last. Ran into their man in Boston last month, showed him samples, talked him around." He certainly was not going to tell Johnson, nor did he wish to remember, the frantic machinations of those two days in Boston with Hunt and Slocombe's buyer. He had haunted the Worcester station until the fellow's train came in from the West. He had virtually kidnaped him, carrying him off to the American House where Amos had already engaged rooms, plied him with liquor, provided a little dancer, blandished him, bullied him, told the most outrageous lies about competitors from both Marblehead and Lynn, none of whom got to see the fellow at all. Yes, it was almost funny now, that the plan had worked, but it hadn't been so easy to hide the desperation under it all, to keep from showing by the flicker of an eye that the order from Hunt and Slocombe's was the last hope.

"We'll get going tomorrow," said Amos. "Carload of fancy Morocco hides 'll be in from the tanneries on the morning train."

"They'll wait to be paid?" asked Johnson, quickly.

Amos nodded. "I showed 'em the contract when I was in Salem yesterday. I guess I better talk to the hands, when I go around the factory tomorrow, stir 'em up, and promise 'em a bonus."

"Yeah—" said Johnson, grinning. "You can forget it later, when the order's gone out."

"Maybe," agreed Amos reluctantly. "I try to play fair with them, but I've got to ease things off at the bank first, and then of course my personal expenses are very heavy, with Mrs. Porterman's condition and all. Monthly nurse coming next week—and she's not been so well, poor girl. I'm thinking of calling in that special woman's doctor in Boston."

"Too bad," Johnson clucked sympathetically. Had hard luck with his wives, the chief did. The first Mrs. P. had certainly been as wishy-washy a piece of ailing womanhood as you could find. But this one—a big strapping girl and had done the work of two in the stitching room, way back that time when she worked there. You'd never think she'd turn out sickly. But the chief, he *likes* to coddle her—thought Johnson with a flash of insight. Maybe he got in the habit in his first marriage. And then he's so grateful to have kids. Always was crazy for kids of his own.

"It's a funny thing—" said Amos suddenly. "I could swear these papers aren't in the order I put them." Following his own train of thought, he had unlocked the built-in strongbox drawer, in his desk. Here he kept all private papers, deeds, policies, mortgages, and now he placed with them the new contract.

"Well, ain't you the only one has a key?" answered his foreman without much interest.

Amos nodded. "I've got the only key." He glanced at it as it dangled from his heavy watch chain. Thank God, I won't have to sell this watch chain now, he thought. Hes would have noticed that all right. "I wouldn't want anybody to get a look at those papers—" he said with a spark of grim humor. "Between you and me, Sam, they might give the idea Porterman's is a bit shaky."

"Well, there ain't nobody had a look at 'em—" said Johnson, "so quit frettin', sir. You forgot how you placed 'em. Anybody's apt to do that."

"I guess so—" said Amos. He slammed and locked the drawer. "I suppose the night watchman's all right?" He knew it to be foolish but he was still a trifle uneasy. Queer about those papers, queer that memory should be so mistaken.

The foreman frowned. "Oh, Dan's honest as daylight, but he's gettin' on. Don't hear so good no more."

"Fire him," returned Amos promptly. "Get a younger man."

Johnson nodded. "I'll look around next week." Reckon he'd been lax in keeping Dan on, but the old man had a wife and a feeble-minded grandchild to support. Well, he could go on the town, like many another, only Dan was an old Marbleheader, and prouder than Lucifer, had been captain of his own fishing schooner once, donkey's years ago. Still there was no use being soft.

"I'll be off now, sir—if there's nothing else. Got to get after them sole cutters."

"I won't be back here this afternoon—" said Amos rising and pulling down the roll top on his desk. "Doctor Flagg said Mrs. Porterman'd be able to risk an airing, now the weather's turned so good. I'm going to take her down to see the Regatta."

"Well, rather you than me, sir," Johnson remarked, opening the door. "Can't see no point to watchin' a lot o' boats chasin' each other around rocks in the bay."

Amos was inclined to agree with him. He had no interest in sailing or fondness for salt water, but this regatta interested him for other reasons. It was held by members of the Eastern Yacht Club which was composed of wealthy Bostonians, and Amos considered that it would be very good business for the town if the club decided to settle permanently in Marblehead. During the seven years since the club was founded it had shown a regrettable fickleness in its choice of waters for the annual regatta, and the last three years the race had been sailed from Swampscott. Now it was back in Marblehead again, and the town's more progressive citizens earnestly hoped that the club would buy a site on the harbor side of the Neck, and settle down.

Amos mentioned this viewpoint to Hesper, as Tim drove them carefully down Pleasant Street toward the town. At first she had not at all wanted to go out on this expedition, but her health was better than it had been during the last months, and in the face of Doctor Flagg's recommendation and Amos's persuasion, she could find no excuse for refusing.

"So you think they'll put a clubhouse on the Neck?" she answered Amos politely. "I guess there's quite a few foreigners 've bought over there, lately."

"Foreigners!" repeated Amos. "Frenchies and Russians and Japs, I suppose!"

"I'm sorry, dear," said Hesper, touching his gloved hand with her gloved one. The Marblehead term had slipped out, though she knew how Amos disliked it, and with reason. "It's a beautiful day—" she added quickly. "I'm so glad I came."

The matched bays walked slowly and evenly under Tim's able driving, and Hesper found the motion of the open Victoria soothing. She was conscious of looking well in her best summer hat—a golden leghorn straw, adorned by two bronze bird's wings and an edging of blond lace. It had been bought in Boston last year for the holiday in the White Mountains, and was becoming and fashionable enough. Under the blended golds and yellows, her hair repeated the bronze of the bird's wings on a redder note, and beneath the lace-edged brim her skin lost its excessive pallor and glowed as it did in her girlhood. An embroidered taupe plush mantle covered her bust and shoulders, falling in long fringed points to her lap and concealing the distortion of pregnancy. Though, in truth, considering that the baby was due in five or six weeks, she had not gained excessively. That was the advantage of height, and a well proportioned, long-boned frame.

The carriage emerged from the shade of fresh-leafed elms and maples along the upper part of Pleasant Street, into the glare of hot sunlight in the business section, by the depot and shoe factories. Here between the newly erected monument to the Revolutionary hero Captain Mugford, and the flimsy old Marblehead Hotel, the Porterman carriage was impeded by a crush of Friday noon traffic—a procession of Payne's Express wagons loaded with cases of shoes, and bound from the factories to the depot for shipping on the afternoon train.

"We'll have to wait a bit, till they get by," Amos said. "Better put up your parasol, Hes, you don't want to get a headache in this sun."

Hesper had been enjoying the sunlight, had been gazing around her with a freshness of interest long unknown to her, thinking that the Mugford shaft of granite was really imposing, that it was good to see people again, and that the loungers in front of the Marblehead Hotel and adjacent Glover firehouse looked contented and kindly as they basked in tipped-back chairs, some smoking, some chewing on wads of tobacco, some merely gazing up into the blue sky.

"You don't want to take any chances—" continued Amos, surprised that she had not obeyed him. "Your first outing in so long. You feeling quite all right, Pussie?"

"Oh yes—" she said, but as she said it her head startled her with a dull throb, and she was conscious of a faint return of the giddiness which had afflicted her all winter. She put up the parasol.

The carriage began to move again, and both Amos and Hesper leaned forward to look at his factory around the corner on School Street. The four-story frame structure towered above the Rechabite building next to it and loomed impressively against the sky behind. Big, thought Hesper with satisfaction, biggest factory in Marblehead except the Harris's. Through the open windows there came the whir and clatter of machinery, they could see figures passing and repassing inside.

"To think I ever worked there—" Hesper burst out involuntarily, moved by the extraordinary changes life could offer. "I hope you've a better forelady in the stitching room than Miss Simpkins was."

Amos's lips compressed; he turned his head from contemplation of the factory and stared stiffly between the near horse's ears. "I don't know of any objection to Miss Simpkins. As a matter of fact, I believe we've taken her back. She's most able." And cheap. Didn't fuss if her pay check was overdue, like the last woman.

"But she wasn't honest—" persisted Hesper, aware that she was annoying him, but unable to stop. "At least she used to extort fines from us for the stupidest things. I told you about it, and she—"

"Hesper—" cut in Amos, "I may be presumed to run my business as I think best?" Had he spoken in anger, her own temper might have flared, but she heard a genuine note of hurt. She understood that from her he could bear no criticism. She was aware, too, that his antipathy to remembering that she had worked in the stitching room ran deeper than snobbery. Something to do with his picture of the ideal wife. Something to do with Lily Rose perhaps. And Hesper had never been jealous of Lily Rose. Justice had prevented that from the beginning. For had not she and Amos each come to the other scarred by an earlier marriage? And how much greater than hers his forbearance had been in cherishing a woman tarnished by divorce, as well as by an irrational and ill-omened passion.

For it was thus, in shame and revulsion, that she now thought of her marriage to Evan.

"Why, of course, you know best, dear," she said gently with a faint smile. "Oh, I thought we were going over to the Neck to watch the race from the Point!" she added, surprised, as the carriage turned down Washington Street.

"Thought we'd stop and ask your folks did they want to drive over with us," answered Amos accepting her change of subject. "There's plenty of time. Thing won't start till two, it said in the paper."

"Oh, of course," she answered. "That was thoughtful of you." Amos had always been a good son-in-law.

They drove down Washington Street over the hill of the old training field, crowned now by the huge, nearly completed red-brick Abbot Hall. Across the Square, Charity emerged from her house and waved to them before climbing into her little surrey, flicking the horse and driving herself briskly off to Lynn. Hesper waved back, feeling a sudden warmth for Charity who had called a few times throughout the winter, and though her complacent optimism was trying, her visits had been a distraction. And I have no other friend, thought Hesper; not that it matters, my family's enough.

The horses slowed to a walk as they descended the hill past the sea captains' Georgian houses, built a hundred years ago in the day of Marblehead's greatest prosperity. Hesper, gazing up at them from beneath the flounced brim of her parasol, suddenly saw her town with new eyes. She did not see the architectural beauty which a later generation was to discover in these stately houses, with their characteristic corners quoined like checkerboards in panels of lighter wood, their delicate fanlights, their carved cornices and Ionic porticoes, but she did feel for the first time in her life a thrill of objective pride.

"The Town House—" she said musingly to Amos, as the carriage squeezed along the narrow street beside the little yellow wooden building which had been Marblehead's Town Hall for a hundred and fifty years. "There's been a lot of history made in there, it's heard the declaration of three wars, and Marbleheaders made their mark in all of them."

Amos snorted. "You sound like your father, Hes. Darned old shack wants a coat of paint if you ask me. Be a good thing when Town Meeting moves to Abbot Hall." Amos had no love for the Town House, scene of many a row in Town Meeting, in which he always seemed to be in the minority. And he'd long ago recognized how hopeless was his earlier ambition to be elected selectman.

"Turn down State Street, Tim—" he called out suddenly to the coachman—and to Hesper he explained, "I believe I'll have a look at the sail loft, seeing as we're so near." This was the sail loft he had been buying eleven years ago, the night she crossed over from the Neck with Evan. Amos rented the business out to an old sailmaker, but there was mighty little call for a sail loft in Marblehead any more, and the sailmaker was behind with the rent. Amos intended to look the premises over again, with a view to selling—if I can find a buyer, he thought glumly.

They turned down State Street and Hesper felt a constriction around the heart. Leah's house stood in the middle of the block. She saw from Amos's preoccupied expression that he either had not thought of this, or considered it unimportant, and she was silent, shading her face from Amos with her parasol, and staring at the house with painful interest. It looked as it always had, four-square and porticoed, a smaller edition of the handsome houses on Washington Hill. Leah's pink and red hollyhocks were beginning to bloom at each side of the steps. There were no shutters to close, but each of the seven front windows was masked by a black paper blind, as they had been left after the burial. It seemed to her that one of them on the corner of the second floor moved a little.

They passed the house, and Hesper turned her head still watching. The three windows on the harbor side of the house were shrouded too, but as she looked she saw movement again, then one of the blinds in the upper story fluttered, the lower corner was pulled aside, and though she could not see clearly she received the impression of a gaunt, brooding face.

Amos turned at her smothered exclamation. "What's the matter, Hessie?"

"Is Nat back in town?" she whispered, unwilling to have Tim hear. "I could have sworn I saw his face up there at the window."

Amos craned around and looked back at the house. There was no one to be seen, and he shrugged his shoulders. "I doubt it, but what if you did? It's his house. No reason why he shouldn't live in it."

Yes, of course, Amos was right, unimaginative, practical and right.

Leah's dreadful death had happened half a year ago. Nat might very well have recovered completely from the shock in that time. And, as Amos said, if he were back what difference did it make?

And yet while she thought this another voice spoke in her mind. It said, "Go in and find out! Nat's a human being, no matter how twisted a one. He's never hated *you*. Maybe you could help him—maybe you could fend off—"

"Draw up over there by the wharf," said Amos to the coachman. He got out of the carriage, smiling at Hesper. "I'll be right down again."

She nodded and watched him ascend the stairs to the sail loft. The voice in her head became silent. Silly, she thought, "makin' a whale out o' a minnow." She turned her back on State Street and looked out over the harbor. It glittered with white sails. She had not seen it so filled with boats—since—since I was sixteen, she realized with shock, and the bankers and riggers were setting out in the spring. Superficially there was resemblance to that other long-past gala day. Today as then, streamers of colored bunting fluttered from many harborside windows, small boys tooted on old fishhorns and penny whistles. The rocks and ledges of Skinner's Head and Bartol's Head, as far as Redstone Cove, were dotted with Marbleheaders, happily ensconced with bottles of beer and picnic lunches—waiting to see the schooners sail out. But the schooners themselves—ah, they were as different from the weathered old bankers as swans from ducks. No broad beams and bulging, gaudy striped hulls on these schooners, they were long and slender and white as birch trees, and above them the unfamiliar and complicated rig seemed to Hesper as flimsy as so many pocket handkerchiefs. These toylike alien ships had brought with them a galaxy of satellites; an excursion steamer from Boston bearing Eastern Yacht Club members and their ladies, steamers from Salem and Beverley, and a hundred small pleasure craft from scattered points along the North Shore.

As she watched, the band on board the Boston steamer broke into a raucous march tune, and all the steamers blew their whistles moving out toward the starting-point at Marblehead Rock in the wake of the ten contesting yachts.

"It's a pretty sight—" she said quietly, as Amos reappeared. "No, it doesn't matter if we don't see them start. We'll get out to the Point in time to see them come home." She paused a moment and corrected herself. "I mean finish."

Amos did not notice the correction, nor hear the faint quiver in her voice. He had no means of knowing that for an instant she had slipped back to her girlhood, and had been standing right here on this wharf watching Johnnie sail off in the old *Diana,* amongst the rest of the fishing fleet. Her heart that day had been a shrunken ball of fear, and in the breasts of all the waving, cheering women there had been the same tight ball. The horns had tooted, the church bells had rung, and the bunting had fluttered from the windows even as now, but it had been a gaiety of gallantry and purpose, not a gaiety of sport.

They drove along Front Street toward the Hearth and Eagle, and Amos pulled a newspaper clipping from his pocket. "Here's a list of the yachts that're racing," he said. He ran his eye down the names of the boats, *Magic, Halcyon, Romance, Madcap*. "Mighty influential Boston men own 'em," he added, impressed. "Sure hope some of them decide to build homes on the Neck."

They both looked across the harbor to the Neck. Its rounded slopes were still barren of much vegetation except scrub pine and beach grass, but above these twenty or so new summer cottages reared their peaked and fretworked roofs against the horizon. Along the harbor beach by the ferry landing, there were a few tents and log cabins, remnant of the Nashua and Lowell Tent Colony, which had come and dispersed during the last ten years.

"Do you remember," said Hesper thoughtfully, "how short a time ago there was nothing on the Neck but a couple of farms, and that beach there was covered with fish flakes?"

"Progress—" Amos assented with satisfaction, but there was cause for discontent too. Why hadn't he had sense enough to buy up land on the Neck, or in any of the town's waterfront outskirts, while it was yet cheap? But this new and growing passion for a sea view on the part of summer people had not occurred to him. As it had never occurred to him to build his own house anywhere but inland on the highway.

Still, he thought, there's hope yet, soon as I get straightened out a bit and can lay my hands on some cash again, I'll buy some land.

The carriage drew up with a flourish before the side entrance to the Hearth and Eagle, and Amos stared gloomily at his wife's old home.

One sure thing, there'd never be any market for the crazy tumbledown houses like this in town. When the old folks go, he thought, Hes and I'll tear it down, maybe sell the land, or put up a good modern hotel. He had long since given up his earlier ideas for improving the actual structure. Just putting illuminating gas in had proved that it was hopeless. The house resisted improvement, with a nearly human cunning. There was no room to lay pipes, except in the open, the heavy oak carrying beams rejected new nails as though they had been iron girders, there wasn't a straight line in the house, not a door, not a floor, not a ceiling, and not one room plumb level with the next.

Hesper had long known and agreed with Amos's views, and now that she again actually saw the long hump-backed silvery old house, the vague fears and mystical aversions and hostilities with which during the last months she had endowed it, all vanished.

She descended slowly from the carriage, leaning on Amos's arm, and walked up the beaten dirt path toward the taproom door, noting with some amusement that Susan had planted sunflowers by the picket fence. There had never been sunflowers in Hesper's girlhood, because they somehow produced old maids. "Where sunflowers grow, beaux never go."

She opened the taproom door, and was annoyed by the cracked jangle of the bell. Ma should have a girl to answer the door, she should in any case give up the taproom. Undignified. The very word "taproom" had a raffish, outmoded flavor—and with half of Marblehead gone temperance already—but Ma was bull-headed always. Hesper perceived however that there was nobody in the dark taproom, nor in the kitchen either. After a minute, Susan appeared from the parlor, and found her daughter and son-in-law standing uncertainly in the entry.

"Well, I'll be gormed—" she said, advancing towards them across the floorboards. "If it ant Hes and Amos. I didn't hear the carriage." Her still-keen eyes glanced through the window. "But I see it's there." She surveyed Hesper, noting the modish hat, the best embroidered mantle and the parasol. "So you've perked up enough to venture out, have you!"

Of course Ma would use that tone. Never had a day's illness in her life. Seventy she was now, and still the picture of stout health.

"I'm feeling better—" said Hesper coldly. "We came to see if you and Pa would like to drive over to the Point o' Neck and watch the regatta."

"Oh—" answered her mother after a moment. "Aye, the regatta. 'Twas kindly meant of you both. But Roger he's still ailing, his heart's not so good, he's resting upstairs—and I've company."

"We'll be getting on—we won't disturb you then—" said Hesper quickly, hurt by her mother's attitude. Susan had been standing with her back to the parlor door in an unmistakably defensive manner, and far from showing gratitude for this long-delayed visit, the Porterman appearance seemed to be an embarrassment.

Susan had no difficulty in reading her daughter's thoughts. Her heavy shoulders hunched themselves under the black alpaca, she moved from the door, and the puckers around her mouth flattened into a grim smile.

"It's naught but Peg-Leg and Tamsen Peach—" she said, "and now you're here you'd best come in and greet them."

Hesper glanced at Amos, and she saw that although the reason for her mother's hesitance was now quite clear to her, Amos was neither enlightened nor interested.

Peg-Leg Dolliber, of course, was Hesper's uncle, and he had been exceedingly outspoken in his opinion of Hesper's two scandalous marriages; egged on by Mattie, he had loudly averred amongst the tight circle of old Marbleheaders that he for one washed his hands of the dom-fool gur-rl, and preferred to forget she was blood kin.

The prospect of meeting Tamsen Peach was even more disquieting. It was not only that Mrs. Peach had been Johnnie's mother, and that Hesper had always an uneasy impression that Tamsen looked upon Hesper's subsequent loves as a betrayal, but also, rightly or wrongly, Hesper knew that all the Peach connection attributed Lem Peach's death from consumption to Amos's tyrannical factory system.

"No—" said Hesper sharply. "We'll be getting on, Ma." She arranged the fringes of her mantle, and slipped her hand through Amos's arm. He patted it, and turning to go was startled by the change in Mrs. Honeywood. The old woman drew herself up until she seemed taller than her daughter, her broad fat face assumed the sternness of a Buddha.

"I said—you'd best come in and greet them, Hes!" she said, weighting each word. "You can't go on hiding all your life, my girl."

Amos felt Hesper stiffen, heard her sharp, catching breath. "Oh come now—Mrs. Honeywood—" he said with a small awkward laugh—"that's a peculiar thing to say. If Hessie doesn't want to meet those folks, I don't know why she should. I don't want her upset." He saw with alarm that Hesper's face was flaming red, and she pushed his protective arm aside.

"Who are those old folks to upset me—" she said through her teeth—"Ma making a stupid pother about nothing, as usual."

She shoved past her mother, burst open the parlor door, and swept in. The two people on either side the fireplace looked up in surprise.

"Good day, Mrs. Peach. Good day, Uncle Noah," she flung at them, standing in front of the center table and glancing down at them with an angry defiance. Her mother's guests passed from a shared astonishment into two divergent reactions.

Peg-Leg shifted his wooden stump, took his unlit pipe out of his mouth, put his mug of rum flip down on the hearth tiles by his chair, and exploded into cackles of laughter. "Jesus—" he choked. "Look wot the tide washed in! If it ain't the high and mighty Mrs. Par-rtermon, fancy bunnit, sunshade 'n all!"

Tamsen Peach said nothing for a moment. She had never been a pretty woman, but she had known deep love from husband and from her brood of children, and now at fifty-five her faded little face shone with a calm fulfillment. Suffering, poverty, and loss had left no bitterness, though they had extinguished all the laughter of her girlhood. She had never felt hostility toward Hesper, but she had never felt affection either, even during the betrothal to Johnnie. The girl had always been too self-contained, too deeply immersed in the egotism of youth to awaken response in a mother's jealous heart. And there had been that, too, Tamsen had long ago recognized that she had been a little jealous of Johnnie's love for Hesper. She looked at Hesper now, and saw her condition as Peg-Leg had not, saw the flushed defiance for the bravado it was, and she spoke softly. "Good arternoon, Hessie—'tis foine to see ye once again. And Mr. Par-rtermon—too," she added, nodding to Amos who had entered with Susan and now stood uncomfortably by the door. Her gentle brown eyes expressed no judgment of him either. It was true Lem's cough and the night sweats had got worse after he contracted to send all the output of his little shoe shop to Porterman's factory, but Tamsen had never been one to blame. If it hadn't been Porterman's it would have had to be another factory, and maybe it was the shoe shops themselves bred the consumption, stooping all day long over the bench, and breathing in the chalk and smoke.

Amos did not recognize Mrs. Peach—the town was full of Peaches, nor did he connect her with Hesper's youthful love affair, of which indeed he knew very little. He bowed vaguely to her, and to Peg-Leg whom he knew to be one of Hesper's hard-bitten, shell-backed relations, sat down on the edge of a chair indicated by Susan, and waited impatiently for Hes to finish off this unwelcome interruption to the day's outing.

This she seemed in no hurry to do. That curious flash of temper left her as suddenly as it had come; she sat down beside Dolliber on the sofa, and accepted from her mother a glass of dandelion wine. Soon the room thickened with Marblehead gutturals, even Hesper, whose speech was, like her father's and most of the younger generation, nearly free from the burr and the peculiar transposition of *o* and *a* sounds, fell into a way of talking that he had not heard from her in years.

The truth was that Hesper, having met friendliness from Tamsen, and no worse than ridicule from Peg-Leg, had felt a great relief and a desire to make amends. She asked after her uncle's garden, sure method of restoring his temper. Peg-Leg was growing larkspur and cinnamon roses—"the Gawd-dom biggest roses in Morblehead." He'd had to give up dory fishing at last on account of his rheumatics, but he wouldn't sell his old dory, he'd put her in the front yard and filled her with earth, and grew simples in her, marjoram and rosemary, and mustard and wormwood and pennyroyal. The salt and the fish gurry that had sunk into the dory's hull seemed to flavor the herbs and make them grow bigger than anyone else's.

"Have you tansy, Peg-Leg?" inquired Susan. "Mine is scanty this season, and I'd take it kindly could I have some to give Hessie."

Tamsen nodded gravely; tansy tea was well known to promote easy labor.

"Aye—" answered Peg-Leg, "Oi have some. So that's the way the wind blows." He surveyed his niece with a kinder look, drained off his rum flip, and clamped his tough old gums on the pipestem.

"Come, Hes," muttered Amos fidgeting. "We'll miss the race altogether."

She turned to him hastily, murmuring apology. She had quite forgotten the race, unaccountably soothed and sustained by chatter she perceived to be boring to Amos.

"I should think you'd want to watch it too—" said Amos politely to Peg-Leg, "you being such a sailor, and it's a fine day."

Peg-Leg snorted. " 'Tis naught to me which one o' them fancy boats beats fir-rst to Morblehead Rock, and 'tis not a foine day."

"Why, there's not a cloud in the sky—"

The old seaman gave him a look of amused contempt. "Weather breeder—it'll star-rm afore mar-rnin'."

"Aye—" said Susan suddenly, "and there's worse than storm in the air. Did you hear the 'screechin' woman' last night?" She looked at her brother and Tamsen, and she asked the question as casually as one speaks of any disagreeable manifestation of nature—"Did you hear it hailing last night?" But Peg-Leg and Tamsen both started, frowned, and considered the statement distastefully.

"Did ye, Susan?" said Peg-Leg. "She's out o' season. But mebbe 'twas boys imitatin' her screeches. Oi had a tur-rn at thot meself, sixty years ago."

Susan shook her head. " 'Twasn't boys. I heard *her* plain screeching,

'Ha' mercy! Ha' mercy! Oh Lord Jesus save me!' Like she always does. There's bad luck coming."

Hesper knew she should laugh; Amos's expression of bewildered annoyance was funny in itself, her mother's belief in a shrieking ghost was funny, but she could not laugh.

"What in the name of heaven is the screechin' woman?" Amos demanded. The three old Marbleheaders turned and looked at him somberly. They had forgotten him.

"Furriners don't hear her," said Peg-Leg in a grumpy voice, and he clamped his jaws again on his pipestem.

"It's an old legend," explained Hesper hurriedly. "A couple of hundred years ago a high-born English lady was captured by pirates and forced ashore here at Marblehead. The pirates murdered her just up the street in Oakum Bay. Some people," she glanced at her mother's impassive face, "some people think they can still hear her screams for mercy."

"She screeches—" said Susan, calmly, filling Peg-Leg's mug from a pitcher. "Sometimes on the night she was slaughtered, and sometimes when there's evil coming to Marblehead."

"That's roight," agreed Tamsen. "Oi hear-rd her in '73 two days before the town was strick with the smallpox, and so did many another."

Amos stood up abruptly, ignoring Mrs. Peach and addressing his mother-in-law. "I am surprised at a sensible woman like you, talking like that." It pained him to have to revise his long-held respect for Mrs. Honeywood, pained him the more as this nonsense somehow reflected on Hesper. He had always soothed the disquiet occasioned by her father's undeniable whimsies and fantasies by the reflection that she took after her robustly practical mother. Susan still further disquieted him by smiling tolerantly and saying, "You sound like Roger. He was grouty with me for saying I heard her, but he heard her too, despite his deafness. I could tell by the jump he gave and the look on his face. But he wouldn't own to it."

"Of course not—" snapped Amos, reversing his usual position. "He's a sensible, well-educated man."

Susan sat still with her fat mottled hands clasped on her ample lap. "Funny thing about Roger—" she said, in a saddened almost gentle voice. "He hankers after the past, sets such a store by past things—but when the past really comes through to him like it does sometimes—he's afeared, and he won't listen and he won't see."

Maybe that's true—thought Hesper. Her mother's words gave her a strange shock. The past comes through, not only the evil in the past like the screechin' woman—but good too—like Arbella's letter—the past always there, flowing beside us as we journey, like a river hidden by mist. It seemed to her for one second that she was close to both her parents, understanding their viewpoints, which were not opposed, as she had always thought, but the two sides of the same shield.

She hurried upstairs to see her father, but she found him fast asleep, propped up against the headboard of the old spool bed in her parents' room. His spectacles had slipped down his nose, the inky pen had fallen to the counterpane, and across his lap there lay open and half covered with his scratchy writing—the second volume of the "Memorabilia." She kissed the top of his head where the pink scalp showed through the white hair. She took off his glasses, and eased the pillows under his head. He stirred and smiled a little, but his deafness prevented him from hearing her. Last she put the pen on the oak chest by the bed, and lifting the heavy volume off his lap, she glanced at the page he had been writing. First there were several lines in parenthesis. "(This incident refers to April, 1814, when the British frigates *Tenedos* and *Endymion* had been three days pursuing our *Constitution* which took refuge in Marblehead Harbor and was thereby saved, by Fort Sewall's doughty cannon. I saw this myself, being a lad of eight, and great was my perturbation, since my father, Thomas Honeywood, was a seaman on the *Constitution* and amongst those Marbleheaders who piloted her to safety.)"

And he had written one stanza.

> Old Ironsides, fleeing from pursuers
> Shelters in our harbor still.
> Adds one more glory to our story,
> "Marblehead is Marblehead, has been and always will."

Hesper's eyes filled with tears. She shut the volume gently, marking the place with the pen, and she stole out of the room.

Amos and Hesper left the Inn, re-entered the carriage, and drove over to the Neck across the causeway at Riverhead Beach. When they reached the squat white lighthouse on the Point they found a crowd of people crowded around its base. Though Marblehead youngsters were perched amongst the rocks, and the Portermans recognized a few acquaintances like the Browns and the Harrises, the crowd consisted mostly of strangers, the summer cottagers on the Neck, and excursionists who had not wished to remain on the steamers.

Amos drifted off to speak to Mr. Harris, and Hesper sat alone in the carriage beneath her sunshade and watched the distant white yachts sail in past the stake boat off Marblehead Rock. Near the carriage there stood a young couple from Lynn. The man wore a blue-and-white-striped jacket with gold buttons, and a blue cap with a shiny visor and an anchor embroidered above it. He had a spyglass, and he informed his lady of the progress of the race, in a loud, confident voice. That was *Halcyon* coming first, followed by *Magic.* The young man was a trifle dejected, because he'd bet Ned two dollars on *Latona,* but *Latona* had run into trouble past Halfway Rock, and parted her port main shrouds, so she was out of the race.

Hesper sat and perforce listened, but the sun poured very hot from out that cloudless sky, the violet haze on the horizon shimmered before her aching eyes, and the depression which had lifted from her that morning returned again. Pretty boats with pretty names, a charming spectacle to watch as one watched colored lantern slides of romantic scenery. But Marblehead was more than a convenient screen on which to project an alien spectacle, no matter how charming.

She felt a sudden fierce resentment, jealous for the harbor as it had been once, teeming with the bankers and the riggers and the coalers and the ballast lighters. It was *ours* then, she thought, the sea and the town were united in purpose, integrated with each other. She looked out toward the fairy yachts, slipping now one by one into the harbor, their sails half furled and strings of rose and green lanterns festooned between their masts. From the Boston steamer there floated the delicious and sensuous strains of the Blue Danube.

Get out—she cried to them all, go away, with your waltzes and your fairy lanterns and your make-believe races. You don't belong here. And like the cat's-paw of wind that skimmed across the harbor, something whispered in her heart—"And do *you* belong here, either? Isn't your life, too, a pretty colored lantern slide?" But she scarcely heard the whisper, before it was gone. Amos came back, and they drove home together through the dusk. He was concerned because she looked very tired, and indeed she felt drained and empty. Her head ached now in earnest and she longed with singlehearted yearning for the moment when she might again slip between her cool lavender-scented sheets, and sip the sugared lemonade that Annie would have waiting.

CHAPTER 16

THE STORM prophesied by Peg-Leg duly arrived in the night and it blew and rained all Saturday and most of Sunday. Hesper spent those days in bed. She and Amos thought it wise to rest after the fatigue of the expedition; neither was there any particular reason for getting up, even on Sunday, for it had been years since she had gone to church. Amos was no churchgoer. Right after their marriage they had gone to the Old North, but they had not enjoyed the buzz of whispers that accompanied their appearance, and once it became apparent to Amos that the effort would produce neither social nor financial results, they gave it up.

Except that Hesper ate her meals off a tray sloppily prepared by Annie, Sunday plodded by much like all other Sundays. She read Henry a Bible story, then questioned him on it. She leafed through a couple of Ladies' Magazines, she played a hand or two of euchre with Amos. After dinner she napped and dreamed about the baby, seeing it as a rosy, laughing little girl. They were on a ship together, she and her little girl, the ship was Johnnie's old *Diana,* but it looked like one of the Boston yachtsman's schooners, and it was bound for a soft southern country far away where they were to live in a little white temple amongst a grove of flowered trees.

She awoke from this dream, and lay staring at the ceiling, listening to the rain until Amos came in from a trip to the stables, and coming to the bedside asked affectionately how she was feeling.

"All right—" she said, smiling up at him. "I was dreaming of the baby."

He sat on the edge of the bed, taking her hand in his. "You're not too worried, Pussie—about, well—your ordeal? It's awful that women have to go through those things."

"I'm not much worried—" she said, and she could see the admiration in his eyes. Though in fact Henry's birth had not been bad. It had been methodical and expeditious as Henry himself, and she had had whiffs of chloroform all the way through.

"I've told Doctor Flagg to get hold of that special woman's doctor from Boston—" said Amos. "Should have had him for Henry's birth, but I didn't know about him, then."

"Ah darling—" whispered Hesper, much touched, and her hand closed around his. "You're good to me." Far off in the back of her head she heard Susan's snort of derision, and she heard her mother's voice as though she stood in the room—"So even me and the monthly nurse and Doctor Flagg and chloroform a'nt enough to birth a strapping healthy woman!"

But I lost the first baby, Hesper reminded her mother's image sharply. You never make allowances.

Amos bent and kissed her. She looked young and pretty, lying there against the pillows with the two curly auburn braids falling down her shoulders against her blue swansdown jacket. He no longer noticed the heavy straight black eyebrows which had once disconcerted him with their startling effect of strength in a face otherwise very feminine. He saw only that her hazel eyes looked softly at him, and that her lips had an appealing and wistful curve.

"Of course I'm good to you, my girl. I'm fond of you," he said gruffly. Her heart swelled. It's for this—she thought—for this. Why do I ever feel discontent—how dare I feel an emptiness? We have so much, Amos and I.

"Amos, dear—" she said, after a moment. "Are things still going well at the factory?"

He looked surprised and indulgent. "Certainly. Very well indeed. Just got a big new order. Why do you ask?"

The real optimism in his voice convinced her. She answered hesitantly. "Do you think, maybe, you might—sell the factory—someday—we might move from here?"

"Well, I suppose I might," said Amos, still indulgently, though he was startled. "You don't like it here, Hes? Why, it's your own town and—" and he glanced around the luxurious room, "and this is our home."

"Yes, I know, and it's beautiful. But—we aren't really part of the town, are we?"

Now it was out. The thing they never mentioned, and she had said it so quickly and casually that he hardly heard her. He put her suggestion down to a whim born of her condition. The time had passed when he cared what the town thought of him. As long as there was money to be made from it. Cheap labor and now this new prospect of profitable real estate. As soon as the factory was on its feet again, they could travel more, perhaps buy a winter house in Boston if she wished it. And soon as money flowed in again, as it surely would.

"We'll see, Pussie," he said. "I guess you'll be far too busy with the new baby to think of moving yet awhile," and he went out again to go down-town and make a final quick inspection of the factory.

At five, Hesper decided after all to get up for supper. She rose languidly and put on a summer house gown, made of white muslin, with a loose, flowing overdress of leaf-green silk edged with black braid. The weather had begun to clear and it was growing warm. It tired her to raise her arms for long. So it was too much effort to rebraid her hair after its perfunctory brushing, or to arrange the little lace "breakfast" cap which should accompany negligée.

She wadded all the stubborn curly red mass into a black net and tied the black ribbons in a bow on the top of her head, ending with a quick survey in the rosewood cheval glass.

I look pretty good, considering, she thought, surprised. The long flowing lines of the green overdress hid the thickness of her waistline. This burden that she carried forced her body to a proud, even magnificent carriage, with head and shoulders well back to balance the forward pull.

Her skin glowed with the fine-grained luster sometimes bestowed by late pregnancy. I do look handsome in green, she thought, and yet for many years she had avoided the color because of its painful associations with the green dress Evan had bought her in New York. The dress in which he had tried to paint her and failed.

She turned from the mirror. It was never wise to think of Evan. Pain and failure must be thrust back again at once behind the protective wall. Or they might be denied existence, as Charity said. "Evil is nothing but illusion, Hesper, it has no reality. You must think only sweet loving thoughts, for the sake of the little one, if not your own."

Hesper sighed. Well, maybe. Charity was certainly a good example of her own preaching. Healthy, bustling, and complacent to the point of smugness. No more feverish yearnings and clutchings for her, no doubts or self-distrust.

She heard the front door slam and moved to the head of the stairs, calling greeting to Amos, who ran up to her boyishly. "So you're all dressed, Pussie! Sure you feel up to it?" and she noticed that Amos was in his happiest mood.

He and Johnson had been inspecting every room in his factory, and found everything in topnotch condition for the start of the great effort tomorrow. The stitching machines and the buffers and the channel turners were all cleansed, oiled, and in working order. The cutting tables and the lasters' benches cleared from back orders and ready. And in the basement stock room he had been delighted with the quality of the new shipment of tanned and dyed black Morocco hides. He congratulated Johnson, who nodded and admitted that the hands were showing a good spirit. He'd told the cutters to show up at five-thirty tomorrow morning and they'd agreed without fussing. It was the promise of the bonus had done it, that and the thrill of optimism communicated downwards from Amos.

There had been only one puzzling little incident to mar the pleasure of this final inspection. Amos had been standing in the making room on the third floor near the new buttonhole cutter which had just been installed. The buttonhole cutter was set up by the back southwest windows, and Amos had happened to glance out. "Hello—" he said, "there seems to be someone in that old shed down there. I thought it was kept locked up."

Johnson joined him at the window. Below them there lay a small muddy lot cluttered with tin cans and cast-off leather shavings. It was bordered on two sides with the backs of buildings which fronted on Pleasant and School Streets—a feed and grain shop, the Marblehead Hotel, the Rechabite building which contained a small shoe factory as well as the Rechabite Assembly rooms, and, largest of all, Amos' factory.

The lot was bounded on the north by the railroad tracks, and on the west by the General Glover firehouse and a small reservoir called the Brick Pond. Besides mud and refuse, the lot contained the ramshackle shed which stood within twelve feet of Amos' building and was a great annoyance to him, since it partially blocked access to the back entrance of the factory, and hindered loadings and deliveries. Amos had, of course, tried to buy the shed, but its owner, who also owned the feed and grain store, was obdurate. He kept supplies in the shed, and had no interest in obliging Amos.

"I don't see nobody—" said Johnson.

"Looked to me like a man darted in carrying something," Amos explained, frowning. From where they stood they could not see the shed door.

"Well, what if he did? Prob'ly someone wanted an extra pail of oats in a hurry. Jesus, Chief, it ain't like you to be jumpy."

"Hate to have anyone break in and get those fine hides," said Amos, half joking. "I wouldn't put it beyond some of those fly-by-night shoemen down the street."

Johnson received this with a sardonic chuckle. "You want me to stay here nights and sleep on them precious hides? Or maybe we should hire a troop o' watchmen?"

"You haven't replaced Dan yet, I suppose?" said Amos smiling.

"Hardly, in two days. But he's all right, sir. And so are our locks and bolts." Johnson permitted himself an amused and paternal grin. "You go home to the missis. I'll have another look around afore I leave, and speak to old Dan special."

So Amos rode contentedly home through the late afternoon sunlight.

At six, he and Hesper and Henry sat down to family supper. While Hesper ladled the split-pea soup out of the silver-plated tureen, she noticed a film of grease around the rim of a soup plate. She frowned and wiped it with her napkin, and now she saw that the silverware was dingy and the tablecloth spotted. There were dust-pussies clustered behind the bulbous feet of the mahogany-veneer sideboard, and a filmy cobweb drifted from the fretwork cornice of the mantelpiece.

"Annie—" she said, when that young woman clumped back from the pantry bearing a platter of fried steak, "the cloth and silver aren't clean, and when did you dust the dining room?"

Annie twitched and tossed her head with a scarcely veiled impertinence. "I didn't know you was comin' down to supper—" she answered. "I've too much to do as it is. Me and Bridget we need a kitchenmaid, and a chambermaid too—come to that."

Hesper opened her mouth to answer that the care of three people was not much work, and that in any case the situation had not changed in the four years Annie had been there, but she did not feel equal to a scene. She was baffled by the girl's new hostility and she thought weakly—all my trays and perhaps there would be too much work while the monthly nurse was here, and the confusion of the lying-in period. When Annie had flounced back to the pantry, she said to Amos, "Perhaps we *should* get another maid? I'd hate trouble with Annie and Bridget just now."

Amos cut another strip of fried steak, and poured catsup over it before answering. He knew the secret of Annie's insolence was that he hadn't yet paid her May wages. He settled all the household bills directly from his office, leaving to Hesper only the disbursement of her generous dress allowance.

"We'll see—" he said pleasantly. "Maybe next time I run up to Boston. Don't worry your head about it, Hessie, I'll see that the servants behave."

"Annie spends a lot of time in the stable with Tim," remarked Henry suddenly, as one who offers a helpful sidelight. "They hug and kiss."

"That'll do!" cried both his parents in a stern chorus.

Henry subsided. They finished their supper with a Queen pudding of bread, custard, and jam, then repaired as usual to the library.

Hesper had never admitted to herself how much this elegant room depressed her, even more so than the drawing room. It was papered in a purplish maroon pattern of leaves shaded in black along the edges so as to appear embossed, and the fumed-oak woodwork in here had been darkened to the shade of mahogany. The east wall was lined with sets of books, behind glass doors. A set of Scott in tooled umber, a twenty-volume set of *Little Gleanings from the Classics* in green calf and marbleized half-covers; an Encyclopedia and a Longfellow. There were three rosewood armchairs and a settee all upholstered in horsehair. The carpet was dark brown to match the woodwork, and even after all four bracket gaslights were lit, the room was gloomy, as it was meant to be. There should be no frivolity about a library.

Hesper had been very proud of it when she came to the house as a bride, and she was still proud of it, but she was not comfortable in it.

They followed the nightly custom, settling themselves in the prickly chairs while Amos read out loud. He enjoyed reading aloud, and did it well in a slow and sonorous voice. In the past he had read them *Ivanhoe* and *Quentin Durward,* but he considered Scott too melodramatic for Hesper at present, and had been reading from the placid pages of Mrs. Dinah Maria Mulock.

Henry while listening was allowed to occupy his hands by coloring pictures, which bored him, but he had no more thought of rebelling than had his mother. It was good of Papa to read to them, and this was established law for the after-supper hours.

At nine o'clock Amos looked at his gold watch and shut the book. "Time for bed, son."

Henry slid down from his chair and kissed his parents.

"You too, Hessie?"

She nodded and rose with difficulty. Amos steadied her arm.

"I'll be up presently. I'll just finish the article in the *Transcript.*"

Hesper and her son started across the parquet floor toward the stairs, when the front-door bell rang. They paused in surprise, and waited, watching while Amos opened the door.

A shabby urchin stood on the mat, blinking in the sudden light.

"Well—" said Amos. "What do you want?"

Annie stuck her frowsy head around the corner of the hall in answer to the bell, but seeing her master and mistress there, disappeared again. The boy advanced into the hall, dragging his feet.

"I've a message for Amos Porterman—" said the boy, staring vacantly at the floor. "He said t' big house near t' for-rk fur Salem, an' a stuffed deer in t' front yard."

"Yes!" said Amos impatiently. "This is the house, I'm Mr. Porterman. What do you want?"

The boy, raising stupid eyes to Amos's face, considered this. He took off his cap and twisted it in his fingers. "He said fur you t' go t' fact'ry. Immedjate. T' hurry."

Amos stiffened. Now what's the trouble, he thought, his lips tightening. *"Who* told you?" he demanded, though he hadn't a doubt it was Johnson.

"I dunno," said the boy. "'Twas some man stopped me on the street. He give me two bits. Said he'd wait till you come."

"All right—" said Amos. "I'm coming," and he would have given him a dime but the boy, having had his say, stepped back through the door and walked away.

"It's nothing," said Amos hastily to Hesper who looked troubled. "I suppose Johnson wants to show me something. I guess I'll walk. It's a lot quicker than getting a horse hitched. Now, go to bed and don't stay awake. I might be late and I want you to get your sleep." She nodded, watching him take his hat from the antler hatrack, and wind his black silk muffler around his neck.

"Good-bye, dear—" she said, and the little phrase echoed in her ears. Her nerves gave a faint quiver, shrinking like the sea anemone from an invisible vibration. Then she turned briskly to Henry. "Hurry on off to bed, my lad."

"What did the dirty boy want with Papa?"

"Oh he was just a messenger from Mr. Johnson. You know sometimes Papa does go back to the factory at night when they're very busy."

Henry was satisfied. He trudged upstairs, and allowed his mother to tuck him in, and even sing "Rock-a-bye Baby" to him—a foolish indulgence which he usually denied her.

Hesper went into her bedroom. But she was no longer sleepy. She moved restlessly around the room. Finally she lay down on top of the covers, still dressed in her house gown. She turned up the gas jet by her bed, and began to read. For a while the story occupied the surface of her mind, and then she lost it in a growing uneasiness. This is ridiculous, she thought, nerves again. She put the book on the table, turned the gas low, and closed her eyes. After a while she dozed, and from the shadowy layer between two consciousnesses, sinister faces peered at her; they shifted like dark water, these pointed faces, watching her with yellow eyes that vanished into the blackness of rocks behind them. And then it seemed to her that from these rocks water oozed in an oily and serpentine coil. It gathered speed and size as it oozed toward her, until she heard an advancing roar and it towered above her, a wall of evil black water surging and roaring toward her flattened body.

She jumped up and awoke. She was trembling and the palms of her hands were wet.

The nightmare terror passed slowly, though she brought to bear on it all the arguments of common sense. It was too warm in the room, her supper had disagreed with her. She should have gone properly to bed as Amos had told her. He'd be cross when he came back to find her awake and still dressed.

There was no clock in the bedroom, and she lay a few more minutes without moving, profoundly reluctant to know the time. At last she got up and, walking to her dresser, turned over the little enamel watch which she had placed earlier in the pin tray. It was one o'clock.

"But there's nothing in that," she said aloud. "A dozen things may have delayed him."

She went into the bathroom and washed her face with cold water, and while in there she heard through the wall Henry muttering in his sleep. She went into his room, lit the night light, and pulled the blanket over him. He stirred and half opened his eyes. His room faced the east and was cooler than hers, for a breeze blew in from off the sea. She walked over to the window, intending to close it a little, but as she put her hand to the sash, she stopped with a stiffled exclamation, shoved it up, and leaned out.

A ruddy glare illumined a section of the eastern sky. Her straining eyes saw a high darting tongue of flame, and faint on the breeze she smelled the acrid odor of smoke. She leaned on the windowsill to ease the sudden panic of her heart, and she heard the distant jangle of alarm bells from the South Church steeple.

"What's the matter, Mama?" called Henry from behind her. He always awakened alert, and in full possession of himself. He pattered out of bed and edged in beside her.

"Fire—" she said beneath her breath, scarcely conscious of him. "In the business section."

Henry peered through the window with lively interest. "Near Papa's factory?"

"It looks near—" she said in the same hurried voice. She still leaned on the sill in a paralysis of indecision. Something not clear, something more than fire . . .

"Marblehead has lots of fires," said Henry with satisfaction. "I like to see the engines. Did Papa go down-town on account of the fire?"

"No," she said. "No." And the deadlock broke in her mind. There had been no fire when Amos left, she would have seen it when she opened Henry's window, nor would Johnson have sent a summons like that had there been fire.

But that boy's message didn't come from Johnson. It came from Nat!

"Oh my God—" she whispered—"you fool, you fool. Nat's trapped him. I know it."

And in that second of anguish, she saw herself for a coward and a weakling. How deaf she had been to the inner voice, how many warnings had she evaded, how many compromises accepted for the sake of ease. If I had gone with Leah that night, or kept her here. . . . If I hadn't let myself be lulled again and again, if I'd gone in to see Nat Friday—when I know I saw him at the window—if I'd stopped Amos tonight—

"Mama—what are you doing?" Henry shrilled, running after her, for she had left his room and already reached the landing.

"Go back—" she said. "Stay in your room." But he saw she had no awareness of him; he darted into his room for his slippers, put them on, and clad only in his nightshirt, scurried after her down the stairs. He was a little frightened by her face, chalk-white and her eyes fixed and angry, looking like the picture of the terrible Egyptian queen in his Bible, but he had also an impulse to be near her, and he wanted to see the fire.

He slid out the front door behind her, and down the drive to Pleasant Street where she turned toward the town. On the street's firmer surface her steps accelerated almost to a run, and Henry, panting, finally tugged at her arm. "I didn't know you could walk so fast—" he said plaintively. "I didn't know you could walk much at all. You're always in bed."

By the light of the half-moon overhead, he saw her lips move in a bitter smile. She stopped a moment. "Henry—you shouldn't have come. Go back!"

He shook his head. "I want to stay with you."

She made an impatient sound, and began to run again. "All right, but I can't look out for you. Papa's in danger. You'll have to rely on yourself." He accepted this as fair, and was silent.

They crossed the railroad tracks near the little Devereux depot and now they were joined on the road by other hurrying figures. Hesper's breath came harshly through her nostrils, her heart hammered against her ribs, but she did not feel her body. Her feet moved of themselves, sure and fast.

As they neared the town, the glare ahead of them grew lurid, and the air resounded with a dull roaring. The church bells clanged incessantly. Then from behind them up the road they heard quicker, sharper bells, and the approaching thunder of horses' hooves. Hesper and Henry ran for the side of the road with the dozen other men and women who were heading toward the fire. "Gorm—" cried a man, near Hesper. "They've telegraphed for the Salem steamers, fire *must* be bad." Salem's red fire engines streaked by, and the sparks from metal horseshoes flew up to meet the sparks that drifted down out of the sky.

They hurried on and reached the juncture with Washington Street, and here they were stopped by a volunteer fireman, who flourished a long pole. "You can't go no fur-rther down Pleasant. Tur-rn bock—all on ye!" And he waved the old leather buckets with which he was trying to wet down the corners of the nearest houses.

The crowd hung back, gaping, all but Hesper. Ahead of them the left side of Pleasant Street was a mass of roaring flames.

"What buildings are afire?" cried Hesper, grabbing the fireman's arm. He started to shake her off, then looked again.

"Why, Hesper-r—is it you?"

She did not recognize Willy Bowen, mate on the *Ceres* and long ago friend of Johnnie's. "What buildings?" she cried again, shaking his arm.

"Morblehead Hotel, an' the feed store, an' ye can see for yourself, Glover Engine House's caught, though they got the steamer out, but the Brick Pond water's already biling hot and useless."

"Is Porterman's burning?" she cried with anguish.

"I dunno. I think it started there first in the back, but the east wind's pushed the fire this way—wind's shifting though—"

She shoved him aside, and ran down the flaming street. Henry tried to follow her, but Willy Bowen stretched out his foot, tripped him and seized him by the back of his nightshirt. "Oh no ye don't, my lad! You stay here. D'you want to be fried to a crisp? Here, missis, you hold him." He thrust Henry towards a goggle-eyed woman. But Henry no longer struggled, he stood quiet by the young woman, staring with all his eyes after his mother.

Hesper clung to the houses on the right-hand side of the street which had not yet caught. Across the street the four burning buildings sent out a blast of furnace heat that seared her throat and eyeballs.

She held her breath, shut her eyes, and ran through the worst to the corner of School Street. Here the fire engines were clustered, Marblehead's old hand tubs, its steamer, the General Glover, and Salem's newly arrived steamers. The hoses writhed across the street, on the hand tubs the crews of men pumped up and down frantically; but even as she stumbled amongst the engines, there was a cry of despair while flame and smoke sprang from Pope's Block across the way. The fire had jumped Pleasant Street.

She cared nothing for that, she saw only that School Street was not yet in flames, and though the smoke was so dense that she could hardly see its outlines, the front at least of Amos' factory was not burning.

She ran toward it past one of the Salem steamers which was playing a thin stream of water on the smoldering Rechabite building. She ran to the foot of the outside stairs which led up to Amos' private entrance, when a rough hand fell on her shoulder.

"Jesus, Mrs. Porterman! What in the name o' God are you doin'? The factory's on fire!"

She looked up into Johnson's soot-streaked, haggard face. He too held a bucketful of water with which he had run from the nearest pump.

"Where's Amos?" she cried. "Have you seen Amos?"

"No!" he shouted, staring. "Ain't he with you?" He dashed the bucket of water at the building, crying to the nearest firemen—"Turn your hoses here, boys, for God's sake!" But the Salem firemen were cursing the feeble water supply and did not hear.

"Amos is in there!" Hesper cried, pointing at the factory. "I know he is. Hurry, you fool, we've got to hurry!" And she started again up the stairs.

"Mrs. Porterman, come back! You're crazy. The place's on fire, I tell you. He wouldn't be in there."

Hesper reached the top of the stairs, and twisted the knob, throwing her shoulder against the door. It would not yield. She looked wildly back at Johnson's blank face. She saw him clutch at her again, thinking her truly crazed, and she raised her head and screamed "Help!" at the top of her lungs.

The Salem firemen turned, saw her, and came running. They swept Johnson ahead of them up the stairs. "Break it in—" she shouted, pointing to the door.

The men lunged together and Johnson with them. The door cracked and gave. They stumbled into the dark smoke-filled room; through the open door the glare lit up a figure prone on the floor by the desk.

"My God—" whispered Johnson. "She's right." The three men seized the limp figure, and coughing and choking they carried it down the stairs and across the street to a clear space by the railroad tracks.

"He'll be all right, ma'am," said one of the firemen. "He's breathing. Just overcome by smoke. Let him lay quiet a bit, but you better get him out of here soon. Christ—" he said, turning to his companion, "look at that depot roof, that's caught too. There won't be nothing left of this town."

The two men started off running, back to their hose.

Amos stirred and moaned, as Hesper and Johnson knelt beside him. The foreman muttered, "Thank God, he's comin' to. We'll have to walk him out of here, unless I find someone else to help carry him." He was now dazed, he had ceased thinking or wondering. Across the street he saw the flames beginning to lick through north windows of the factory. That would be in the stitching room, he thought, just about by them new boxes of fancy buttons.

"Yes, he's coming to—" said Hesper. "But he couldn't walk like this. Have you a knife?"

"Knife?" repeated Johnson, pulling his hypnotized gaze from the burning factory. He stared at the crouching woman, her hair, dark in the red glare around them, streamed down her shoulders to the ground beside her husband. Her green overdress was torn, and her left shoulder showed white through the rent. But her cheeks and hands were blackened like a minstrel show, he thought vaguely.

"Have you got a *knife?*" she shouted with a vehemence that penetrated Johnson's daze. He fumbled in his pockets, and brought out a small clasp knife.

"Cut these—" she said through her teeth. Then he saw that she was rolling up the bottom of Porterman's trousers. He looked down and said "Sweet Jesus—" very softly.

Amos's ankles were bound together by a solid band, made from turn after turn of fine, unbreakable fishing line. Johnson sawed through the lines with his knife, and the ankles fell apart limply.

Hesper started chafing them. "The wrists too," she cried. A spark fell on her skirt and she brushed it off impatiently.

Johnson muttered while he cut through the wrist bonds. "But who done this? Who would have done such a terrible thing?"

Hesper said nothing. Amos stirred again, lifted his head a little, and opened his eyes. She slipped her arm around his neck, holding his head against her breast. "You're all right, dear—" she said in a low, clear voice. "Amos, do you hear me? You're all right."

His body gave a convulsive shudder, and his head jerked back, pressing painfully against her breasts. He looked up at her. "Hessie?" he whispered. "What are you doing here? Your face is dirty."

"I know," she said. "Now I want you to stand up, see if you can walk."

She moved from him, stumbling awkwardly to her own feet, regained her balance at once, and bent to take one of his arms, while Johnson pulled up on the other. Amos stood up swaying, leaning on Hesper's shoulder.

As they stood there, one of the Salem firemen raced toward them. "My God, ain't you out o' here yet?" he shouted. "Get back. Quick!"

They obeyed him without thought, Hesper and Johnson pulling Amos with them, and their ears were deafened by a tremendous roar and crash.

A hundred yards away across School Street, there shot up a geyser of flame and burning brands and sparks. The entire north wall of Porterman's had fallen in.

"My factory?" said Amos in the same startled questioning tone he had used to Hesper.

"There's plenty more burning than your factory," said the fireman. "We got the Lynn steamer now, but she don't do no good neither." He vanished again into the smoke.

"Come," said Hesper to Johnson. "This way. Help me with him across the tracks until we get to Elm Street." Her voice was calm and controlled. Amos obeyed it mechanically, limping a little but walking between them without support. He had as yet no memory of what had happened. The roaring and crackling and the crashing of walls behind them, the lurid red glare, the heat, the smoke that swirled around them and cleared again before puffs of wind, all came through to his oxygen-starved brain as meaningless confusion, in which Hesper's voice was the only security.

"Where're you goin'?" asked Johnson, as they picked their way over the tracks where some of the ties were already smoldering.

"Home," she said.

"But you're goin' the wrong direction."

"No. I mean my home."

They turned down Sewall to Elm Street, and here the fire had not yet reached, though the sky was filled with flying sparks and small glowing embers borne by the shifting wind to sections as far away as Barnegat.

And now Hesper stopped, and glancing at Amos who stopped when she did and stood silent, his head lowered and his eyes fixed on the ground, she drew away from him, and said very low to Johnson, "I'll get him home all right now. I want you to go back down Bowden Street, skirt the fire until you come to the western edge of it. Find Henry, and bring him to me."

"My God, ma'am," whispered Johnson. "Is the boy out in this?"

"He followed me, but he'll be all right. Henry has sense."

Johnson opened his mouth and shut it again. He stared at the soot-blackened, disheveled woman. She's got guts, she has—he thought. Keeps her head wonderful. And then he remembered her condition. "But, ma'am—you ain't strong enough to walk all that way down to the harbor—let alone caring for *him*. . . ."

She raised her chin and looked not at Johnson, but past him with a strange level look. "I am—" she said. "I'm plenty strong enough. I've more strength than I've ever used."

She turned and put her hand under Amos's arm, and they started to walk again. In all the houses along Elm Street and then Back Street as they neared the water, there were lights, and pounding footsteps and sometimes weeping. Panic-stricken men, women, and children rushed about the streets, dragging out their household goods and piling them futilely by their doors, and swarming the roofs with pails and pitchers of water, crying to each other that all the churches had caught, that the fire was leaping down Washington Street, that the whole town would surely go.

Fear and shouting and turmoil all around her, and yet in Hesper there was an inner stillness. The town will not go, she thought, not the real town. God won't let the evil go that far. Yet even as she thought that, a deeper honesty rebelled. For suppose He did let the evil go that far and farther, if in fact He did not concern Himself with evil, what recourse then for us?

And it seemed to her as she and Amos came at last in sight of the sea, stretching limitless and calm in the gray dawn behind her home, the old hump-backed house which had endured so many years through good and evil—that she knew the answer.

CHAPTER 17

SUSAN, in her nightgown and flannel wrapper, was in the kitchen, heating water on the little cookstove for Roger who had taken a sudden turn for the worse.

She heard the sounds at the back door and moved towards it with the candle. "Lord a mercy," she whispered, as she recognized her daughter and Amos. "My God, what's happened?" She stared at Hesper's streaming hair, the blackened faces, and the torn clothes. "Come in—set down, the two of you. I'll hot up some coffee. Is it the fire?"

"It's bad, Ma," said Hesper quietly. "All the business section's burning—" She glanced at Amos who had sunk down on the settle, his arms resting on his knees, and was staring at the floor. She spoke very low. "The factory's gone."

Her mother met her eyes with startled dismay. "That *is* terrible," she whispered. "What's the matter with Amos? Was he hurt?"

Hesper nodded. She took the coffeepot from her mother, poured out a cup, and brought it to Amos. "Drink this, dear. You'll feel better." She sat beside him on the settle and held the saucer while he drank.

He finished the coffee, and suddenly threw his head back, staring at Hesper. "It was Nat," he said in a puzzled voice. "Nat Cubby. He was hiding in my office when I got there. It wasn't Johnson sent the message."

"Yes, I know," said Hesper quickly. "Don't try to talk about it yet."

Amos glanced down at his big hands, and back to Hesper; he continued in the same groping voice. "I'm a strong man, I'd make two of Nat, but he jumped out at me so suddenly I fell down—he kicked me on the head."

Hesper gave a soft cry. Now for the first time she saw a bluish bump above Amos's right ear. "I'll get arnica—"

He shook his head impatiently. "It isn't bad. He didn't want it to be, just stunned me long enough so he could tie me up with the fishing line."

"Gorm—" whispered Susan again, staring at him openmouthed. "What was Nat trying to do?"

He turned his head towards her, and some of the vagueness left his eyes. He answered in a surer tone. "He was trying to murder me. He fired the factory and thought I'd burn up with it."

"But why—" said Susan soothingly. "Why would he want to do that?" For now she thought Amos still dazed.

"He said Leah told him to. He said Leah'd been with him every minute of these six months that he's been wandering around the country, he doesn't know where. But then she'd told him to come back to Marblehead and deal with me. So lately he'd been making plans. He'd hide in the factory nights and sneak past old Dan. He made a duplicate key to my strongbox, and read all my papers. He knew exactly when to strike. He got into that shed in the back lot and laid a trail of kerosene from it to the factory basement. He knew he'd been clever. Nobody could ever've guessed he set it, if I'd burned up."

"The wind," said Hesper faintly, "held the fire a little. It jumped first to the hotel, and the feed store."

"Do you mean this is true?" whispered Susan, staring at her daughter, who bowed her head.

"But where's Nat now?" cried the old woman. She licked her lips and her head trembled. "I can't hardly believe . . ."

"I don't know," said Amos. "He said he was going home to Leah. He locked me in, he left me there on the floor, trussed like a chicken. I could hear the flames crackling."

"Don't!" Hesper cried. She jumped up from the settle, poured more coffee for both of them, then went to the sink and pumped water into a basin. She brought this to Amos with a towel. "Let's wash your face," she said, "and let me see that bump."

He submitted obediently to her ministrations, and Susan watching felt a new amazement imposed on the horror of the story Amos had told. Hessie so strong and sure. And Amos leaning on her like a little boy, letting her care for him.

After a moment the cold water and the coffee cleared his head. The protective curtain of shock melted away. He stumbled to his feet, looking down at Hesper with full awareness.

"My God—" he said. "Your dress is burned. Hessie, why aren't you home? How did I get out of the factory?"

"Johnson and I," she said, "and some Salem firemen. I—I guessed you'd be in there."

He shut his eyes a minute. Then he touched the naked skin of her shoulder where it showed through the tear. "You ought to lie down. Please go and lie down. Where's Johnson now?"

"He's back there . . ." she gestured with her head. "Finding Henry. The boy followed me, but I know he's all right. Johnson'll find him. Oh, don't go back—darling," she cried, as she saw the expression of his face.

"Of course I'm going back. I'm all right now. Do you think I could sit here? Take care of her. . . ." he said to Susan, and he flung out into the waning night.

The two women sat silently in the kitchen. The candle guttered and Susan snipped the wick. "D'you think he's after Nat?" she asked fearfully.

Hesper clenched her hands hard together; a spasm twisted at her mouth and she sat waiting. Then her hands relaxed. "I don't know—" she said. "He'll find Henry first. Love is stronger than hate, isn't it? But they're both strong."

Her mother glanced at her sharply. "You must get some rest, Hessie. I'll find some sheets, we'll make up your old bed."

Hesper gave a strange soft little laugh. "No," she said. "We'd best make the bed up in there," and she pointed to the paneled door beyond the fireplace. "In the borning room."

Her mother started. She put the candlestick back on the table. She came over to her daughter. "Is it so? It's begun? Oh, my poor lass." Lord, she thought, this is dreadful. Roger so sick, Amos and the boy God knows where, the town burning. She was very tired, and her fat old face sagged suddenly with a frightened bewilderment.

Hesper seeing this put her hand on her mother's arm. "Don't fret, Ma dear. I can manage. Help me with the bed. Find me a nightdress while I wash."

Susan's bewilderment passed. She saw the shining of Hesper's eyes, the exaltation in the pale soot-streaked face. Aye, she's buoyed to her task, she thought. We must trust in God. Her normal efficiency returned to her. She helped Hesper into bed, and tearing a sheet in two, fastened it to the square wooden bedposts so that she might have something to pull on in the pains. She went upstairs and dressed herself, at the same time telling Roger only that Hesper was in the house, resting in the kitchen bedroom. He smiled feebly, but did not open his eyes, and she was not sure he understood. His pulse was very rapid and thready. His lips had a bluish tinge. She shook her head, and came downstairs again to her daughter's bedside. "How often are the pains, Hessie?"

"Not so often—about every five minutes, I think."

"I'm going out to find the doctor. For your Pa as well as you. I'll hurry all I can, but you'll have some time yet."

"Oh, Ma. The doctor'll be at the fire. Don't go down into that . . ."

"Don't be afeerd, Hessie—I'll get back in time. Here's a pitcher o' tansy tea. You sip that between pains. It'll ease 'em."

Hesper's eyes opened wide, and to Susan's surprise there was a spark of humor in them. For Hesper thought of the trained monthly nurse, and Doctor Flagg, and the special woman's doctor Amos had ordered from Boston. What would they think of tansy tea?

"I'm not afraid," she said. Her gaze wandered around the little low-beamed room. "The house'll take care of me—like so many others . . ." she added, but Susan had hurried out, leaving the door open.

Hesper lay quiet listening to the measured tick of the banjo clock in the kitchen, and the distant lap of water against the rocks. She heard the mewing of the seagulls as they circled over Little Harbor watching for incoming dories with their loads of bay fish. Through the small-paned casement window she watched the gray sky become streaked with rose. The strengthening light fell softly on the little pine dresser, the narrow rush-seated chair, the low, sturdy bed which had been built by Isaac Honeywood for his wife's first lying-in.

I was born in this room, she thought, and Pa, and back and back. When the pains came she clutched at the twisted sheets, gritting her teeth and holding her breath, while the sweat pricked out on her forehead and along her scalp. When they receded she lay quiet again, staring up at the rich dark beams. On one of the beams, the axe that had hewn them had left marks something like an anchor. She stared up at the little anchor, wondering if any of the other laboring Honeywood women had ever seen it. Sometimes she raised her head and took a sip of the bitter tansy tea.

The banjo clock whirred and then bonged five times, and as though it had been a signal the pain leaped at her with a new frenzy; it bit at her like a tiger, twisting and shaking her shuddering body in its bloody jaws. And she heard her own voice from far off, mewing like the distant seagulls. "Oh God. Help me!"

The tiger backed off a little, waiting in ambush. She saw its cruel yellow eyes watching. Panting and throwing her hands before her face she tried to hide from it.

She heard a step by her bed, and a voice say—"Hesper!" But at first she would not open her eyes, thinking it a trick of the tiger's. And then she felt a hand on her forehead and looked up, to see her father bending over her, his lips trembling, his eyes blurred with tears.

"Pa, you mustn't—go back to bed—" she panted, and then the tiger jumped on her again. She clutched at the thin old arm in the nightshirt, holding on to it frantically.

She hurt him but he did not feel it. "There—" he murmured. "There, there, child—it'll pass. I'll not leave you."

"Endure—" she whispered through her clenched teeth. "A sturdy courage to endure." She did not know that she was quoting from the letter about Phebe; the words to which she had been forced to listen by her father had long vanished from conscious memory. But now against the agony and the mounting fear there was no other shield. Not sympathy, nor prayer, nor even love.

Roger could not hear her. He was far too ill to wonder how she came to be here this night. But as he had lain alone upstairs, drifting through a land of shadows, it seemed to him that he had heard her voice calling. He had not heard it with his dulled ears, but it seemed to him that her voice had cast out the shadows with a ray of brilliant light. He had seen the light shimmering throughout the dearly loved house, and he had known its source and followed it to the little room which had always been the gateway to the Mysteries.

He pulled the rush-seated chair over by the bed and tottered onto it, crooning to her as he leaned over her. "There, there—don't, dear. It'll pass. . . ." Feeble, meaningless words. But as he talked to her, new words came, words such as he had never been able to find in a lifetime of searching. Their music filled the little room with the song of birds and sunlit winds, and the melody of the sea, and it seemed to him she listened. The tossing of her body stilled a little.

And then her mouth opened wide as though she screamed, but he heard no sound. She flung her arms back above her head, seizing the headrail, and then lay quiet looking up into his face. "Pa—" she whispered. "It's born."

He read the motions of her lips and a great joy shone in his eyes. He would have moved to help her with what must be done, but her face shimmered and slipped away from him. He sighed and leaned forward on the bed, resting his head on his arms.

When Susan and Amos and Doctor Flagg rushed into the kitchen five minutes later they heard the plaintive wailing of a baby. They ran into the little room, to see Hesper sleeping in profound exhaustion, and they saw Roger who seemed also to be asleep, but he was not.

Hesper lay for ten days in the little kitchen bedroom and she had great need of the glimpse of inner strength that she had attained to on the night of the fire and the baby's birth. For there was not only the sorrow for her father, the desolation of the funeral, and the grief that she was not able to follow him to his last resting place on Burial Hill amongst all the other Honeywoods, but there was sharp worry about Amos.

For some days he tried to hide his situation from her, speaking with forced heartiness when he came into her room, fending off any questions by loud admiration of the baby boy who had a headful of dark curly hair and was heavy and strong as a little bulldog despite his early birth.

But Hesper was no longer willing to be lulled for long. On the morning after Roger's funeral, she awoke to a determination born of increasing physical strength. She raised herself on her elbow and looked into the little pine cradle which stood next to her bed. The baby was still sleeping. She heard someone stirring in the kitchen, and called "Ma?" softly, through the half-opened door.

But it was Tamsen Peach, not Susan, who responded. Tamsen had moved down the hill from her own Barnegat home to help the Honeywoods as soon as the news of the birth and death reached her.

"Mar-rnin', Hessie," she said, approaching the bed with a cup of steaming coffee and a slab of fried johnnycake. "Yore ma's not down yet. Clean tuckered out, pore thing. How d'you rest?" She freshened up Hesper's bedclothes, and poked an inquiring finger at the baby to see if he were wet, and her gentle serious face puckered with concentration as she changed him.

"Fine," said Hesper. "Mrs. Peach, you're awful good to us."

"Good Lard, Hessie—" said Tamsen, astonished. "We allus help each other-r in a jam."

I haven't, thought Hesper, and she thought of all the years that she had avoided Tamsen. Quick tears stung her eyes.

"Now, ye mustn't go grievin' fur yore pa, child," said Tamsen, seeing them. " 'Twill tur-rn yore milk. Ye know he went real easy, an' 'twas a stavin' foine funeral. All the town to do him honor-r."

Hesper nodded. She knew that they had all gathered round him at the burial service—the old Marbleheaders whose lines stretched back nearly as far as his own—the Selmans and the Picketts and the Cloutmans, and the Tuckers and the Ornes and the Gerrys and the Brimblecomes, and others too, besides, of course, the Peaches and Dollibers. And this would have pleased him, no matter how he had shut himself off from them in life.

"I'm not grieving any more," she said. "I know he was ready to go." She finished her coffee and johnnycake, and Tamsen picked up the awakened hungry baby and laid him in her arms. He fed lustily with greedy gulping noises, and the two women looked at each other and smiled.

"Is Henry still asleep?" asked Hesper, and when Tamsen nodded, she added after a little pause, "and Amos?"

The older women hesitated, then she said, "No. He left here torrible early, just as Oi come down meself. Said he'd be bock later-r. Oi reckon he has a heap o' worry from the foire." She had not meant to say this, for Amos had warned her and Susan that Hesper must not be disturbed by any mention of the fire. And Tamsen had felt sorry for him. Outside of his wife's room he had acted like one distracted these last days. Refusing food with which she tried to tempt him, forever flinging out of the house on unexplained business. He had not even attended his father-in-law's burial, but had come in some time later haggard and silent, only to shut himself up in the Yellow Room upstairs which he was temporarily occupying. Of course he'd lost his factory, but plenty of others had done that too, and Mr. Porterman was a rich man.

Hesper shifted the baby to the other arm and said quietly, "Are there any newspapers in the house? I'd like to see an account of the fire." And also see if there's any mention of Nat, she thought. During these sorrowful days when Roger's body had been lying in the parlor, and she had been in the exhaustion of emotional strain and childbirth, she had not questioned anyone, but now she knew that she must find out what had happened outside the Hearth and Eagle.

"Well, there is some," answered Tamsen reluctantly. She went out and brought back a copy of the *Salem Observer,* and the Fire Editions of the *Marblehead Messenger.*

Hesper thanked her and after the satisfied baby had been lowered back into his cradle, she began to read.

The figures were shocking. The entire business section in the new part of town had been destroyed, and more too. The South Church was gone, and the depot, and the Rechabite building and the Allerton Block, and thirty houses and twenty shoe factories. In fifteen square acres there was not a structure left standing. But there had, fortunately and remarkably, been no loss of life; one or two minor injuries, but that was all.

There was no mention of Nat Cubby, though the *Messenger* contained one pertinent paragraph to the effect that a jury would be appointed to investigate the origin of the fire, as there were some dark rumors circulating, and possibly suspicious circumstances.

There was no mention of Amos either except the listing of his factory as one of those completely destroyed.

She folded up the papers and lay thinking. Nat had caused a far greater devastation than he intended, even though he had not succeeded in destroying the one life which had been his aim. But if he should try again . . . she thought with sudden terror. And what has Amos been doing these past days?

Fool, she cried to herself, letting things slide again, hiding your head in the sand.

"Ma!" she called sharply, peering through the door into the kitchen. "Ma. Come here!"

"What's all the pother?" said Susan appearing in the doorway. "Hessie, lay down!" For her daughter was half out of bed. "What's got into you!"

Susan pushed her daughter down against the pillows, and retucked the covers, then she sat down on the bed, and surveyed Hesper with the grim amusement her daughter sometimes inspired in her. Susan had mourned deeply for Roger, she would miss him all the rest of her life. But she was never one to wear her heart on her sleeve, and now well rested, thanks to Tamsen, she had turned her face resolutely forward.

"Ma—" said Hesper. "I've got to know. D'you know what's happened to Nat? Did Amos ever find him that night?"

Her mother's face changed. She got off the bed, walked to the pine dresser, and mechanically straightened the wash bowl and pitcher. "You worrying about Amos?"

"Yes. I've got to know. How could I," she cried with rising vehemence, "have been so soppy lying here in a sort of haze just thinking about the baby, and—Pa."

Susan came back to the bedside. "You've changed quite a bit, Hessie, got a lot more spunk than I thought for. Now don't go swinging the other way feeling responsible for everything. You had a right to a few days o' peace. Yore body needed it."

"But what *happened,* Ma?"

"Amos he forbade me telling you," said her mother, frowning. "Still, I can't see it his way. We all got to face up to things. Most o' the harm done in this life comes from not facing up to things, seems to me."

Hesper gave a sharp sigh, but she waited.

"Amos found Nat that night," continued her mother slowly. "He first located Henry, just as you said he would; he found the lad with Johnson well out o' the reach o' danger having hot malted milk in Eben Dorch's drugstore. That's where I found Doctor Flagg, too, filling up his medicine bag with fresh supplies. I told Johnson not to hurry with Henry on account o' your state, and the doctor and I started back down Washington Street." She paused, glancing at Hesper's strained face.

"Well, when we passed State Street, you may be sure I looked down it, and saw Amos as I'd thought I might. He was turning in the gate o' the Cubbys' house. I run down that street like a scalded cat, the doctor tearing after me, thinking I'd lost my wits. The door was open and I wasn't much behind Amos clambering up the stairs. I screeched to him, but he didn't hear me, he was opening doors and searching, and I prayed then . . ."

"Ma—" whispered Hesper.

"Well, we found Nat," said Susan, with a crisp matter-of-factness. "Hanging from a beam in Leah's room under the scuttle. He'd hanged himself with a strip from her old black shawl. And now you know what happened."

Hesper's stiff body relaxed, she sank back on the pillows. Thank God —she thought, thank God.

"I reckon he thought Leah told him to join her, like she told him to fire the fact'ry," said Susan dryly. "I can't help feeling a mite sorry for the two of 'em, despite what Nat did. They was always like a couple o' cockatrices in a hen-yard, an' I don't know as they could help it."

"Yes," Hesper breathed, wondering how much her mother knew. Yes, there was pity. She had felt great pity for Leah, and now that Nat was no longer dangerous, now that Amos was saved forever from any more consequences of that weak moment, when he had allowed himself to be swung into an orbit so hostile to him—

"Aye," said Susan, watching her daughter. "It's a relief, isn't it! I knew Amos was wrong. You're a sight tougher than he thinks."

"He doesn't quite understand . . ." said Hesper.

"He don't understand Marbleheaders an' that's a fact. He hasn't the sea and the wind and the rocks in his blood, an' he hasn't the fierce pride o' being rooted with your own kind. But he's a good man for all that.

"Yes," said Hesper softly. "But, Ma—there'll be an inquest now, won't there—on Nat, I mean? And the papers, it'll all have to come out, Amos testify—badgering him—"

Susan shook her head. "There'll never be a word about it. The sheriff'll hush it up. D'you think we'd give a lot o' furriners the chance to gape and poke and pry into our troubles? Thing's finished, Hes, since punishment's now in God's hands."

Hesper nodded. She had no doubt her mother was right. Marblehead had never been one to let the outside world see it wash its dirty linen. And there was many another scandal that had been hushed up. No, the danger for Amos was past, she knew with devout gratitude, and now there remained only to reassure him and help him forget the horrible thing that had threatened. Oh, they'd have to economize, of course; the loss of the factory had been a heavy blow, but it might have been so much worse. Amos had other property, in Danvers and even in Marblehead, and he always managed. We'll probably have to give up the carriage, she thought, and let Annie go for a while. Bridget and I can manage very well. I was getting awfully lazy.

Or maybe this would be the time to move from Marblehead; he probably wouldn't rebuild here anyway. She thought dreamily of a little flat in Boston, or maybe some place like Worcester—anything Amos wanted.

She dozed a little until Henry came in. He was dressed very neatly in the black serge suit he had worn to his grandfather's funeral, but all his flaxen sausage curls had been clipped off close to his head.

"Oh, Henry—" cried Hesper staring at the prickly wisps in dismay. "Your hair!"

"I cut it off," said Henry. "Grandma said she wasn't going to bother with all that dom-fool curling every morning, and I think she's right. When are we going home, Mama?"

"Oh, pretty soon, I guess. When I'm up and around." And though she too had been thinking of the return to their mansion on Pleasant Street, she felt an unpleasant pang. "Don't you like it here, dear?"

"Oh, it's all right," said Henry indifferently. "Only I miss my bank game, and I was building a toy village in the stable. Tim was helping me."

"Couldn't you build it in the barn, here?"

"Too small."

"Why don't you go down to the harbor, learn something about the boats while we're here?" persisted Hesper; "that's what most Marblehead boys like to do."

"I did," answered Henry. "I've been out twice with Ben Peach in his dory. He says I row real well. But I'd rather build the village. It's what I set out to do. I like to finish things."

Hesper gazed at her son with a mixture of respect and irritation. He's certainly got character, she thought, and she looked down at the lusty dark-haired baby, wondering about him. It seemed to her that this one was far more vigorous than Henry had ever been. Certainly he cried louder and oftener and appeased his appetite with a more single-minded vehemence. For a moment she regretted the gentle little girl baby for whom she had longed, and then stifled the regret forever. For the new baby had brought with him a special kind of love, born with him in the turbulence of his birth night.

"Here—" said Henry suddenly, thrusting a squeezed and wilted bunch of pansies at his mother. "They're for you. I forgot." His grandmother had suggested that he pick them, but he had been quite willing. Since the night of the fire, his placid affection for Hesper had been deepened by a tinge of admiring awe. He knew that she had done a very brave thing, for Johnson had told him so. To be sure, here she was lying around in bed again, but the new baby apparently somehow explained that.

"Thank you, dear," said Hesper, much touched, and spread the bruised pansies on the counterpane. She ran her fingers softly over the golden brown and purple faces. "They're for thoughts," she said. "Some people call them 'Heart's-ease.' I wrote a poem about pansies once. I guess it wasn't very good."

She stared down at the pansies, wondering why her first pleasure at seeing them had dissolved into a dull pain. And suddenly she remembered that she had read the pansy poem to Evan one day at Castle Rock before their marriage. Read it with pride and a quivering expectancy, totally unprepared for the shock of his expression as she looked up for praise at the end. He had been looking at her with embarrassed pity, then quickly turned his head, murmuring "Charming."

But she had pressed for an opinion, and he had finally said, "There's nothing real in it, Hesper. It's just a lot of flabby little words." Nothing I did ever really pleased him, she thought.

"You're hurting the flowers," observed Henry, mildly disapproving. "Gramma says it's naughty to pull them apart."

Hesper looked down at the scattered gold and purple petals on the counterpane. "It is," she said. "Run out and play, dear. It looks like a lovely day."

"I guess I'll take the ferry over to the Neck," said Henry. "There's some boys over there who like to trade."

"Summer people?" she asked, surprised. "How did you ever meet them?"

"Oh, I meet lots of people when I want to," said Henry vaguely.

"Have you money to pay the ferry?"

"Sure. Papa gives me plenty."

Hesper smiled and held out her arms, and Henry submitted to her kiss, even hugging her in return, before he escaped.

Amos was so generous and good to them, she thought, reaching down for the baby who had awakened suddenly with an indignant demanding roar.

"Hey—can't you even wait one minute?" she said laughing down at the thrashing scrap on her lap, and she longed for Amos to come back so that they might laugh together, taking pride in the vigorous new son they had created.

But when Amos came back and entered her room in the late afternoon, she saw there would be no laughter.

"Hello, Hessie," he said dully. "Feeling all right? How's the little one?" But he did not look at the baby which she held in her arms. She had brushed all his abundant brownish hair into little peaks, and dressed him in some exquisitely embroidered baby clothes Susan had brought down from the attic, and she had been amused again to see how his rampant masculinity triumphed over the delicacy of his robes.

Now her gay greeting died on her lips. She saw that Amos had lost weight. There were furrows in his cheeks and lines around his eyes. His broad shoulders were slumped forward under the pearl-gray broadcloth suit, which was rumpled and spotted. She noticed with startled dismay the absence of the massive gold watch chain he always wore.

"Sit down, dear, and talk to me," she said, carefully putting the baby in his cradle, so as not to wake him.

"We're both fine—" she added, answering Amos's questions. "But you don't look very well. You're worried, aren't you? Tell me about it."

She felt the resistance in him, saw that his impulse was to go out again.

"Please—" she said.

He hesitated, then looked at the rush-seated chair. "Isn't a comfortable chair in this house."

"On the bed," she said quickly, moving over. "Sit here."

He obeyed reluctantly, sat staring at the wide glossy floorboards.

There was a silence and Hesper cast around in her mind to find the best opening. Then she rushed into speech before she lost courage.

"The loss of the factory's a heavy blow I know, and the dreadful way it happened. But it's over now. I mean Nat. I know about that, Amos. Only thing to do is start fresh, never looking back."

He turned his head then and looked at her, and she caught her breath, for his eyes were chill and remote as the winter sea, and he gave a bitter laugh. "Start fresh with what?"

"Why, Amos—" she faltered. "You had lots of other interests. You have property, I know, besides our house, and then the insurance on the factory. I read about that in the *Messenger,* the factories were covered by insurance. It said so."

"Mine wasn't."

She stared at him blankly. "I don't understand. You've never told me much about the business, but the papers said they were starting to build again right away and . . ."

"Then I'll make it clear to you," he interrupted, in the cold hard voice, "since if you're reading the papers, it's obvious I can't spare you much longer. I am totally and completely bankrupt. I owe thousands of dollars I can't pay. I let the insurance lapse because I couldn't afford it, and took a chance until a big new order paid off. You'll see by Monday's papers that the bankruptcy court has taken over everything I ever owned."

He turned his head back and once more stared down at the floor.

Hesper swallowed. The room swirled around her, spiraling down to Amos's averted face. "Oh, my poor darling . . ." she whispered. No, she thought, that's not the way.

"Well—" she spoke in an even tone. "It's a shock, of course. But we're still pretty young, and you *can* start fresh, Amos, after the—the bankruptcy business is finished. You made money before, you can do it again."

I didn't start from nothing before, he thought. I didn't start from ruin and I wasn't forty-five. But he was grateful to her, and the bitterness in which he had encased himself cracked a little.

"It's for you and the boys—" he said on a softer tone. "Failing you like this—how to provide for you now. I've nearly gone crazy trying to think what to do."

"But surely it's very simple," she said after a minute.

"What?" he asked, raising his head.

"Why, we'll stay on here for a while until you can get on your feet. This house belongs to Ma and me now. They can't touch that, can they?"

"No," said Amos slowly. "They can't. Mr. Honeywood willed it to your mother for lifetime tenure, then reversion to you. But Hes, you always hated the place. Dilapidated. Uncomfortable. I was so glad to get you out of it. To give you—"

"I don't hate it now," she interrupted. She looked at the baby in the old cradle and at the rush-seated chair where her father had sat beside her that night. Far more truly home than that great, glossy mansion on Pleasant Street. She had never been alive there, always a thinness and an emptiness. But this she knew she could never say to Amos. She watched the defeat in his face change to a bleak resignation, and knew that for him this house and the interwoven richness of generations of Honeywoods would never be home. His next words proved it.

"You might sell, I suppose," he said, sighing. "If you could persuade your mother. But who'd buy it? Wrong part of town."

"I wouldn't care to sell," she said quietly though she had been conscious of a little spurt of anger. "We need a home. I find I like hearing the sea again. It's—" She paused, searching for a word to express the sensation of release she had been feeling as she lay listening to the beating rhythm, forever unaffected by puny human struggles. "It's comforting," she said at last.

Amos turned his head and stared toward the window. "Is it? I hadn't noticed." He drew in his lips with a sharp sound, and reaching behind him found her hand. He held it tight. "Oh, Hessie, you're a good wife. I haven't said—I haven't told you—you saved my stupid life that night." His voice thickened and he stopped.

Underneath the gratitude, there was the added twist of humiliation. Hessie, whom he had sworn to protect, delicate, bearing his child, finding him trussed like that on the floor, leading him out like a baby—the strong one. . . .

Hesper watched the back of his down-bent head, and felt the quiver of his hand as it held hers. And she understood. She bent over and laid her cheek against his hand.

"I love you—Amos," she said.

He turned and gathered her into his arms.

They lay quiet together, not speaking, while outside the little window the twilight deepened over the sea and the rising night wind slapped the mounting waves against the shingle.

They were aroused by a vehement wail, and Amos, drowsing in the first surcease he had known since the fire, gave a start, and said, "What's that!"

"That's our baby," said Hesper, laughing. "He's hungry again. Light the candle, dear—will you?"

Amos pulled himself up from the bed and complied. He held the old pewter candlestick down to the cradle and inspected his son. "He's got good lungs." He put the candle on the dresser and picking up the squirming baby handed him to his mother. "What shall we name him, Hessie? You'd like Roger Honeywood, wouldn't you?"

Yes, she had certainly thought that the baby would be named for her father, and Susan and Mrs. Peach had already assumed so. But then she had not known the situation, nor realized the extent of the mutilation Amos's pride and self-respect had suffered.

"Hardly," she said, smiling. "Pa's name doesn't fit this young man at all. I can't picture him writing poetry."

"Nor I," said Amos, smiling a little at last. "What then would you like?"

She considered a moment. Henry, of course, had been named for Amos, Amos Henry Porterman. "We'll name him Walter, for your father. Suit you?"

"Yes," said Amos.

He stood looking down at them. The bent head, copper-tinted in the candlelight, the tender brooding of her mouth as she watched the baby, the curve of the white blue-veined breast from which his son drew abundance and security.

Amos flushed, and leaning over, kissed the white parting between the waves of hair. "I'll make money for you, Hessie, again. I'll get out of here. We'll start fresh in some other place. Out West maybe. I'll take care of you better than I ever did. You and Henry and little Walter. You'll see."

She raised her eyes from the baby, and the tender indulgence in their shadowed depths did not change as they rested on her husband. "I know you will, darling," she said, but in her ears as she spoke, stronger than the voice of any human love or yearning, she heard the fateful and omnipotent pounding of the sea.

CHAPTER 18

On the twentieth of September, 1909, Hesper dispatched the last of her summer boarders, hung a neat black-and-white "Closed for the Season" notice in her parlor window, and went back through the taproom—now the boarders' dining room—into the old kitchen to wait for Carla. Hesper still called it the kitchen, though of course Eleanor referred to it as the living room, and a new compact kitchen had been built from the old buttery in the rear.

Hesper sat down in her rocker by the crackling fire. It had turned chilly out, and the southeast wind was beginning to blow harder from a tarnished pewter sky. The glass had been falling all day. Maybe the line storm.

She pulled her rocker nearer to the great hearth, watching the flames leap high above the tall black andirons. Walt had laid this fine fire for her, before he went down the path to Little Harbor to look to his lobster pots. She sighed and rocked slowly, feeling the content of fire and rest. Glad to be rid of those boarders, though they were all good people, and mostly regulars from summer to summer. But how delightful to have the house to oneself again. Just Carla, and Walt and me, she thought, savoring it.

To be sure she'd have to put up with Henry and Eleanor too for one night, but not, praise be, that mincing French governess this time. Even Eleanor wouldn't try that again. Or Henry. Henry, she thought, sobering. Was he happy? And why not? . . . He had achieved everything he set out to do. "I mean to be rich, Mama—not just rich in Marblehead, rich in the whole world," and he was; in banking circles his name would be recognized anywhere. He had married great wealth, but he had made it, too. A millionaire.

Strange that my two boys should be so different. But they aren't boys any more, she thought with astonishment. Henry's forty, and Walt is thirty-three. She stopped rocking and sat up straight, listening to the banjo clock's tick and staring into the fire.

All those years—where had they slipped to? Looking back she saw her life flowing like a long river through this house, and yet there was a sharp break in the middle when she had left the river and strayed far from it into a different land. The time with Evan in New York, and then the years with Amos on Pleasant Street.

Perhaps the house had known all the time that she'd be back. And without its shelter and the comfort it gradually distilled for her out of its memories, she could not have endured watching Amos's deepening unhappiness through the years that he tried to fit himself into a life he hated. He had been brave and scrupulously honest throughout the bankruptcy proceedings, and in this town which had always excluded him he awakened some sympathy at last. Some of his Marblehead creditors refused to prosecute, and in the end it developed that though everything else was gone he might keep possession of the little sail loft on the wharf.

Amos had taken it over and doggedly tried to run it, much helped by his old tenant who stayed on for a while out of kindness and taught him the business. The sail loft did begin to make a tiny profit, thanks to the increasing numbers of summer people and their pleasure craft. But the drive had gone out of Amos. He faded before her eyes into a beaten old man, and she, powerless to help him, had watched and grieved.

And then came a day at the end of the summer like today, when Amos came home to supper and told her that Mr. Thompson of Boston, owner of the *Black Hawk,* had given an order for two new suits of sails for his yawl.

"But that's wonderful!" she had cried. "Aren't you glad, dear?"

She had never forgotten the tone of his laugh, and the startled way the two boys looked up at their father.

"He called me 'Cap,'" said Amos. "He slapped me on the back and told me to get a move on. He asked me to come over to his house on the Neck sometime when his family wasn't there. Said I could bring the missis and kiddies along for a treat. It'd be fun for them to see all the elegant decorations and imported furniture."

She had smiled uncertainly, saying, "But he meant well, Amos, I'm sure, and that's a big order."

"It'll bring in enough to take me to Cincinnati."

It had been a shock at first, but she had never questioned the rightness of the move for him. He had got wind of a small shoe business there, a young man who might be talked into taking on an experienced partner. A little hope returned to Amos, and the days before he left they were very close to each other. He was to send for her and the boys as soon as he could. And in a month the summons came, but not from Amos. It came from the Commercial Hospital where he lay dying of a pneumonia he had caught tramping the cold wintry streets in search of an opening that would exactly suit him, for the young man's shoe business had not.

She had traveled day and night on the train and reached him in time. He had died in her arms, and just before the end he had recognized her, and murmured something about the boys. "Henry." And she had known he had meant Henry would take care of her.

Hesper sighed, leaning back again in the rocker. Heartbreak. That crazy old Aunt 'Crese on Gingerbread Hill fifty years ago. Had she really seen into the future or had she simply guessed at a pattern for a woman's life from the wisdom of her own years? "Yo'll think yore heart'll never mend, but it will. De heart's tough, honey."

Yes, it mends—glued together somehow by hard work, and time and necessity. The cracks are always there, but the organ functions again. And she had had help with the mending—the boys to raise, and the house, and Ma—for five more years.

The Inn had kept them going, though the type of guests changed as the town changed. After the fire of '77, some of the shoemen built again and tried to carry on the shoe business, but it was a losing battle to Lynn. And after increasingly violent labor troubles and another disastrous fire in '88, Marblehead ceased to compete. In '85, when the town went completely dry, the Inn could no longer get a license, and Hesper had started to take boarders. It was the summer people who kept the town going now, much as most Marbleheaders resented their intrusiveness and careless patronage.

So Marblehead after its brief and fruitless compromise with industrialism had reverted to making a living from the sea again. Not the way it used to be, though, not like the fishing fleet, with Marbleheaders working for themselves. This was the sea at one remove, purveying for and tending other people's pleasure craft. But there was no use resenting it, or despising the yachtsmen who had pulled them out of economic distress, as once she had despised the shoemen who had saved them all from starvation when the fishing declined. "Face up to things" and accept them, as Ma had always said. And the town itself had not changed, not intrinsically. My house hasn't changed, she thought. What deep comfort that growing realization had given her through the years. There were minor changes, of course, the new kitchen and the two bathrooms upstairs, but its structure and its essence had not changed. And it seemed incredible to her that she had during so much of her youth been deaf to the beauty of its sustaining voice.

The banjo clock coughed and finally struck once. Hesper glanced at it absently. Five-thirty. They'd not be here yet awhile unless Henry had a sight better luck than usual with the automobile. Tires forever popping and the road was muddy out of Swampscott.

She went to the woodbox, picked out a large log, and threw it on the fire. Praise be, I'm near as strong as I ever was. Not run to fat like Ma's people. When she sat down again she was conscious of the leanness and vitality of her erect body under the black watered silk. Her hair was still abundant and just as hard to manage. It had turned very quickly after Amos's death to the translucent pearl-white peculiar to auburn hair, but her eyebrows had not turned, and the heavy dark brows gave an impression of youth, which occasionally astonished her when she remembered to look in the mirror.

She had looked this afternoon, coiling her hair into a loose bun against a little jet comb, and putting on a high-boned embroidered net collar that made angry little welts on her throat, because Carla liked to see her dressed in Sunday best. Bless the child, she thought, how I wish Amos could have seen her. Though he'd never said so, she knew how much he too had wanted a daughter. He would have adored this grandchild—if Eleanor would have let him.

She shook her head and smiled. Trust Henry to get himself a wife like that; exactly what he must have had in mind since he was old enough to wear long pants.

Eleanor's father was Carl Willoughby Norton, Third, and he was one of the first to build himself a summer palace on the Neck. That was in '81, the year they opened the Eastern Yacht Club, and Mr. Norton was as zealous a sailor as anyone, thanks to a two-hundred-foot steam yacht, an English captain, and a crew of eight. Mr. Norton and his elegant Eleanor never actually did anything on board but sit in wicker chairs on the after deck under a striped awning, and chat with privileged guests.

"Lord, Henry—" Hesper had burst out once while he was courting Eleanor. "How can you stand mudgeting around all day on your backside in that floating teakettle—and you a Marbleheader! Why don't you take that girl out in an honest sloop or even a dory—give her a real taste of the sea?"

Henry had looked patient. "Eleanor wouldn't care for it, Mother. Nor do I consider myself a typical Marbleheader. At least I don't intend to get stuck in this backwater all my life. Look at poor Father." He hadn't meant to be unkind; he simply stated facts, and of course he was right. After Amos's bankruptcy Henry had lived at the Hearth and Eagle, because he'd had to. But he never joined any of the boys' gangs. She'd never had to wash his mouth out with soap for saying "Whip" and other dirty words as she had Walt's. He'd never filched cod splits off the flakes, and there still *were* a few flakes when he was little. He'd never played hooky, like Walt. No, he'd forged quietly ahead in his studies, top of his class at the Academy, got himself a scholarship to Harvard and graduated summa cum laude. After that he had had no trouble in finding an excellent financial job in Boston. And then in '95 he had married Eleanor.

The memory of that wedding tickled Hesper now, though she'd been mad as fire at the time. As you got older it took a mighty bad thing to seem tragic, or even exasperating; more and more you learned you couldn't run life or even people, just sit back and be amused.

Eleanor had had herself a regular tidderi-i of a wedding. No mother to guide her, but her father had imported some sort of aunt, and anyway Eleanor did all right by herself. "Braeburn," the thirty-room turreted mansion on the Neck, had been swaddled in flowers sent up from Boston. Even the yacht had had white streamers on her, and Japanese lanterns. She steamed in from Boston the day before stuffed with wedding guests up to her plate glass and engraved brass port holes.

The ceremony took place in Marblehead in Saint Michael's little church on Frog Lane. The Nortons were Episcopalians, and Eleanor thought the church just too quaint and dear for words. Eleanor thought lots of things about Marblehead were quaint, including the Hearth and Eagle, and it developed at the wedding—her mother-in-law.

Hesper had been sitting with Walt behind a rose-festooned pillar during the reception at "Braeburn" when she heard Eleanor's high clear voice explaining things to some of her young cousins from Providence. "Daddy was quite horrified at first at the idea of my marrying—well, you know, a 'native.' But Henry's such a dear, Harvard, of course, and after all they are a very old family. The Honeywoods actually came over with the Winthrop fleet. Why, that's before the Nortons came even. They've got the sweetest old house over in the town. Too romantic. I'm dying to get my hands on it, but Mother Porterman—"

Here the voice was lowered a trifle. "Well, you saw her in the receiving line. Quite a character. Honestly, I tried to get her a different hat. But you know she's practically never been out of Marblehead. Can you imagine? Live on year after year in the same place, nothing ever happening. But my Henry's not like that."

The bride broke off and blew a kiss to her husband. He smiled gravely at her across the heads of the milling guests, and Hesper's annoyance had subsided. In their own way they were in love with each other. And she could and had forgiven much to Eleanor because she had somehow managed to produce Carla.

I mustn't be a fool about that child, thought Hesper. She jumped up from the rocker, went into the new kitchen, and lit the gas stove. They should be here any minute now, and Eleanor would want tea. Henry and Eleanor were tea drinkers, she and Walt were coffee drinkers, and that's the way it was right through.

The water was boiling, it boiled mighty quick on gas, when she heard the excited honks and roaring of gears approaching down Franklin Street.

She turned the gas low, hung up her apron, and hurried out the kitchen door and down the path. The wind whistled through the remaining leaves on the huge chestnut tree, and instinctively she noted the crash of mounting breakers on the Front.

The great yellow Packard touring car, liberally besplashed with mud, drew to a wheezy stop before the gate. The headlights flickered and dimmed. The chauffeur and Henry clambered down from the front seat, and opened the door for Eleanor. All three figures were shapeless in flapping dust coats, and the pink chiffon veil which anchored Eleanor's hat streamed back in the wind and for a moment covered the small figure which followed her. But Carla had seen, and ducking under her mother's arm she flew at Hesper, crying "Marnie—Marnie, we've come!" And for a moment, before Eleanor came up to them, Hesper held the child tight to her breast.

"How d'you do, Mother Porterman," said Eleanor, bestowing a touch of the lips on Hesper's cheek. "We've had an excruciating trip, wind and mud, all the way. Henry, I do think something should be done about the roads. Can't you speak to the senator? Carla, do be still, dear, you'll deafen your grandmother if you squeal like that."

Carla, who had been trying to tell Hesper all in one breath about the two puppies they had seen in Lynn, instantly became quiet. Mama and Mademoiselle taught obedience; Marnie did too, but it was different. And Mama didn't like her to use that baby name of Marnie, for grandma. I won't forget again while Mama's here, she thought. Poor

Mama, she had a lot to worry her. It was a dreadful bother getting off on a trip to Europe, and Granpa sick in Brookline, besides.

Carla drew back, waiting while Papa greeted Marnie, and the chauffeur staggered up the path bearing a load of valises.

The child's blue eyes danced with greeting to the dear familiar place. The horse-chestnut tree—she strained her eyes through the twilight to see if the tree house was still there, way up high. She sniffed the salt wind and licked her pink lips. Surely that was spray blowing in. She looked with love at the humpbacked old house, crouching like a camel with its ears back, blown by the wind.

She followed her elders inside. They went in the ceremonial front door and entered the parlor. Carla sniffed again voluptuously; every room here had its special smell, and all of them pleasing, though she found the parlor the least exciting smell in the house. It smelled of gas and brass polish and the lavender sprigs Marnie kept in a green speckled jar on top of the what-not. There were many old friends to be greeted here. The spinet with split yellow keys would give out a cracked tinkle when Marnie let her play on it. And there were queer things on the what-not, little carvings on pieces of bone and wood. Scrimshaw they were called. Honeywood men had made them on trips to the Grand Banks.

On the center table, resting on the fringed plush throw, there was the fat Bible, and fatter album with its curly silver clasp. The album wasn't very interesting. Except for two pictures of Marnie when she was young, everybody looked alike. Marnie laughed and said that was because they were mostly Dollibers. Far more exciting was the stereopticon and its box full of faded twin views; Niagara Falls, the Great Pyramids, and the Leaning Tower of Pisa. Carla had seen the real leaning tower last year with Mademoiselle, on the summer trip to Europe. And she had been disappointed. It was more vivid, more magic, in Marnie's stereopticon view.

Mama and Papa and Marnie were all sitting by the little tea table near the fire so she couldn't crowd in to greet the blue and white Bible story tiles that ran around the fireplace. Jonah and a funny-looking whale like a pug dog. Jael hammering a spike like a pencil into Sisera's head, the spike dripping with blue blood. Marnie had told her all the stories, but Mama did not approve of the bloody ones. Carla had always known and accepted the knowledge that there were lots of things Mama and Papa did not approve of about the Hearth and Eagle, and Marnie. They didn't say so, of course, but you could feel it. Like Mama's voice now. The voice she used when she was trying to be patient.

"Thank you for the tea, Mother Porterman. It's most refreshing. Your—uh—guests have all gone?"

Marnie nodded briskly. "Cleared 'em all out today. The Front Room and the Yellow Room 're redded up and waiting for you."

Mama and Papa never slept in the same room.

Papa put down his teacup, and frowned a little bit. "I do wish you wouldn't keep boarders, Mother. You know perfectly well it isn't necessary. If you'd only let me—"

Marnie gave a funny little laugh and made a face almost like one Carla herself would have made. "Oh, I know, Henry, you're both very generous. But they're company for me, and I like to keep busy."

Mama's pretty mouth tightened, she put her teacup down too. "But how you can stand a houseful of strangers—in your own home. It seems so—you're so individualistic too, so proud of the old place—I can't understand the psychology—"

Mama always used long words when she was mad, they floored most people, but Marnie didn't turn a hair.

"Well, you know, Eleanor," she said mildly, "this house has always been an Inn. I like to share it."

Mama and Papa looked at each other, and Papa shrugged his shoulders. But Mama never gave up easily. "Apart from everything else," she said, "there are some incredibly valuable heirlooms in this house. I should think you'd have to consider damage or loss from strangers. Of course a lot of the stuff is hodgepodge, but when I get back from Europe, I wish you'd at least let me weed out the old, really good pieces and—"

"Do what?" asked Marnie.

Mama flushed up under her powder. Carla remembered hearing her tell Papa how well that marvelous carved Jacobean chest would look on the stair landing at Brookline. That was Phebe's bride chest. But Mama didn't mention the chest, she said—"Why, the Massachusetts Historical would be enchanted to display them, care for them properly."

"I dare say." Marnie smiled but her eyes looked sharp and green. "Lately lots of people have come moseying around. They want to put a historical plaque on the house, and I guess that's all right. But this is my home, it's not a spectacle. And as for what you call the 'valuable heirlooms,' they weren't built to be heirlooms, they were built for use. They belonged to real people, not a museum. Just because two, three hundred years have gone by, doesn't change that any. Far as I'm concerned they'll stay in use and wear out too if they've a mind to, right here where they belong."

Carla's heart swelled with a passionate conviction. Marnie was right. There was happiness in belonging. The queer old house, and all the things in it, new and old, and the rocks and the sea and the town outside, all belonged together. And that was safe and right. Troubles never seemed so bad here. Like two years ago when she was visiting here and the kitten died. The whole house had seemed to hold her close, the way Marnie did, whispering and comforting.

You couldn't feel that in the Brookline house, or "Braeburn," or in hotels or boats. They all had a hurrying feel to get somewhere else.

"Well—" said Papa, smiling a little. "I guess that's that. You can't change the Marblehead mind, Eleanor. Mother, isn't Walt back yet? I thought we'd all go up to the Rockmere for dinner. Save you the trouble of cooking, since you seem to be servantless as usual."

Marnie sighed and began to stack the tea things on the tray. "I let Dilly go home to Clifton for a holiday. I had fixed supper for us, but it'll keep. I don't know when Walt'll be in. He went out in his boat over to Chapel Ledge to look at the traps. But it's blowing up pretty bad. He should be back."

"And doubtless smelling most charmingly of fish and alcohol," said Mama, laughing. She didn't like Uncle Walt at all, and she sometimes told Papa about it. "Henry, really my worst enemy couldn't call me a snob; it isn't that your brother is a lobster fisherman, but he looks so uncouth, his clothes—and he swears so. I was terribly mortified when the servants told me he'd turned up drunk at the back door of 'Braeburn' peddling his lobsters in a wheelbarrow."

Papa had been cross too, but Carla knew very well Uncle Walt had done that for a kind of joke. He was very shaggy and big, and unless he was mad he didn't say much, but sometimes he did funny things and chuckled to himself.

"Help your grandmother with the tea things, dear," said Mama, folding up her pink veil and picking up her gloves and pocketbook. "Papa and I are going upstairs to freshen up for dinner."

Carla asked nothing better. She followed Hesper through the back passage to the old kitchen, and here it smelled as it always did of burning pine logs, and baking beans and gingerbread. "Oh, Marnie—" she cried with delight. "You're using the old brick oven!"

Hesper smiled, a trifle rueful. "I guess it's silly, when the gas is so quick, but beans are no good at all with gas, and—it's a lot of work, but sometimes I like to cook in here still."

"I love it—" said the child, "and you didn't forget the candles! Can I light 'em?" This was a private and recurrent ceremony on first nights of Carla's visits. Hesper had placed beeswax candles in the pewter wall sconces and the branched Sheffield candelabra that stood on the oak dresser.

She turned off the gas jet, while the child, chewing her lips with concentration, lit the candles. "Now—" she said with a happy sigh. "Isn't that the way it was when you were little?"

"Not always. Candles cost a lot and were awful tiresome to make. Mostly we had an oil lamp right there on the table, or just the firelight."

Carla looked at the table and nodded. She sat down on the three-legged stool just within the great fireplace. Carla's stool, but once it had been Hesper's stool, and before that Roger's.

The child looked up, her gentian eyes expectant under the wings of soft brown curls held back by blue butterfly bows. "Tell again the stories your father told you—about the pirate's cutlass mark on that table, and Phebe's andirons."

"Not now, dear. We'll have plenty of time for that. Wash these cups for me, and mind the handles, they break easy."

Lord, how many times Ma said that to me, thought Hesper. But I didn't care then, the way this child does. A violent gust of wind shook the house, and whistled down the chimney scattering fine ash on the hearth. I wish Walt would get back, it's the line storm for sure. Suddenly fear touched her, and she leaned against the sink, chiding herself.

Walt was an expert boatsman, he'd been out in dozens of storms. His broad-beamed catboat was staunchly seaworthy and the auxiliary engine brand new. There was no excuse for this foreboding.

"What is it, Marnie?" asked the child, watching. "You look sort of scared."

"Nonsense!" Hesper snapped, turning sharply. She saw Carla's face fall in hurt bewilderment. Why, that snappishness was like Ma, too. She put her hand under Carla's chin and kissed her. "I didn't mean to be grouty, dear. Somehow this night makes me remember one long, long ago when I was half your age. There was a great storm, a hurricane I think it must have been. My mother was terribly worried."

"What happened?" The child looked up at her, big-eyed, as little Hesper had on that far past night, quick to grasp the communicated fear.

"Oh, nothing much happened here at all," said Hesper briskly. "It was fun in a way, the waves came over Front Street right to the house."

"Would they again?" Carla tried to picture the harbor waters escaped from their proper place, rioting and tossing outside the door.

"Oh, I don't think so." Hesper hung up the tea towel and fitted the slender pink luster cup handles over their hooks. "There's the wall built now and all those rocks. Anyway the house would stand."

Ma said that too, she thought. "The house'll stand." Things change, people change, but it seems like the pattern doesn't change much. But there've been many storms I've not even noticed. And *my* son isn't a thousand miles away off the Grand Banks. There's no excuse for getting into a swivet. Still the uneasiness persisted. The wind whined and whistled past the windows, the rain came and lapped in gusts against the panes. And whenever there was a lull, she heard the heavy muffled booming of the waves as they hurled themselves against the sea wall.

Eleanor pushed open the back passage door and entered the kitchen from Moses's wing. "What a night!" she said. "I guess we can't get to the Rockmere after all. Sorry to trouble you, Mother Porterman, and you know Henry's so fussy about his food."

"I ought to know," said Hesper grimly. "But he used to relish clam fritters, and baked beans and gingerbread with sauce. I guess they won't hurt him any now."

"Well, it sounds very good," said Eleanor with a vague smile. She rustled over to the Windsor armchair, emitting a faint odor of French carnation. Her dark pompadour was sleekly shining, pearls glowed at the lobes of her large ears, diamonds and sapphires formed the crown brooch and tiny watch which were pinned to her Irish lace blouse. "Can I help you?" she murmured, looking at the fire.

"No. I've got everything ready, and Carla'll set the table. She knows how. Company dishes, dear—" Hesper said to the child, nodding toward the oak-leaf Staffordshire set in the china closet. When they were alone they still ate off the pewter.

Carla obeyed earnestly. She loved the great blue platters with their pictures in the middle, of the frigate *Constitution,* of President Washington on a horse.

The door opened again and Henry came in. "The Packard won't fit in the barn," he said to his wife. "I've had to send Briggs up-town to try and find a decent place to put it in. He wasn't any too pleased."

Eleanor's pretty face creased in a worried frown. "I do hope he isn't too upset. We don't want him giving notice just as we're sailing."

"Shall I set for Uncle Walt?" asked Carla, pausing by the table with a handful of thin rat-tailed spoons.

Hesper put the china sugar bowl down with a plop. "Of course, he's sure to be in soon."

"Bad weather, all right—" said Henry unexpectedly, looking out of the window, "but Walt's a regular sea dog. He could sail through the Ledges blindfold in a pickling kench."

Quick warmth flooded Hesper. She gave Henry a startled smile. So he hadn't completely forgotten his boyhood, and he was not as far from her in spirit as she had thought. He was half Honeywood after all despite that he resembled Amos, a big, blond man not quite so big as his father, but sharper cut and with a channeled self-assurance that Amos had never quite attained. She touched her son's arm as she hurried into the new kitchen to turn the clam fritters.

"Have you some oilskins around someplace, Mother?" asked Henry, following her. "I might go down to Little Harbor and take a look, see if there's any news."

She nodded. "I wish you would." She felt her mouth tremble and averted her face.

Eleanor watched her husband struggle into the spare oilskins with stark disapproval. "For heaven's sakes, Henry, Mother Porterman's got supper on the table. You just said Walter could take care of himself, and what on earth could *you* do, except get soaked and start up your asthma? Anyway, he's probably sitting happily in some fishwife's cottage."

"I doubt it," said Henry. "If Walt'd been forced in somewhere, he'd find a way to telephone. He'd know Mother'd be worried." He went out the back door to the garden path that led to Little Harbor.

Eleanor looked puzzled, staring at the door. "I wish Henry wouldn't—he's not quite over that bronchitis. It's just an ordinary storm—isn't it? Why, I've been out in some myself here, and nobody ever got excited."

Maybe not in a two-hundred-foot steam yacht, Hesper thought, but she smiled. "That's true," she said.

Carla crouched on her stool, her intent gaze traveling from her mother to her grandmother. They waited.

The fire flared up and died down. The wind had worked loose the shutter on the borning-room window and it banged monotonously. Hesper listened for the sound of the sea. Thank God the tide was nearly on the turn. Mostly the wind changed then.

Henry came back. He stood on the mat in the back entry, shaking water off the oilskins, and stamping the high rubber boots.

"No news," he said. "All the boats are in but Walt's."

Cold went through Hesper's stomach. "Thank you, Henry. We'd better eat." She dished up the clam fritters, put the brown crockery beanpot on the table.

They sat down. Hesper filled the plates and left her own empty. Henry and Carla did not eat much. Eleanor started by picking at the clam fritters which she cut into tiny pieces, but she finished everything. "Well, I'm sure there's no use worrying," she said, accepting another spoonful of the crisp golden-brown beans, "there's sure to be some reasonable explanation."

Hesper gave her daughter-in-law a quick look that held something of pity. Eleanor lived in a world of reasonable explanations. In her sheltered haven there were no surprises. She had never yet had to pit her reasonable explanations against the rocks and the sea and the tempest. She hadn't learned how vulnerable we all are. She had never seen the sudden black face of death.

Eleanor sipped up the applesauce and ate her gingerbread. She reproved Carla for large mouthfuls, and finally with the effect of coaxing difficult children, she gave her silent husband and mother-in-law a heartening smile. "This gingerbread is delicious, Mother Porterman. Don't you think so, Henry? Do give me the recipe, and I'll get Marie-Louise to try it."

"I'll copy it for you," said Hesper. "Mind she puts just a dash of coffee in. Brings out the flavor."

The banjo clock whirred and struck eight. The shutter banged faster, and loose window panes rattled. Outside there was rushing roar and movement in the unquiet night. Even the stalwart house, accustomed to so many assaults on its endurance, shook under the blasts.

Eleanor shivered suddenly. "There's a terrible draught. Carla, run upstairs and get my little fur cape. Oh no, I guess you'd better go, Henry. I forget there's no lights on."

Henry nodded and went, seeming glad of action.

Dear Lord, Hesper thought, why doesn't Walt get back!

Eleanor, bored by the storm and her mother-in-law's silence, cast around for a topic. After all if the poor thing was worried it was only kind to try to distract her. Even Carla, who was usually such a chatterbox to her grandmother, crept about the room like a scared mouse, putting the silver away.

"I've got the new *Century Magazine* with me," said Eleanor. "It has several charming reproductions of paintings by Evan Redlake. The great American artist, you know. Some of them reminded me of Marblehead, and the article said he once did some painting here."

Really, I wonder if she isn't beginning to fail, Eleanor thought, seeing a curious blankness settle on her mother-in-law's face, and the wide firm lips twitch into a mirthless smile.

"Did you ever hear of him?" pursued Eleanor gently but without expectation.

"Yes," said Hesper. "He stayed here at the Inn once, when I—when I was a girl."

"Oh? That's interesting. Though I don't suppose you remember much about him, if it was so long ago? Last month Henry and I were invited to a dinner at the Gardeners to meet him. I was quite pleased. But you know he never showed up. Dreadfully rude. It seems he's a regular hermit. Has a cottage somewhere on the Maine coast and hardly ever leaves it."

"Indeed," said Hesper, rising from the table and sweeping into her hand some crumbs overlooked by Carla.

That's the trouble with her, thought Eleanor, pitying. She isn't interested in anything outside of this narrow-minded little town. But she persisted with the topic. Now that they had a Sargent for the Brookline library, it would be nice to own a Redlake marine, for the drawing room at "Braeburn."

"Did he stay here long?" she asked. There might be some anecdote that would amuse the Art Society. "My husband's family, the Honeywoods at Marblehead, you know. Well, Evan Redlake used to stay with them . . . and . . ."

"No," said Hesper. "Not long." For a moment she almost yielded to impulse. What would happen to that pretty, well-bred tranquillity if she said baldly, "I was married to Evan Redlake once. I bore him a child." Disbelief? Shock? Gratification? The silence of forty years was not worth shattering for those. And it wasn't I, this old woman, torn with anxiety for her son, who knew Evan Redlake.

Eleanor abandoned hope of any reminiscence. "Of course—" she said, entirely for her own pleasure at having assimilated the conversation at the Gardeners, "though he was *the* American pioneer in Impressionism, some people consider him a trifle old-fashioned. Still, the Museum of Fine Arts just paid ten thousand dollars for his "Fisher Girl at Great Head." The highest they've ever paid to a living American artist."

Henry came back with the mink cape and put it around his wife's shoulders. Eleanor thanked him and looked over at Carla on her stool. "Darling—it's way past your—"

Hesper interrupted, "Is that painting you just spoke about pictured in the *Century* too?"

Eleanor was surprised. "Yes, I believe it is. Henry, that copy of the *Century,* I put it in my dressing case—will you—"

"Never mind," Hesper interrupted again. "I can see it some other time."

She spoke with sharp decision, and turning her back on them she pushed aside the curtains at the window and stared out into the night. The storm was passing, and the rain had nearly stopped. She strained her eyes, peering through the darkness along the path to Little Harbor.

"Fisher Girl at Great Head." Great Head was the chart name for Castle Rock. But there were other Great Heads along the coast, and many fisher girls for Evan, no doubt. What did it matter?

Why don't I pray? she thought, pray for Walt out there. But she could find no words with which to dull the piercing fear. God up there in the darkening sky, was he ever a God of tenderness or balm? Was he not rather as inexorable as the sea, and as indifferent to human desires?

I'm tired of standing things, and standing them and living through them and going on somehow. Tired of it. She leaned her forehead against the window, and the weight of all the separate losses through the years pressed past this new pain. Johnnie, Evan, Amos all gone from me. And Ma and Pa too. Each time I lived through it and found some content. I can't do it again if Walt—

"Mother, please come back and sit down by the fire. I'm sure there'll be word soon."

Hesper let the curtains drop. She stiffened her thin body, and walked back to them. "Sure to be. How'd you like a mite of the '72 port, Henry?"

Carla jumped up from the stool. Marnie was acting so worried and strange, and her face was pulled down at the corners and showed a lot of wrinkles it didn't usually. "Can I get it for you, Marnie—Grandma—it's in the decanter in the pantry, isn't it?"

Hesper looked down at the eager child, the little heart-shaped face between its bunches of curls and bows, the soft blue eyes full of instinctive sympathy. Yes. There was Carla, too.

"We'll get it together." She took the plump hand in hers.

"And then really the child must go to bed—" said Eleanor. "I do hope you won't let her stay up till all hours, Mother Porterman, will you? Mademoiselle keeps her on a strict régime."

It was while she and Carla were in the dark pantry, searching the back shelf with a candle, that they heard noise outside on the path from Little Harbor. Footsteps and voices, light from a lantern flickered into the pantry. Hesper put the candlestick down on the shelf. She stood listening. More than one person. Were they then carrying something? Thunder beat in her ears.

Carla had run to the window. "Marnie—" she cried, "there's three people coming up the path. And one of 'em's Uncle Walt! I reckernize him."

Hesper moistened her lips. "Are you sure?" Even as she asked she heard the sound of Walt's deep voice.

She jerked her head, wet a dish towel at the tap and slapped the cold wetness to her face.

She hurried to the kitchen entry and flung the door open. Walt came up the steps. She realized that he was supporting someone, and followed by someone else, but she saw only his big dark face, and the hazel eyes like her own looking tired but triumphant. In his stiff yellow oilskins and sou'wester he blocked the doorway.

He shook his head when he saw Hesper's face. "You've been fretting, Ma. You ought to know by now you can't sink a lobsterman." He reached out his left hand and gave her an affectionate squeeze on the shoulder. She saw now that his right arm was around a girl. The invisible face drooped against Walt's crackling yellow sleeve, but there was a mat of black hair, long and glistening.

Walt pulled his burden into the kitchen, while the others crowded around, exclaiming. And a boy followed behind him.

"Ma, get a blanket and some brandy," said Walt. "These kids 're half drowned." He deposited the girl on the hearth rug before the fire. She slid down into a wet heap, giving a little sighing moan. The boy sat down on the settle. His teeth were chattering.

"Fished 'em out of the South Channel," said Walt, flinging his oilskins and sou'wester into a corner, and shaking himself vigorously. "Fool kids thought it'd be fun to go boating in a line storm, I guess. They were somewheres off Cat Island when their skiff swamped."

"Poor little things—" cried Eleanor, shaking her head. "I knew there was some reasonable explanation for your being late. Poor Mother Porterman was so upset."

Walt gave his sister-in-law a look of speculative amusement. "I had a hell of a time getting back," he said. "God-damn bitch of an engine failed twice."

Eleanor winced. "Walter—please—at least think of the children—" She indicated Carla, and the sighing heap on the hearth rug.

But it developed after Hesper had administered brisk treatment to the girl, rubbed her down, and changed her clothes in the kitchen bedroom, that she was not a child. Eighteen at least, and a voluptuous, rounded little body. When she was covered by Hesper's old green-sprigged wrapper and a blanket and brought back to the fire, still silent and dazed but walking without support, they all made a further discovery. She was exceedingly pretty, with huge sleepy dark eyes, and her drying hair curling on her shoulders in a black cloud. The dark eyes rested on Walt and stayed there, following his movements as he poured out brandy for the boy, who was now also dried and regaining color. The girl accepted her share of brandy with the same gravity, her somber gaze still on Walt's face.

Nobody seemed inclined to say anything, and Eleanor, whose social code did not admit the silences which never seemed to bother the Portermans, leaned forward and said gently, "Now that's better. You certainly must have been thankful when Mr. Porterman found you. It must have been a dreadful experience."

"Yes, ma'am," said the boy. He was rather nice looking, curly brown hair, tall, and with a pleasing clean-cut leanness. He looked about sixteen. The girl said nothing.

"Where do you—uh—young people come from? What are your names?" Eleanor addressed the boy.

He answered courteously. "We both live over in Devereux. My name's Tony Gatchell. My father's boss mechanic at Burgess's new aeroplane factory on Gregory Street. Her name," he pointed, and the girl looked at him briefly then returned her gaze to Walt, "is Maria Sylva. Her father's a Portugee."

"Oh—" said Eleanor. The Portuguese who had during the last quarter-century infiltrated all the Massachusetts coast were considered by the summer people to be several cuts below the Italians and Irish.

Walt poured himself another large drink of brandy and swallowed it in two gulps. He settled himself in the massive chair his father had used, lit his pipe, stretched his long legs, and gave a gusty relaxed sigh. His eyes met the girl's steady gaze, and he grinned. "You feeling better, kid?"

Maria lowered her magnificent lashes, her red lips parted in a slow smile. "Yes. Much better." Her voice was low, a trifle sibilant. She raised her lashes and added with an intimacy that excluded all the others in the room. "You are wonderful."

A dull red ran up through Walt's weather-tanned cheeks. Hesper, watching her son and still glowing inside with the ecstasy of relief, felt a shock. She had never seen Walt look like that, startled and aware. In in his teens and twenties he had had many girls, but they had been brief, lusty affairs—soon forgotten. She had thought once or twice that there might be marriage. But nothing ever came of it and for years now no thought of an outsider had disturbed their relationship.

"You two better let your folks know you're all right," said Hesper. "Anybody got a telephone near your home?"

The boy nodded. "Yes, ma'am, I was thinking of that. Bartlett's drugstore'll be open. They'll deliver a message."

"You'll stay here the night, I've plenty of room," Hesper continued, nor did she miss the flicker of delight in the girl's eyes.

The boy looked doubtful. "That'd be a lot of trouble for you, ma'am. I reckon the cars'll be still running. We can get back."

Maria turned her head; all her motions were soft and graceful. "No, Tony," she said. "I am very tired."

"Of course, she is! The poor kid," cried Walt. "And Ma—you must have some vittles someplace? Looks like she needs feeding."

"Yes. I'll fix up something," said Hesper, and to the boy she said, "The telephone's over there behind the pantry door. D'you want me to work it for you?"

"No, *ma'am,*" he shook his curly head. "There's hardly a mechanical dingus been made that I don't have the hang of." He went behind the door and they heard the rattle of the handle and ringing burr.

"Well!" said Eleanor laughing. "Somebody certainly thinks well of himself. Henry, I'm utterly exhausted. We'll be wrecks tomorrow. And as for you, Carla, I only hope you don't get a tummy ache from staying up so late. Say good night to Grandma and Uncle Walt."

The child rose and threw her arms around Hesper's neck. "Marnie—" she whispered. "Don't you think that's an awful nice boy?"

Hesper kissed the child and murmured something; her eyes were on the girl and Walt. They weren't looking at each other now, but across half the room, Hesper could feel the tension, the awareness.

"D'you think it would be all right tomorrow—" whispered the child anxiously, "if I asked him to show me an aeroplane?"

Hesper nodded as Eleanor said, "That's enough, Carla. Stop dawdling."

Carla kissed Uncle Walt, who smelled good, of salt and smoke. He gave her a playful slap on her behind. "You better scat, little one, your mama's all boogered up!"

Eleanor sent him an angry look. Henry bade them all a quiet "good night."

Hesper was left alone in the kitchen with Walt and the flotsam the storm had sent her. The quiet nice-looking boy called Tony Gatchell, and the smoldering dark-eyed little beauty, Maria Sylva.

She fed them both, and made up beds for them upstairs in the new wing. The girl tried to be helpful, and followed instructions silently and quickly. But whenever possible, she edged back into the great kitchen near Walt, who was drinking much less than usual, and once when Maria bent over his chair to offer a plate of the gingerbread, Hesper saw his hand reach out and touch the cloud of soft dark hair.

She longed to ask the boy what he knew of Maria, but fear restrained her. She did not want to know. By ignoring the foreboding it might be made to vanish into the limbo of all foolish worries. Ridiculous, she thought. The girl's too young. She's a Portuguese. He's never seen her before. Just because he's saved her life, and she stares and stares at him like a sick calf, doesn't mean anything. Walt isn't like that. But underneath she knew. The fear of loss, which had terrified her while Walt was out in the storm, had been true after all. Not, thank God, the most fearful loss of all, but from this night Walt would no longer be free. All his life at intervals, Walt had fulfilled his impulses. He drank and wenched and fought when he pleased, and she had learned to accept, certain of his eventual return, and of his innate love of home. But this was different, and never before had there been a humble, bewildered look in his eyes as he gazed at a woman.

She saw the long message they exchanged without words, as they parted on the upstairs landing, when she finally sent the girl to bed. Oh, I wouldn't mind, she cried against the sharp pain, if it was one of our girls here, Sally Pickett or Madge Peach, I'd be glad. But this sleepy gypsy with the hot passionate eyes, the dark skin and the foreign voice . . .

Of the boy, Tony Gatchell, she did not think at all, but Carla did, before she drifted off to sleep in the little old east bedroom that had once been Hesper's.

CHAPTER 19

It was not until the following March that Walt and Maria Sylva were married, though for all that Hesper saw of him during the winter, they might as well have been married the day after the line storm that had brought them together.

Walt spent every waking instant, when he was not caulking and painting his boat or tinkering with his lobster traps, at the Sylvas' yellow frame cottage in Devereux.

The Sylvas were devout Catholics, and Maria's choice of a Protestant angered them. The delay in the marriage was caused by their prolonged refusal to consent.

Maria had a somewhat equivocal reputation amongst the youth of Marblehead, though Hesper resolutely closed her ears to the rumors, knowing well that nothing would stop Walt, whom Maria handled shrewdly despite her passionate desire for him. She would neither disobey her parents, nor give herself to Walt without the ceremony.

Hesper, seeing little hope of happiness for either of them, had sometimes been guilty of wishing for the latter solution, so that their physical obsession might eventually cool and everyone be spared the muddle and heartaches already bred of this headstrong alliance.

But the Sylvas at last gave in, and Maria Sylva became Mrs. Walter Porterman in the rectory of the Star of the Sea, the handsome new Catholic Church on Atlantic Street. Maria wore a looped and puffed white net dress bought readymade in Lynn, and a wreath of glittering wax orange blossoms on her stiffly waved and heavily brilliantined black hair. Nevertheless she was beautiful. Hesper, seeing Walt's face as he greeted her, felt a final clutch of jealousy and desolation, then tried to put these unworthy emotions behind her. The thing was done and Walt was gone from her. He had bought himself a tiny cottage near the shore at Dolliber Cove. He wanted to be alone with Maria. Hesper had

had too much sense to hint that there was plenty of room at the Hearth and Eagle.

She stood in the corner of the priest's parlor and watched the unfamiliar ceremony. Across the room Maria's parents and a handful of cousins genuflected at intervals and whispered once or twice in Portuguese. They looked pretty glum. Maria should have married her own kind, like Sancho Perez, a rich man, an importer of wines. He would have taken her back to Lisbon for the wedding trip. There would have been a real church wedding with hundreds of people, and High Mass.

So nobody was pleased but the principals. Hesper had tried to explain this to Eleanor whose reactions to Walt's marriage had ranged from outraged disbelief—"even Walter couldn't do a thing like that"—to tight-lipped disgust. Which would not have concerned Hesper, though she was exceedingly tired of storms and explanations, except as it affected Carla.

"Of course, I'm delighted to have Carla visit you now and then, Mother Porterman. She loves it and you're so fond of each other. But she's at a very impressionable age right now—and please forgive me for being quite frank—you know, mixed up with the Portuguese—and she talks a lot about that Gatchell boy—didn't you exercise any sort of supervision over her last fall?"

So Carla was not making her regular spring visit to the Hearth and Eagle. It was a bitter disappointment for Hesper, but she had not blamed Eleanor, who was expressing a real maternal anxiety, untempered by Henry's calmer judgment, for Henry was attending a conference in London.

Maybe, thought Hesper sadly, I *didn't* "exercise enough supervision." She had let Tony Gatchell ride Carla on his bicycle to the little aeroplane plant and see his father at work upon one of the new flying machines.

And she had let Tony take the child sailing in Walt's catboat. Walt had promised to do that himself, but he had been too much occupied with Maria. Tony was a nice boy, he had been kind to the child, treating her obvious admiration with bluff elder-brother humor. Gatchell was an old Marblehead name, nearly as old as Peach or Honeywood. But from Eleanor's point of view, he was not a desirable playmate for Carla. His father was a mechanic and his mother during the summer months had waited on table at the Nanepashmet Hotel on the Neck. The Gatchells lived over a grocery store on Smith Street, and though Tony did very well in high school, he sometimes made slips in grammar.

Carla did belong to a different world. The world of great wealth. The world of travel, of speaking French as soon as English, of Miss Prynne's Finishing School, and then débutante parties on Beacon Hill. It was not a question of better or worse, higher or lower. It was a question of difference. Oil and water, both very good things, but they don't mix.

Carla *had* shown a rather excessive attachment, tagging along after Tony, even slipping down to Gregory Street to wait for him outside the aeroplane plant. But Carla was only ten. Yet, thought Hesper with astonishment, I loved Johnnie when I was ten, and I never stopped. Ah, she thought with dismay, Eleanor was right and I was stupid.

And it seemed to her in the mood of depression into which she drifted after Walt's marriage that her whole life had been punctuated by stupidities and errors of judgment.

She was entirely alone now at the Hearth and Eagle, and she had plenty of time to think. The boarders were not due until June and she found herself dreading their advent this year, for what alleviation could a houseful of alien pleasure-seekers give to this painful recognition of emptiness and futility? Sooner or later it came to most people, the bitter knowledge that nobody needed them any more, but to Hesper wandering around the honeycomb of rooms in her old house, there came further and more melancholy doubts. Had she ever in the past accomplished anything worth doing in a lifetime of clutchings and strivings?

Her life now seemed to her a long succession of dead-ends. The love that she had given to three men—what good had it done any of them, and where was this love now? Finished. Gone from the world as though it had never been, except in her own restless and unshared memory. She thought of her sons. Henry had never needed her, nor would she have been able to help him if he had, so essentially different were their patterns. And Walt. Through all the years he had been with her, had she not with foolish love blinded herself to the truth about him? He was a rash and feckless misfit, nor had she ever been able to help him at all.

One afternoon she went up in the attic and unearthed the old Pansy Album into which she had copied the poems she had written in her girlhood. She remembered well the way they glowed for her on the pages, and how she had thought them beautiful. But they were not. She read them now, the limping stanzas, the forced and fleshless little metaphors, and her face grew hot with an embarrassed pity. For in this too how lamentably she had failed, nor ever even tried enough. Like poor Pa, she thought, and reminded of the "Memorabilia," she hunted and found it at the bottom of the same trunk. She opened the dog-eared pages covered with Roger's cramped, tiny writing. He had always meant to have it copied properly some day.

> Marblehead denizens ever must be,
> Nutured and soothed by their Mother, the sea.

Hesper smiled faintly; her eyes moved to the attic window and the misty gray-blue horizon far to the east. Maybe that's true. I thought so once.

She read on about the founding of the town and the arrival of the Honeywoods. The first winter as Roger had imagined it and the birth of little Isaac. The first community enterprise, the building of the *Desire* in Redstone Cove. She turned the pages, reading the history of her town. Roger had omitted nothing that he could learn from town records, from Moses Honeywood's journal or from legends. And as she read she felt astonishment and a dawning pride. Roger at least had not entirely failed, for somehow through the stilted waltz-time couplets there emerged a recurrent pattern of struggle and victory, a starkness of courage and idealism as rugged as the town's weather-beaten little houses and the sea-torn rocks it clung to.

I must get Henry to have it printed, she thought. Not for the public, she added to an echo of her father's lifelong fear of ridicule. But there must be some who would not laugh.

The light in the attic grew dim and she closed the "Memorabilia," laying it tenderly back in the trunk. She walked down the stairs to the kitchen. Though it was May a penetrating chill had begun to drift in across the water on a fog bank. The lighthouse on the Point o' Neck began to honk its hoarse, mournful bray.

The fog and the cold made Hesper's joints ache a little. She threw a knitted shawl over her shoulders and hesitated by the great fireplace. The fire had been laid in readiness for the fall. Suddenly she scratched a match and lit it. Who's to care? she thought in answer to the guilt born of years of thrift and her mother's spartan rule.

She watched the driftwood spurt into iridescent flame. The orange and blue and green tongues darted up into the chimney's black throat. She sat down in the rocker. It was nearly seven but she had no interest in getting supper. Who's to care? she thought again. She reached around to the work bag which dangled from one of the rocker posts and fished out her crocheting. She was making an afghan for Carla, who would probably never use it since her bedrooms at Brookline and the Neck were superabundantly furnished. But it brought Carla closer.

She sighed and began to rock, listening to the purr and crackle of the flames. The hearth fire gilded the old kitchen, and it lessened the loneliness.

The foghorn blared and died away across the harbor, and in the silence she heard a small scuffling noise outside the east window. She looked around to see two plump bespectacled faces peering at her through the window panes, two round mouths slightly ajar.

Lord a mercy, thought Hesper, exasperated, they're starting early this season! She walked across the room and whipped the curtains over the window, and the vacant, faintly aggrieved faces.

This happened often now, since the Historical Society had put a tablet on the house wall. "Honeywood House. Earliest part built in 1630 by Mark Honeywood, one of town's first settlers. Later parts added about 1750."

Sometimes tourists rang the bell and demanded to be taken through the house. Sometimes they just goggled through the windows.

Walt always used to give his raucous chuckle. "Oh, let 'em be, Ma. They get pleasure out of gawking like they were at the zoo."

But Hesper never got used to it. The Marblehead Historical Society was refurbishing the old Lee Mansion on Washington Street. Let the tourists go there if they craved to gape at the relics of a past in which they had had no part.

Hesper sat down again in the rocker. She thought of making some coffee, but lately coffee bothered her at night.

She finished the brown stripe on the afghan, pulled a tight pink ball from the bag, and began a new stripe. Might move in to the parlor and listen to some music—liven me up. Henry and Eleanor had given her a gramaphone for Christmas, and some new records. But it took too much effort to move into the chilly parlor away from the fire.

I should get out more, see more people. Maybe take the next meeting of the Arbutus Club here. But the Arbutus Club, under the capable leadership of Mrs. Orne, was deep in Browning.

> Grow old along with me!
> The best is yet to be,
> The last of life, for which the first was made: . . . . . .
> What I aspired to be,
> And was not, comforts me. . . . . . .

Bah! thought Hesper violently. Doesn't comfort me any. She finished several more rows. The banjo clock struck eight, cracking on the last notes as it always did now. If Charity had a telephone, I'd call and ask her to come over and sit a spell till bedtime. Queer how old friends came closer to you through the years even though they weren't very congenial to begin with. But it was Wednesday night and Charity would be running a Divine Healing meeting. That's where I ought to be, at our own Prayer Meeting. But she had never been able to get the comfort out of churchgoing that her mother had, though of late years she had seldom missed a Sunday at the Old North. The hymns were always moving, and sometimes there was a sermon that gave you a glow of determination. But it was hard to believe in a gold-paved Heaven. Hard to believe that Jesus kept a loving, helpful eye on every discouraged lamb.

I guess I'll hot up some milk, she thought, should be something in the stomach before going to bed.

She went into the new kitchen and lit the gas ring. Almost right away the milk bubbled up around the edges of the pan. That would have taken a lot longer on Ma's little old stove. Gas saved time. Automobiles saved time, telephones and steam ships saved time. Time for what?

She carried the glass of hot milk back to her rocker by the fire. There were some new novels on the shelves over what used to be the old stone sink, boxed in now to make a cabinet. Henry was thoughtful. He'd left a standing order at the Corner Book Store in Boston. They sent all the new books. She glanced up at the titles that had arrived last Monday. *The Rosary* by Mrs. Barclay. *Bella Donna* by Robert Hichens. Maybe I'll start one of them tomorrow. She sipped the milk slowly. A big log burned through and fell to charred embers between the andirons. A spark flew out and expired on the wide hearthstone.

She heard a crunch on the gravel, slow footsteps coming up the path. If it's another one of those prying tourists . . . Her mouth tightened and she listened for the thud of the brass knocker. But the footsteps paused, then came around the corner and up the kitchen path. There was one sharp tap.

She walked to the entry and opened the back door. She saw a tall caped figure under a wide, slouch hat. She had an immediate impression of shabbiness and eccentricity. Tramp, she thought with some disquiet, conscious of the great empty house behind her.

"Yes, what do you want?" she said, holding the door.

"Mrs. Porterman?" muttered the man, not moving. His voice was low and harsh. She saw that he rested one hand on a gnarled blackthorn stick, and in the other hand he carried a square black bag.

"Yes?" she said again. "What do you want?"

The man raised the stick and poked the door open from under her hand. "Let me in—" he said peevishly. "I'm tired." He came up the steps and walked into the kitchen. She retreated uncertainly.

He stood in the middle of the floor in the full light of the gas jet. The wide hat shadowed his face, but she saw a thin, jutting nose and a gray mustache and pointed beard. He wore a voluminous brown cape with a velvet collar, and a tiny red ribbon gleamed in the buttonhole of his suit coat.

Her heart beat fast and she watched him, puzzled; though her fear was subsiding she edged toward the telephone. He stared around him in a leisurely way, his eyes under the wrinkled lids passing over Hesper with neither more nor less apparent interest than they did the furniture.

"Place hasn't changed much," he said. "Though we have. Why in the name of God did you paint the floorboards? Looks like hell."

He took off his hat and cape and put them on the table. He had thick iron-gray hair, and one lock fell over his forehead.

Hesper's mouth dropped open. "Evan?" she whispered. She reached out and gripped the rim of the Windsor chair. Her throat closed down on a choking desire to laugh.

He shrugged and made the old semi-derisive sound through his nostrils. "Museum dragged me down to Boston for a fool banquet. I thought long as I was near I'd take another look at Marblehead, seeing that the canvas they've just acquired was done from memory." He sat down, leaning on his blackthorn stick. "Where's your husband?"

Hesper sat down; the moment of hysteria passed leaving a sardonic amusement, not apparently unlike his own. "Amos has been dead over twenty-five years. And for all you knew so might I have been?"

She put it as a question, wondering if he had ever bothered to find out anything about her since her brief note to England telling him that the divorce was final and that she was marrying Amos.

He crossed his legs, and she noted that his right dragged, he moved it painfully. "Never occurred to me you weren't right here at the Hearth and Eagle, same as ever. You can put me up for the night, can't you? I want to get over to that rock on the Neck in the morning. I remember a certain shade of greenstone across the porphyry, I'd like to check it."

So he didn't come to see me, she thought. Inside, under the gray hair, the sharpened face, the stooping shoulders and dragging leg, he was unchanged. But people didn't change much inside, while their bodies did. The only thing that really vanished was passion. It was a pity other emotions did not vanish with it. Yearning and regret and the capacity for humiliation.

"Well, I'm alone here," she said with crispness. "But I guess you can use the Yellow Room. The one you had before."

She shut her mouth tight, annoyed at having added that. Something ridiculous and slightly shameful about popping out with a reminder of —of forty-four years back.

He nodded without interest. He leaned over and began to rub his knee. "I've been sick—" he said querulously. "First time in my life. Had a dizzy spell last month and fell down. Did something to my leg."

"I'm sorry—" she said. "What does the doctor say?"

"Oh, stupid young know-it-all. Says to keep off it. I'll give it a rest when I get home to Thursday Cove, peace and quiet." He looked up at her suddenly. "Don't you tell anybody I'm here. I can't stand being pestered." His voice rose in vicious imitation. "'Ooh—Mr. Redlake, would you please give me your autograph?' 'Ooh—Mr. Redlake, wouldn't you let me have just one little tiny peek into your studio?' Blithering idiots."

There was a silence. Evan rubbed his knee.

"Yes. You're a famous man, now," said Hesper quietly. "I suppose you'd like something to eat, or drink, before you go to bed."

"I would," said Evan. "Couldn't eat at that banquet. They kept at me and at me for a speech. Seems I'm Dean of American painting. What do you think of that?" He tugged at his beard and cocked his head, looking up at her.

"I think you've accomplished what you set out to."

The twinkle left his eyes. He shook his head. "That's where you're wrong. You never do, you know."

"Don't you?" said Hesper. What more had Evan wanted than painting and recognition—and freedom?

He frowned into the red embers of the fire, not answering. She went out to the other kitchen and fixed a tray. She brought it to him, and threw a log on the fire.

He ate and drank in silence. She sat in her rocker and watched him. Here they sat, two old people in an old room, bound by no tie except memory. Memory of brief passion and long grievance.

Why did he come? she thought; why did he have to push into my life again with his selfishness and his painting? stirring up a lot of pain I'd thoroughly buried. Why did I say he could stay here?

He finished everything, wiped his mustache on the damask napkin. She got up and took the tray. Her face was hostile.

"Thanks," he said suddenly. "Tasted good." And he smiled. Despite the beard and the mustache the quick smile still startled by its ironic sweetness. The flash of a searchlight across a brooding cliff.

"You've still got beauty, Hesper," he said. "You had good bones. That's why. They never let you down. Good proportions stay, unless one gets fat. But why must you swaddle yourself in muddy gray and black? You never did have the slightest feel for color."

She glanced at her gray percale housedress, the knitted black shawl. "I'm a widow," she said coldly. "And I'm an old woman. Are you ready to go up to your room?"

He struggled up from his chair, leaning on his stick. She picked up his square valise preparing to show him the way.

"Don't touch it!" he snapped. "I always carry that myself. Can't bear people touching my things."

She shrugged her shoulders and put the bag down.

That night in her bedroom above the old kitchen, she lay awake for a long time staring into the darkness.

The next morning the fog had blown away and a clear rich sunshine sparkled on the ripples in the Great Harbor. A southwest breeze gentle as the May fragrance it spread over the town—the fragrance of lilacs and chestnut blossoms—blew through the open windows of the Hearth and Eagle.

Hesper awoke to the feel of Maytime, and though the derisive inner voice jeered at her, she took pains with her hair. And she put on her only colored dress, a lavender dimity, crossbarred in white. It was quite warm enough for a summer dress.

She started breakfast, and promptly at eight, Evan appeared. She greeted him and set a chair at the big oak table in the old kitchen. She was shocked by his looks. Perhaps it was natural that during the night when she thought of him lying there in the Yellow Room, she had seen the Evan who had once lain there on a bridal eve. And the readjustment was difficult. No, it's not only that, she thought. It's because he looks sick. His color was bad, the grayish skin drawn tight over his cheekbones and forehead. He ate with effort, frowning as he slowly propelled the fork towards his mouth.

"Did you sleep all right?" she asked.

He put his fork down and smiled at her. "Pretty fair, except for the hauntings. Ghosts, you know."

"Ghosts?" she repeated uncertainly. The boarders sometimes reported ghosts, shadowy figures in Puritan costume, pirates, a Revolutionary soldier. But these manifestations always appeared to those who had learned something of the house's history and who believed that every old house must have a ghost. Hesper never argued with them.

"Memories," said Evan, pushing back his plate. "What's the best way for me to get across to the Neck?"

Hesper stood up and began to stack dishes. Ah yes, you sentimental fool, she said to herself, did you think the memories were of you? He came here to check on the shade of the greenstone as it runs through the porphyry at Castle Rock.

"I'll get a message to Walt, my son," she said. "He can take you there in his lobster boat at high water, right to the beach by the rock. You'd never walk across the Neck with that leg."

"Very well," said Evan. "But you come along, Hesper."

"Whatever for? I know what the Rock looks like though I've not gone there in years. And I'm too old for junkets."

Evan sighed. "Maybe I am too. I don't want to trouble you, but do come. I detest being alone with a stranger."

Oh, so that's it. But why *not* go? The sea and the sun and the joy of motion on the water were not restricted to the young.

Walt was impressed by his passenger. Maria had a calendar decorated with a picture by Redlake, called "Breakers Ahead," and Walt had read a story about him in the Sunday supplement called the "Hermit of Thursday Cove." It had smeary photographs of his Maine cottage, perched on a cliff over the sea, and told how he lived alone and wouldn't let anybody in, and how he particularly hated women, though there was a photograph of a painting of a naked girl lying on a beach. This, of course, had made Walt read the article in the first place. It said this painting was hanging in a museum in Paris.

So Walt greeted his mother and the painter with considerable curiosity. The tide was in and he had brought his boat up alongside one of the Little Harbor wharves. His mother scrambled in and sat down by the tiller. She was pretty spry for her years, but Redlake had a bad leg and needed help. He sat down forward of the housing on a stack of lobster pots.

Walt started up the engine. "Handsome old coot," he muttered to his mother. "What in hell's he doing at our place?"

Hesper looked at Evan. He sat erect, one hand on his blackthorn stick. He had folded his arms into the brown cape to keep it from fluttering. He reminded her of a dimly remembered picture of an Italian duke. The narrow dark face, the haughty nobility of bearing.

"Oh, he was here once long ago," she said. "I guess he didn't know about the other hotels."

Walt was satisfied. His thoughts reverted somberly to Maria, her avid, passionate beauty and her sulkiness. The boat chugged along between Gerry's Island and the ruins of Fort Sewall, heading toward the lighthouse on the Neck. Already the Great Harbor was filling with summer craft. Yawls, schooners, and ketches rocked at their freshly painted moorings off the two Yacht Clubs, the Eastern and the newer Corinthian. And the smaller boats, the sloops and cats and an occasional cruiser, were sprinkled thickly on the turquoise water.

"Going to be a good season," said Walt. "Sell all the lobsters I can trap." His face darkened. "Been having trouble with that bastard Ratty Dawson again. He's swiping from my pots."

"Well, you better not beat him up this time," said Hesper grimly. "Let the harbor police handle it—"

"Codshit!" said Walt, and he jerked the tiller. "They want witnesses, and they want proof, and they want papers filled out, and then they don't do anything. I can handle Ratty myself."

Evan suddenly turned his head and his amused gaze rested on Walt's scowling face. "I'm afraid you're an anachronism, Mr. Porterman. Our civilization seldom does anything direct any more."

Walt looked blank and Evan continued, "By the look of that harbor, Marbleheaders don't even take their sailing direct any more. Many townsfolk own those boats?"

Walt shook his head and shrugged. "But I don't know as it matters. They spend a lot of money in the town. And you can bet your last dollar we don't let 'em swindle us."

They rounded the lighthouse and passed over Lasque's Ledge. The little boat rocked on the long swells of the open ocean. Evan stared at the shoreline, the smooth green lawns, the turrets and gables and battlements of the period mansions. "I had no idea it was so built up," he said, "and why must they build so colossally ugly?" He raised his stick and pointed at the largest of the houses, an improbable mixture of the Alhambra and Balmoral Castle.

Walt grinned, glancing at his mother. "That one happens to belong to my sister-in-law. Mrs. Henry Porterman. She thinks it's mighty elegant."

Evan looked startled. Hesper felt his frowning gaze pass over her. He said nothing.

Walt anchored in the cove just south of Castle Rock, the cove where Evan had pulled Hesper out of the waves on the day they met. But neither of them mentioned this. Walt rowed them to shore in his dinghy. "I'll wait in the boat," he said. "Got a couple of nets to mend."

He was mildly amused at the expedition, but he assumed that his mother was accompanying Mr. Redlake to make herself useful. He watched them move over the shingle and start up the rise of ground that led to the rock. Two tall figures, thin and erect, except for Redlake's limp. Ma always did know how to handle queer people, Walt reflected, and whistling through his teeth, he went to work on a lobster pot, splicing together the meshes of string torn by a powerful claw.

Evan toiled up the slope until they reached the beach grass and cluttered piles of rose rock that had split off from the main mass. She heard his breathing sharpen, and saw that his skin had suffused with a dark red. He staggered and caught himself on his stick.

"Here—" she said. "Sit down, Evan."

He obeyed, slumping onto the nearest rock. He leaned forward, resting his forehead on his hands as they clasped the stick.

"What is it?" she said. "Dizzy?"

He raised his head and beneath the drooping lids, his eyes rested on the lavender haze that shimmered along the far horizon.

"I'm going to die, Hesper."

She put her hand on his knee and drew it back. "Nonsense. Everyone gets faint spells."

He jerked his head. "My dear—spare me the rubber-stamp conventions. I didn't come here for that."

The sun shone down on them. Two little boys with fishing rods ran down the path and disappeared on the other side of the massive rock. Near Hesper's foot under a clump of grass there was an empty beer bottle and a fragment of white paper. Below on the beach low waves creamed over the rattling shingle.

"What did you come for?" said Hesper.

He was silent so long that she was frightened, but she saw that he had lost the dusky color and his nostrils no longer flared in the struggle for breath. When he spoke he did not look at her, and his musing voice drifted out toward the water.

"All my life I've tried to capture something. An essence of reality. Many times I've thought I had it. Now I don't know. Of late years I've been repeating myself. Painting over old canvases. That "Fisher Girl" that Boston's got . . ."

She waited. A sandpiper hopped along the beach. Faintly from the anchored boat she heard Walt's whistle.

"That was you, Hesper. I've been painting you in some phase ever since I left you. You were in the gentle English meadows, and the plodding, French peasants, you were in the pine mountains of the Adirondacks, and you are in the storms and the calms of the ocean that I paint now. I never was sure of it until today."

Her heart trembled and paused. Soft, healing water flowed over the barrenness in her soul. The soft water rose to her eyes. She shut them and turned away.

"Have you seen any of my work?" he asked. She shook her head and he gave a mordant chuckle. "Ah well, you never did understand it anyway. It doesn't matter. I'm going to die very soon. But first I want to go home and paint one more picture. I think I can now. I needed to see you and Marblehead again."

"Thank you—" she whispered. "Thank you for telling me that our marriage was not all a terrible mistake, and that somehow I did help you become a great artist."

He heard the poignancy in her voice through the naïve little words and understood her need as he could never have done in the past. He took her hand and raised it to his lips. "I told you once, Hesper, that what love I had was for you. It was true. It still is."

Stay here with me, Evan—she cried to him silently, as once she would have cried it aloud. We're two lonely old people. I'll take care of you. Stay with me— But the cry never reached her lips. Even now, without the turmoil of passion, she knew there could never be sustained closeness between them. I always wanted more from him than he could give. Learn, learn, learn at last, stupid heart.

He studied her face. "What the years have given you of serenity and inner strength!" he cried with wonder. "More than I ever would have dreamed."

"Strength and serenity?" she repeated sadly. "Oh no, Evan, I haven't found either of them."

He smiled at her and struggled to his feet. "Perhaps you've never known very much about yourself, my dear. Let's go back across the Harbor. This place is no longer part of us." He glanced at the surrounding mansions, and the smooth velvet lawns.

They called Walt and went back to the town, and as they approached her home from the Little Harbor side, Evan became silent. Nor did he speak again except to say good-bye during the remaining minutes of his visit. They parted very simply, and she stood quiet as he had left her, watching at the door as he limped down the path to the buggy which was to convey him to the depot. She turned back into her home, deeply grateful to him for having released her at last from a long humiliation. But Evan was in the end to give her far deeper cause for gratitude.

Two months after his visit, she read of his death in the *Boston Tran-*

script. And she was unprepared for the violent shock of pain and loss it gave her. Even the boarders noticed that Mrs. Porterman's usual brisk cheerfulness was replaced by heavy-eyed silences, and wondered a little. And Carla, who escaped from Eleanor's supervision at "Braeburn" and ferried across to the town whenever she dared, was troubled by the sadness she felt in her grandmother.

But some days later the sadness lightened, though Carla never knew why.

Hesper received a small shallow crate by express, and a terse covering letter from a Maine lawyer stating that Mr. Evan Redlake's will directed that the accompanying package be sent to her at once upon his death. She carried the wooden crate to her room and locked the door. When she had pried up one of the slats she saw a letter pasted to the back of a canvas. It was addressed to her, and she sat down on the bed and opened it with shaking fingers.

It began without salutation.

> I leave you no money, my dear, since your son Henry has plenty, judging from that monstrosity on the Neck. Instead I send you this, my last picture, which is of and for you. It's the best thing I ever did, and I hope that it, at least, will have meaning for you.
>
> Evan

She sat a long time looking down at the letter. Then she released the canvas from its wrappings, and when she saw what it was she gave a faint cry. For Evan had painted the Hearth and Eagle much as he had painted it long ago in the picture she had stared at in the New York gallery, but there were differences in the painting, and in her.

Again as in the earlier painting the house was bathed in light, but in this picture the shadows were not violent. They blended in exquisite harmony with the earth and the chestnut tree and the limitless blue ocean behind the house. And here a dim figure stood in the doorway, the arms held out in offering and welcome. The figure was that of a woman, ageless, and the features barely sketched, yet in the reflected light the upturned face shone with a quiet strength.

But it was the house itself behind the figure that drew Hesper's startled gaze, and as she looked, its meaning for her grew and expanded. It seemed that the silver clapboards became transparent as gauze and behind them there was moving life. It was peopled with gentle spirits not imprisoned but forever slipping through the house on an endless journey. They were all there and alive, the familiar names, and they slipped through her mind as they slipped through the house, like vivid jewels on an everlasting chain. Phebe and Mark and little Isaac; Lot and Bethia; Moses and Melissa and Zilpah; Richard, and Sarah, who was Gran; Roger and Susan.

And all the children. She saw them clustered around the great fireplace, yearning for life, their hands outstretched both to joy and suffering. And she saw the baby Hesper sitting on her stool amongst them, neither more nor less embodied than the rest.

Timeless minutes flowed by as she looked at the picture, and she understood at last what Evan meant by the essence of reality he had striven all his life to interpret. For here was more than a masterly portrait of an enduring old house, as the picture so long ago had been. Here, far more beautiful and grander than actuality, he had evoked the matrix of human experience—the ideal image of home, rooted in the earth and rocks and trees, washed by the sea.

She turned at last from the picture and looked again at Evan's note, rereading it with a tender smile. Yes, my dear, she thought, this at least has meaning for me, and I thank you.

And it seemed to her that he heard and understood, and that through the medium of his art they had at last found true communication.

CHAPTER 20

ON A WARM Indian summer day of early November in 1916, Hesper sat in the sunlight in a deck chair Walt had put out in the garden for her, under a gnarled old apple tree. It was good to sit and rest. The dull pain up her left arm was gone for the moment, eased by the pills the doctor had given her.

Little Harbor was quiet this afternoon. The summer people had gone home and the town had become itself again. It lit its kitchen and parlor fires, smoked or chatted peacefully with blinds undrawn, free for eight months of admiring artists and sightseers. The Great Harbor, too, was nearly deserted. The yacht clubs were closed now. The graceful pleasure craft that had made Marblehead the country's foremost yachting center were all put to rest in various boat yards for the winter.

Hesper listened to the diminishing put-put of a lobster boat, and thought how beautiful the foliage still was on Peach's Point. Clumps of fading gold amongst the somber green of the pines. And the water a crisp, diamonding blue that you only saw at this time of the year. She listened to the music of the ripples on the beach, and the plantive mewing of the seagulls, and thought what quiet treasures of the senses age brought in return for the passion it removed. Mauve smoke drifted toward her on the northwest breeze, perfuming the salt air with the smell of burning leaves. She had never realized what a lovely smell that was before. Perhaps there was nothing in the world so rewarding as tranquil awareness.

Then the back door slammed, and Walt shambled around the corner of the house toward her. He wore dirty blue jeans, an antique pea-jacket, and a blue officer's cap with gold insignia, pushed way back on his coarse, grizzling hair. He had won the cap shooting craps with the mate on Eleanor's steam yacht and he wore it incessantly. What with Hesper's good cooking and his continual drinking he had put on weight since he came home, and his jowls and paunch and sardonic humor suggested a joviality that fooled strangers.

"Carla just phoned," he said brusquely to his mother, shifting a quid of tobacco to his cheek. "Coming down on the afternoon train, wants to stay a spell. Seemed upset. Says you've got to help her. Reckon she's ducking out on something."

Hesper sighed. Peaceful enjoyment shattered as it always was. Even the prospect of seeing the beloved child could not quite atone.

"I wonder what's the matter," she said, rising slowly from the deck chair. "You better meet the train. And for heaven's sake shave first."

She walked up the back steps into the great kitchen. Walt followed her. "Carla can take the depot hack," he said, slumping into the Windsor chair. "I'm not in the mood to get all goddam prettied up."

Hesper turned and surveyed him. There was a bottle of rum on the floor beside the chair, but he wasn't drunk yet, just enough to be stubborn.

"Then will you go out to look at the traps?" she asked. "It'd be nice to have lobsters for supper. Carla loves them."

He hunched his shoulders, scowling, reached around the chair and pulling up the bottle of rum, took a long gulp. Then he spat a brown stream of tobacco juice into the fireplace.

Suddenly anger spurted through Hesper. "Get that bottle out of here!" she cried. "Out of my—out of this room. Go make a swine of yourself down along at the harbor like you always do. I won't have it here."

He looked up startled; he had not heard her raise her voice in years. She stood tall and straight and very pale, her lips tight and her chin thrown back. His bitter inward-gazing eyes cleared and focused on her.

He gave her a dim replica of his old grin. "Why, Ma," he said. "You think I'm polluting the house? This old place has seen plenty of drunks before. Plenty of everything."

She expelled her breath and the anger left her. Yes, I suppose it has. What's the use of fussing. You can't *make* people do anything.

"Well, try to pull yourself together while Carla's here. I really can't blame Eleanor. . . ." She sighed. The scandal and near tragedy three years ago had been pretty bad for everybody. Maria had run off with the Portuguese, Sancho Perez, who had once wanted to marry her. Walt had followed and tried to shoot them both. But he had been stopped by the hotel detective before he even got to the room. The papers had been full of it for a day, and then forgotten, hushed up probably by Henry's money. People forgot so quickly anyway. The waters of life closed over the hole made by the stone. Unless you were the stone on the bottom, she thought, looking sadly at her son.

He shook his head, and returned her look with a rueful affection. He ran his hand over the stubble on his chin. "Sorry, Ma. I'm a bad boy. I don't wonder you get riled. You know what?" His voice rose to a mocking singsong. "We're an old, old family and they run to seed. That's what I heard one of those lady artists say. She was sketching our house, and she saw me sitting on the stoop. Run to seed, she said, looking at me, Ma. She stole one of the old hand-wrought nails right out of our clapboards too, picked it out with her little pocket knife. You know what else she said?" He gave a muffled hiccup.

"Oh, Walt, get along with you. Go on out to the traps."

"This lady artist she saw old Cap'n and Martha Manson walking by with their dog, and she said, 'Aren't they just precious! The town's just full of the cutest eccentrics.' You wouldn't want me not to be a cute eccentric, would you, Ma?"

Suddenly he heaved himself up from the chair. He drained the bottle. "To hell I pitch them all!" He flung the bottle into the trash basket, wiped his mouth on his hand, and slammed out the door.

Hesper turned wearily toward the pantry. Born out of his time, as Evan said that day on the way to the Neck. Walt should be allowed to fight it out with his fists. He should have been the lusty, brawling skipper of a windjammer.

She moved around the old kitchen and the little new one, getting ready for Carla. Dilly came every day now and helped with the work, so there wasn't much to do. But Dilly always went back to Clifton in the afternoon. Henry and Eleanor couldn't see that at all. They thought her a stubborn old woman, because she wouldn't let them provide her with a couple of maids who would sleep in. Their lives were so different that it was hard to make them understand a dread of idleness. Better wear out than rust out, and it was so good to have the house to oneself in the long, quiet evenings. She had finally given up the boarders three years ago at the time of Walt's trouble, when he came back home. And that had been a relief. The house, without its chattering roomsful of strangers, had grown even nearer to her, an understanding third with herself and Walt. A friend.

She went into the borning room, where she slept now. Wise to move downstairs, the doctor had said, avoid all unnecessary exertion. Henry and Eleanor had been very sweet and worried. They wanted to enlarge the room, to refurnish it. She would let them do nothing except give her a fine hair mattress for the old bedstead, and an easy chair to supplement the straight ladder-back. In this room, unchanged from the night on which she had borne Walt and her father had died, unchanged before that for all the births and deaths of the long generations, she found support with which to meet the inevitable.

On the wall beside the bed, she had hung Evan's picture of the house. Nobody, not even Carla, had ever known the story of the picture, and few had seen it, since she jealously guarded the privacy of her room. But Eleanor had, of course, and her amazed curiosity had been hard to quench. "Why, Mother Porterman! What a lovely painting of the house! Where in the world did you get it? It looks almost like a Redlake, only softer somehow. And that looks like E. R. down in the corner!"

"Does it?" asked Hesper. "Someone gave it to me." And she had changed the subject with a finality that Eleanor could not budge. And Eleanor soon forgot about the picture. She and Henry came seldom to Marblehead these last years. They had not opened "Braeburn" for two summers, had rented a huge villa at Newport instead. Since with the war going on in Europe they couldn't go abroad. And though no one ever said so, Hesper knew that Marblehead had become painful to Eleanor, because of Walt's scandal, and because of the trouble with Tony Gatchell. Poor Carla, poor baby, thought Hesper. She had acted a lot older than her scant sixteen years, and had taken the fuss with a kind of dry-eyed suffering that was frightening. It had been very hard for Hesper to side against her with Eleanor's vehement—and Henry's more temperate—decrees, but from any sensible angle it was the only thing to be done.

Anyway Tony had immediately ceased to be a menace, for he had gone out West, and had not been in Marblehead these two years. And Carla seemed to recover rapidly, as her elders knew she would. She finished up at Miss Prynne's school in Boston, she danced and flirted and had beaux and apparently enjoyed the Newport summers. On her brief Thanksgiving and Easter visits to the Hearth and Eagle, she never mentioned Tony's name.

Hesper, knowing the vagaries of the afternoon train, had timed her preparations, and when she heard the sound of wheels outside she lit the great hearth fire, opened the back door for Carla, and stood waiting. There was unusual hesitance in the girl's approach. She came in silently, giving Hesper a subdued kiss, then dropped her little suitcase on the floor, and went to stand by the fire, greeting it and the unchanging old room with a wistful half-smile.

"Glad to see you, dear," said Hesper, watching the little figure with loving amusement. Carla looked a trifle defiant, and altogether pretty. She wore a blue velour suit that matched her eyes, an ivory crêpe de chine blouse and the short string of magnificent pearls Henry had given her for graduation. Her dark hair was puffed out over her ears in the new fashion. The puffs of hair and the embroidered blue velvet toque might have overshadowed her small features, except for the long-lashed gentian eyes, and the rose lipstick which accented the firm little mouth, somewhat to Hesper's disapproval. But she had kept her disapproval to herself. The girls in Carla's world used make-up now. And Carla was not vain.

"Are you going to tell me?" asked Hesper, after a minute. "Or shall we start supper. Uncle Walt's out. I was hoping he'd bring some lobsters, but I guess not."

Carla made a distracted little gesture. "No, sit down, Marnie, please." She indicated the rocker, and Hesper complied. Carla flung her hat onto the settle, pulled the three-legged stool from the hearth, and sat beside her grandmother. "I sort of ran away—" she said, staring into the fire. "Mother thinks I've gone to visit Betty Walton in Hingham. I had to come here to you and the house. Things are clearer here, and besides—oh, I know there's honor and self-respect and all that, but you've got to understand—" she stopped.

Hesper put her hand on the girl's soft hair. "I certainly don't understand anything yet. What *are* you talking about?"

Carla threw back her shoulders and turning her head looked up into her grandmother's smiling eyes. "I'm talking about Tony."

Hesper stiffened, and her smile faded. Beyond the unwelcome surprise there was dismay at the tone in which Carla had spoken. A tone of hardness, almost implacability.

"What about Tony? He's out West at college."

"No—" said Carla. "He's back here."

"Then you've been hearing from him! He broke his promise."

"Promises!" said Carla bitterly. "He didn't need any promises, he never wanted to see me again, after that night. The shame. The awful things Mother and Father said. Telling him he was after my damn money. Thinking he was— Marnie, you sided with them later. It hurt me terribly. We weren't doing anything that night, by Castle Rock, when Mother found us. We weren't even kissing. Tony wouldn't. He loved me. And they acted as though he . . ."

"Oh, my dear child!" cried Hesper with shocked pity, for they had all thought Carla too young to understand. "Nobody thought there was anything wrong, at least— You must be fair, dear. You were a little girl not yet sixteen, and Tony was twenty-one. Your parents had to protect you. And when they found you'd been seeing him secretly too."

"But I had to. Tony didn't know the way they felt about him. Though he learned all right. They made it ugly. Horrible. And I was so frightened and bewildered that night, I couldn't speak. I know Tony thought I agreed with them. When I tried to find him next day, he was gone."

"You didn't see him again?"

Carla shook her head. "I wrote him one letter. I tried to tell him how I loved him, and if he'd only wait till I got older. Oh, it was terrible to be so *young*. You wouldn't any of you believe how I felt. Tony didn't believe. He never answered the letter. I waited and prayed and waited for weeks."

She got up off the stool and walked back to the fireplace. She took the iron poker and adjusted the logs which had burned through. And there was maturity about this withdrawal.

"How do you know he's back now?" asked Hesper gently.

"Because I ran into Sam Gerry at the Yale game Saturday, and I asked him if he'd heard of Tony, and he said he'd just come back after finishing up at California Tech. That he was going to M.I.T. this fall."

Yes, thought Hesper. She had heard that Tony had been putting himself through a Western college, training to be an engineer. Though he had been earning good money helping his father in the Burgess Airplane plant, in the years after he finished high school. That trouble with Carla probably did him good, she reflected, spurred him into making something of himself. But she scarcely knew the boy, though she had always liked him, and she dreaded hearing the answer she now saw Carla would give to her next question.

"And what is it you want, Carla?"

The girl leaned the poker on the bricks inside the hearth; she turned with dignity and only her hand clenched in a fold of her skirt betrayed her. "I want to see him again. Oh, I know he may not give two straws about me any more. But I want to see him and then I'll know. I want you to ask him here, Marnie. Don't tell him why. I have some pride. If we meet here and there's nothing—it can be sort of casual."

"But my dear—are you *sure* you want to see him again? You've done very well without him—it seems so foolish."

Carla's restraint broke. Her face twisted and the blue eyes upturned to Hesper filled with hot tears. "I haven't got on without him! Oh, I've been to lots of parties, I've had fun with other boys, but never one I didn't wish was Tony. There's never been a night or a day go by these two years, that I haven't thought of him."

Lord, thought Hesper shutting her eyes. This is *real.* Somewhere long ago in this very room, she had had that sudden blinding certainty after a period of disbelief. Over there by the broom closet that led to the pirates' hidey-hole, the night they rescued the slave girl. She had been forced out of her reluctance—made to recognize fear and danger, and take action about them. Ah, but she was old now and tired of answering other people's emotional needs. Too tired to stand by and see Carla hurt as she might well be. Heartbreak. I've lived through my own, why must I be forced to share in this child's too?

"Marnie—" whispered the girl. "I'm sorry. Don't look like that. I can take it, you know. I have guts."

Hesper started, staring into the small face that had drawn near hers. Not a child's face but that of an understanding woman.

Hesper's mouth pulled into a rueful smile. She got up from the rocker and walked to the telephone in the pantry. May God forgive me for a meddlesome old fool, she thought, as she twirled the handle and asked Central to connect her with the Gatchells. God and Eleanor, she added grimly.

Tony had answered the phone himself and though obviously astonished to hear from Mrs. Porterman had said he'd be over right after supper. The two women waited, not talking much. They had some coffee. Carla went upstairs to her own room, and came down again in a simple gray wool dress, and Hesper saw that she had taken off the pearls. She was very pale, and her blue eyes were strained. They heard footsteps come up the path toward the old taproom door, and the girl's face suddenly grew old and haggard. "You go, please—" she said to Hesper, and she walked to the settle at the far side of the fireplace, sitting down in the corner where she was in shadow.

Hesper opened the door. "Good evening, Tony—" she said. "It was nice of you to come." And she eyed him narrowly. A slim young man, hatless, with curly light-brown hair, a thin brown face, and gray eyes that returned her scrutiny with puzzled wariness. A truculent jaw, held high, a defiant set to the head.

"Nice of you to ask me—" he said. "I hardly expected a welcome home from Portermans. Father sends his respects."

Hesper's heart sank. A sharp edge under the polite manner, and a resentful question—"*Now* what is it you people want of me? Let's get it over with."

She silently led the way into the great kitchen. She stepped aside and Tony, frowning, glanced around the low fire-lit room. Then he saw Carla, sitting on the settle.

"Hello—" she said in a husky, carefully casual voice. She leaned forward a little. "Hello, Tony."

Hesper could not see the boy's face. She saw the stiffening of his back, the almost imperceptible quiver that seemed to run through all his muscles like an electric shock. He stood without moving, staring at Carla.

Hesper held her breath. The room seemed to gather itself into a listening stillness beneath the purring of the fire and the ticking of the banjo clock.

She saw the change in Carla's face that must have answered his. The set smile vanished from her mouth. She gave a little sigh and rose slowly from the settle, moving toward him, her hands outstretched. For one more moment he hesitated, then he said "Hello, Baby" in a harsh, breaking voice and gathered her into his arms.

Hesper stole away from them, and from the old kitchen lit now not only by hearth fire but by the eternal radiance. Tears stood in her eyes, and she walked blindly through to the parlor and gazed out at the sea.

For the next days the force of Carla's love propelled them all. On the night of their reunion the two young people had talked until past midnight in the old kitchen, and they had decided many things. The next morning Carla phoned her father at his office, and Henry came down to Marblehead by the afternoon train.

They had a conference, the three of them—Carla, Hesper, and Henry, and he had listened gravely to his child. When Carla had finished he turned to Hesper.

"What do you think, Mother?"

"I think that they love each other, and as they're not suggesting marriage right away, I think you and Eleanor better be reasonable too, and get to know Tony."

Henry nodded, unsmiling, though his eyes softened as they rested on his daughter's glowing face. "But it'll be a bitter blow to Eleanor," he said.

"I don't see why!" cried Carla passionately. "Tony's done awfully well at college. When he gets his degree next year, he'll be able to get an engineering job most any place. And as for being a Marbleheader, why you were a townie yourself, Father!"

Henry's heavy face did crease then into a faint smile. "I was, but I doubt your mother'll think of that. Well, let me talk to this young man. I'm sorry we all got off on the wrong foot two years ago, and after I've seen him . . . don't worry, Carla. I'll break the news to your mother. But maybe you better stay down here a while till she calms down."

Carla laughed and kissed him. The music of her happy laughter echoed through the old rooms and even affected Walt. He stopped drinking, bathed and shaved, came home to meals, and spared his niece the bawdy cynicisms with which the spectacle of young love usually inspired him. Carla went up to Brookline for a couple of days then returned, reporting that Eleanor was still non-committal, but coming around gradually. Tony was to spend part of the Christmas vacation in Brookline, a prospect he endured for Carla's sake. At present he was commuting from Marblehead to Boston and his studies at M.I.T., but he saw Carla evenings in the parlor—the proper place for courting, since the weather had grown too cold for the traditional outdoor trysting places. And soon Carla's joy bubbled into a natural youthful expression. She wanted a party. An early Christmas party. "Marnie—yes. The house hasn't been gay for a long time. It'll love it. I'll do everything. I don't want you to get tired or worry about it."

Hesper was tired; the dull pain in her left arm and breast had lately become more persistent. It was perhaps this oppression and tiredness that gave her a curious reluctance to granting Carla's very natural wish. Perhaps too it was because Carla wanted a costume party, costumes of the periods that the house had seen. Yet that was natural too, in view of the trunks full of old clothes in the attic. And Carla was efficient and eager to handle everything. There were no valid objections, and Hesper of course consented, ignoring a quiver of foreboding which persisted.

The party was set for December 18, and the guests invited. Not many, for Carla knew few of the Marblehead youngsters, and the only Neckers would be young people from two families who had heated houses and opened them for Christmas.

But the people did not matter to Carla as long as Tony was there. She was possessed to fill the house with gaiety and light and music, and to re-create for it the days of its greatest glories.

She spent an energetic day in Salem, buying dozens of bayberry candles, red streamers, and provisions. She sent to Boston for holly wreaths and mistletoe. She went to the Abbot Hall library and looked up books on the American past. She reluctantly gave up the idea of having syllabubs, and port flips, but she bought a huge turkey which must be stuffed with chestnuts and oysters, and cooked on the spit in the old way, and the brick oven long disused must be fired again to bake the beans. She unearthed Zilpah Honeywood's recipes for Christmas cake and brandied mincemeat and mixed them herself, though the prescribed aging must be omitted.

Several days before the party, Carla and Hesper went up to the attic to look at costumes—which were not costumes but real clothing worn by Honeywoods.

It was fairly warm in the attic, heated by the great stone chimney, and a startled wasp buzzed feebly amongst the rafters. The great hand-hewn rafters were furry with dust and giant cobwebs quivered between forgotten dangling bunches of dried rosemary and dill.

"Mercy on us—" said Hesper, smiling, and attacking the nearest cobweb with an old twig besom she picked from a corner. "Ma'd have had a fit if she saw this. I'm afraid I never have been a good Yankee housekeeper."

"You are too," said Carla, laughing. "And you're a wonderful cook."

"Oh, that's nothing. A dash of this and a grummet of that. It's a knack; besides, you will be too."

"Do you remember—" said Carla, twirling a creaking spinning wheel, "how we used to tour the house when I was little? You told me stories about the Honeywoods—made everything seem so real. Of course it *was* real. About my own ancestors. That made me very proud."

She walked to the east corner and touched the hood on the long, outsized cradle. "Gran's cradle," she said with amusement. "Did you really rock her in it when you were small?"

Hesper nodded, leaning on the broom handle. The pain ran through her chest and down her arm. I must be more careful, she thought, waiting for it to pass. Once the child's party's over . . .

"Yes, I did," she said. "It kind of scared me then. Seemed so crazy. But now I don't know. You get old, Carlie, and all you want are the old things you've always known—and rest."

"Well, I can understand that," said the girl. "I've always felt so safe here. Really home." She threw open a trunk lid, said "Whew" to the wave of camphor, and began to rummage through piles of quilted bodices and homespun petticoats. It was not the trunk she wanted. She was looking for the rich brocaded and panniered clothes from Moses Honeywood's time. These homespuns were from an older day, maybe even Phebe's. As she dropped the lid she spoke reflectively.

"I sometimes think of Phebe. It seems so strange to have her things—when she's been dead for hundreds of years. Where's Arbella's letter about her, Marnie?"

Hesper thought a moment. "Why I guess it's in that wooden chest with the iron hinges over there by the warming pan. I've not looked at it in ages. I always meant to put it someplace safer in case of fire, but I don't know where would be safer—is it there?"

Carla had lifted the stiff, heavy lid, after dragging the whole chest over by the window. She nodded, pulling out a long, yellowed envelope, inscribed in Roger's cramped hand. "Portion of letter written in 1630 by the Lady Arbella Johnson to her sister Lady Susan Humphrey, concerning my fourth greatgrandmother, Mistress Phebe Honeywood. The letter is apparently written from Salem."

"Well, read it aloud, if you can make it out," said Hesper sitting down on a trunk. It was good to rest; she leaned her head against the wall.

The girl crouched over the letter, frowning at the faded brownish ink, the unfamiliar spellings and s's. She read slowly, guessing at some of the words.

"No word yet from home, so I write thee again . . . by the Master of the 'Lion.' I try to keep my thoughts from harking back, but . . . I can not, this is my shame for there be many here who are braver.

"There is great sickness, and I pray for the babe I carry. I . . . endeavour to strengthen my spirit in the Lord God who led us here. He . . . hath vouch—vouchsafed to me a friend. This, one Phebe Honeywood, wedded to one of the adventurers, a simple yeoman's daughter and a most brave and gentle lass . . . a fine delicate spirit, and God is closer to her than she knows. She hath been an inspiration to me, having a most sturdy courage to follow her man anywhere, and found a lasting home.

"O my dear sister, it is such as she who will endure in my stead, to fulfill our dream of the new free land, such as she whose babes will be brought forth here to found a new nation . . . while I—too feeble and faint-hearted . . ."

"That's all," said Carla softly. Her eyes glistened, and she folded the letter and put it back in Roger's envelope. "Arbella did die, didn't she?"

"Yes," said Hesper.

The girl was silent a minute; then she burst out. "But *why?* It doesn't seem fair. You can see she was a wonderful person. Why couldn't she be happy too? Why can't we all *stay* happy!"

Ah, I forget how young she is, thought Hesper. Why do we all have to start with rebellion, and frantic strivings? How long it takes to get over the sentimental delusion of "fairness."

"I don't know, Carlie—" she said, "but we can't. Have you found the clothes you want?"

The girl shook her head; she stared down with troubled eyes at the rough dusty floorboards. "Marnie, Tony thinks we're going to get into the war. He told me last night, he wants to go. He's going to train to be an aviator."

Hesper sank back on the trunk. So that's it. Again and again and again. The long years melted, and sharply against the attic wall, she saw Johnnie in his blue uniform, standing at the depot platform with a hundred others, and chiding her for tears. But though he had not returned, most of the others had. And though the pattern repeated, its interwoven strands were never the same.

"Well—" she said with deliberate tartness. "If there's a war, he doubtless will. If there's reason to fight, men fight."

"But we've just found each other again. I can't bear—"

"Fiddlesticks, Carla. You've got as much grit as anybody. Right here in this house there's been plenty of people bearing things, from Phebe on down. And it helps to think about the others, because we're never really alone, we're part of all those that are gone, and here now, and coming. I think you'll learn that quicker than I did, because you've got more sense to start with."

"Marnie!" Carla gave a startled choking laugh. Their eyes met for a moment, in that flash communication that transcends the barrier between all human beings; then they both turned at once, and looked at the still uninvestigated boxes in the corners of the attic.

"I wonder if that pink satin dress isn't in that cowhide thing over there," said Carla, and knelt down to investigate.

All Saturday the house was in an uproar, as Carla and her helpers prepared for the party that night. Dilly was there from Clifton, and Dilly's sister too, and Walt was pressed into unwilling service. Carla, noting how pale and drawn her grandmother looked, had insisted that Hesper remain quietly in her room, only interrupted every few minutes by anxious consultation. Would they have had flowers around for decoration in the old days? Certainly not in December, said Hesper. . . . What on earth were you supposed to do with the grease and drippings off the spitted turkey? Catch them in the tin trough that must be stacked with the other unused hearth furniture in the bottom of the oak dresser. . . . Uncle Walt had forgotten to build a fire under the brick oven as he'd promised. Was it too late to put in the beans now? No, said Hesper, they'd be done by nightfall.

Through her half-opened door she heard Carla relay this to Walt in the kitchen, and his sulky thick-tongued rejoinder. "What d'you want to go to all that trouble for! God-damn old oven's got a crack in the back of it anyhow."

"Oh please, Uncle Walt. The beans taste so much better, and I promised Tony I'd show him how it worked."

"Tony!" repeated Walt in disgust. His few days of reform had worn off, and his fondness for his niece by no means balanced the effects of the rum he had been drinking half the night.

"Walt!" Hesper called imperatively. He slouched to the door, and stood scowling on the threshold.

"You know how to fix the bricks in the back of the oven. You used to do it for me. Then please build a fire for Carla. She's got her heart set on having this party like the old days."

"Oh whip!" muttered Walt. "She going to serve a stinking hagdon stew, and send her guests out to the privy like the old days too?"

"Do as I say!" said Hesper sharply. "There's little enough I ask you to do around here."

Walt hunched his shoulders, gave her a bleary look, and as he turned he stumbled. She gazed after him with resigned pity knowing how painful must be the contrast now between the two he had fished out of the storm seven years ago. Carla's happiness with one must increase the bitterness of his failure with Maria. Later she saw him shambling in from the wood shed with an armful of firewood, before she shut her eyes for a few minutes' nap. The sense of foreboding very often accompanied a weakened heart, the doctor said, and had no more sinister basis. She might live for years with rest and medication. Nothing very wrong organically. Yet no amount of reasoning entirely vanquished the persistent quiver of apprehension. I've got the shogs, she thought, smiling back through the years to Susan. I'll be hearing the screechin' woman next. She slept for a little while and awoke refreshed.

The guests arrived at six, and the old house, all its rooms opened and cleansed and garnished, gave them a glowing welcome. A welcome of candlelight, and hearth fire. All the doors were decorated with holly wreaths and, inside, all the rooms were fragrant with pine boughs. Carla had hung mistletoe bunches from the center beams in the taproom and kitchen and from the chandelier in the parlor. Though her historical researches and Hesper's memory had disclosed that Christmas trees were never part of the traditional ceremonies until after the Civil War, she had not been willing to forego one, and a seven-foot spruce stood near the spinet in the parlor, its dark branches sparkling with gold and silver filigree balls, festooned with ruby strings of cranberries, and the fluffy white of popcorn. Each branch was tipped with tiny candles.

The whole house was lit with candles, and the perfume of bayberry mingled with burning cedar on the hearths, the smell of the browning beans, and of the mammoth turkey. Golden brown and luscious, it still rotated on the spit, run by the old clockwork pulley Carla had several days ago persuaded Walt to set up. And the house greeted its guests with soft Christmas music, not from a squeaky fiddle or the cracked old spinet—Carla's respect for the past had not gone that far. She had rented a small piano and hired a pianist from Lynn, establishing them in the taproom which was cleared now of tables for the dancing later.

The dozen or so young people from the Neck arrived first with their house guests. Carla had lent the girls some clothes from the attic, and they had enthusiastically adorned themselves in a medley of quilted skirts, brocade bodices, earrings, and poinsettias in the hair, for a picturesque if hardly authentic result. Of the young people invited from the town, Cloutmans and Bowens and Peaches, the girls had ransacked attic trunks as Carla had, and most of them wore their mothers' or grandmothers' wedding gowns. The young men were mostly Tony's school friends, and he had rallied them for Carla's sake into overcoming the normal male objection to dressing up, by a simple compromise. The result was a shock to Hesper.

She sat on the mohair sofa in the parlor next to Charity Trevercombe, and together they watched the arrival of the young people. As the Marblehead boys came up to pay their respects, Hesper gave a stifled exclamation. She did not see the polite young faces, bowing in front of her, she saw only the heavy leather pants, the red flannel shirts, black scarfs, and knitted "Gansey" jackets—the Sunday best clothes of the old Marblehead fishing fleet.

"Charity—do you remember?" she whispered.

Charity nodded. "Yes—it takes one back a long time!" And she put her puffy beringed hand for a second on Hesper's. An unusual gesture and admission from Charity, whose philosophy permitted no mention of age. She had grown very fat, and still dressed as she pleased in youthful styles. She used rouge on her cheeks, and she tinted her white hair to a faint straw color. For all that, she had achieved a true serenity, born of the years' determined practice of it. The warmth of shared memory helped Hesper to smile a little over the unexpected stab of nostalgia—for that other party the night the slave-catcher came, the night before Johnnie and the other young seamen sailed off for the spring fare. Only *those* young men had not been in costume.

"Fifty-eight years ago, Charity—" she said. "We were sixteen."

But Charity was not prepared to go that far. "There is no age in eternal life, Hesper," she said severely. "We're no older than our thoughts."

Hesper smiled, watching the young folks. Carla looked lovely in Zilpah Honeywood's imported London gown of brocaded rose satin trimmed with lace ruffles. She had powdered her hair and the two little curls that hung down her neck. So delicate and porcelain-like did Carla look in the Watteau style of 1750, that it was astonishing that she could eat so much turkey and beans, thought Hesper with amusement. Astonishing too that later when she danced with Tony, the clumsy fisherman's clothes did not seem incongruous next to the brocade. But the clothes suited the boy, or rather Tony's personality would always eclipse his surroundings. Now that love had banished the truculence he had shown earlier, his intelligent face was extremely attractive. He was a doer, not a dreamer, but his sense of humor would always counterbalance the streak of rashness and stubborn pride. She watched him maneuver Carla under the mistletoe as they waltzed together, and saw the tenderness of the quick kiss they gave each other, and she felt in her own heart a warmth and gladness.

Charity continued to eat luxuriously of the moist black cake and little green mints, but Hesper watched the young people as they waltzed and one-stepped in the taproom, occasionally collapsing for breath in the parlor. And she heard snatches of their conversation. The Neckers talked of the sailing races they had won that summer, and of the yacht clubs, and they talked of their little boats, the "Brutal Beasts," the special Marblehead class. They all talked of football games and college, and during an intermission in the dancing they talked a little of the old house. At least Carla started it, and the Neckers, raised in the new self-conscious worship of family lineage and the accompanying craze for antiques, demanded to be taken all over it. The Marbleheaders, most of them possessed of old houses themselves, were not so interested, until Carla to Hesper's embarrassment told the story of the slave girl and her grandmother's part in the rescue.

Then everyone begged to be shown the pirate's hidey-hole.

"Please, Marnie—" cried Carla, her eyes shining. "Just tell me again how to find the pin."

Hesper hesitated a moment and then complied. There was no longer any reason for secrecy about the hidey-hole, and no reason beyond a sentimental one for a shrinking wish to protect it from curiosity. Besides, the house would be Carla's some day, and her love and respect for it might be trusted to shield it from any cheapening. It was Carla's pride in it now that made her want to show it off in all its individual features. And the house, Hesper thought, as she listened to the squeals of laughter and heard the running footsteps of a game of hide and seek, had the strength to be tolerant of all youthful giddiness, looking upon it with the uncritical tenderness with which it had looked at so many human emotions.

When they all tired of dancing and hide and seek, they gathered around the piano and sang carols: "Oh, Little Town of Bethlehem," "It Came Upon a Midnight Clear" and the ever beloved "Holy Night" which produced in them all its magic of wondering awe, until Carla dispelled the mood with "snapdragon." For this traditional Christmas game she had loaded the largest of the pewter platters with candied fruits swimming in blue brandy flames. And the party broke up at last in mock terror and gales of laughter while the guests snatched at the burning sugarplums.

Hesper accompanied Charity to the front entrance and watched her clamber into the livery-stable hack. The two old friends had kissed each other good-bye with unusual warmth. "Thanks, Hessie," said Charity, "it was charming. A lovely Christmas party," before she waddled down the path to the hack.

The only person left who calls me Hessie, thought Hesper, and once we despised each other. Dear Amos, she thought, remembering, but he seemed remote as the stars that twinkled in the ink-black sky. The air smelled of coming snow. It was turning cold and the wind was rising. In the darkness across Front Street she heard the suck and splash of the water amongst the rocks; then it was lost in the honking of two motor cars sent by parents over from the Neck to collect their youngsters.

Hesper turned back into the house to stand beside Carla and say good-bye. The Marbleheaders all walked home to their near-by houses.

Tony went last. "Thanks a lot, Mrs. Porterman. It was swell. I always was crazy about this place since the night Walt dropped me in here like a drowned rat."

"And then see what happened!" said Carla. "He *never* should have done it." She gave him a naughty and adoring look under her eyelashes, and Hesper smiled, leaving them alone. She walked through the kitchen, on the way to her room, giving it a desultory glance. After-party mess, but could be dealt with tomorrow. All buoyancy had drained out of her, leaving her to a dull exhaustion. She could scarcely drag one foot in front of the other. She undressed, took three of the white pills, and sank thankfully onto the bed. Through the ceiling she could hear the sound of heavy snoring. That was Walt, who had never appeared at the party, but had gone to his room in the afternoon and refused to come out.

She sighed and listened a few minutes to the sound of the wind and water outside. Then she slept.

At four o'clock she was awakened by a confusion of sound and someone yelling. She sat up dazed, clutching at the bedclothes. Then she realized that her room was stifling hot and filled with the acrid smell of smoke. She jumped from the bed and put on her wrapper and slippers; she heard Carla's voice from outside calling frantically, "Marnie," and then through the wall in back of the bed she heard the sharply remembered sinister crackling. "No," she whispered under her breath over and over again. "No. No. No." But she acted by instinct, without conscious thought. She took Evan's picture from the wall, and held it tight against her side. She opened her door. The old kitchen was full of smoke. It was behind the chimney and between the old stairwell and the taproom that the fire was burning.

She dashed across the kitchen, slid the bolt on the back door, and ran outside. Carla was there, her horrified face dim in the dawn light; she had been beating at the door with her hands. "Marnie darling—" she cried. "Thank God you're safe. It's awful—I ran down the other stairs. . . . Thank God there are the fire engines!"

People were gathering, neighbors, the engine from the near-by firehouse. There was a tumult of shoutings and orders.

"Where's Walt?" cried Hesper sharply. "Is he out?" Even as she spoke Walt appeared at the window of his room, someone ran with a ladder, and he wedged himself through the window and descended slowly.

"You all right, Ma?" he said, coming over to her where she stood by the barn. He was in his shirt and pants as he had fallen asleep. He did not look at the burning house.

There came the pound of hooves down Franklin Street, and another fire engine drew up.

"How could it have happened? I don't see how it happened," Carla moaned. "I was so careful with the candles. Tony and I put everything out."

"It was the brick oven, I guess," said Walt; his heavy face looked stupid and vacant.

"Didn't you make it tight?" cried Hesper, watching the hissing streams of water and the running firemen.

He shook his head. "I didn't think it mattered. I was fuddled. One of the embers must have fallen through to the wood and smouldered a while." Suddenly he sat down on the ground and buried his face in his hands. Hesper stood frozen beside him. Then the paralysis of shock released her. She leaned down grabbing Walt's shoulder, shaking it savagely. "Go and help!" she shouted. "What's the matter with you!"

He muttered something, staring up at the tall, thin figure in the flannel wrapper, the terrifying eyes beneath the straight black brows and disordered gray hair. He jumped to his feet and ran toward the house. Carla and Hesper ran after him.

They reached the path by the open taproom door through which the hoses writhed. He plunged through the clouds of smoke where the two women would have followed him, but a fireman held them back. The women stood silent just beyond the bare horse-chestnut tree, watching. Carla was crying softly though she did not know it. In Hesper there were no tears; her soul was filled with a stony hatred. *This I will not stand!* she cried to the senseless blindfolded god. There was then no pity or indulgence in the universe if the shelter of ten generations might be consumed in an hour by simple carelessness. Fool, she cried into the relentless void, fool to have ever believed in soft, tender things, in help or comfort.

Once through the stony hatred she tried to pray, but she saw a little tongue of flame dart up through the roof and lick at the side of the great chimney, and the prayer froze hard within her. For what was there to pray to? The little lick of flame disappeared. She watched the spot on the roof where it had been. The minutes passed and they heard shouts from within the house. Carla crept closer to her grandmother. "It's spreading," she whispered. "Marnie, I can't stand it—I can't."

Hesper said nothing. Neighbors pressed near them, murmuring and sympathizing. She did not hear. Suddenly Walt stumbled out of the house; coughing and holding a handkerchief to his face. He ran toward them. "It's okay now, Ma!" he shouted. "We've got it out! It just burned up the stairwell, and along the back of the chimney to the roof. The old shack's tough all right!"

Hesper saw his eyes shining with a fierce exultation in his soot-blackened face, and she heard the ring in his voice. She gave a soft sigh, and Walt's face and the murmuring voices and the lanterns and the pressure of Carla's arm about her all merged into darkness.

When she opened her eyes again, she knew at once that she was lying in her own bed, in the borning room. She knew because her gaze rested on the beam above her head and the little knot in the wood that was shaped like an anchor. She knew too that there were people around her bed, but she did not look to see who they were. She turned her head to the right wall and saw that Evan's picture again hung there as it always did. The picture she had clutched all during that dreadful hour in the night. I saved that, she thought—the only thing I tried to save.

How strange. But as she gazed up at the picture, she knew that it was not strange. For if the house itself had been destroyed, she would still have had this—the symbol of the ideal that could never be destroyed. She looked at the mute, ageless figure in the doorway—its arms outstretched in welcome. She looked beyond the jeweled and living house and saw that they were still all there inside, the people who had built it into an enduring pattern, and that behind the house there lay, forever incarnated—the image of the eternal sea.

She turned her head at last and saw the anxious faces of those by her bedside. Her doctor was bending over her, and next to him Carla knelt by the bed. Behind them, she saw Walt and Henry, and Tony and Eleanor, all crowded together in the narrow doorway.

Yes, she thought, as she tried to smile to them all, it's coming now, very soon. But she felt no fear. Her eyes wandered past them to the window. She saw that snow was falling against the distant line of black trees along Peach's Point. She heard the quiet lapping of water on the shingle of the Little Harbor.

And then she heard another sound near her; and after a moment she knew what it was. The sound of Carla's muffled sobbing.

And this roused her from the clinging gray peace that was falling around her as softly as the snow fell against the window panes.

"Don't, dear—" she whispered, though she thought she spoke loud. She felt the girl take her hand and press it against a wet cheek.

"There *is* comfort—" she whispered to Carla. "There *is* pity. I thought there wasn't. But there is."

But she saw that the girl, deep in grief, could not understand that, and she groped for words to express the new security in her own heart. "The andirons—" she whispered urgently. "Phebe's andirons. They mean home, and even if the house *had* burned, they couldn't have burned. Because they're strong. Do you understand that, Carla? 'A most sturdy courage to endure.' That's what really matters. Do you see, dear?"

She did not hear the girl's answer, but she did not need to, for it seemed to her that the little room became illumined with a golden light. She knew the light came from the house, and from the sea outside, and from beyond the sky that covered them all. But it seemed to her that the light flowed brightest of all from the ever-replenished lantern that is passed down from hand to hand and shines upon the symbols of the enduring hearth.

THE END